BAEN BOOKS by TRAVIS S. TAYLOR & LES JOHNSON

Back to the Moon • *On to the Asteroid* • *Saving Proxima*

BAEN BOOKS by TRAVIS S. TAYLOR

THE TAU CETI AGENDA SERIES
One Day on Mars • *The Tau Ceti Agenda* • *One Good Soldier*
Trail of Evil • *Kill Before Dying* • *Bringers of Hell*

WARP SPEED SERIES
Warp Speed • *The Quantum Connection*

WITH JODY LYNN NYE
Moon Beam • *Moon Tracks*

WITH JOHN RINGO
Into the Looking Glass • *Vorpal Blade*
Manxome Foe • *Claws That Catch*

Von Neumann's War

WITH MICHAEL Z. WILLIAMSON, TIMOTHY ZAHN, KACEY EZELL, JOSH HAYES
Battle Luna

BAEN BOOKS NONFICTION BY TRAVIS S. TAYLOR
New American Space Plan • *The Science Behind The Secret*
Alien Invasion: How to Defend Earth (with Bob Boan)

BAEN BOOKS by LES JOHNSON

Mission to Methone • *The Spacetime War*

WITH BEN BOVA
Rescue Mode

ANTHOLOGIES
Going Interstellar (edited with Jack McDevitt)
Stellaris: People of the Stars (edited with Robert E. Hampson)

For a complete listing of Baen titles by Travis S. Taylor
and Les Johnson, please go to www.baen.com.

SAVING PROXIMA

SAVING PROXIMA

TRAVIS S. TAYLOR
LES JOHNSON

SAVING PROXIMA

This is a work of fiction. All the characters and events portrayed in this book are fictional, and any resemblance to real people or incidents is purely coincidental.

A Baen Books Original

Baen Publishing Enterprises
P.O. Box 1403
Riverdale, NY 10471
www.baen.com

ISBN: 978-1-9821-2550-9

Cover art by Dave Seeley
Models used for cover art by John Douglass
Timeline graphic by Carol Russo

First printing, August 2021

Distributed by Simon & Schuster
1230 Avenue of the Americas
New York, NY 10020

Library of Congress Cataloging-in-Publication Data

Names: Taylor, Travis S., author. | Johnson, Les (Charles Les), author.
Title: Saving Proxima / Travis S. Taylor, Les Johnson.
Description: Riverdale, NY : Baen, [2021]
Identifiers: LCCN 2021021989 | ISBN 9781982125509 (hardcover)
Subjects: GSAFD: Science fiction.
Classification: LCC PS3620.A98 S28 2021 | DDC 813/.6—dc23
LC record available at https://lccn.loc.gov/2021021989

Pages by Joy Freeman (www.pagesbyjoy.com)
Printed in the United States of America
10 9 8 7 6 5 4 3 2 1

We can figure this out.

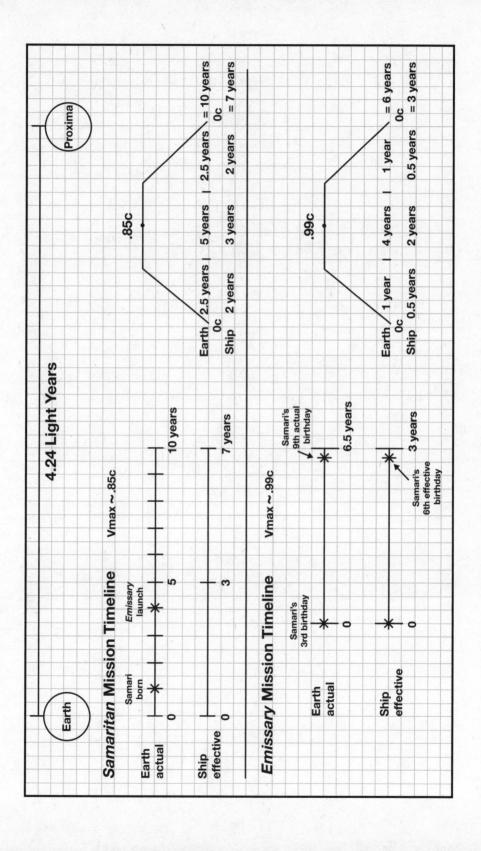

CHAPTER 1

February 29, 2072

To Lorraine Gilster, the Lunar Farside Radio Observatory was the most beautiful thing she had ever seen. From the moment she arrived, she fell in love with it. When the brilliant, unfiltered by atmosphere sun was shining, as it did every two weeks for fourteen days straight, the light reflecting from the ten-square-mile array was dazzling. The yellowish plastic-like film in which miles of antenna wires were embedded contrasted with the gray lunar soil in a way that shouted, "I'm not natural! People placed me here!" As if anyone looking at it could ever believe it was a natural construct. The three large segmented optical telescopes that stood just on the horizon added to the majesty, and sense of amazement, as only massive objects standing in stark contrast with the blackness of space that provided their backdrop could.

Lorraine, or "Rain," as her friends and colleagues called her, stopped at the observation window on her way to the data analysis and control room as she did at the beginning of every shift. She did not think she would ever grow tired of the view and, even though her current stay at the observatory was just short of half over, she fully intended to stop and stare every chance she could. Today was no different from yesterday, or the day before. The lunar night was just three Earth days in the future and then the other majestic view would be hers to see—the dark, desolate lunar night. All fourteen days of it. It was just as majestic and beautiful as the daylight view, but completely different.

She was abruptly shaken from her reverie by the nearby

1

communications link buzzing and demanding her attention. On each wall and in every room at the observatory there was an old-fashioned, fiber-optic, hardwired intercom. No radios or wireless communications were allowed anywhere near the precious radio-quiet zone that was home to the Farside Radio Observatory. Being away from terrestrial radio sources, artificial and natural, was why it had been placed on the lunar farside with the mass of the moon providing all the radio frequency shielding needed to make it the most radio-quiet place in the inner solar system. Allowing personnel to use wireless communications this near the extremely sensitive radio antennas and receivers would compromise the environment and potentially introduce radio noise that would drown out the very faint signals they were there to collect and study.

Rain reached for the button to activate the intercom, cursing under her breath as she did so. This was *her* time. She wasn't on the clock yet and had planned her day to allow ample time to look out the window undisturbed.

"This is Rain. What's up?" She tried not to sound terse, but she knew that whoever was calling could probably tell they had interrupted something.

"This is Stephan. I'm sorry to bother you, but I thought you'd want to know that the ICC just denied Lunar Global their constellation permit. The vote was five to four."

Rain sighed. The vote was closer than she liked but winning was winning. One of these days, though, they were likely going to lose. Gone were the days of unanimous support for keeping the lunar farside free of radio interference. The Interplanetary Communications Commission demonstrated they were still on the observatory's side by voting down Lunar Global Corporation's proposal to build a constellation of lunar-orbiting, high-bandwidth communications satellites—again. But how many more votes could those who wanted to keep the radio spectrum here quiet and free from interference win? One of these days, the lunar real estate developers would win and the satellites would be launched, ruining big swaths of the radio spectrum for science. Apparently, there was only so much one could do with miles and miles of fiber directly connecting the many lunar bases and outposts to one another.

"Thanks for telling me, Stephan. That means we're safe for another three years or so. Anything else?"

"Yeah, you owe me a dinner. When can I collect?"

"How about tonight? After my shift."

"That would be great. Come by my room at nineteen hundred. It will be the best meal on farside," said Stephan.

"See you then," Rain said as she closed the connection. She liked Stephan, but not in the same way he liked her. Rain knew when she bet him on the outcome of the ICC vote that she would probably win and that she should not have accepted the wager. She felt like she was leading him on. But his offer of a home-cooked meal, instead of one of her usual freeze-dried moon-meal specials, was definitely not one to ignore. Stephan was a good cook and good company. She just wasn't romantically interested in him the way she knew he was with her. *Relationships are just so complicated.*

She glanced out the window one more time, catching the ghost of her reflection in the thick, multi-layered glass. With her salt-and-pepper hair cropped short, brown eyes, and high cheekbones, she knew men found her attractive and she was certainly interested, but not to the point that any man had ever been become more important to her than her career. Stephen was no exception. *Maybe someday,* she mused as she looked one more time at the image of herself superimposed over that of the moon and resumed her walk toward the control room. *But not as long as I've got the moon.*

The control room wasn't nearly as spectacular as the view out the window, but it was pretty in its own way. Instead of a window showing the lunar landscape extending to a somewhat disconcertingly close horizon, the walls were covered with displays showing the engineering status of the various telescopes and spectrum analyzers scanning multiple radio frequencies from across the visible sky. Everywhere Rain looked she saw data, glorious data, and she knew that it was going to be a good day. She just didn't know how good the day would end up being. After all, who could know such a thing? Who knew what great discoveries were yet to be made? That mystery was what had gotten Rain interested in science in the first place.

Modern radio astronomy, like just about every other aspect of modern astronomy—and science, for that matter—wasn't "real time." The vast amount of data collected by the radio telescope as it scanned huge swaths of the sky was collected across thousands of discrete frequencies, recorded, analyzed, cross-checked with previous similar data to look for changes or discrepancies, reanalyzed, and archived for future reference. Artificial intelligence systems, especially designed for the purpose of analyzing data, made the processing seamless and nearly transparent for its human creators and operators. Rain's presence wasn't required in the control room for data analysis but for troubleshooting and decision-making. AI systems were great at sorting, assessing, and presenting data, but they weren't yet capable of the innovation and quick decision-making that humans were so good at. Rain wasn't so certain as to when that might change, though, because the newest quantum processor-based cluster that housed over a million tiny protein-based nanoscopic processors used for pattern recognition in the signal data was getting smarter and smarter every day. There was talk of a new system coming out soon that would house a hundred million of the quantum physics-based processors. Who knew when such systems would start getting close to mimicking the human brain and make her obsolete and out of a job?

As the AI did its job, Rain busied herself looking over the data summaries generated during the last shift that would keep the teams of university scientists Earthside busy writing papers for the rest of their careers. The recent data collected ran the gamut, from new radio galaxies, quasars, and pulsars to the logging of yet another elusive Fast Radio Burst—this one from a galaxy "only" three billion light-years distant. But one bit of data caught her eye: the interference report. On and off during the last several months, a pesky UHF signal was encroaching on the gigahertz radio observations and the team from Beijing was not too happy about it. The signal was obviously artificial; the carrier wave was clearly modulated using some unregistered code. The AI had been running coincidence analysis, trying to figure out whose satellite was leaking radio signals into the array in clear violation of international treaty. Once they figured it out, there would be hell to pay for someone. Most modern spacecraft and satellites could fairly easily direct their antenna so that this kind of leakage didn't occur. Someone was just being lazy or perhaps their system was malfunctioning. Whatever the reason, once they figured out who was responsible, they would have to fix the problem or face a heavy fine or, at the least, some political backpedaling.

Rain couldn't figure out why it was taking the AI so long to determine the source. Every spacecraft operating in Earth orbit and throughout the inner solar system had ICC-registered transponders. Most used optical comm, which was much more efficient than radio and also highly directional. Laser comm basically had no leakage, unless the receiver wasn't in the right place to intercept the message, in which case the signal would head off into deep space. The AI had mapped the timing of the signal being detected and compared it with the locations of all the registered spacecraft and bases and come up empty. There was no correlation. But there was regularity. The signal appeared on a regular interval that coincided with the lunar farside having unobstructed views of the same region of sky.

The same region of the sky, she thought.

And along the spiral arm. Where there are a lot of stars. And planets.

UHF was in the so-called water hole of frequencies that was the Holy Grail in the Search for Extraterrestrial Intelligence, or SETI, and had been the part of the radio spectrum studied so intensely for over a century as various groups searched the sky for evidence of alien life. Radio astronomers called it the "water hole" because of the radio signals emitted by hydrogen atoms and hydroxyl molecules that float in free space. Hydroxyl, being an oxygen and hydrogen atom combined, only needs one hydrogen atom to make water. Hence, the hydrogen and hydroxyl signals were from the "water hole" as per those clever SETI astronomers of the past. Clever or not, the answer had remained the same since the beginning: nothing. No one was broadcasting, or at least no one was broadcasting with a signal strong enough for humans to detect.

Until now. Was it possible she was listening to an extraterrestrial signal? ET?

Perhaps the UHF signal wasn't coming from any of the registered spacecraft now crisscrossing the solar system; maybe it was coming from *outside* the solar system. Maybe it was artificial. Rain made the leap from worrying about placating the Beijing team studying gigahertz-emitting sources in nearby galaxies to wondering how she could determine if the signal was from an artificial extraterrestrial source. But which source? Where, specifically, was the signal coming from? To answer that question would take some analysis, but given the speed at which the AI could sift data, she was sure it wouldn't take too long. All they had to do was fine-tune the correlation with what specific stars were visible whenever the signal was received, look at the signal's dispersion from traveling through the interstellar medium to get an idea of how far away it originated, guess at the relative motion between that star and Earth to make any required Doppler-shift corrections to the data, and look for similar detections in other radio telescope data archives that might perhaps allow her to narrow down the region of the sky from which it came. Maybe, just maybe, she could identify its likely star or stars of origin. *If it is really alien,* she thought. *There is no way, not after all these years, that I'm the one finding a message from ET. No way, right?*

If she had found ET, then she was determined to get as much information about their location as possible before going public. It never occurred to her to try to decode whatever message was contained in the signal.

The incessant buzzing of the intercom was finally more than Rain could ignore. She'd been buried in data for the last several hours and had successfully ignored all the distractions she could, until now. Whoever was trying to reach her happened to finally have the good fortune of their attempt coinciding with her need to go the bathroom. She stopped mid-sentence in her annotations of the anomalous UHF signal and accepted the incoming call.

"Rain? Finally. Are you okay? I thought you were going to be here half an hour ago." Stephan sounded concerned and more than a bit annoyed. She had completely forgotten about his dinner invitation.

"Me? No, I'm fine. I just got wrapped up in something and forgot. Give me a few more minutes to wrap up and I will be right over. I have something I'd like to share with you. I need an independent set of eyes and you're just the person to provide them."

"Okay. But be ready to eat when you get here. The food is on the table and the wine poured."

"I'll be there as soon as I can," she said as she broke the connection. Stephan would be a good person to provide an independent look at what she was thinking. He, too, was a radio astronomer and, better still, one that she could trust not to scoop her on the discovery. His infatuation with her would see to that. She signed out of her account and moved toward the hallway and the bathroom she now urgently needed, barely acknowledging Ka-Lok, her control room replacement for the next shift, as she exited. She wasn't even sure she had acknowledged him when he arrived to relieve her nearly an hour before. Her mind was again wandering to the signal and its repercussions. She was now sure that the signal originated from *elsewhere*.

Fifteen minutes later, Rain was walking down the sterile, gray, downward-sloping corridor that led to the residential section of the moon base, buried ten meters below the lunar surface to provide its inhabitants maximum protection from the solar and galactic radiation. Without an atmosphere or magnetic field to shield the surface from the at-times deadly streams of solar radiation and long-term, cancer-causing, very-high-energy galactic cosmic rays, having the crew's living quarters underground was the best possible solution to keeping them alive and healthy. Rain hated it because there weren't any windows providing views of the surface, just display screens showing whatever scenes the local residents wanted projected there and the occasional outside view from a surface-mounted camera. Today it was a view of the Grand Canyon. Awe inspiring, for sure, but the blue sky above the dramatic rock formations seemed incongruous with the low gravity that reminded them they were far away from the real thing.

She arrived at Stephan's cabin and quickly moved through the door to enter. Stephan, like most everyone at the base, kept his cabin spartan and utilitarian, with wall screens showing various pictures of people and scenes from home. Bigger than the galley on most interplanetary cruisers, the room was nonetheless much smaller than a typical apartment back on Earth. Each resident's cabin had two rooms—an all-purpose kitchen, living and bedroom area, complete with a Murphy bed that could be pulled down at the end of the day, and a bathroom. With the exception of the images on the wall and the occasional knickknack on the table, it could just as easily have been Rain's cabin.

Stephan McGill, looking well-groomed as was his custom, greeted her with a smile and barely an indication that he was upset at her for being late. From his full head of brown hair without a hint of gray, to his high cheekbones and nearly perfect stature and proportions, he exemplified many of the benefits that came from being a member of the Earth's elite. Now in his mid-forties, Stephan had been born in the early days of the designer-baby genetic engineering revolution. He was perfect. Which meant he was too perfect for Rain. To her, he wasn't real. She didn't know what she was looking for in a man, but she was sure that "perfect" was not on the list. At least, not for a romantic relationship. As a friend and colleague, "perfect" was just fine and she did consider him to be both.

"Food is on the table, so I suggest we go ahead and eat before it gets cold," said Stephan, motioning to the small table upon which there were two place settings and a hot, steaming casserole. "I hope you don't mind a vegetarian meal. I just couldn't bring myself to cook another meal with synthetic chicken again."

"Vegetarian is fine. I'm famished. And while we eat, I have something to run by you. I need someone else to tell me if I've gone off the deep end or not," Rain told him as she moved toward the table, noticing that Stephan had also poured each of them a glass of red wine. The bottle was labeled as being from the lunar vineyards, which was fine; she loved the local wines.

As expected, the meal was fabulous. She and Stephan were able to eat small bites in between their discussion of the data she pulled up on the table's built-in screen, moving the casserole dish more than once to uncover a specific signal spectrum that she wanted to reference. She laid out all the data for him, going over in detail all of her leaps of logic. Sometimes the utilitarian design of the base was truly annoying—having one's dinner table also serve as their primary computer display was some efficiency engineer's dream and a practical user's nightmare. *Let's look at figure number three—there—just under the spaghetti noodle.*

Rain patiently walked Stephen through her leap of logic that pointed toward the signal being extraterrestrial. And waited for some reassurance that she wasn't nuts.

He nodded, asked a few probing questions, which she answered easily, and finally, taking the last of his third glass of wine and leaning back in his chair, commented, "Rain, the data is incontrovertible, and your logic is perfect. The signal must be extraterrestrial. If it were coming from any of the bases or ships in the outer solar system, the timing of its detection by the array would have been totally different. The only correlation is with an extrasolar source. And you've narrowed it down to a fairly small region of the sky. In the old days of SETI the first thing they would do is compare the sidereal motion of the stars with the signal, but all that was taken out by the various AI filters which actually made your problem of verifying harder. The simplest thing to do would be to look at the raw data once again and have the AI filter out everything without sidereal motion. With corroborating measurements from other observatories, we might be able to narrow it down to a few dozen star systems as opposed to the few thousand that are in the line of sight you've identified—maybe even better."

Rain's excitement from his affirming words was barely contained. She felt the same adrenaline rush as when she learned she'd been selected for assignment at the lunar array. It was an intellectual high. The observatory hadn't been built for searching for alien signals, although it was always considered one of the lower-priority applications that could be running in the background while the real science was being conducted.

"There's more," she said. "The signal strength varies on an eleven-day cycle. It peaks on day zero, decreases for a little more than three days, and then disappears completely only to return near the end of the seventh day to peak again on the next cycle. I think the source is orbiting something that blocks its line of sight to us on days four to six."

Stephan reached for his now-empty wineglass, stopped, leaned forward, and stared intently at Rain.

"What I don't understand is why you haven't analyzed the signal itself. It may be weak, but it is consistent and measurable across the sampling interval. From what I can tell, it looks like a frequency-modulated UHF signal similar to what our grandparents' generation used to listen to radio and watch television back before everything went fiber. Here, let's put it through the speaker system and see what it sounds like."

He swiped across the screen, tapped a few virtual buttons, and looked up at Rain.

"Here goes. Let's listen to what your ET is broadcasting," he said.

Sound filled the cabin, but it certainly wasn't the sound they were expecting. Instead of the chirps, bleeps, and Morse code-like sounds that were audible from data-encoded broadcasts, they instead heard melody and rhythm. Instead of incomprehensible noise, they heard what sounded like piano, strings, and what might be brass. Instead of confirmation of an alien signal, they heard what sounded like some sort of new music genre from an all-too-human-based composer. What they heard could *not* have been created by aliens. It was too familiar. Too human.

"Are you sure about your analysis?" asked Stephan, as he paused the music.

"I'm sure. And now not sure. I know this signal came from deep space, outside the solar system—light-years outside the solar system. But how could it? That isn't a song I know, or even a style I'm familiar with, but it sure doesn't sound like it's from aliens."

Stephan resumed the playback and they listened to music play for another thirty seconds before it faded.

"Rain, I'm sorry, but this just can't be what you think it is. I mean, that sounds like some new classical piece straight from Carnegie Hall. Is some startup company testing a deep-space relay station and just didn't register it? Or maybe it's a pirate radio station, like the ones the CIA used to run off the coast of Cuba back during the Cold War. I don't know what it is, but you'll have to eliminate all these possibilities before you claim to have discovered an alien radio broadcast of a Mozart concert."

"Let's play another segment of the data—from a few hours earlier," was her only reply. Rain didn't doubt her data analysis in her head; her gut was another thing entirely. That sinking feeling that one got at the bad news of a loved one's death was the closest thing she could think of to describe what she was experiencing.

Stephan removed the casserole dish from the table, scanned the signal profile, and selected a new data set to send to his speakers. He leaned back after selecting the play icon on the screen.

What they heard was absolutely, without a scintilla of doubt, a human voice. A male human voice, complete with inflections, variations of intonation, and even a few "ums." The language was clearly not English.

"That nails it. This must be some rogue station out in the asteroid belt or one of the most complex pranks ever devised. The speaker is clearly human, but I don't recognize the language. Do you?" asked Stephan.

"No," said Rain. She almost didn't reply. Her mind was racing, trying to figure out what language the speaker was using.

The lunar base was a miniature United Nations, with scientists and engineers from just about every country on Earth. In the hallways and cafeteria, she would hear a cacophony of speakers, each using their native language and shifting to English only when they needed to interact with someone from outside their native culture. She'd gotten used to the various accents and could, most of the time, discern the speaker's native language. She could tell Belgian French from the French spoken in France. Puerto Rican Spanish from Costa Rican. But this accent she couldn't place.

They played more data from different times, some going back more than a week. They heard more music and more speakers. Each bit of music was clearly different, but the instruments used were still basically recognizable: strings, brass, drums, and even what sounded like a piano or harpsichord. And then there were the speakers: male, female, male and female speaking together in what sounded like some sort of foreign-language debate.

The evening long-since passed and Rain discovered that it was after midnight, local time. With no window, she couldn't tell the difference between the time she arrived, nearly four hours previously, and now. She fiddled with the display controls to get a view from outside. She then saw the same, unchanging lunar surface extending toward the horizon that couldn't care less about her being exhausted and elated at the same time. The moon was as close as possible to something eternal and unresponsive as any human could ever hope to see and experience. It's *alienness* reaffirmed her belief that what they were hearing was from somewhere else.

"Stephan, I need to go to bed soon. I'm exhausted. But before that, I think we need to discuss what we're going to do with this."

"What *you* are going to do about this. *You* made the discovery; I'm just along for the ride."

"Stephan, I appreciate your gesture, but if it weren't for you, I would only be announcing the detection of a signal. Instead, we will be telling humanity that we've found what sounds like an alien culture not dissimilar from our own—at least in the way they speak and the music they like. Which, by the way, is really quite unbelievable. It just doesn't make sense."

"Maybe we'll be able to make better sense of it after a good night's rest. It wouldn't hurt to get some independent eyes and ears on this before we tell the solar system. Deborah would be a good place to start. She is the director, after all. And she was a competent radio astronomer before she went into management," Stephan said.

"I agree, but I don't want to sit on it too long," Rain replied.

"Agreed. But there is a protocol for this sort of thing and we need to follow it. Let's get together over breakfast and figure out how we're going to tell her and everybody else. Seven o'clock?"

"Seven o'clock," she confirmed.

"Try to get some sleep," Stephan said as he leaned forward and kissed Rain on her forehead.

Rain was pleasantly surprised at the chaste kiss. It made her feel...respected. And loved. She needed that affirmation and support now, at this time, more than she thought she did. It gave her peace.

"Thanks, Stephan, I will."

CHAPTER 2

March 1, 2072

After their heady seven o'clock breakfast of eggs, locally grown hydroponic grapefruit, and some blah bread, Rain and Stephen found their way to the office of Deborah Kirkland. Kirkland was also the product of the designer baby boom. Her finely chiseled facial features and perfectly groomed hair accentuated her toned physique. Her clothing appeared to have been perfectly tailored to fit her and accentuate her African heritage. She was smart, affable, and beautiful. She was also the boss.

Kirkland, though now firmly entrenched in the all-too-necessary bureaucracy of running a lunar base and research facility, greeted their news of alien discovery with a healthy bit of scientific skepticism and some surprisingly astute questions. Questions to which Rain and Stephan had reasonable and reasoned answers—up until the one that was the eight-hundred-pound gorilla in the room.

"Are you saying the aliens are human? Like us?" Kirkland asked, using her best manager's "you have my attention" stance, slightly leaning forward in her chair, right hand nestled on her chin, and her gaze focused on Rain's face.

"No, I'm not saying that. At least physically; that's just flat-out impossible. What I am saying is that they, whatever they are, use language in a frequency range similar to our own and they have music—again, similar to our own. And they can't be more than one to two hundred years away from us technologically," replied Rain.

"Okay, let's not jump to conclusions. Before we say anything about this to anyone else, we need to get independent confirmation of everything—of the detection, the signals, the decoding, and just where in the hell it is coming from," Kirkland replied, with extreme excitement evident in her voice. She leaned back in her chair and gazed at the photo on her wall. There, prominent on the wall to the left of her desk, was a photograph of the Arecibo Radio Observatory in Puerto Rico taken in the early days of radio astronomy. Rain guessed the image might date from 1970s, when everyone thought detecting a signal from ET could happen any day.

It was difficult for Rain to remain still while Deborah pondered, but the reassuring hand of Stephan on her shoulder helped. She glanced at him and he returned the glance with a subtle wink. It was both flirtatious and conspiratorial. Rain smiled.

"I'm going to pull the logs, check the database, and listen to the signal myself. I'm also going to contact Space Command to see if they have any new comm sats in the line-of-sight from here to where we think the signal originates that could be spoofing our systems. Don't worry, I won't give anything away. We just need to make sure we've eliminated all the more credible alternatives to your interpretation of the signal as we can before we go public. None of us want to announce this and then have some kid at MIT or Shandong find out we overlooked a perfectly normal, mundane source." Kirkland then rose and walked from behind her desk toward the door of her office, beckoning Rain and Stephan to follow. A clear indication the meeting was over for now.

"When?" asked Rain as she arose to follow Deborah.

"I should be able to get back with you later this afternoon with my results."

"We aren't going to go public with this until we get independent confirmation," Kirkland warned, after summoning Rain and Stephan back to her office. It hadn't taken long. Barely four hours had passed between the time she sent them on their way after the initial briefing until now. Deborah's hair wasn't as perfectly groomed as it had been that morning. She now sported the look of an anxious, harried scientist who was putting in too many hours at the lab. Rain couldn't help but speculate that the discovery had put her boss out of the management lifestyle and back into that of a researcher—at least for a short while.

Rain noticed that the excitement in Kirkland's voice was tempered by... anxiety? Rain couldn't be sure. But she didn't like it and wondered if the need for "independent confirmation" would have been there if it had been someone else who made the discovery, like Stephan. Intellectually she knew that sexism was mostly a thing of the past, but the thought did still cross her mind. It shouldn't have. Both were women, and didn't women stand together?

"Independent, as in... what?" asked Stephan. "I've looked into the protocols and they are pretty clear what to do in a case like this. According to treaty, we are supposed to send a message to the International Astronomical Union. That's when others will try to find the signal and give us all the independent confirmation we need."

"I know. I looked it up myself," replied Kirkland. "But once we do that, the credibility of this entire laboratory will be questioned. Frankly, I'm not sure I believe the data and I want to be damn sure it's real before putting our necks out there."

Rain's blood pressure began to rise. *Is she questioning my integrity? Does she think I made this up somehow?*

"What about the data don't you believe?" asked Stephan before Rain could calm herself down enough to speak.

Kirkland leaned forward in her chair and stared at them as if they were in a courtroom about to be sentenced for a crime, with her as the judge.

"If you had come to me with a simple spurious signal, claiming it to be of extraterrestrial origin, that would have been one thing. Simple. Extraordinary? Yes. But simple. We would double-check everything here at the base and then send it out as proscribed by the treaty. But you didn't come to me with something simple and straightforward. You came to me with hours of data that ends up being like a mid-twentieth-century radio broadcast, complete with orchestra and an announcer. It is, quite frankly, completely unbelievable."

"You think we planted the data," said Rain.

"You, or somebody else. I shudder to think that our data security has been breached, but that is a far more likely scenario than the one you presented to me. Before we make ourselves the laughingstock of the science community, a future case study to the hacker community, or a target of the politicians who are always eager for a soundbite of some outrageous waste of intergovernmental money, I've got to be sure it's real."

"Okay, I get it. I know we didn't plant the data, but, like you, I can't be sure someone else didn't. It would be good to get confirmation from some other system that isn't linked to ours. That way we can be reasonably sure the data, if it is still there, isn't planted," Rain said, calming herself down and listening, as difficult as it was, to the more rational side of her brain.

Kirkland leaned back again and said, "I'm glad you agree. I've got a call in to Riku Tanaka at the Japanese space agency. They've got a spacecraft nearing one thousand astronomical units that should have the sensitivity to detect the signal. Since their ship is almost a thousand times farther away from us than the sun, the terrestrial background noise should be minimal."

"I know of Riku, but I've never worked with him," said Rain. Stephan shook his head in seeming agreement. "I've read some of his papers; they're solid."

"I'll only tell him what to look for after I've gotten his word that the information will be kept under wraps pending some sort of official announcement from us. If it is real, then I won't let him go public until we are ready," Deborah said.

"Are we finished here?" asked Rain. She was eager to get this disappointing meeting behind her and back to trying to learn more about the signal.

"No, we're not. I want you to walk me through the whole thing again, from the moment you found the signal to the minute you walked in here to tell me about it," Deborah replied.

They didn't finish for three hours.

Traveling at 186,282 miles per second, light takes just over one second to travel from the Moon to Earth. If the Sun were to suddenly vanish, people on Earth might not realize it until eight minutes later when the sky would go dark and Earth would fly off into deep space, no longer bound by the Sun's immense gravity—or at least that's what some textbooks stated. Other theories suggested that gravity might be instantaneous and humans would feel the effects of losing the Sun before seeing them. Space experiments had long shown that gravitational waves traveled at finite speeds and the evidence pointed to the speed being that of light, but no one as yet had proven the actual speed of gravity itself.

Though it took less than a day for the base commander, Deborah Kirkland, to find and brief Riku Tanaka at the Japanese

Aerospace Exploration Agency's spacecraft control center in Tsu-
kuba, it took the signal from Japan another five and a half days
to reach their *Interstellar Voyager* spacecraft that had just crossed
a symbolic milestone—passing one thousand astronomical units.
With one astronomical unit, or AU, being equal to the Earth-to-
Sun distance, *Interstellar Voyager* was farther from home than
any other object made by humanity. *Interstellar Voyager* was also
moving faster than any other spacecraft ever launched, taking
advantage of the new photon drive invented at the Samara State
Aerospace University in Russia just nine years previously. This was
the shakedown cruise for the drive and, so far, it had performed
admirably. Taking only ninety-two days from launch to reach one
thousand AU, the drive was poised to change space exploration as
profoundly as the invention of the rocket many centuries before.
But today, the Samara Drive was irrelevant. The communications
system onboard the spacecraft was highly relevant.

Once it received the command signal from home, *Interstellar
Voyager* turned its eight-meter gossamer radio antenna toward
Proxima Centauri to search for the signal detected by the radio
telescope back on the Moon. If there, the signal it would detect,
and record, would have been traveling at the speed of light for
many years, perhaps hundreds or thousands of years.

Interstellar Voyager listened for approximately one Earth day,
twenty-four hours, and then sent the data it collected back toward
Earth. It took another five and a half days for the signal to reach
Japan, where it was automatically forwarded to the observatory on
the lunar farside. Nearly two weeks had elapsed since Rain made her
discovery and she was more than ready to find out if she had been
fooled or made the greatest discovery in the history of the species.

Rain and Stephan were called to Deborah's office just after
the evening meal. Rain knew the message would arrive any day,
any hour, and she dropped everything when her apartment's
intercom flashed, alerting her that she had an incoming call. She
didn't have to find Stephan. She ran into him in the hallway on
the way to the director's office. He had apparently just returned
from the gym, sporting running shorts and shoes and a sheen
of sweat. Both agreed that there wasn't time for him to clean up
before meeting with the director, so he walked in lockstep with
her as they made their way forward.

Deborah Kirkland was waiting on them and wearing an expression that caused Rain's heart to sink. It wasn't the look of a woman bearing good news. Rather, it was the look she imagined Deborah would wear when dismissing an employee for malfeasance. Rain hoped that wasn't the case here, but she certainly wasn't sure.

After motioning for them to sit, Deborah walked to the front of her desk and leaned against it, still wearing the dour expression Rain noticed when they first arrived.

"The data from Tanaka arrived this morning. I've spent most of the day discussing it with him, the US ambassador to the United Nations, and, a few minutes ago, with the director general herself," Deborah revealed, pausing to gauge the duo's reactions.

"The UN? Does that mean that the Japanese satellite confirmed the detection? Is the signal real?" asked Rain as her heart nearly skipped a beat. She unconsciously reached over to Stephan and gripped his hand as she asked the question, realized what she'd done, and then quickly withdrew it—all before Kirkland could reply.

"The signal is real. Whatever it is, it isn't ours." As Kirkland spoke, her stern appearance was replaced with a big smile.

"Oh my God!" Rain exclaimed. Her mind was racing. She'd found intelligent life beyond Earth. Real, honest-to-God aliens. Her mind skipped rapidly from the scene before her, to the moment in the control room when she had the epiphany that the signal might come from outside the solar system, to a brief imagining of herself receiving a certain medal in Stockholm, Sweden. But then she returned to the present and glanced expectantly at Stephan.

Stephan was quiet. He was an observer here; the story, the discovery, and the moment were clearly Rain's.

"What's next? What did the director general say?"

"What's next is you are going to Earth on the next shuttle to New York. It departs tomorrow morning at oh-seven-hundred sharp. Once you land at LaGuardia, there will be a car waiting to take you to the UN where you'll be met by a team they're pulling together. I've sent them all the data, but I want you to carry it on a memory cube as well. In this case, redundancy is good."

"And what, exactly, will this team do?" asked Stephan. It was the first words he'd spoken since the meeting began.

"They're going to review it, parse it, turn it back into bits and reassemble, analyze, and decompress every bit so many times that no one will question its authenticity. And if it is fake, they will skewer this facility, likely fire me, cut our budget, and make sure both of you are never again employed in a scientific field anywhere in the solar system," Kirkland said without a trace of sarcasm.

Rain was sure she was serious and that didn't bother her one bit. She knew she hadn't faked any data and she was confident that they'd ruled out any reasonable probability of fraud or fakery. The signal was real, since they'd now logged many hours of it—humanlike voices, music, and noises all the while.

"I'll be ready. And I don't expect to be fired any time soon," Rain said as she rose from her seat, barely keeping herself from leaping for joy. *In one-sixth gravity such a leap would cause my head to hit the ceiling*, she told herself as the temptation passed.

"Stephan, you can go with her if you want. There is an extra seat," Kirkland said as she eyed first Stephan and then Rain, waiting on their answer.

"Well, I, um..." stumbled Stephan.

"I'd be honored to have my codiscoverer go with me," interjected Rain. As she looked at him, all she could think was how much he looked like a kid being picked up and swept away by a tornado. Not that she'd ever seen a tornado in person, but she could imagine. She suppressed a smile.

"Okay then, you'll both be on the seven o'clock shuttle. You'd better go pack and try to get some rest."

Stephan rose and accompanied Rain out the door, remaining one step behind her as he did so.

Rain looked around the Luna Shuttle as she strapped herself into her acceleration chair next to Stephan and eight other passengers bound for Earth. She wasn't sure, but she suspected their having two seats with such short notice resulted in someone else being bumped to a later flight. She couldn't imagine that the craft would fly unless all the seats were occupied and fully paid for.

The shuttle wasn't exactly spacious, but it was comfortable enough. In addition to their seats, where they would also eat all their meals and spend most of their awake time, she and Stephan had adjacent microsuites to use during their trip to Earth. Though hardly spacious, the microsuites had everything possible to make the three-day journey back as pleasant as possible. Measuring five feet on a side, the enclosed suite had a personal virtual reality entertainment system, a private video link with which they could call anyone on Earth or in the solar system ("*The first ten minutes are free!*"), and a wall-hanging sleeping bag into which they would zip themselves into each night if they wanted to sleep. Since after the initial boost from the lunar surface the ship would coast with no acceleration until the Earth entry burn was required, they would be in zero gravity, making "up" and "down" distinctions completely arbitrary. Sleeping zipped into a pouch was required to keep them from drifting around the cabin and bumping into the walls with the air currents from the life-support system as it stirred the air. Everyone aboard—the two pilots, one steward, and ten passengers—shared a common two-seater toilet in the back of the shuttle.

As they departed the surface and flew within sight of the Apollo 12 Historical Site, Rain couldn't help but think about the "room" used by Alan Bean, Pete Conrad, and Dick Gordon on their journey to and from the moon. Cramped into a tiny capsule, the trio didn't even have room to stretch.

Late in the first day of their trip, just before dinner, Rain found a popular press article about the Japanese spacecraft that had confirmed her findings. The *Interstellar Voyager* was built in Japan (where else?) by an industrial consortium that included the big aerospace tech giants from the USA, Europe, Japan, and China. They all wanted in on the flight because of the new space drive that propelled it—the Samara Drive. She found it ironic that the country home to Samara State Aerospace University, Russia, didn't have a company in the consortium. According to the article, once the Samara Drive was proven in deep space on missions like *Interstellar Voyager*, it would be put into use on just about every other spacecraft in the system. From what she could tell, if they had the new drive on their shuttle, they would not need microsuites with sleeping quarters. The trip to or from the Moon would take only a few hours, not days. Now *that* she was looking forward to.

Rain noted that poor Stephan was still looking as confused as the day before when Kirkland offered him the chance to accompany Rain on the trip to Earth. Deborah clearly thought they were a "couple," even though Rain had tried extremely hard to *not* give anyone that impression. Stephan, Rain knew, wanted very badly to be part of a couple with her, but that just wasn't in her playbook right now. And she'd tried to make that clear to him. Having him accompany her on the trip didn't help.

As they belted into their seats in the common area, located centrally between the two rows of passenger microsuites, dinner was served by their steward. Jon, as he introduced himself, was about thirty, spoke with an Israeli accent, and appeared to be normal born, not genetically engineered. She surmised this when she saw his already thinning hair and slightly off-center, but very real, grin. She liked him immediately.

Stephan and Rain had spent most of the trip so far not talking about the signal, instead focusing on the excitement of the launch and the spectacular view as they departed the Moon. Rain never tired of the views from space, even after spending so much time on the Moon. She felt a compulsion to be there and experience every second as if it were going to be her last. Most people she had met in the "space business," she had come to learn, didn't share her bonding with the infinite. For them, the science, technology, and engineering challenges posed by space exploration provided the motivation. She was, for all practical purposes, married to her job, which was how she rationalized and explained her not having any emotional attachments. Truth was, she was desperately lonely and dreamed of finding her soul mate. But THE criterion that soul mate would have to meet was a shared love of space and a desire to spend as much time there as possible. Any commitment without that would, she feared, keep her from spending so much time away from Earth.

After the meal, Rain retrieved her datapad and pulled up on the screen her latest analysis of the alien signal.

"Stephan, I've been thinking about the origin of the signal and I'd like your opinion," Rain said, looking up from the pad, glancing out the window briefly before fixing her gaze on the man beside her.

"Me, too," he said, pulling out his own datapad and unlocking it with his thumbprint.

"First of all, the source can't be all that far away. The signal-to-noise ratio is surprisingly good and it isn't broken up with too much interference. That means there aren't many energetic sources between us and the origin along the line of sight," Rain said, scrolling through a seemingly endless stream of numbers with her right index finger.

"The Centauri system," Stephan said with a growing smile.

"What? Why do you say that?"

"Well, first because of what you just said. I didn't sleep much last night and, well, since I couldn't rest, I thought I'd do some additional data analysis before we get peppered with questions at the UN. I made a list of the nearest stars, ones with planetary systems and planets we think might be habitable. I omitted those that weren't in the general direction of where we think the signal originates. Then I looked at the signal strength and did a quick regression analysis to see what the output signal power would have to be for us to get the signal we recorded and that eliminated all the stellar systems that are more than twenty-five light-years away. If the broadcast came from one of them, their output power would have to be enormous and likely directed toward us—something I just don't think is happening. I feel like we are eavesdropping on a planetary broadcast meant for local consumption, not for us."

"That sounds reasonable, but why jump to the conclusion that it originates in the Centauri system? Because it is the closest?" she asked.

"Triangulation. We have the position of the *Interstellar Voyager* and we know where its antenna was facing when it recorded the signal. Combine this with our data and the stellar systems close enough for us to get the signal-to-noise we're measuring, and we have triangulation on the origin. Simple geometry. So simple, I did it by hand," Stephan said as he pulled a sheet of laboratory notebook paper from his trouser pocket and unfolded it.

Rain eagerly leaned over to look at his handwritten note filled with triangles and a few simple trigonometric formulas. The math was simple and the conclusion he reached so basic and straightforward that she used her right hand to slap her own head after reading it.

"Proxima Centauri," she said, looking up from the paper and excitedly at Stephan.

"Proxima Centauri," he replied.

"Do you know which planet?" she asked.

"There's not enough fidelity to triangulate on a particular planet in the system, but I can hazard a guess. We've known since the early 2000s that there are stable planets around Proxima Centauri and the mostly likely candidate is Proxima Centauri b.

Proxima is a red dwarf star and not as luminous as Sol. The planet is in the habitable zone, which at Proxima Centauri places it really close to its parent star. We're about twenty times farther away from Sol than Proxima Centauri b is from its star. And guess what? B has an orbital period of eleven days. That would explain your eleven-day variation in the strength of the signal. Halfway through, the planet is behind the star and the signal is completely blocked."

Rain started to say something and instead she did something she never thought she would ever do. In her excitement at the news, she kissed him, and immediately regretted doing so. *There I go again, leading him on. Dammit!*

ased ultra-
All were
ervatory
ce and

heard
ima
ble
y,
d

CHAPTER 3

May 2, 2072

"We don't know much about aliens, but we know about humans. If you look at history, contact between humans and less intelligent organisms has often been disastrous from their point of view, and encounters between civilizations with advanced versus primitive technologies have gone badly for the less advanced. A civilization reading one of our messages could be billions of years ahead of us. If so, they will be vastly more powerful, and may not see us as any more valuable than we see bacteria.' Stephen Hawking said this in 2015 and he was right. We should not reveal our existence when we don't know what's out there," said Joaquin Luce, his voice quavering only a bit as he concluded his remarks to the committee.

Joaquin Luce was among the last of several experts called to testify at the UN Special Committee on Proxima Centauri—specifically, on the problem of the radio signals received from Proxima Centauri and what to do about it. Would the UN send a message in response? That was the big question. As the director of the European Southern Observatory, Luce spoke with authority. He was clearly used to speaking his mind and having people listen. At fifty-two, he wasn't the youngest-ever director of the ESO, but he was, by far, the most successful—technically and programmatically. The Observatory was flush with cash, using the money raised by Luce to upgrade all the instruments and data processing systems at all the Observatory's optical, infrared, and radio telescopes throughout Chile as well as their lunar optical

telescope. Within two years, ESO's new flagship space-b
violet telescope would be ready for launch into space.
the results of Luce's tireless efforts on behalf of the Obs
and its researchers. Luce was passionate about space scie
astronomy and had given his life over to the pursuit.

"Professor Luce, don't we know what's out there? We've
a great deal these last two days about the signal from Prox
Centauri and all the scientists agree that whoever is respons
for it are over one hundred years behind us technological
roughly at the stage we were in around the year 1950. It woul
seem to me that we are the more advanced species and they the
primitives. Shouldn't we be worried more about contaminating
them?" The speaker was the Honorable Kiania Oliveira, chair of
the UN special committee. Oliveira was Brazilian, but her English
was nearly perfect, betraying only a slight Portuguese accent.
Leaning forward in her seat, it was clear that she, too, was used
to speaking in public and getting her way. She exhibited just the
right amount of ignorance and humility in her question to show
deference to the scientists in the room, but not enough to appear
weak in her resolve to understand the real situation at hand.

Luce mentally conceded that Oliveira was correct. They'd been
listening and trying to understand the signals coming from near
Proxima Centauri for almost two months now and were not much
closer to translating their all-too-human-sounding language into one
that people from Earth could understand. Other than correlating
some words and phrases that always seemed to precede music or
what the experts said was most likely news, they were still woefully
ignorant. No interstellar Rosetta Stone had yet been found.

"Ms. Oliveira, you are most likely correct. What we're detecting is almost certainly radio leakage of a civilization much like
our own in the last century. We are more advanced than they
but we're assuming that the 'they' we are listening to is the real
'they.' How do we know this isn't some sort of ruse? Furthermore,
if we beam a message to Proxima Centauri with sufficient power
to be noticed, we cannot guarantee that only 'they' will be listening. The signal isn't so focused that it will only be detectable on
their planet. No, it will continue to propagate through space for
quite some distance and be detectable by anyone else out there
for many years to come. Like Dr. Hawking, I don't believe we
should make our presence known."

The proposal to send a message from Earth to the denizens of that planet near Proxima Centauri had considerable backing from many countries, including two of the most powerful—China and the United States. Still, all nations agreed that something of this magnitude would affect all countries and that the decision should rest with the United Nations. This committee was merely the first step toward a vote in the General Assembly. A recommendation to send the signal, or not, would carry a great deal of weight when it finally came to a vote. Luce would do his very best to get the committee, and then the General Assembly, to vote "no." His personal experience observing the indigenous peoples of South America still trying to catch up with their colonist-descended cohorts convinced him of that. The native peoples of the Americas had been first contacted nearly six hundred years ago and they still had not recovered. He didn't want the same fate for all of humanity.

Luce looked around the large assembly room and it was packed. It had been packed since before the gavel struck early that morning to begin the meeting and it looked like no one had left. Luce was sure the press gallery was equally filled and God-only-knew how many people were watching on the 'net.

"The chair recognizes the speaker from the United Nations Permanent Forum on Indigenous Issues," said Kiania Oliveira as she diverted her attention to the representative from a sister committee to her own.

Speaking of indigenous peoples . . . thought Luce as he sat back and rested in his chair, eager to hear what the experts in dealing with the aftereffects of historical first contacts had to say.

The new speaker, a man who looked to be in his early forties with a wide face, high cheekbones, coal-black hair, and a demeanor that one would immediately mistake for that of a much older man, rose to his feet.

"Madam Chair, my name is Chayton Jonathan Williams, Chayton is my tribal name and means 'falcon,' but I go by Jon or Mr. Williams. I am descended from the Lakota Nation in North America and a representative of the United Nations Permanent Forum on Indigenous Issues. I am honored to address this committee and bring to it the perspectives from my committee's deliberations on this matter. I should mention that the UN Forum on Indigenous Issues has members from indigenous peoples' groups from around the world and, because of this, our members' views are no more monolithic than those of the other peoples in this room. With one exception. On this issue, we stand firmly against sending a message to the people of Proxima Centauri." Chayton Jonathan Williams paused, looked around the room as if waiting on a question, and then continued.

"The peoples we represent in my committee are all the victims of imbalanced first contact and, as the previous speaker aptly noted, most have not yet fully recovered. Even if the indigenous peoples of the world had not been the victims of horrific diseases and physical conquest, their cultures would nonetheless have suffered, perhaps irreparably, from even a peaceful first contact with a more technologically advanced culture. In nearly every case of such interaction throughout human history, the indigenous peoples have suffered. It is for this reason that we oppose sending a message. We should honor the native inhabitants of Proxima Centauri and not subject them to the same sort of disruption that my people experienced in North America. We do not have the right to force ourselves upon them, potentially doing them and their emerging culture substantial harm."

The room was silent after Chayton Jonathan Williams finished his impassioned speech. Luce, while grateful for the support, was surprised at the rationale behind it. The reverse consequences of first contact had never occurred to him and, for that, he felt guilty. And the fact that it had never occurred to him made his opposition to sending a return message more strident.

The committee was soon to break for the day. Tomorrow would be closed-door deliberations with a full committee vote scheduled for the day after. There was only one speaker remaining on the agenda, the discoverer of the signal, Lorraine Gilster. Luce had met Lorraine only last month when her data was presented at a special UN meeting called for the purpose of reviewing and assessing the radio broadcasts she received and recommending what the next steps should be. She seemed reasonable enough, but he was inherently suspicious of her and her motives. She had made it clear in those early days that she was in favor of sending a message in response to the alien broadcast and she didn't appear to have given the consequences of doing so much thought at all. *Reckless* was the word that came to mind. Brilliant, affable but *reckless*.

"The chair recognizes Dr. Lorraine Gilster," said Oliveira.

Rain, with her name tag hand-altered to read "Rain," instead of "Lorraine," leaned forward to the microphone, cleared her throat, and began speaking.

"Ladies and gentlemen. I had the honor and good fortune to be the first person to learn the nature of the radio signal coming across to us from Proxima Centauri just a short time ago. It seems like yesterday but so much has happened since that first 'ah ha!' moment I had at the Farside Radio Observatory. What we heard that day, what we learned that day, is extraordinary. We are not alone. Let that sink in for a moment. Since the dawn of history, when our ancestors were looking at the night sky and imagining that the lights they saw were the campfires of people like themselves, looking toward them, pondering their own existence, we have wondered about life elsewhere.

"You heard the scientific basis for making contact this morning and I won't be redundant. I'm here to make the case on a deeper level, from a human level, from the perspective of sentient beings here and *there*. Whoever sent the signal we received is obviously sentient and perhaps I'm anthropomorphizing here, but if we wondered such things as we gazed at the sky, then how could they not also have the same questions? Aren't they most likely looking outward wondering if they are alone? Personally, I cannot imagine making this discovery and saying, 'Isn't that interesting, now let's have dinner.' To dismiss this opportunity to communicate with another self-aware species is unconscionable, and, I would argue, inhuman. I urge this committee to approve sending a response message as soon as possible."

A door in the back of the committee chamber opened, and an olive-skinned man made his way down the main aisle. He walked like a man on a mission. His appearance, from his jade-encrusted bolo tie and sport coat to his straight black hair worn long and in a ponytail, screamed of a man who meant to be noticed and heard.

"Thank you, Dr. Gilster. I know everyone here is ready to go to your hotels and get some rest, but we've had a last-minute shuffle to the agenda with an additional speaker this evening. The chair now recognizes the speaker from the United States Space Economy Committee, Ambassador Charles Jesus," Kiania Oliveira said as she read the name from the screen in front of her without looking up.

"It's pronounced Jesus, Madam Chair, just like the Christian's savior. Not 'hey zeus,'" the man said lightheartedly as he settled into his seat. He adjusted his microphone and then took a sip of water from the glass before him. There was a light, embarrassed chuckle from the chairwoman. "I am here as a pragmatist and in some ways nonbiased in the decision either way to send a return contact signal to Proxima Centauri. Dr. Gilster and Professor Luce both made very interesting arguments for both and Mr. Williams's speech, while historically correct, left out large portions, and dare I say important and fundamental components, of the positive side of the history of first contact. While it is true that millions of natives around the world and throughout history died due to accidental disease exposure, conquest, war, and exploitations of various sorts, the long-term results and economic benefits of contact are historically clear. The North American Natives made it clear early on that they were very interested in the technologies being brought by the explorers, as they quickly put aside their bows and arrows and picked up black powder weapons. The fur and domestic farming trade industry arose from the contact between the various natives and explorers and business peoples. It is true that cultures mingled, mixed, and some even vanished, but that is true of all cultures throughout history and has very little to do with first contact and everything to do with change, adaptation to circumstances, and simply time. We are certainly not going to be 'accidentally infecting' these people anytime soon as they are light-years away and we know of modern microbials, antibiotics, and antivirals. We could have a very slow cultural, scientific, philosophical, and economic exchange across the distance between the stars. Imagine, what if we can electronically invest in them and they in us? The wealth, the commerce, from information exchange alone could spark business on both worlds as to yet completely unimagined levels. So, I say, Madam Chair, and to the members in this gathering, and to the world, we should not dismiss the opportunity of a lifetime, of all times, here and now. Contact with these people might be the biggest investment we can make for our future and theirs. Thank you for your time."

The ambassador from the US leaned back and looked across at both Rain and Mr. Luce with a look of satisfaction on his face. Luce glared back at him, disappointed in himself for not having thought of adding counters to the "economic argument." Between Jesus and Gilster he was concerned that he had not been strong enough in his counter. Jesus's speech was based on dollars and with many of the UN-based organizations being socialist it might not be as effective as the "cultural negatives" of Mr. Williams's arguments. But the astronomer's arguments were emotional and philosophical—two very powerful debate weapons. To top it off Gilster's speech was not only emotional and articulate, but also, Luce had to admit, convincing. *He* wasn't convinced, but he could tell by looking at the faces of the committee members that they were sympathetic to what she had said, and he now knew the vote would be close. He might even lose. If that was to be the case, then he feared for the future of every human on Earth. *Stephen Hawking was right,* he thought, *and these fools can't see it.*

CHAPTER 4

May 4, 2072

Luce received the news of the committee's vote just as he and his wife were sitting down to have a quiet dinner at home. His wife of nearly twenty years, Maria, had prepared his favorite: lasagna, spinach salad, and a full glass of pinot noir. His AI, affectionately called Roberto, interrupted his second bite with its customary and polite, "Excuse me, Dr. Luce, but you have a call from one of your approved contacts, Dr. Felix Asiago."

"Thanks, Roberto, I'll take it on the speaker," replied Luce, after getting an approving nod from Maria. Maria was used to the interruptions. After all, they happened almost daily.

"Joaquin, we won. The UN Committee voted against recommending sending a message to Proxima. And it wasn't even close. I think the plea from Chayton Jonathan Williams sealed the deal. Once the scientists were up against *Star Trek*'s prime directive, they were bound to lose," said Felix, his rapid speech betraying his excitement.

Luce was surprised and elated. He had sincerely thought the vote was lost after Ambassador Jesus's economic appeal and Dr. Gilster's emotional speech just before they adjourned. But fortunately, more cautious heads prevailed, and Earth wouldn't be loudly announcing its presence into the great unknown—at least for a while.

"Felix, is the full council set to vote next week as originally planned?" asked Luce, his elation momentarily subsiding while his political mind reengaged. Though they'd won the committee

33

vote, they still had to win the vote in the General Assembly and there was absolutely no guarantee that it would follow the committee's lead. It was likely, but not guaranteed.

"Yes. And you can bet that the US and Chinese delegations will be lobbying heavily to win. Both will likely start calling in favors. The multinationals are lobbying heavily in favor of making contact. They smell new ideas, new technologies to patent, and new products to sell."

"I don't buy that last argument, Felix. We've discussed this before. If their tech is really over a hundred years behind ours, what can they possibly have to tell us we don't already know? Other than their religion or philosophy, or perhaps their own version of the Kama Sutra, our science and technology are almost certainly way ahead of theirs," said Luce, taking another bite of lasagna and washing it down with a large sip of wine.

Luce's wife winked at him, nearly causing him to choke.

"The point is, we don't know what we don't know and isn't that the whole point in not making contact? God only knows what sort of wonder weapon they've developed and that could be unleashed here. Talk about a potential for disruptive technology!" said Felix.

"I'm right there with you. We may not have the money like our opposition, but if the public opinion polls are accurate, then we have the majority of the world's population on our side. The numbers I saw yesterday had the 'no contact' side up with about sixty-seven percent. The other side was at twenty percent with the rest 'undecided.' If the politicians are listening to their constituents, then they'll have to ignore the big-money corporations on this one and side with common sense and caution, just like the committee recommends."

"If I know you, however, you aren't going to take a win for granted. Shall I reconfirm the appointments you have set up over the next few days?"

"Yes, please. And let me know if anything else comes up that might influence the vote. We don't want to take anything for granted. Goodbye, Felix." Luce ended the connection.

"Cause for celebration?" asked Maria, draining the last of the wine from her glass.

"For today, yes," said Luce.

"Roberto, hold all calls until tomorrow morning," said Maria as she scooted her now-empty plate of lasagna toward the middle of the table. She leaned forward and kissed her husband on the forehead, adding, "Let's celebrate. I'm all yours and you are all mine."

Luce looked at his still-uneaten meal and said, "There's always the microwave..."

"Damn, damn, damn," Rain cursed as she looked across the table full of take-out Chinese food in its customary tidy, small, and individually packaged white boxes. Stephan, her once-again dinner partner for the evening, looked back. Rain thought he looked wistful, but she was still seeing red.

"Rain, I'm so sorry," Stephan said.

"The committee voted three days ago, and I haven't thought of any meaningful way to negate Chayton Jonathan Williams's isolationist revisionist history he gave in the General Assembly. If it weren't for him, the vote would probably have been 'yes.'" Rain said. "It's like they didn't even listen to that ambassador's speech."

"Agreed. I would have thought that the data showing we've been announcing our presence for a century and a half to anyone nearby listening would have swayed them. After all, anyone within one hundred and fifty light-years would have a chance of picking up one of our own early radio or television broadcasts. If they had sensitive enough equipment, of course," Stephan said.

"Play the odds. Someone would have to be listening, with sensitive enough equipment, at the right frequencies, and at the right time. If they stopped listening before 1920, then they would be convinced there was no one out there and be blissfully ignorant of our existence. And to pick up our earliest signals out that far is a long shot in and of itself. They would be awfully dim at those distances and mostly lost in the noise due to all the other, much more energetic radio sources out there. No, the Proximans might have been able to pick it up, but they didn't have the tech yet," Rain countered.

"And now we're mostly quiet," Stephan nodded.

"And now, thanks to fiber and laser comm, we don't emit nearly the radio noise we did a hundred or so years ago. And you know, as a radio astronomer who up until a few months ago fought against what radio noise we still produce, I was elated. Now, not so much."

"Yeah. If the Proximans are listening, they won't hear much. Our peak signal years happened too long ago. Technology marches on. Their signals aren't even digital, for God's sake. It's still analog and probably created using vacuum tubes," he said.

Rain stopped chewing her General Tso Chicken and looked straight at Stephan.

"Technology marches on. Technology marches on," Rain said after swallowing her half-eaten bite.

"You've got something," said Stephan.

"Your comment made me think of those odd, almost-digital signals we started picking up on the carrier wave from Proxima two days ago. When did the code breakers at the National Security Agency get them to do their magic?" she asked.

"Not until this morning. I wouldn't expect to get anything back from them for a week or more," said Stephan, cautiously.

"Your mentioning old technology made me think of something. What if we're trying to be too 'high tech' in looking at the data and in trying to figure it out? The intelligence community will be running their best code-breaking, AI-enhanced algorithms trying to figure it out. What if we need to look extremely low tech?"

"Go on," Stephan said.

Rain reached to her side and pulled her tablet computer out of the bag from next to her seat. She was never far from her purse or her access to the data from Proxima.

"Here's one of the new data sets," she said, holding up her tablet and pointing to the rows of numbers. "Let's not look at this as some sort of binary code to break, but as a simple binary encoding similar to what our technological forebearers had to work with. Let's send the data to the image processor and tell it to render all the zeros as black and the ones as white and to arrange it into a single image."

Rain's fingers flew across the tablet as she had her computer do just what she said. Then, she stopped and stared at the screen.

"Oh my God," she said, finally.

"What? What have you got?" asked Stephan, starting to rise out of his chair.

"It's a picture. We picked up a fax machine transmission. They've got bloody fax machines!"

"What's it a picture of? Don't keep me in suspense," Stephan exclaimed.

Rain turned her tablet display around so Stephan could see

the image. On the screen was a black-and-white picture of a man holding what looked like a fish. He was wearing some sort of robe. He appeared to be in his early adult years, perhaps in his twenties, with features that were clearly Asian.

Both were speechless for several minutes. The room was so quiet that Rain could hear the sound of water dripping out of a faucet in the hotel's nearby bathroom. *Drip. Drip. Drip.* It was almost a mocking sound to Rain's ears.

"They're human," said Stephan.

"But that's impossible. Parallel evolution toward bipedal shape, bilateral symmetry, and all that I can buy. But parallel evolution to looking just like us is simply...impossible," Rain replied.

"We need to look at the other binary data sets. There are hundreds by now. How could we have missed this? How could the code breakers have missed this?" asked Stephan, now getting out of his chair and moving toward the hotel room's desk where he had put his tablet.

"I don't know, but let's see what else we have," said Rain, already scrolling to the next bit of data.

Two hours later, they had a collection of photos depicting different people, animals, buildings, and page after page of illegible text documents. It seemed that the Proximans used their radio fax-machine technology in much the same way those on Earth had—to send and receive documents. The additional images confirmed what they had seen on the first one: the Proximans were as human as Rain and Stephan, shared features that on Earth would be considered Asian, and they had cities and towns that anyone on Earth would recognize as such. There were humans just like them on a planet more than four light-years distant.

Five days later, the UN General Assembly, with hundreds of images received by fax from Proxima Centauri before them, voted nearly unanimously to prepare and send their new neighbors a greeting from Earth.

Though not a linguist, of which there would be plenty on the assembled message team, Rain Gilster was named the technical advisor. They were given one month to develop the message that would change the course of history for two worlds—two worlds inhabited by humans.

❖   ❖   ❖

Not quite ten months since the discovery of the signals from Proxima Centauri, using a radio telescope in Australia modified for sending a message and not just receiving one, the people of Earth began sending their greetings.

In addition to mirroring some of the radio broadcasts that had been intercepted, as a way to get the Proximans' attention, the message contained verbal and visual information about the people of Earth, its languages, cultures, arts, and, of course, its science and technology. It was the latter upon which most of team pinned their hopes of beginning a dialog: mathematics and physics had to be universal. Using the work of the late Carl Sagan and others from the 1970s as a starting point, they developed a message that used prime numbers as a starting point, followed by various universal principles and facts of mathematics and science, each building upon the previous. An *Encyclopedia Mathematica*.

Many members of the message team argued that communicating with *these* aliens ought to be relatively simple since they were, for all practical purposes and without having one to test and observe close up, human. The linguist developed a verbal and written language dictionary filled with common images and the associated words to describe them that almost any elementary school child would recognize: beginning with dog, cat, and house, the dictionary ended with more complex definitions like love, forms of government, and the performing arts. The result was probably the lengthiest and most complex fax ever sent.

The message, traveling between the stars at nature's speed limit, light speed, began crossing the interstellar void and losing strength almost immediately. No matter what the broadcast power, the signal strength at any distance from the source dropped in proportion to the square of the distance, meaning that by the time it arrived at Proxima Centauri, the signal would be relatively weak. Much weaker than the local broadcasts. That meant there was a chance it would not be detected for quite some time until someone stumbled across it. For this reason, the signal was set to repeat indefinitely. No one wanted the Proximans to miss it just because they weren't listening at the "right" time.

Two-way radio communication across four and a quarter light-years would take some time.

CHAPTER 5

April 14, 2082

After the flurry of activity surrounding the release of the news that humans weren't alone in the universe, including all the excitement of briefing the world's politicians, astronomers, anthropologists (who were the most excited at the news), philosophers, ethicists, laypeople, and just about every community group she could imagine, Rain had returned to her office on the Moon and her beloved radio telescopes. Like before the discovery, she would stop daily to admire the telescope array and its contrast with deep space. This time, she imagined she could see others out there, looking back.

Most people on Earth went about their daily routines without giving the humans on Proxima Centauri so much as an extra thought. There were bills to be paid, babies to be made, and places to see—just like there had always been. Before the discovery, some had thought there might be widespread panic at the news that humans had found life elsewhere. That there would be riots, people would finally give up religion, people would become more religious, or that the aliens would become an obsession to change people's lives forever. None of that.

Even the world's religions mostly took it in stride. The Christians were mostly curious as to whether the aliens had "fallen" into sin like we humans and if they had a redeemer. The Mullahs proclaimed that the aliens must "worship and be accountable to Allah," though not to Mohammad—he was only for humans on Earth. The Hindus embraced the news and, like the Christians, were curious as to how the aliens worshipped their gods. The Mormons, on the other hand, simply replied saying, "We told you so." There were pockets of deniers in just about all of the religious camps who, despite their theological differences, shared the general opinion that the Proximans couldn't really be human and therefore must be demons or some other nefarious creature that should be avoided at all cost.

After the initial shock, most people simply filed it away like they would the daily stock market report and moved on. Except, of course, for those who had a vested interest in studying and learning from the newly discovered aliens on Proxima Centauri b. Rain was, of course, among them. Her world had changed dramatically.

Rain was now the technical assistant to the director of the Lunar Farside Radio Observatory. The previous director, Deborah Kirkland, had long since retired and been replaced by a dynamic, much younger, and much more politically savvy woman named Samineh Bensaïd. Samineh had studied at Oxford and later at Nanjing University. Rain liked her much more than her predecessor and their respect was mutual.

Rain's discovery and fame, combined with Samineh's acumen and connections, landed the Radio Observatory its first major upgrade since its initial construction two decades ago. The array was being expanded by a factor of four, with all-new electronics and the latest AI-assisted signal processing. They also had secured management of the newly funded Solar Gravity Lens Telescope being placed six hundred astronomical units out, in the direction opposite to Proxima Centauri. The SGLT would allow direct optical imaging of Proxima Centauri b and extremely sensitive radio reception of their signals thanks to the amplification of electromagnetic radiation emitted from the distant planet by the sun's mass. The distortion of gravity around the massive sun would bend space-time and allow radiation passing through the bending to focus on the detectors they were building to send to six hundred astronomical units for just that purpose. Rain liked to describe the sun as acting like a magnifying glass, allowing select regions of the electromagnetic spectrum to be focused on their detectors like the magnifying lens would fry ants, if placed the appropriate distance from them on a sunny day.

Thanks to the Samara Drive, the SGLT would be on station

in only a few months after launch. *You can get places quickly if you can accelerate at one gee and use light as your reaction mass,* thought Rain. Initially there were concerns that the intensity of the light emitted by the drive would adversely affect the Earth's upper atmosphere, but those were mostly dispelled when limits were agreed upon to prevent the highest energy drives from being used anywhere near the Earth and Moon system. Most robotic missions and small crewed tugs fell into the category of having allowable emissions for use near the Earth. Larger ships, like the new mining ships and those bound for Mars, had to wait until they were much farther away to take advantage of the Samara Drive. Thus, like she had predicted nearly a decade ago, her trip times between the Moon and the Earth now took less than a day. *Not bad. I can even go home for the occasional weekend.*

Rain's day started, like so many before it, with a quick shower and breakfast, followed by a brisk walk around the perimeter of the base where all of those who maintained the Lunar Farside Observatories (it was now more than one) lived. Her warm-ups and cooldowns were, of course, at the large observation window overlooking the radio telescope's array. She never grew bored of the sight.

Rain liked her morning runs. Aside from the obvious health benefits, like keeping her cardiovascular system healthy in the Moon's paltry one-sixth-gravity environment, it gave her time to think and reflect. Today was one of those days she could sink into melancholy if she weren't careful; she was pondering her life that almost was, her own mortality, and what her next career steps might be.

Rain's thought train began as she finished her warm-up at the observation window and reminisced about her time with Stephan. He'd finally grown weary of Rain's lack of interest, left the observatory staff, and found himself a job working at a nearside university teaching astronomy. She missed him and sent an occasional message informing him of the latest scientific discovery—just before the details were published and widely available. It made him feel like an "insider" and kept their friendship warm. There had been no one significant in her life since him and she was fine with that—most of the time. Today, her next thought was what it would have been like to marry Stephan and start a family. This one didn't last long since Rain had extreme difficulty intellectually reconciling the demands of family, husband, and children with her work. She knew which one would take priority and, if she had taken this path, that the likely outcome would have been acrimony and divorce. A path, she admitted to herself, that was probably best not taken. Even if it did make her sometimes feel lonely.

By the time she was in her cooldown, Rain had moved on to thinking of what she would do after her time on the Moon. She was now near the maximum allowable lunar stay time. Despite her morning workouts and the many pharmacological treatments given to those on the Moon for more than just a few weeks, her heart was still losing strength, her bones were weakening, her muscle tone declining, and her total radiation dose from solar and galactic cosmic ray exposure was ticking inexorably upward. Every lunar facility adhered to these universal health guidelines and they would soon catch up with her, forcing her return to Earth and... *what?* It was her thinking about the "what" that made her melancholy.

She thought that looking at the moonscape through the observation window would bring her out of it, and it did, but only by changing what she was thinking about. It was as beautiful as ever, stark, desolate, and mostly unchanging.

Unlike the Moon's nearside, which always faced the Earth, giving those back home the same constant and unchanging view of the Moon to which they were accustomed, there was little or no commercial activity on the farside. To maintain the pristine, radio-quiet environment that had led to the discovery of the Proximans, the UN's ban on farside development remained intact and no orbiting radio communications relay satellites were ever approved. Keeping the farside pristine was now a widely recognized "good idea" that was almost universally supported by the world's politicians and public.

Lunar nearside was a vastly different story. With the advent of the Samara Drive, the Moon was far more accessible both logistically and financially than ever before, with bases, hotels, universities, and research facilities being built there at a prodigious rate. With a land area roughly equivalent to Asia, there wouldn't be a lunar land shortage for quite some time.

Today, Rain was back in the control room, but instead of

being the one directing—or, more accurately, watching—the AI direct the day's observations, she was simply there to discuss with one of the operators how the new parts of the extended array would be integrated with the existing system as the new segments were completed. They had discussed this many times in the design phase, but now was the tricky part: putting the plans into action. And, like a general's battle plan becoming useless once the battle was engaged, sometimes the best-designed interface would have unexpected problems. Rain was trying her best to avoid having that happen.

She and the operator—a slim, inexperienced but eager female post-doc named Margie, from Ontario—were just getting into the details when the observatory's AI interrupted. The AI had a male voice and, Rain long ago concluded, a very male personality. It was the latest generation general-purpose AI, meant to resemble a human when in direct interaction, and designed to fool just about anyone who tried to give it a Turing Test. Most AIs resembled men, Rain had noted many times, thinking that the reason might be its inherently linear thinking. Women's thoughts tended to interconnect with everything, shaded with nuance and too holistic for most men to really understand. Men's thoughts, however, tended to be much more focused, one topic at a time, with an almost conscious effort to not follow the obvious interconnected thoughts. AIs, being software and still mostly based on simple "if/then" coding, were also linear. Hence, the male thinking pattern that she perceived.

"Dr. Gilster. We are receiving a new transmission from Proxima Centauri. I am sending the translation to your station."

Rain, now excited by the news so blandly reported by the AI, moved away from the wide-eyed Margie and to her station just to the left of the picture window that overlooked the massive array. Rain moved so quickly she nearly stumbled, easily recovering thanks to the low gravity. After she unlocked the device with her thumbprint, the contents of the message began to scroll across the display.

A parroting of their own message, just like they had parroted the aliens' message in the first part of theirs.

More parroting. And yet more. The replay extended for several pages and then... something new.

A grayscale picture of what looked like a human family, sort of—two men, a woman, and five children, all male, standing next to what looked like an ocean or lake. Two men? She wondered what people would make of that. It was clearly a disarming greeting intended to show their humanity. The people were all dressed in robes and they held their palms upraised. Was this the equivalent of an Earth family waving?

Next were photos of trees, fields filled with flowers, lakes, mountains, and some fairly large cities with tall, concrete-and-glass buildings. And then came the animals, from what looked like insects to small mammals to large mammals and reptiles.

And then, the text, in somewhat broken and stiff, but understandable, English:

GREETINGS EARTH. PEOPLE OF PROXIMA CENTAURI HELLO.

The Proxima Contact Team was large, led by the UN-appointed Dr. Julia Coetzee. Coetzee, a native of South Africa, was clearly the UN's compromise candidate to lead the team. Well credentialed (she earned her PhD in linguistics from Cambridge) and well respected, she rose to the top of the list because she was from nonaligned South Africa. Coetzee opted to conduct the meetings of the Contact Team virtually, with most of its twenty-eight members participating from their home institutions around the world and, in Rain's case, from the Moon. Until now, which meant for the past eight or so years since the team was formally established, they'd been studying the Proximans' solely by their electronic eavesdropping—listening to the radio broadcasts and attempting to read their transmitted faxes.

So far, they knew that the Proximans were most definitely human. The anthropologists and sociologists were at first disappointed with this fact but over time grew excited over the prospect of studying the societal and cultural development of an isolated human civilization. They knew human biology and roughly how people think; now they got to apply this knowledge to the study of a culture that had developed in complete isolation from Earth's humans and that was not yet contaminated by the knowledge that other humans even existed. What were their social constructs? How did they differ from Earth's human cultural and social development? How were they the same? They'd let the biologists argue over how it was even possible for humans to exist in evolutionary isolation.

And argue they did. For most, it was an established fact that humans had evolved on Earth by natural processes taking billions of years. Natural selection had tried various survival traits over these years and had, after a fashion, spawned a species of mammalian bipeds with large brains and opposable thumbs, leading to the development of an intelligent, tool-using species—Earth's humans. For this group, it was simply inconceivable that the parallel processes, operating completely independently on a world four and a quarter light-years away, could lead to the identical evolutionary product at about the same time. These processes took millions and billions of years. The likelihood of parallel evolution happening, at the same time, was essentially zero. Yet there they were—Proximan humans.

Their existence emboldened a minority group of biologists who adhered to the idea of panspermia—that life on Earth, and perhaps Proxima Centauri b, were related because of the past instances of Earth, and presumably other worlds, being smacked by asteroids, sending pieces of their planet into deep space. Some may have carried life, perhaps with the same DNA, to another world where evolution would continue. But even their theory didn't account for the facts. The bacteria or other simple organisms that traveled through deep space would still have to evolve into an identical species. Even this minority view had serious shortcomings.

And then there were those who said the whole thing was absurd. In their view, panspermia was science fiction and parallel human evolution a fantasy. They looked at what was known about Proxima Centauri, the star, and Proxima Centauri b, the planet, and concluded that advanced life there was simply impossible. Earth's Sun was over eight times heavier than Proxima Centauri and one thousand times brighter. That meant that the planet's habitable zone, where liquid water could exist, was twenty-five times closer to Proxima Centauri than the Earth was to the sun. Being that close to its parent star, there was a good chance the planet was tidally locked, meaning that one side of the planet was always facing the star and the other deep space—much like the Moon was to the Earth—making it a very complicated system for harboring life. In this group's view, too complicated. Red dwarfs also tended to fire off powerful flares—which can destroy a planet's atmosphere and bathe it in harmful radiation—more often than sun-like stars do. Considered together, the "absurd" group simply refused to believe any of the data. However, they were unable to provide an alternative viable theory to account for the signal. Yet.

The scientific community, across the board, had learned much about the Proximans since the first signals were detected, but much remained to be learned. They were all hoping that the two-way information exchange would be... enlightening.

There was much debate, and Coetzee, for the most part, reveled in it. She loved a good old-fashioned academic debate based on observable facts, not biased conjecture, and the topic of the Proximans' humanity was just such a debate.

The sociologists and political scientists had their own theories based on the intercepted message and texts. They surmised that the Proximans lived under a single government, spoke a single language, and developed a legal and governmental bureaucratic system much like our own. While they didn't understand the specific contents of the many faxes they studied, they were able to conclude that the vast majority were transactional, functional, the very same kinds of data that companies might digitally exchange in modern times.

Without a Proximan Rosetta Stone, they were extremely limited in what they could say with high confidence about the inhabitants of Proxima Centauri b.

That all changed with the arrival of the message two weeks ago. Not only did it contain an extensive dictionary of their language, but also what appeared to be a gigantic historical encyclopedia of their history and culture. The contact team decided to call it the Proximan Encyclopedia. There hadn't been enough time to parse all the data, but some high-level information was coming to light that merited discussion among the contact team, all of whom agreed to share the data among themselves. The data was embargoed until a majority of the committee voted to release it. The steering committee could, at least temporarily, bar the release of any information deemed "incendiary" or "politically destabilizing" to the world at large. So far, nothing the committee found had ever been permanently embargoed.

Coetzee saw that everyone was online and called the virtual meeting to order. The minutes of the last meeting were read and approved, and a vote was taken to dispense with regular business to begin a discussion of the recently received data dump from deep space. Coetzee knew that trying to have a firm, fixed agenda with a large group of scientists was impossible, but she tried. She first recognized the lead from the biology subteam, Dr. Felicia Hernandez, for a preliminary report.

"The biology subteam has no initial findings, but rather a few observations. From what we can tell from the data they provided in the Proximan Encyclopedia, they don't have a well-developed field of evolutionary biology. And the data provided on biology is extremely limited. We believe that information about their biology and biological history were redacted from what was sent. The gaps are obvious and can only be explained by deliberate omission," Hernandez stated. Her body language spoke volumes—she was clearly disappointed in the lack of usable data in the transmission.

"Madam Chair, may I interrupt?" asked Dr. Wang from the archeology and anthropology subteam. Wang was online from his university in Hong Kong.

"Certainly, Dr. Wang. Go ahead," said Coetzee.

"My team obviously hasn't had time to dig deeply, but we do find many entries in the Encyclopedia related to their cultural evolution. They have records going back at least as far as the oldest manuscripts here on Earth, perhaps further. Their cultural evolution seems somewhat parallel to ours in that they record their beginnings as hunter/gatherers near the planet's tropical regions, with the development of civilization following rather quickly after they discovered agriculture. There seem to be many instances of the all-too-human wars and conquests similar to those we endured, which, I might add, my team found to be disappointing and oddly comforting at the same time. It reinforces their basic humanity—the good and bad. Their path paralleled ours with early agricultural beginnings, following by warring city-states, leading to more complex social and cultural organization, and resulting in their current worldwide government. As best we can tell, the latter, the coalescing into one single government, is a rather recent event. The reasons for it are not completely clear—at least not yet. The bottom line is that until about ten thousand years ago, they were nomads on their world, much as we were. A parallel societal evolution, if not a biological one."

"Thank you, Dr. Wang. Can you tell us your level of surprise at this? In other words, given their development in assumed isolation from us, would you expect such similarities?"

"The committee is mixed on this, I am sure. But I can give my opinion. No, I am not surprised. Human beings are human beings—with the same basic needs of food, water, procreation, and control over one's own destiny. The possible solutions that lead to stable civilization are few and we humans have experienced many variations of them, at least as a species, here on Earth. I would have been surprised if they had come up with solutions significantly different from those proposed and tried here on Earth."

"Dr. Wang, do you have anything to add?"

"Yes, as a matter of fact I do, but it is more of a question for the biology subteam."

"Proceed," she said.

"Dr. Hernandez, what do the Proximans eat?" he asked.

"Now that is a surprise. Their diet appears to be quite similar to our own. In fact, from what we can tell, their biosphere is remarkably like ours—they grow wheat, corn, soybeans, and many other crops that would be recognizable to anyone here on their dinner menu tonight. They raise pigs and cattle, which, amazingly enough, look remarkably similar to those here on Earth. The few differences can probably be accounted for in the selective breeding they've done since implementing agriculture and farming. Simply stated, it isn't just the Proximans that appear Earthlike, but much of their biosphere could have easily been lifted from here to there with only subtle changes. It is a puzzle," she said.

This latter comment caused quite a stir among committee members, many of whom had to mute their microphones to silence the spontaneous discussions breaking out in the various conference rooms between team members and their local support teams at this most recent biological bombshell being delivered.

"Madam Chair, when our response is crafted, the biology team will have many questions to include. And we have a lot of data yet to sift through," said Hernandez.

"I'm sure you won't be the only ones with questions, Dr. Hernandez. And we will be collecting the questions from every team member as time passes and before any such new message is crafted," Coetzee said. "Next, we will hear again from Dr. Wang for the archeology and anthropology subteam."

"Thank you, Madam Chair. The archeology and anthropology subteam spent much of the last week looking at a topic to which the public seems to be showing extreme interest: religion. Specifically, do the Proximans have religion and, if so, then what is it? The answer was found in the Encyclopedia and it is yes.

The Proximans do, most emphatically, have religion. They seem to have many religions of the usual types: shamanic, monotheistic, Olympian, and atheistic. Of the four, monotheistic seems to be dominant. From what we can tell, none of their religions are historically similar to those found here on Earth. There are no figures comparable to Mohammad, Christ, or Buddha in their teachings, though the tenants of some of the religions seem to be roughly similar to their Earthly counterparts. If people are hoping or expecting our neighbors to answer one of the most vexing questions in our own history—what is the mind and plan of God?—then they will be sorely disappointed. The Proximans seem to be divided and seeking answers to the same questions as we."

"Except for their origins," commented someone from a hot microphone. Hernandez couldn't figure out from whom the comment came, but she wasn't really that concerned. She had the same thought herself. It was THE question.

Five months later, the first batch of questions from Earth was sent on its way to Proxima Centauri b. Along with them was Earth's version of an Encyclopedia.

Instead of redacted entries on biology and evolution, however, the Earth-human encyclopedia excluded just about everything on technologies beyond what could be ascertained as compared to the Proximans' own state of development. Generally speaking, this meant the removal of much of the scientific development of the twentieth and twenty-first centuries: quantum mechanics and technologies that grew from it were redacted, including nuclear power and nuclear weapons, transistors and semiconductors, lasers, etc. Even vacuum-tube television technology was omitted since the radio leakage observed thus far seemed to be audio only and they were not sure they yet had the technology. If not, they were certainly close. It was impossible to omit mentioning some of these technologies, but no technical details were provided.

Also omitted were entries on the mapping of the human genome, genetic engineering, and the cures of many of the diseases that had ravaged humanity since the species first arose. There was a fear that the detailed knowledge provided to the few that were involved in the interstellar communication loop could be misused.

After considerable debate, most of the violent history of

Earth's civilizations remained in the encyclopedia, including World War One and World War Two—minus the bit about dropping atom bombs on Japan, remembering the intentional omission of nuclear weapons and power. The decision to include these less-than-admirable events in human history was not unanimous. They were included to show reciprocity with the Proximans, who had been quite open about their own less-than-stellar history of conflict in what they sent.

The world waited on the response, or what the Proximans might have sent in the time after their first intentional message to Earth. Conducting a meaningful, consistent two-way conversation, if done serially, would take quite some time with about nine years between each successive message. Perhaps the messages would not be serial, and more data might be already on its way...

CHAPTER 6

August 12, 2086

In the four years since the original exchange, there was no new information from Proxima Centauri b. After Earth's reply was on its way with its series of questions and the Earth Encyclopedia, a second message was prepared. It was simply a collection of additional questions that no one thought to ask in the first one—an addendum. The UN team continued to meet, review the data provided, and parse it out to the entire world, open and freely available on the global internet to any who wanted to review it. Thousands of technical papers and many more popular press articles were published about the Proximans, their humanity, and their culture.

It was a busy year for Proximan culture on Earth. There was a play on New York's Broadway about a Proximan family in crisis due to a missing child; VR stories were created that allowed the viewer to experience what could best be pieced together about life on Proxima Centauri b, and concerts devoted to performance of Proximan music. For a while, it became fashionable to wear the long flowing robes that so often adorned the Proximans in the photos received thus far.

It was late in the year that Rain Gilster moved back to Earth after reaching her maximum allowed time on the Moon. She wasn't happy to leave, but she knew the rules and that it was for the best. She formally left the staff of the Lunar Observatory and accepted a position as Eminent Scholar of Astrobiology at Emory University in her hometown of Atlanta. She found it amusing that a physicist radio astronomer should be given a plumb emeritus position at a prestigious university in a field that was not her own, just because she was the one lucky enough to discover the existence of the Proximans. But since the job allowed her to remain on the contact team as an active member, she didn't complain. She didn't even have to teach regularly—just provide a few lectures each semester, bringing faculty and students up to speed on the latest discoveries from deep space.

It was after one such lecture, a joint event between Emory and Georgia Tech, that she met Enrico Vulpetti. He approached her after the last of the student questions and as she was packing up her belongings from the podium in the lecture hall. Despite the predictions that higher education would become virtual, making real-life university lectures a thing of the past, many colleges persisted and thrived. It seemed that people learned more and better in the physical setting of a university lecture hall. And Rain was glad for it. She loved the idea that she could VR with most anyone in the inner solar system from the comfort of her own home, but she found interacting with students in the here and now was something she enjoyed immensely. Of course, all the students' AIs were recording the lecture and, consequently, some students tuned out during her talk. But most did not, and it was for them that Rain would willingly go the extra mile.

"Dr. Gilster, may I have few minutes of your time?" asked Vulpetti with a smile. It wasn't a "how are you I'm glad to meet you" smile, but more of an "I'm friendly, can we talk?" smile. A smile that totally disarmed Rain and kept her from hurrying off as was her custom after a lecture.

"Sure," she said. She had noticed him approaching the podium and wasn't totally surprised by his introduction.

"My name is Enrico Vulpetti and I'm in the aerospace engineering department at Georgia Tech. My specialty is advanced in-space propulsion," he said.

Rain liked his voice. It was deep, purposeful, and conveyed confidence, but not arrogance. She didn't know the man, but she already liked him. He was probably ten to fifteen years her junior and she liked his overall appearance—tall, at least six feet, a full head of black hair, and just a bit of a five o'clock shadow that had to be intentional. She couldn't tell if he was bioengineered. Just enough facial hair to be masculine, not enough to look unkempt.

She momentarily wished she were younger. Especially when she noticed he wasn't wearing a wedding ring.

"How may I help you, Dr. Vulpetti?" she asked.

"Please call me Enrico. My students call me 'Dr. Vulpetti.'"

"Alright then, how may I help you, Enrico?"

"Have you been keeping up with the work on the Samara Drive?"

"Only to the extent that it made my last few years on the Moon much more tolerable and is the reason we're now sending people all over the solar system. I remember the 'good old days' of chemical rockets taking us from here to the Moon and I cannot say that I miss them," she replied.

"I'm on the team that's working on the next-generation Samara Drive, one that doesn't require the same amount of input power to derive thrust. Basically, we're improving its overall performance and simultaneously reducing the power required to use it. We've got a major test next month that I believe you'll be interested in."

"Why so?" she asked.

"Because, if it is successful, then we can start thinking about building a ship to go to visit the people on Proxima Centauri b instead of just sending them radio messages."

"I read a few years ago that we could already do that, or so I thought."

"You probably read about the robotic probe that the research group in Bremen came up with. Until now, there were limits on the ultimate speed a ship with Samara Drive could achieve that depended upon the weight of the ship and the availability of onboard power to drive the propulsion system. The Samara Drive's limits at the time kept the trip time to about one hundred years because it would have stopped accelerating when it reached about twenty percent the speed of light. As the ship's mass grew, the trip time increased and the maximum speed the craft could achieve dropped—if the power available remained the same. Unfortunately, if you want to have more power available onboard, the size and weight of the power system grows, making it more difficult to go faster, etcetera. To go faster, you need more power, which makes things heavier, which make them slower and requires more power, etcetera. The system begins eating its tail, as it were, and we're stuck with a century to send a robotic probe—one way."

"And that's changed?" Rain asked.

He smiled and said, "Oh, yes. Our new design is much more compact than its predecessors and the drive doesn't require nearly the input power. In addition, the Chinese have come up with a new compact fusion reactor design that we believe can fit on a large spacecraft, large enough to carry people, and accelerate it to at least 0.4c, maybe even as much as 0.9c, with possible trip times of under twenty to even ten years."

"Twenty years to Proxima Centauri? That's amazing. But for humans? Why not just send the robotic mission and cut the trip time even further? Wouldn't that be simpler? And if you're traveling that fast, shouldn't you get there a lot sooner than twenty years?" Rain asked in rapid-fire succession, her mind racing and now thoroughly engaged in the conversation, his thoughtful and penetrating gaze notwithstanding. She wasn't going to allow herself to be distracted by his good looks.

He smiled. "I'll try to answer your questions if I can remember them all. Yes, twenty years to get to Proxima Centauri. Yes, that would be for sending a ship carrying about a dozen people along with all the supplies needed to keep them alive for the trip. We propose a human mission because I—I should say *we*—don't believe that a robotic-only mission will have the support that a human mission would have. People are fascinated by the aliens at Proxima Centauri b and they want to go there and meet them. That might now be possible," he said.

"I'm impressed, but you didn't answer all my questions. Why is the trip time so long? If you are moving at forty percent the speed of light, then you should get there a lot faster than twenty years," she replied.

"If we want to stop at Proxima Centauri, then we will have to slow down. We'll accelerate to a maximum of about 0.4c at the halfway point and then turn it around and begin decelerating. Newton's Law says that it will take us just as long to decelerate as it took us to accelerate, lengthening the overall trip time."

"I get it. And why are you telling me?" she asked.

"I think that should be obvious. I want your support in the UN contact team when we bring it before them next month."

"And how long before this ship of yours could be ready to launch?" Rain asked.

"Not before the next message cycle. Three to five years. And that's if we can get the funding lined up quickly."

"I'm definitely intrigued, but before I can make any commitments, I will need to do my homework. Can you send me your contact information?"

"Already done. My AI proactively did that before we even began our conversation. I hope you don't mind. It can sometimes be, well, a bit pushy."

"I'm sure AIs don't get that kind of trait from their owners," Rain said with a smile.

"Of course not. Thank you for your time. I look forward to hearing from you."

"It was my pleasure," said Rain, looking wistfully at young Dr. Vulpetti as he walked away. *All that and brains too.* Once again, she found herself wishing she were a decade (or so) younger.

Later that night, after a mostly vegetarian meal and sinfully delicious chocolate cake dessert, Rain got on the 'net and did her homework about the Samara Drive, Chinese fusion reactor research, and Dr. Vulpetti. All three were very real and very impressive. She noted that Vulpetti was not just a propulsion researcher at Georgia Tech, he served as the Endowed Chair of Advanced In-Space Propulsion at Georgia Tech and directed the Advanced In-Space Propulsion Division at a major aerospace conglomerate. His credentials were impeccable and the more she learned about him and the nascent plans to build an interstellar-capable spacecraft within the next few years, the more she came to believe that it all might just be real.

She also came to the realization that it might also be premature to be thinking of a trip to Proxima Centauri. There was simply so much they didn't know about the Proximans and their world. Why were they keeping their knowledge of biology a secret? Without more biological information, any physical contact between Earth and Proximan humans would be dangerous—for both parties. She was reminded of the words spoken by Chayton Jonathan Williams in the committee hearing a decade ago and of her knowledge about the earliest contact between Europeans and the indigenous peoples of North America—before Christopher Columbus sailed the ocean blue.

That thought took her to one of the many reports, books, and briefings they'd been given to read since joining the contact team—a book about the same first contact Williams's ancestors experienced. The conclusions were not encouraging.

It was now known that fishermen from northern Europe contacted Native American fishermen in the North Atlantic and along the coast of North America long before Columbus convinced the Spanish monarchy to support his journey across the ocean in 1492. The two groups of fishermen didn't fight with each other, but the result couldn't have been any deadlier for the Native Americans. European diseases, to which the natives had no immunity, spread widely and wiped out significant fractions of the local population. Much of the pre-contact Native American population was already dead or dying when Columbus arrived in Hispaniola. It was first contact of the deadly kind.

The risk of disease being exchanged between Earth humans and Proximan humans was very real. If both were truly biologically human, then each would be susceptible to the diseases that afflicted the other. And, from what she knew about how rapidly viruses could mutate to get around any immunities that might exist, she doubted that either side would have experience with the illnesses that might be common and mostly harmless on their individual home worlds. A common cold for an Earth human might cause respiratory arrest in a Proximan human never exposed to a similar virus and vice versa. Or they might not. Humans were humans after all and the human immune system adapts. There was just no way to be certain on either side of that argument.

There truly was no way to know if this was a real risk, or not. The Proximans left out from their Encyclopedia just about everything related to their biological past, including common diseases. Earth decided to omit from its Encyclopedia any information about genetic mapping and engineering since it was assumed the Proximans would not yet have discovered this was possible—trying to not give away too much technological information too soon. Without these tools, without the common languages of modern biology and epidemiology, it would be impossible to know the risks. A ship full of Earth humans arriving at Proxima could be the catalyst for a global pandemic there, wiping out millions or billions of people. Or not. However, such a trip could prepare for just that scenario with a couple medical epidemiology experts, stores of vaccines and pharmaceuticals, and the means or technology to produce new treatments as needed all taken along for the ride. Another possible approach might be to ask the Proximans for volunteers to stay in quarantine with the Earthlings for a few weeks to watch for symptoms on either side. While it might be premature to jump to a manned mission, there were ways to do it safely. Or at least with lower risk.

Five weeks later, the idea of sending a crewed ship to Proxima Centauri b using the newly improved Samara Drive came up for consideration by the first contact committee and failed—by a slim margin. The suggestion would therefore not be sent to the General Assembly by the committee for a full vote unless one of the members of the Security Council decided to bring it up themselves. Of course, not everyone in the world agreed that the UN had jurisdiction over such matters and Enrico Vulpetti knew who many of these people were—and he had a "Plan B."

Two weeks after the committee vote, Enrico Vulpetti met with a group of angel investors in the Hotel Palácio in Estoril, Portugal. He requested they meet in Portugal, and this particular hotel, because Vulpetti was putting into play a plan that might not be well received by the rest of the world, particularly the world's political leaders, making him feel positively "cloak and dagger." It was here that the novelist Ian Fleming had supposedly penned the first of his James Bond novels and as the plan Vulpetti was pulling together became clear, he felt more and more like a character in one of those ancient novels. One of the villains, to be exact. Though he didn't feel like a villain, he gave the project a codename: *Spectre*.

Together, the three investors who met with Vulpetti controlled nearly one trillion dollars in assets. Their clients were the ultra-wealthy who either felt truly blessed to have so much money and were eager to share their good fortune with the masses, or they were the ultrawealthy who believed they could achieve a sort of immortality if they were to use some of their excessive wealth to the betterment of the species. Either way, what Vulpetti proposed piqued their interests—selfish or not.

By the time the dinner was over, and the chocolate mousse and aperitif were consumed, the deal was made. Design and development would begin immediately for the world's interstellar ark to carry her emissaries to Proxima Centauri—the UN be damned. As far as Project Spectre was concerned the governments of the world had little reign over the final frontier. Oh, the United States, Russia, and China each had their space forces but they were there to protect their national assets and industrial complexes and infrastructures in and throughout the solar system. Deep-space exploration was pretty much like the wild western frontier of the 1800s in North America. And there were few, actually a total of zero, US Marshals out there to do anything about...well, anything. Project Spectre would begin in secret and remain there as long as possible to avoid premature legal challenges that could slow them down or ground them altogether.

The plan was audacious. The ship would be built in the open, in the same lunar orbital shipyard that was now building the next of many interplanetary arks soon to be bound for the many planets, asteroids, and moons of the solar system. Only this one would be built to unique specifications, unique for a ship taking a multidecade-long voyage to Proxima Centauri at a significant fraction of the speed of light. With luck, no one would uncover the ship's true purpose until well after it was launched—when it was too late for any government to stop it. There was a lot of work to be done between now and then. Three years and some months was a long time for anyone to keep a project of this magnitude secret for very long. But it had been done in the past by military operations, video game industries, and moviemakers, so Project Spectre would do it as well.

At the end of the meeting, Saanvi, the investor who represented a multinational pharmaceutical consortium, asked Vulpetti the question that each of the meetings' attendees had been wondering about, but not willing to ask—until now.

"What's in it for you? Why are you putting your career, possibly your life as a free man, on the line to make this mission happen? Granted, you have the technical expertise to make it happen, but why? Once the world finds out about the project, won't you likely be arrested and put on trial on some charge or another? You might even be tried for treason against humanity, if there is such a thing. We'll make sure we are safe and untraceable. Our money will be laundered so much that it will look bleached by the time you receive it. We know how to do things like that. You don't and, in this case, can't. What is *your* angle?"

"It's quite simple. I want to go. If I'm on my way to Proxima Centauri they can't very well put me under arrest and lock me up, can they?" Vulpetti said, sipping the last drop of his Aperol. "And besides, I don't buy all that nonsense. There's no law keeping a citizen of most any country from deciding to leave the planet or solar system if they have the means. Show me the law."

The man on the other side of the table burst out laughing, held out his hand, which held his flexible AI interface pad, and said, "Pay up. I told you he would want to go on the trip." Looking resigned to his fate, the other investor took out his own AI pad and touched the two together.

"The funds are transferred," the second man said, now bursting into his own smile. "I'm not totally surprised, but I can't stand to turn down an interesting bet. And Dr. Vulpetti, you make a particularly good point about the laws. In fact, we might start paying some lawmakers and media conglomerates to start emphasizing and socializing that idea so that it will certainly appear legal, as far as everyone on Earth will believe, when the time comes."

"I'm glad that I lived up to your expectations," said Vulpetti, looking only slightly annoyed at being the brunt of their fun.

"Our expectations won't be met until you are on your way to Proxima Centauri. And remember, we get to pick fifty percent of the crew," said Saanvi, looking Vulpetti squarely in the eye.

"I remember. And you remember the crew members you select can't be a bunch of fat bankers. Whoever you select must have a skill that's needed, and they must pull their own weight on the trip out, and back, if they then choose to return to Earth." Vulpetti paused, briefly sizing up the investors. "I have one more requirement."

"And what is that?"

"I want my stepmother and my sister to be given forty-two million dollars each, tax free, and no questions asked. I want to be assured that they will be taken care of once I leave the planet. They're the only family I have."

"Why forty-two?" Saanvi asked with one raised eyebrow looking over a martini glass.

"First, I calculated about how much they would need to never have to work again and maintain a moderate low-end upper-class lifestyle for the rest of their days." Vulpetti smiled and finished with, "And I like Douglas Adams's writings. As old and antiquated as they are, they're still funny to me."

"Not familiar with the reference." Saanvi eyed his cohorts as if they were speaking telepathically with one another. Vulpetti guessed that their AIs were passing information back and forth and displaying them on virtual displays on their contact lenses or through their audio ear patches.

"We'll agree to those terms provided you deliver and agree to ours," Saanvi replied.

"It's a deal."

With that, the four nodded and stood from their chairs, said their goodbyes, and went their separate ways. Vulpetti headed for the casino across the street. He wasn't yet finished with his spy-novel adventure. Not until he found a wealthy and attractive blueblood to share the rest of the evening with him.

CHAPTER 7

December 02, 2086

It was a beautiful winter's day in Tampa, Florida, and Rain was enjoying every minute of it. Emory was taking its winter break and she was taking her own break in warm, sunny south Florida. The temperature was in the mid-70s, the sky was blue with barely a cloud visible, and Rain was on her way to meet with two fellow first-contact team members for an unofficial gathering in a quaint bar near the Tampa Museum of Art. Rain could taste her first margarita of the afternoon already, even though she was still ten minutes away. Strolling down the Tampa Riverwalk, Rain cleared her head and thought about as little as possible, other than where she was going, as she enjoyed the day. It was a good day.

As she came closer, she saw Julia, who still chaired the committee, sitting with Dr. Roger Young, one of the committee's recent additions. Both already had their afternoon drinks in hand as she approached. They waved her over.

"Julia, it's good to see you," Rain said, leaning over to hug her longtime colleague.

"Hi, Rain!" Julia seemed excited to see her.

"And Roger, it's a pleasure to see you again as well," she added as she gave him a less familiar, basically perfunctory, hug.

"Have a seat." Julia motioned to a chair.

They exchanged pleasantries until after the waiter had taken Rain's order and returned with her Charred Orange Margarita.

"Okay Julia, what's this all about? You didn't come to Tampa just to share drinks with me along the bay," Rain said, getting to the point.

"Rain, you're correct. Roger and his team have uncovered some information from the Proximan data that you need to know about. It's interesting and, if his conclusions are correct, will have major repercussions. Major ones," Julia said.

"Dr. Gilster. What do you know about human population growth over time, particularly in the twentieth century?" asked Roger.

"Not much, other than at one time people thought we were on the cusp of population doomsday and that Thomas Malthus was going to get his revenge," she replied.

He laughed. "It is a common misconception, you see, that the Malthusian model has any correlation with reality at all. The model claims exponential population growth that really doesn't represent any known species, especially if you include species competition. Fortunately for us, Malthus didn't take into account the miracles of modern agricultural productivity and the fact that educated and/or working women tend to have fewer children. And that wars, famines, pandemics, and other nonlinear forcing functions get injected randomly into any population. The Earth likely reached its peak population a few decades ago and the population growth rate has since become negative. Our numbers have been declining at a steady but manageable rate especially with the exodus to the Moon, Mars, the Belt, and other places throughout the system."

"Uh-huh," Rain nodded.

"We didn't outstrip the planet's food-bearing capacity and just about everyone's standard of living has been increasing for over a hundred years. But in the 1950s we didn't know that would happen. The population was increasing, thanks to modern medicine increasing everyone's lifespan generally, and children's in particular. Childhood mortality dropped dramatically as we discovered and began using antibiotics, vaccines, etcetera. The intelligentsia of the world wondered if we could, in fact, continue to outrun Malthus's predictions as the world population seemed to be exploding. Even the Nobel Prize-winning physicist Enrico Fermi fell into the fallacy of the Malthusian exponential population growth model. Of course, the Lotka-Voltera model, the more modern Dupuy models, and those of Lanchester's Laws predicted much better what was going on and what may or may not happen. God only knows why Fermi had never heard of Lanchester's Laws as they were developed in the early nineteen hundreds—but I digress." He paused to accept the refill on the drink the waiter had brought. "Thank you."

"Hang in there, Rain. It gets more interesting," Julia assured her.

Roger continued, "The math of Malthus was shown to be highly flawed and even the basis of the old nonsensical Fermi Paradox from the twentieth century. The Proximans have certainly laid that silly paradox to rest for us and therefore a final nail in the Malthusian model's coffin—as if it needed it. Fortunately for us, we were able to predict better with the more accurate and actual data-based models what resources needed to be where and so on over the decades. In the end, Mother Nature and the solar system have provided us with far more than our population needs at the moment and for the next, maybe, thousand years or even longer? Hard to predict that far out."

"Go on, I'm listening," said Rain with a slight grin. "I'm not a population expert apparently."

"What was the world's population in, say, 1900? Would you like to guess?"

"About a billion?" Rain replied, tentatively, uncomfortable guessing at something outside her realm of knowledge and expertise like a contestant on a gameshow.

"Close. A little more than one and a half billion. What about in 1960?"

"That was the time we had the medical breakthroughs you just mentioned, correct? Penicillin, the polio vaccine, etcetera. So, I'd say it doubled. Three billion," she said.

"And you would be correct. In 1960, the world population was three billion and growing. By 1980 it was about four and a half billion and by 2015 it was over seven billion. Everyone in the world could see the 'population bomb,' as they called it, coming right at them. At that time, our population was still growing mostly along the simplified Malthusian model, but it did start to change about five decades later."

"Thanks for the demographic history lesson. Are you trying to tell me the Proximans are facing their own Malthusian population crisis or something?" Rain asked, looking at Julia.

"Let him keep going. You need to hear the whole story before you begin making conclusions," she replied, taking a sip from her drink.

Roger took out his datapad and pulled up some graphs onto the display.

"Look at this," he said, pointing to a curve showing population as a function of what they now knew as Proximan years along the x-axis. "Remember, we estimate the Proximans are experiencing now the basic equivalent of our 1950s: radio, fax machines, industrial automation, cars, aircraft, etcetera. Even the beginnings of a fledgling space program. We've seen it all in the data they've sent. In pictures, stories, and throughout their Encyclopedia—their recent history basically parallels the Earth's twentieth century, minus the world wars. They don't seem to have had as many major wars as we. Not that they are without conflict, they most certainly are not, they just haven't had wars of the scale we've experienced here, which is curious."

Rain looked at the curve and saw a steady population increase until about two earth decades before the present, where the curve went flat and might have even begun to decline.

"It's leveled off."

"Yes. And what does that tell you?"

"They saw the dangers of overpopulation and decided to do something about it. Maybe they decided to not reproduce themselves into a crisis, sort of like the Chinese did with their 'one child' policy."

"That's possible and what I thought when I looked at the data in isolation. But when I looked at other factors, I reached a very different conclusion," Roger said.

Rain looked at Julia, who merely looked back and then nodded toward Roger, gently nudging him to continue.

"Look at these photos from the many faxes we've received. Do you see any interesting trends?"

Rain took his datapad and began to scroll through the hundreds of pictures they'd intercepted that included people. She began with the family picture she'd first decoded in what seemed like another lifetime. She paused as she looked at the two men, the woman, and the five children she had stared at so many times that she had every detail memorized. The next picture showed a group of about fifteen people outside what looked like an apartment building. The next showed a large group of people in some sort of park picnicking. She looked at picture after picture, each showing groups of two or more people, most wearing some variation of the robe style they'd become accustomed to seeing the Proximans wear, until she finally put the pad down, exasperated.

"Okay. The Proximans like to be in groups. I can see that. What am I supposed to see?" Rain asked.

"Look at them again, and this time tell me the rough distribution of men versus women in the photos. Not just adults. Look at the sex of everyone and let me know what you see," said Roger. His face was deadpan, almost ashen.

Rain flipped through the pictures again, saying out loud, "Two men, five boys, and one woman. Twelve men and three women. Five men, one woman, and two boys. Twenty boys, two men, and no women. Three boys. Eight men. One woman. What are they? Misogynist? Have we found a culture that hates or enslaves women?"

"I don't think so. Look again at the pictures and estimate the ages of the women you see. And tell me how many young girls you find."

Rain hurriedly flipped through the same photos and rapidly moved to the next several that she had not looked at previously. Her pace increased as she searched each for the number of women and girls. Finally, she stopped and looked up.

"I didn't see a woman that looked younger than twenty-five years old and no girls. None. What the hell is going on?"

"We don't know for sure, but based on the population data, the pictures, and from what we've pulled from their radio broadcasts, we think they are experiencing some sort of reproduction problem where few or no girls are being born. And perhaps haven't been born for some time. If they are human, and all indications are that they are, then their female-to-male birth ratio should be about the same as ours: one hundred girls born to every one hundred and five males. Roughly fifty/fifty. It looks like their ratio is now zero girls, or close to it, for every one hundred males."

"If that's true, and no girls are being born, then they are going extinct. Rapidly," Rain said.

"That's what we think. I'm calling a closed-door meeting of the committee in two weeks to present this data. From there, if it holds and we haven't overlooked something that causes us to reinterpret it, I plan to recommend that we begin sending everything we know about biology, genetics, and genetic engineering to them as soon as we can. We've got to educate them from 1950s biology to 2080s biology, and soon, or there won't be anyone there left to talk to before long. They will die off," Julia said.

"It's worse than that," Roger said.

"Really. How so?" asked Rain.

"Women keep men civilized. Competition for the affections of women can provoke men to jealousy, rage, and violence. As with any declining resource—if you will excuse my utilitarian terminology, I mean no disrespect—when the supply of a valuable resource gets low, competition can get ugly. Their society may collapse long before the last woman dies off. I give them ten to fifteen years, tops," Roger said, not looking either woman in the eye.

"Roger, in my gut I find your utilitarian language to be insulting. I am not a commodity. But I know that in most of human history, women *were* possessions. Taken during wars to be the sex slaves of the victors. Women were married off to the sons of competing clans to try and keep the clans from fighting each other. In some countries today, women are treated only a little better than property. I won't let my gut overrule what my head tells me and that is that you are, unfortunately, likely to be correct. Our 'civilized behavior' is only as deep as our wealth and prosperity allow it to be. Take away the veneer of that civilization, and we would be no better than our ancestors with the physically strong taking what he, usually a 'he,' wants from whomever he can take it," Julia said.

"Can we bring their knowledge of biology forward fast enough for them to fix whatever is causing this lack-of-women problem?" asked Rain.

"That's a good question. We don't know what's causing it and we're assuming that our technology and medical knowledge are advanced enough to fix it, whatever 'it' is. That might be a bad assumption, even if we do find a way to get them as proficient in bioengineering as we are," added Julia.

"They haven't even told us there is a problem. What if it isn't genetic? What if female babies are being born but they're dying young or born dead? Maybe it's a virus, or a bacterium, or something else in their environment—perhaps their equivalent to Thalidomide," said Roger.

"Thalidomide?" asked Rain.

"It was a drug developed in the 1950s to treat depression. It was widely given to pregnant women and resulted in severe birth defects to a sizable fraction of a generation before it was banned. My point is, this could be an environmentally introduced, completely artificial problem, perhaps an unanticipated effect from some global immunization campaign. Who knows?" said Roger.

"I need another drink," Rain replied, motioning to the waiter.

"Make that two," Julia agreed.

CHAPTER 8

March 3, 2087

Rain sat with Roger and other members of the first contact team in the gallery overlooking the chamber of the United Nations in New York. Instead of tying in virtually, every member of the committee was flown to New York to help Julia prepare for her presentation to the General Assembly. They had been with her ten to twelve hours a day for the past four days leading up to her presentations today. She gave the first one that morning, laying out the case for the crisis on Proxima Centauri b.

The chamber was filled with dignitaries from every country in the world—literally. Rain had been to New York many times in her life but had never taken a tour of the venerable UN Building, which had recently been upgraded and modernized. Rain wondered how much longer it would be before the UN had to update its logo—which for the last century had showed all the continents of the Earth in a stylized, top-down view of the globe—to include the Moon. When she left the Lunar Observatory, there were rumblings among the people living in the various habitats for independence. It wasn't difficult for Rain to conceive of a lunar nation or nations in the not-too-distant future.

The debate following Julia's morning briefing was spirited: The Russian ambassador questioned how anyone could make such dire predictions about the future of the Proximans from so little explicit data and without the Proximans even admitting there was a problem. The ambassador from El Salvador wondered why the UN was so concerned with a people so far away when there was a war in Central Africa in which hundreds, if not thousands, were dying each day as a result of the conflict. Most, however, listened attentively and expressed admiration for the detective work of the first contact committee and sympathy for the Proximans, who were facing extinction.

The afternoon session was the one in which Julia was going to lay out the committee's plan to help the Proximans. On cue, the gavel dropped to call the afternoon session to order and the floor was given back to Dr. Julia Coetzee, chair of the First Contact Committee.

"Ladies and Gentlemen, thank you for allowing me to return to the podium to brief you on the approach we recommend the united peoples of Earth take to help our recently discovered kin on the world of Proxima Centauri b who are facing an existential crisis like no other. Time is short and unless we undertake the paths I will describe here this afternoon, I fear an entire civilization will collapse and die.

"First, the committee recommends that a message be sent to Proxima Centauri b outlining what we believe is occurring there and why, along with an offer to help. We know that getting a return response will take a minimum of nine years, and it is imperative that we not wait on a response from them before we take the additional steps recommended by this committee. Granted, we may be wrong in our assessment. The committee believes this is a low probability and that we should not be deterred in providing what will be, ultimately, a global response to their plight.

"Second, the committee recommends that a comprehensive educational program of study be developed to bring the Proximans from their current state of biological knowledge to a level comparable to our own. The program should begin with first principles, to make sure we begin at a level that is commensurate with the level of understanding of the Proximans. It should be tailored to introduce new material in a logical and coherent fashion to allow their medical and biological experts to understand how the science has evolved, helping them to avoid the many years of research spent in directions that proved fruitless, and to increase their understanding of human biology dramatically and rapidly. The program should place special emphasis on the human genome and how to identify elements in the genome that cause or contribute to various disease states and conditions in the hope that it will help them identify the cause or causes of their fertility problem.

"There will not be time for Socratic dialog. The educational program will need to be comprehensive and not steeped in any single cultural approach to learning. For this reason, we recommend that a multicultural team of physicians, biologists, educators, and linguists work with the world's leading experts on all things Proximan and collaborate on the program of study, and that the first element, described in Attachment One, be completed and sent toward Proxima Centauri within six months. The remaining elements to follow over the next one to two years.

"Third, we recommend that the UN support and fund a medical mission to Proxima Centauri b as soon as possible. We are all aware of the revolutionary developments in space travel that have occurred within the last two decades, beginning with the invention and use of the Samara Drive. The committee was briefed about the recent performance improvements to the Samara system and new onboard power systems that will now enable the transit of large, human-occupied ships across interstellar distances with trip times as short as ten to twelve years. If we begin now, it should be possible to get a medical team, with state-of-the-art medical technological equipment, to Proxima Centauri b in time to avert the total collapse of their civilization. Barely. We estimate that the youngest cohorts of women of child-bearing age will be in their fifties. By any measure, that is very late to be having children—but, biologically speaking, for many it is not too late. And with the state of medical care our team will bring, we have every expectation that both these women, and their children, can be kept in good health.

"An element of the proposed medical mission upon which the committee was divided and unable to make a unanimous recommendation was that the mission would take with them one hundred thousand frozen female human embryos. Population experts believe that this would be a viable floor to maintain Proxima's human population should a cure not be readily found. The embryos could be implanted in willing women, by procedures easily taught to their local physicians, as a last-ditch effort to prevent their extinction.

"We realize these proposals will be controversial and expensive. However, the survival of an entirely new branch of the human species is at stake and we must act, now, decisively, if we are going to save them." Julia completed her introductory speech, took a deep breath, and looked into the gallery at her committee members—eyes seeming to rest upon Rain.

Rain, without thinking, gave her a thumbs-up.

Julia then continued her presentation by pulling up charts showing the details behind each phase of the proposed plan.

The questions, debate, fear mongering, and political grand-standing began.

It was 4:30 and the UN was scheduled to end debate and adjourn for the day at 5:00, none too soon for Rain and the rest of the first contact team. They were exhausted, and they weren't even the one who had been at the podium for most of the day. *Poor Julia must be close to passing out*, Rain thought. *Though she doesn't look it.* Her AI signaled her that she was getting an urgent message.

She pulled out her datapad and saw that the message was from Enrico Vulpetti: WE NEED TO TALK. 7:00 DINNER AT SARDI'S?

She knew what he wanted to talk about. He'd likely been watching the televised UN debate and heard about the commit-tee's proposal to send a ship to Proxima Centauri b. And he had approached her about half a year ago with his own proposal for such a starship. Rain was surprised that he would contact her, given that she was extremely vocal in her opposition to such a ship at the time and was the main reason his proposal never made it to the UN for consideration. Things had changed dramatically since then. Her opinion had changed.

She replied, SEE YOU THEN.

After the UN adjourned, Julia was swamped by the media and didn't get out of council chambers until after 6:00. Rain con-gratulated her on the presentation and told her, briefly, about her dinner meeting with the aerospace physicist from Georgia Tech.

"Find out what you can, but don't make any formal or informal commitments. We're at a critical juncture in the debate and we can't afford any appearance of favoritism toward any one group until the world is committed to our plan," Julia admonished Rain in their brief moment together.

"Don't worry. I voted against his idea the first time, remember?" Rain said with a smile.

"I remember," Julia replied, adding, "Be sure to message me afterward to let me know how it goes."

Rain nodded in affirmation and hurried out the door to catch an autocab to the restaurant. She didn't want to be late. And, of course, it was raining.

Sardi's was a New York landmark. Located in the Theater District, the restaurant was built in 1927 and became *the* place to eat for visiting celebrities. The walls were lined with caricatures of over a thousand celebrities who had eaten a meal there in its one-hundred-sixty-year history. Rain had heard of it, but never eaten there. As she exited the autocab, she saw Enrico standing at the door, looking her way. He still was as handsome as ever. Rain quickly squashed those thoughts to the back of her mind.

"Hello, Dr. Gilster. I'm glad you were able to join me tonight," he said as he opened the restaurant's door for her.

"I appreciate the invitation. Your message caught me by surprise, though it shouldn't have, given our last conversation together," Rain said. "You know there was nothing personal in my decision?"

"Personal? Oh that? Never crossed my mind." He dismissed her halfhearted apology.

"Great, then. Good to see you," Rain said guardedly.

"I watched your colleague's most impressive presentation today and I must say I am the one who should be surprised." He smiled a very bright and toothy smile at her. "Surprised at your turnaround on the issue of sending a starship to Proxima Centauri. But let's not discuss this here in the doorway. We should get our table and at least have an appetizer and glass of wine before we talk business."

"Of course," Rain replied. She immediately realized Vulpetti was on a charm offensive. He was as well groomed and appropriately attired as the last time she saw him and was using his contagious smile to disarm her. And, of course, the "no business talk until after we have a drink" was as smooth and polished as they come. She thought that she would need to be on her guard because, well, damn, it was working.

As she expected, the salmon appetizer tasted as good as the menu described it and the wine was perfect. After placing their dinner order, Vulpetti shifted back into "business mode."

"Dr. Gilster, the reason I've asked you here tonight is to make you aware of the progress we've made on our starship," he said.

"You've begun building it?" she asked, with more than a hint of surprise in her voice.

"The design is complete; we've begun buying the components and lining up the rocket launches that will be required to put it all into space for final assembly. If we remain on schedule, the first component launch will be in just over two years."

"When we last spoke, I thought you were just talking about something that could be done. I had no idea you were already building it. Who's paying for it? I haven't seen anything in the media about it," she said.

"I can't divulge the names of our sponsors, but there is big money behind the project and it is moving forward. We have every intention of going to Proxima Centauri b whether the UN approves such a mission or not. We would rather go with their blessing and support if we can. My investors have a lot of money, but perhaps not enough to make the ship as much as it could be. And, quite frankly, this whole Proximan fertility crisis has changed everything. We want to help. We've got a head start on the starship and we can take the medical supplies we heard about in the briefing today—if we start planning to do so now. The design is mostly complete, but at this stage we can modify it to accommodate the specific equipment you need for the medical mission fairly easily. A year from now, it will be impossible."

"How many people can you take?" she asked.

"Twenty-five. The accommodations won't be luxurious, but they will be comfortable enough. Each member of the crew will have about as much room as you get on a luxury cruise liner," he said.

"For twenty years," she said, remembering the trip time he quoted in their previous conversation. "That's a hell of a long time to be cooped up in a stateroom, no matter how luxurious it is."

"Well, the good news is that we think we can get the trip time down to ten years, like your spokesperson said today, instead of the original twenty. And there will be an option for sleeping part of the way. It isn't the cryogenic sleep you see in the VRs, but more of an induced coma. While the person is asleep, their muscles are electrically stimulated to keep them healthy, their bodies are fed, and wastes disposed of. They will still age, they just won't have to endure the full ten years in deep space. Crew members can choose to sleep all, part, or none of the time during the trip and they can change their minds at any time. And, of course, due to special relativity the trip will seem slightly shorter than ten years to the crew onboard." Enrico paused for effect and drank the remaining wine from his glass.

"This whole story is, well, difficult to believe," Rain said.

"Oh, what we are building is very real and we will be more than happy to provide the details and offer a tour of our facilities if the UN is interested in working with us to make the trip happen."

"May I ask where you are building the ship?" Rain asked.

"The components are being assembled in the United Arab Emirates, but it will be integrated in lunar orbit," Enrico said.

"The UAE has a history of thumbing its nose at the UN. Will you launch from there too?" Rain asked.

"Most likely. The commercial rocket companies are all international these days and the one we're working with has a sea launch platform that they can tow just about anywhere in the world," he said.

"And you want me to be your advocate," Rain said.

"Absolutely."

"Despite me shooting you down the first time," she said.

"You did what you had to do, based on the information you had available. But circumstances have changed. These people are dying unless we get there and help them. Your concerns about biological contamination aren't unfounded and we are trying our best to mitigate the risk as much as possible in our starship design and in our crew selection. Again, we can provide the details if there is interest. But we need to know soon." Enrico looked at her expectantly, turning on all the charm he could muster—which was considerable.

"Shall we have dessert?" he asked nonchalantly, flashing his smile once again.

"Absolutely. I'll take the crème brûlée and a glass of sherry," Rain said.

"Does that mean we have a deal?" asked Enrico.

"It means we're having dessert. But I'll take your offer back to the committee. Tell your team that they'd better be real and have something to show us or a whole lot of important people, very important people, will be extremely unhappy that their time was wasted."

CHAPTER 9

August 27, 2087

Rain's AI received the meeting request from Julia Coetzee while she was sleeping, noted its source and urgency, and adjusted Rain's calendar for the day to accommodate it. In the process, two other meetings were rescheduled for the following week and one was canceled outright. The AI also decided to awaken Rain half an hour early so that she would have ample time for her morning routine, which now always included a brief conversation with her mother.

Rain noted the changes to her schedule as she was preparing her breakfast oatmeal and wondered what the reason Julia might have for calling an emergency, her term, meeting of the First Contact Committee. She would find out soon enough.

Because it was a beastly hot summer day in Atlanta, very typical for this time of year, she decided to participate in the meeting from her home office and not venture to the university. Those online who had visited her home would immediately recognize the backdrop—a room filled with bookcases and stacked with old-fashioned books, paper books, some dating back to the late 1800s. Rain read all of her professional journals electronically, but she preferred the feel of a book when it came to fiction or historical texts. There was something about reading history on paper that made it more real for her.

The meeting began promptly at the appointed time with all but two committee members present. One was unable to be reached, which was quite unusual in this day of everything being network connected, unless one didn't want to be reached. The other was ill and his AI declined the meeting invitation. Julia wasted no time getting to the point.

"Late yesterday, we received a new message from Proxima Centauri b. This one appears to have come from a different group from the one that sent the first message. They made that very clear in their opening. In fact, the message has the look and feel of a less-well-funded minority or dissident group sending a message in secret. It was brief and to the point. Before I begin, please keep in mind that Earth's message to Proxima, in which we disclosed our belief that they have a fertility problem, was only sent a little more than two months ago and our first installment of the Biology 101 tutorial was only sent earlier this month.

"Based on this new message from Proxima Centauri, we believe our assessment of their problem is, unfortunately, correct. There is a fertility problem on Proxima and it has reached a crisis stage. They first noticed the decline in female births about a hundred Earth years ago. At first, the decline was small and mostly anecdotal. Based on their level of technological development, I would guess that they were in the latter part of their version of the industrial revolution and record keeping was basically ad hoc, with an occasional census of some kind or another thrown in. The salient point is that it began then and grew gradually worse.

"According to the sender of the message, who we are now calling 'Dissenter,' the problem grew worse with time until about twenty-five Earth years ago. Since that time, there have been fewer than one hundred thousand females born each year. Far too few to sustain the human population.

"Dissenter went on to tell us that their scientists have been unable to come up with an explanation or even a hint of how to fix the problem. The Proximan government is trying to keep the civilization and the economy working, but it is failing. Families consisting of multiple men per woman are now common. Female kidnappings and rape are at crisis levels, and much of the younger generation appears to be dropping out of the society. They are hopeless and believe there is no reason to plan for a future. Overall, Dissenter paints a very bleak picture of the place. They are experiencing general economic and societal collapse.

"Dissenter sent an extensive demographic database, which is not much more than our census records, and page after page of notes related to the fertility problem from their doctors and other medical personnel. It was an overt plea for help."

"Do we have any idea of who this Dissenter is?" asked Hiro Tanaka, one of the "policy" members of the team.

"Yes. From what we can tell, he is a government official who had access to our interstellar message exchanges and the connections necessary to get his message transmitted. The message repeated only sixteen times before it stopped. We can only surmise that someone noticed the apparently unauthorized transmission and terminated it."

"This means that we are doing the right things to help them," said Mina Lappas, one of the doctors added to the team after the fertility crisis was discovered and the UN intervention plan approved. Rain liked Mina. They had a lot in common and met regularly in person due to Mina being on assignment at the Centers for Disease Control and Prevention in Atlanta.

"I would say so, yes," replied Julia.

"I hate to say it, but it sounds like we are already too late," said the group's only political scientist, Wilhelm Duesenberg. Duesenberg was normally quiet during the committee meetings, which Rain found to be curious. Most political scientists she knew were not exactly the shy and quiet types. Duesenberg normally broke that mold.

"Explain," said Julia.

"Well, they are now at least twenty-five to thirty years into full-blown demographic crisis, which I would prefer we call it. It isn't a 'fertility crisis' at all. Demographics are destiny and their destiny is bleak, as you said. And they know it. Let's say we are wildly successful in our medical tutorial and they quickly understand the information we broadcast. How are they going to do anything with it? Do they have the manufacturing base to build the laboratory equipment, tools, and tests necessary to isolate the cause and determine how to mitigate it? Did we also send the electronics and computer science tutorial to allow them to build the computers they will need to make sense of the data? The success of the Human Genome Project was as much about computing power as it was biology. Do they have the virology labs they may need to insert a fix into developing embryos if, in fact, the 'cure' can be implemented that way? What if the cause is a virus? Or environmental, as we discussed previously? Will they have the tools and the time to use the knowledge we sent in the proper correlation studies? Time is their enemy and they won't even receive the first of our biology tutorials for another four years!"

"And if the female birth rate has dropped even lower, then the biology tutorial will be too little, too late. We need to get a fully staffed, fully functional biolab there as soon as possible," said Rain, her heart breaking as she spoke the words. She feared that it, too, would arrive too late to be of any help at all.

"Rain, the UN did approve the starship relief mission—largely because of you," Julia reminded her and everyone on the team.

"Yes, they did. Let's consider Wilhelm's pessimistic assessment and assume that the ship launches slightly ahead of schedule in two years. It will take a decade to get there. How many women of child-bearing age will there be? Thousands? Hundreds?" Rain asked.

"We don't have any way of knowing."

"With society collapsing and what few women there are being threatened with kidnapping, how many will be healthy and accessible when the ship arrives in twelve years? And arrival is when the work really begins. It may take years to isolate the cause before the team can attempt to do anything to correct the problem," Rain said.

"Don't forget the contamination risk. As Rain mentioned in one of our previous meetings, and as we've talked about several times, there's a good chance we might contaminate them with some virus that would prove deadly to the local population and vice versa. If we go there and inadvertently kill off the natives or they our team, then the whole thing also fails. Remember, this is the sort of stuff I worry about in my normal day-to-day job at the CDC. And there's one more thing," said Mina.

"What's that?" asked Julia.

"The people we send on the starship. They know that we probably can't let them ever come home, right?"

"Because of the viral contagion risk? It's been discussed, but their possible return has always been in the 'we'll isolate you when you come home to prevent contamination' category, not the 'you can't come home' bucket," said Julia.

"Well, you need to move it firmly into the latter. If there is even the slightest chance this demographic crisis is contagious, we cannot take the risk. Even if an isolation period sufficient to rule out any traditional bacterial or viral infection is implemented, it may not be enough. The risk is too great."

"Thankfully, I'm not on *that* committee," said Julia with a sigh.

CHAPTER 10

July 5, 2089

The hardware didn't look like it was assembled and ready for a full-power test. Sure, the connections were made, and no wires or optical fiber cables were obviously loose or disconnected. None of the wires or cables were too long—each was exactly the correct length to connect the various parts of the test cell and they were aligned exactly as the final released drawings said they should be. The pristine, shiny housings containing the extremely sensitive electronic equipment looked like they were pictured in the online catalogs from which many of them had been ordered and the gentle hum of the power supplies waiting to be switched into the system sounded exactly like new power supplies should— they hummed. But Senior Test Engineer Roy Burbank knew that something was wrong. The whole test setup didn't look right, *feel right*, but he couldn't put his finger on what wasn't as it should be. And that bothered him.

Roy Burbank was an engineer's engineer, fastidious in applying proven engineering processes, loath to take unnecessary risks, and a stickler for test plans and procedures. His reputation as a problem solver was widely known and no one had ever been injured—well, severely injured—on any test for which he served as a test engineer. He knew Murphy's Law all too well, and he didn't want Mr. Murphy visiting him or any project he was involved with. This one was no exception. There was something he was missing, and he couldn't figure out what.

They were in lunar orbit, one of many teams frantically

working to assemble the Earth's first interstellar spaceship—*a God-by-damn starship*—and the stakes were high. They had less than a week to go before the *Samaritan* was scheduled to launch toward Proxima Centauri and Roy wasn't about to let his team get on the critical path and cause management to start following their every move. If you were on the critical path, then it meant you were the one whose work would determine when the whole spaceship was ready to go. No, he didn't want his team on the critical path or anywhere near it. Getting the equipment installed and tested today was important, but it was more important for it to not fail.

"I need to hear an affirmative from everyone on the team before we begin the test," Roy said nervously. There was no better way to have a successful test than to have every member of the team verbally agree that their work was complete and ready to go. Ownership of the outcome always led to a better result—in test engineering and in life.

"Mechanical is good to go," said Tad Malone. Malone had worked for a long time with Roy and they were good friends at work and in their personal time. Roy trusted him implicitly.

"Data is ready to go," replied Misha Kuznetsov. Misha, a recent graduate of Tomsk State University in Russia, was new to the team and Roy was impressed with her. What she lacked in experience, she made up for in her eagerness to learn new things. He had been watching her work since she joined the team and found that when she didn't know how to do something, she asked. He liked that. Too many recent graduates thought they were hotshots and would rather screw up than admit their ignorance.

"Power is ready," the final member of the team weighed in. Patrick O'Hearn was a loner, didn't usually crack jokes on the job, and never socialized with the rest of the crew after the workday was done. O'Hearn had only been with the team a short time and had been added to the group by corporate requirements. Roy usually didn't like it when corporate or government big wigs imposed their people on him, but this was a very high-visibility effort. And Roy had to admit to himself that O'Hearn wasn't that bad—at least he wasn't in the way. O'Hearn usually said his goodbyes and then went his own way at the end of each test or workday—always alone. But he did good work and didn't cause problems for Roy.

"Hmm . . . Nigel, I want all the displays of the inputs and outputs from the diagnostic algorithms in my HUD." Roy ran his fingers through his graying red hair and let out a long breath through his pursed lips, making a motorboat sound.

"Aye, Roy." The Scottish accent of his AI data assistant sounded in his ears. Roy looked down at the circuit tattooed on his wrist and laughed a bit to himself. He sometimes wondered if he'd overdone it with the customization of his AI's personality, but Roy was from Scottish heritage and it often reminded him of his grandfather when the AI spoke to him. Suddenly, the requested data screen appeared before his eyes, projected via the wireless contact lenses he wore.

"Okay, start the timer and we'll see how this thing works," Roy ordered as he scanned the hardware one more time using his datapad virtual overlay and the graphs in his own personal field of view through the contacts. With the overlay, he could see the health and status of each major component as their embedded sensors reported it. Integrated System Health Management, or ISHM—pronounced "ish-em"—was being used in the entire ship, with every system and subsystem constantly reporting data to the ship's artificial intelligence. In theory, this would allow the AI to diagnose a systems failure long before it happened by seeing when various components were experiencing performance declines or anomalous behavior long before they were close to failing.

In theory. In theory, if the test were incorrectly set up or a piece of hardware were going to fail, then Roy's datapad should alert him either from the pad itself, his personal view, or through Nigel. And it didn't. The hardware, like the engineers who set it up, reported that all was well. Roy was still nervous. It was times like this when Roy always recalled how, in theory, some idiot scientists in the past had claimed bumblebees shouldn't be able to fly. But in practice? Bumblebees had been flying about for eons. Some theorists were too arrogant to admit that their theory just flat-out sucked and it always fell to the engineer to fix that in practice. Roy was nervous.

The countdown passed uneventfully and the only way they knew the system was successfully powered on was by looking at the ISHM data. As tests went, it was pretty dull. And dull was good—it meant success. It was the interesting or exciting tests that were a problem because that meant there was something that didn't work right. Excitement during a test, in Roy's book, was not a good thing.

The *Samaritan*'s primary navigation system was operational and all functional. Once the complete test sequence was complete, Roy would be able to certify that the Pulsar Interstellar Navigation System—PINS for short—was ready to fly. Without it, the crew wouldn't be able to locate and direct the ship across the 25,280,000,000,000 miles to Proxima Centauri b with any hope of entering orbit around the planet. With the PINS, they should be able to know their relative position to within a few feet at any time during the voyage.

Roy didn't know all the details, his job was to make sure the hardware worked as it was designed; he was not the ship's astrodynamicist, nor did he come up with the idea. All he knew was that the sensors feeding data to the system in front of him were looking for the timing of radio signals from at least four pulsars chosen from a database of thousands that formed a rough tetrahedron with the Sun at its approximate center. Then, using techniques perfected by the early Global Positioning System—GPS—the hardware would figure out where the ship was relative to each.

You can't know where to go if you don't know where you are. And it helps a lot if you know where you've been. The PINS should be able to determine both.

Maybe that's why Roy was so nervous about the hardware. Perhaps he was nervous because so much was depending upon the hardware for which he was responsible. The PINS had to work or the *Samaritan* would not be able to complete its mission and would be forever lost in space.

"The data from the PINS on test run number one shows some anomalous trajectory errors after about two hundred thousand iterations of the filter algorithm on the input from the telescopes," Misha pointed out to him.

"What? Show me the run." Roy didn't like the sound of that.

"Here." Patrick passed a datapad to him and pointed at the trajectory plot in question.

"Misha, are we sure we're putting the right data into the PINS box? If we're not red shifting and/or blue shifting it right the spectra will be wonky and the PINS database will be useless." Roy looked at the chart and then tapped a few icons, opening up other PINS diagnostic processes.

"The telescopes are working," Tad added. "I just zipped through the self-diagnostics on them."

"We're sitting still, right—I mean, for the most part?" Misha pointed out.

"Hahaha, of course we are. Did you start the data red/blue shifting simulation subroutines?" Roy asked Misha.

"I, uh, mmm, I think I did," she replied sheepishly.

"I've got them toggled on now." Patrick nodded, assuring at them.

"Alright then, run it all again. This time with the algorithms running." Roy sighed.

Three hours later, the test all seemed to portray data that was to be expected. In other words, the PINS system was working. For whatever reason, Roy was still uneasy. His unease had no scientific basis as he'd just seen with his own eyes the flight qualification testing pass the required checks. But there was still something...

After some wrestling within himself, Roy had to reluctantly put away his test engineer's intuition, which was still screaming, "Something isn't right!" His team, and the information streaming into his datapad, indicated that the PINS was working fine. So, it was working fine.

"It looks like the PINS is good to go. Let's power down the system, complete the report, and then turn it over to the AI. After that, I say we meet at the Krakatoa for drinks—the first round of pints on me. Any takers?" It was Roy's custom to treat his team to a round of drinks at the local pub after a successful test. He didn't make a lot of money as a test engineer, but he made enough to reward his team for a job well done. And for him, logistically at least, drinks were easier than dinner. Dinner he reserved for his wife, Chloe, and tonight they were celebrating their third wedding anniversary. He didn't want to be late. He hoped that Chloe wouldn't be late either. Once she'd started taking on shifts at the Lunar Docks Trauma Center so she could be there with Roy, she had been working late many nights as well. Fortunately, she was within a month or so of finishing the contract she'd signed with them and she was entertaining thoughts of becoming a small-town doctor somewhere after Roy quit the space testing gig. Roy and she had talked of moving to either North America near his parents, or somewhere warm, or maybe to Scotland. At the present, with all the interstellar space-ship building and testing, Roy was making too much money and having too much fun professionally to retire to the next phase of his life.

As expected, Tad and Misha readily accepted his offer and Patrick declined. Roy knew that one of these days he'd get Patrick to join them, but apparently tonight was not going to be the night. Though Roy always looked forward to time in the pub with friends, tonight was going to be an exception. He had to be back to his apartment in the residential hub before seven o'clock. He and his wife were cooking together and eating in—steak imported from Argentina, lunar merlot, and her special chocolate cake made from her grandmother's recipe. He couldn't wait.

CHAPTER 11

July 8, 2089

Charles Jesus had briefed the presidential staff before, but only a couple of times, and each time it had been an extremely interesting, if not stressful, event. This time, unexpectedly, he was asked to the Oval Office, not the West Wing. That meant the actual president of the United States would be receiving the briefing. But Charles wasn't a hundred percent certain about what the president wanted him to be briefing. He walked cautiously beside and a half step behind the White House chief of staff. He'd have to search her name again later; he was certain, but thought she'd said Tanya Something-or-other Davidson. He uncomfortably paced as best he could to stay with her and continued fiddling with the security badge dangling uncomfortably from his lapel. The chief of staff paid him little attention.

"Right this way Dr. Jesus."

"Uh, okay, thank you." Charles stammered nervously as they passed the secretary and through the door to the president's office—the Oval Office. Suddenly, he realized that more than just the president intended to speak with him. The national security advisor, the chairman of the Joint Chiefs of Staff, the secretary of defense, and the liaison to the United Nations were all present. This was a meeting of heavy hitters. Charles wondered if he'd become a power player as the ambassador for Earth-Proxima Space Economic Interchange to the United Nations and and no one had bothered to tell him.

There were three other men and two women whom Dr. Jesus

didn't recognize. Although he didn't know them, they had the appearance of serious or especially important people, but Charles wasn't even certain what that meant anymore. One thing he noted was that the president was not in the room.

"Have a seat, Mr. Ambassador," the NSA said, motioning to the only empty chair in the room.

"Um, thank you, sir." Charles sat and fidgeted a bit with the tail of his sports coat and then the security badge again. "Is the presi—"

The chairman of the Joint Chiefs jumped up at attention as a door to the side of the desk that Charles hadn't realized was there opened and the president walked through. Unclear of protocol, Charles jumped to his feet as well.

"Dr. Jesus!" The president held out a hand and patted him on the shoulder. "May I call you Charles?"

"Certainly, Mr. President. Whatever you prefer." Charles nodded.

"Have a seat." The president nodded and then leaned on the edge of his desk with a discerning look on his face. "Well, Charles, let me tell you I really hope that we can save those people at Proxima Centauri. And I hope that we can figure out how to make economic windfall with this very expensive endeavor."

"Yes sir," Charles agreed.

"More to the point, I want to. No, *we* have to. We must protect our interests and not bring back to Earth some sort of plague that can't be cured—that is, assuming it isn't already here." The president paused at that statement to see if Charles had caught what he just said. Charles heard it but wasn't certain what it meant. How could a plague from Proxima Centauri make it all the way to the Sol system? The president continued, "Are we certain it's not? I'm not really sure why the scientists of the world haven't seen this or talked about it yet. Maybe because it's not politically correct or some such nonsense, but..."

The president took a long, deep breath and paused again, but only for a brief second. Charles listened intently and wasn't sure where this was going or if he was supposed to say something. The president then broke his silence and pointed to one of the other men in the room.

"Jason, why don't you tell us about your studies with the World Health Organization." The president turned to him but was interrupted by a grunt from the chairman of the Joint Chiefs.

"Ahh yes, the nondisclosure...Tanya, would you have Dr. Jesus sign the form, please..."

"Uh, sir, what's this?" Charles accepted a data pad from the chief of staff. "Nondisclosure of what?"

"Well, you see, Charles, there's a possibility that the...plague, virus, whatever it might be, is already here on Earth and we just haven't noticed it yet. Or, uh, I guess Jason there has noticed it but it is in a particular part of the population that has been discounted as a cultural bias. I dunno. But the nondisclosure is to keep this classified until we truly know what is going on. Otherwise, we could start a global panic and we don't want that."

"Uh, I understand, sir." Charles signed the electronic form and handed the pad back.

"Okay, Jason." The president nodded.

"Hello, Dr. Jesus. I'm Jason Faheem. My parents are from Oman and I'm the first-generation natural-born American in my family. My specialty is population studies and the impacts on pandemics, cultural and situational hunger, and population-based disease propagation. I've worked with the World Health Organization and the National Institute of Health for my entire adult life." The man paused to let his credentials sink in. Charles just nodded in understanding and listened intently.

"What you may or may not be aware of is that there are actually three locations on planet Earth to date that have for generations shown a tremendous gender discrepancy in their population census data. Those are Saudi Arabia, Oman, and a small area in Asia known as Bhutan. At times, the female percentage of the population has dipped as low as thirty-four percent in each of these places. Further study shows there are cultural reasons for fewer women or for women leaving these locations or for great influxes of men into the regions. But a closer look at the birth data shows a significant difference in the number of female babies born versus male babies born each and every year for the past century."

"Oh my God!" Charles gasped. "This is true? That could be devastating long term."

"Indeed, Dr. Jesus." Dr. Faheem frowned and raised an eyebrow. "But there is no need for alarm yet. There are many other genetic populations that have a surplus in female birth that more than make up for the problem. It would appear that Earth's genetic diversity might be protecting humanity from whatever the cause of this is. But if you look at all the imagery and video data of Proxima you will note there is extraordinarily little genetic diversity amongst the population as would be expected."

"How nobody in the press has pointed that out is beyond me," the president added.

"It is quite possible that the cure for the Proximan Gender Plague is actually right here on Earth and we didn't even realize it," Faheem said.

"Genetic diversity?"

"Correct, Doctor." Faheem looked pleased with Charles's quick understanding. "That means in order to save the Proximan population we must begin flooding their population with new genetic material."

"And what's the best way to do that?" the president asked.

"Commerce," Charles agreed knowingly.

"He gets it." The president smiled. "I knew you would, Charles. I've watched most of your presentations to the UN over the past few years and I knew you would get it."

"Thank you, Mr. President."

"But there's a catch, maybe," Dr. Faheem added.

"A catch?"

"Of course, it is only a hypothesis that genetic diversity is a cure. So far here on Earth it is at least keeping the problem at bay. Actually, the problem is almost unnoticeable and has mainly gone unnoticed for more than a century, but it has always been there." Faheem held both hands palms up, gesturing for emphasis. "But what if the reason there isn't genetic diversity on Proxima is because the plague wiped out the other races?"

"But the imagery data and videos are all similar over their history," Charles protested.

"Are they?" Faheem asked. "Their imagery and video technology is less than a century old. Looking through their artwork we did find some interesting paintings of lighter and differently shaded skin colors. Perhaps they existed centuries or even millennia in their past and they died out."

"The point is," the chairman of the Joint Chiefs interrupted, motioning that Dr. Faheem was done speaking for now. "The point is, son, we don't know enough of their history to know if they just died off, were killed off, or some other more troublesome thing happened. And..."

"And, General, we can't take that chance on a guess." The president stood, smiled, and then walked around his desk and sat in his chair. Charles thought for a second that he was going to make a motorboat sound as he leaned back. But he didn't. "We just don't know. So, that is why we are here today. How do we save them, and protect us, and maybe make this good for everybody on Earth at the same time?"

"Mr. President, the mission is one way and none of the people will return to Earth. At least that is the current plan," Charles explained, realizing that he must have known that as soon as he had said it.

"Of course, of course, we all know that's the mission plan for the *Samaritan*," the president replied. Then he followed his thought more succinctly. "But who's to say for sure? We *will not* know what's going on out there once the mission gets going. The way I understand it is that in just a matter of months after they initiate the Samara Drive engine they will be out of touch and out of the control, really, of any government here on Earth. Those crazy, brave souls will literally be on their own, and who knows what decisions they might make along the way?"

"Yes sir, I understand that. But what does that have to do with me exactly?" Charles was confused. He was a commerce ambassador to the United Nations, nothing more. Granted, with the new information he had just been given, he understood the severity and the unknowns of the problem much better. But Charles wasn't sure why he was having this conversation with the president and his senior staff.

"Let's slow down for just a second, why don't we?" The president sat upright and squared himself with the desk. "Mr. Ambassador—Charles, am I to understand that at one point you asked to go along on the *Samaritan* but for some reason you changed your mind?"

"Yes, Mr. President, that is true, but that was before it was decided it would be a one-way trip. I am not sure I'm ready to give up life on Earth just yet." Charles recalled how he had wrestled with himself about the decision to withdraw from consideration on the mission. After he withdrew, he had suggested that somebody who understood history and multicultural commerce needed to be considered as part of the crew, even if it wasn't himself.

"Charles, my sources tell me that you have no family, no

girlfriend or significant other, and as far as I can tell your economic stature isn't extremely good or bad. As an outsider looking in at your life, it would seem that you're not sure what your direction in life is or should be?" The president made it as a statement, but added the slight inflection of a question at the end.

"I still am not sure what I can do for you, sir," Charles replied.

"Well, Charles, I would like you to go Proxima Centauri b as America's first ambassador to the people there with hopes of somehow, someday in the future, bringing new economics to both worlds, and upon assessment of the plague, maybe even bringing them the cure by creating an influx of new genetic material through workers, tourists, immigration, explorers, and such. You'll need to come up with a plan for that."

"Seriously? I'm not sure what to say, sir." Charles was surprised by the request. He was flattered, to say the least, a bit excited, and somewhat uneasy.

"Say yes, Charles. Just say yes," the president replied with a grin.

"It can't be as simple as that, sir." Charles shrugged. "I mean, that is the kind of job that requires a staff, resources, and . . . well, I'm not sure what else. And atop that, the crew of the *Samaritan* might not be too excited about such an addition."

"You're right, Charles, it's not as simple as that." The president paused and looked long and hard into Charles's eyes, and his smile melted away. For the first time Charles could see the age in the man's face. He considered how the job of president must weigh heavy on a person. The president finally let out a sigh.

"Somebody has to make sure that they follow the rules out there. Somebody has to make sure that the crew doesn't go insane. Somebody has to make sure that they don't return to Earth and bring a plague that can't be cured. Somebody has to make sure that a bunch of scientists with lofty notions and unclear understandings of how governments work aren't the only people this new culture sees. Somebody has to go that understands or has the propensity to understand an entirely new form of government and how that must interact with our governments. Somebody—you, Dr. Jesus—needs to go because you understand the full story, the big picture, the behind-the-scenes information that the general public, scientists, and crew does not."

"And you think that person is truly me, sir?"

"Why not?" He almost laughed. "Yes, Charles, I do. I think it's you—with the right team. You will need military advice. You will need economic advice. You will need legal advice. You will need historical, philosophical, and theological advice. You'll have scientists all around you that can't wait to tell you their opinions. And, like any ambassador setting up an embassy, you'll need protection."

"Protection sir?"

"Yes, protection." The president turned to the three men and two women standing along the wall of the Oval Office. "General, please introduce our security team to Ambassador Jesus."

CHAPTER 12

July 10, 2089

Rain had been watching the segments of the *Samaritan* and other ships carrying supplies arrive in lunar orbit for months. The bright specks of light in the otherwise pitch-black lunar sky were a thankfully temporary bother to the optical astronomers, but not even a glimmer of a problem for her beloved radio telescopes. The arriving ships were all communicating with one another using laser-optical communications. It had taken many strings pulled and a rather wordy "release of medical liability" for the powers that be to allow her to return to the Moon for this phase of the project, but she was here and that was what mattered to her. She would not miss this for the world.

She'd flown from the lunar surface to the orbital space dock, arriving barely two hours ago. The space dock provided the most spectacular view of the *Samaritan*. She'd asked to stop there before she was taken through the docking tunnel and into the ship proper. From the space dock window, she saw the majesty of the newly constructed *Samaritan* for the first time and the haphazard appearance of the space dock still under construction. The space dock was being upgraded to what would one day be a self-sufficient construction facility for what was planned to be a series of interstellar exploration vessels like the *Samaritan*. Given the Proximan fertility crisis, completion of the *Samaritan* was a higher priority than the space dock and all the other in-system ships under construction. Evidence of that decision could plainly be seen by looking through the window.

Once complete, the *Samaritan* would use its fusion drive to take it to roughly the orbital distance of Mars before the onboard photon drive would be activated. As she understood it, the drive accelerated by emitting photons, lots of photons, instead of reaction mass. Without having to carry heavy fuel, the ship could accelerate to speeds in excess of seventy percent the speed of light, perhaps above eighty percent. The only drawback was the danger posed by the photons, the light, that accelerated the ship. It was essentially a death ray, a superpowered laser that, if aimed at a spacecraft or even a planetary surface, could do significant damage. The ship had to be sufficiently far away from anything that might fall into the emitted beam when it was operational—hence the need to begin the interstellar journey at or beyond the orbit of Mars.

While the view of *Samaritan* was spectacular, she couldn't say the same for the ship's aesthetic. It wasn't. The *Samaritan* looked like a long-stemmed mushroom with the photons to be emitted from the base of the stalk. In the head were the supplies and the fusion power station. Along the length of the stalk were the crew quarters, the biolab, and the freezer containing the human embryos. It wasn't beautiful, but it was impressive. And it was being built because of Rain and her discovery. She was humbled—and determined. She wondered how Captain Crosby would take the news when she told him. Technically, it didn't matter how he reacted. After all, he was ex-military and was used to taking orders. She hoped, however, that he would take it well. She didn't want to get off on the wrong foot.

Her guide, an extremely talkative man named Artur something or other—Rain hadn't really been paying attention when he introduced himself—was giving her a much-too-detailed tour of the space dock as they made their way toward the *Samaritan*. Since the space dock was spinning, they experienced an acceleration roughly equivalent to that she was used to on the lunar surface. The only difference was the slight dizziness she experienced due to the Coriolis force, causing the vestibular system to send conflicting signals to her brain regarding her orientation and sense of motion every time she bent over or turned her head too quickly.

"...and the ship's Samara Drive, the photon rocket, will make the trip to Proxima Centauri possible in a fairly short amount of time. On the other side of the station, work is beginning on the next starship—which doesn't yet have a name—that is rumored to have a vastly different sort of onboard power system that will enable more rapid interstellar travel. The consortium building it hasn't released much information, so I'm afraid there isn't much I can say about it. However, if you consider..."

I'll bet you find a way to say a lot about it even if you don't really know anything, Rain mused as her talkative guide continued to prattle on without even pausing for much of a breath.

"...then the ship will turn around and begin decelerating. What speeds up, must slow down, you know? Since the ship is therefore under constant acceleration, the crew will experience fractional Earth gravity for most of the trip. The fusion..." Artur continued.

Rain again tuned him out and gazed out the window, admiring both the nearly completed *Samaritan* and her beloved Moon they were circling. She gazed out the window and then noticed it was quiet. Artur had stopped talking and was looking expectantly at her. She had no idea what he had just said.

"I'm sorry, what was that?" Rain asked, trying to look both attentive and apologetic for having missed some nuance in whatever her guide had just said.

"I asked if you were ready to move on. The captain was expecting you on the bridge fifteen minutes ago. We're running late," he said.

"Absolutely. Please lead the way. I will be right behind you," Rain said, motioning in the direction they'd been moving, assuming it was the right way to where they needed to be.

"Great. Then please follow me," Artur said as he stepped forward to lead her in the direction she'd motioned. He continued, "Now, this corridor didn't start out as a walkway to the starships, it was originally used to connect the first lunar orbital node to the power and propulsion module, making..."

"Dr. Gilster, it is great seeing you again." Captain Sam Crosby smiled as he moved toward her and extended his right hand. Rain and Sam Crosby were casual acquaintances, having crossed paths at various meetings on the Moon and in the planning meetings for the *Samaritan*'s first voyage. Rain liked Sam. He was professional, courteous, and open-minded about new scientific discoveries. With his chiseled facial feature, high cheekbones, aquiline nose, and regulation issue soldier's physique, she found him quite attractive—but way too young for him to show any interest in her beyond professional. She might as well have been his grandmother.

"Sam, please call me Rain. You and I are well beyond honorifics at this point. Unless, of course, I need to use your title around your crew?"

"I'd prefer we use first names, here and in public. The crew will understand a visiting scientist not using our vernacular," he said with a still-beaming smile.

"That's great, Sam. Thanks again for agreeing to see me with so little time before departure. Are you still on schedule?"

"We are. We plan to leave the dock in a few days. We will sprint to the Samara Limit, light up the drive, and be on our way."

"This all seems so unreal. It just seems like yesterday that we heard the message for the first time and now here you are, ready to go and meet our cousins at Proxima Centauri," Rain said.

"*You* heard the message and advocated for the trip. This wouldn't be happening if it weren't for you," he said.

"Sam, I'm glad to hear you say that. I hope you still think as highly of me after our discussion," Rain said.

Sam looked puzzled as he motioned for Rain to sit in the chair across from his desk. She sat and tried to look as disarming as possible.

"I'm going with you," she said, deciding to be blunt and get to the point as soon as possible. There wasn't much time to get her gear onboard and familiarize herself with all the ship's systems, so it was just as well that she cut to the chase and get any resistance to her joining the crew out of the way.

At first Sam didn't react. He just stared at her.

"I assume I don't have a say in the matter?" asked Sam.

"Not really. I have a letter of passage from the director general that I will provide. I hope you accept my presence as a plus rather than a minus. I know the Proximans better than just about anyone else alive and I believe my expertise will be invaluable in our first contact with them. I also know that the ship has more than enough room and supplies to accommodate additional crew. I've spent most of my adult life in space, mostly on the Moon, and I am in excellent health." She had also received the full regimen of senescence-retarding therapies, adding at least thirty productive years to her lifespan. But she didn't think she should mention that; even without it, she would be fit and ready for the trip.

Rain knew that the ship's crew of twenty-five could easily be expanded to thirty or more. The cryosleepers would allow her and most of the crew to sleep for the duration of the voyage, minimizing the impact on the ship's food supplies, air, water, etc. Since she had made her decision to force her way into the crew, Rain had been diligently reading everything she could about the ship, working her way through the virtual reality training modules used by the rest of the crew, and passing just about all the physical fitness requirements—still, for a fifty-two-year-old woman who had spent a significant amount of time in the low lunar gravity, she did well.

"Rain, you know I have the highest respect and admiration for you and your work. I also know that you would be a fantastic addition to the first contact team because you *do* know more about the Proximans than anyone else alive. But I must remind you that this is a one-way trip. Your own protocols require that to avoid cross contamination. Once we leave the solar system, there is no coming back."

"I am all too aware of that, Sam. I honestly cannot imagine *not* going with you. I would be miserable remaining here, learning of what's happening at Proxima Centauri four and a half years after it really happened, not being able to contribute anything meaningful as a result. No, I need to be on this ship," she said.

"To be honest, in the back of my mind, I expected you to get yourself assigned to the crew sooner than now. Welcome aboard," he said as he put out his hand.

Rain accepted his handshake, making her grip as firm as she could. She couldn't decide if she was surprised by Sam's acceptance or not. No matter, as she was certainly happy with his reaction.

"Artur's waiting outside. I'll ask him to show you your quarters and give you a personal tour of the ship. I assume you've already taken the VR training?"

"Every single module. I've memorized where you keep everything from the gauze bandages to the duct tape. You never know when you're going to need duct tape," she said with a smile. Rain was relieved to know that she would be welcomed aboard rather than just grudgingly accepted. "You reckon the Proximans have duct tape? I mean, if we run out..."

"Hahaha, we'll take extra. And I would expect nothing less from you, and I guess you are likely as prepared as the rest of my crew. Please be at the all-hands meeting tonight at nineteen hundred and I will inform the crew. It's a shame you didn't join us earlier. This team has been training together for the last five months and it may be a little awkward to have someone new dropped into the mix. But we'll make it work—given who you are," Sam said, still smiling but dismissing her with a wave. "We've got years en route to get acquainted."

CHAPTER 13

July 12, 2089

"Captain Crosby, I really don't think the owners—of which the United States government is one—really are too concerned with any protestations of the scientists in the crew," Ambassador Jesus proclaimed. "This vessel will not leave this solar system without a State Department-sanctioned and United Nations-sanctioned liaison and security team fully acknowledged by the UN as the staff and ambassador of the first-ever Interstellar Relations and Commerce Embassy to Proxima. I hope you can understand this position-slash-predicament." Charles paused to let his comments sink in to the captain. With only four days until departing the Moon for the interstellar insertion point, such an addition to the crew was yet another—this time major—disruption. He only briefly allowed himself to look over the captain's shoulder out the viewport at the silver landscape of the Moon below stretched beneath the stern of the starship. They were currently over a desolate area in the sunlight and there was nothing but the silver- and gray-cratered Moon as far as he could tell.

"Ambassador . . . Jesus—" Crosby stuttered over the name and was interrupted.

"Just call me Charles." He smiled.

"Er, okay. Charles, I asked about governmental liaisons two years ago even before I was named captain of the *Samaritan*. Why now?"

"Simple enough, I guess," Charles replied. "Government moves at the speed of molasses in most cases. And the fact that the president's party is in a precarious position heading into next year's election cycle might have something to do with it. Honestly, we have plenty of time to 'train' along the way, plus, we'll be out of your way unless we can help or the situation requires interaction."

"Adding Dr. Gilster to the roster was difficult enough. This is a big change and it will totally piss off the scientists. That whole 'situation requires it' part. What the hell does that mean?" Captain Crosby was clearly uncomfortable with the circumstances. Charles could see his face growing red with anger. "Am I the captain of this ship or not? Are you going to start interceding in my decisions? Just exactly when will the 'situation require' your interaction, Charles?"

"Sam—can I call you Sam?" The captain just nodded at him. "Sam, I know absolutely nothing about running a space vessel, let alone the world's first-ever interstellar space vessel. You are our first-ever starship captain and I'm not going to get in your way in fear of my own horrible death in space! I can assure you that I'm only here to set up interactions with the Proximans once we get there. And, of course, anything we can do to help along the way."

"Why is your 'staff' and your equipment manifest so filled with weapons and such, then? How can I be certain that you are not here to mutiny once we're underway?"

"Sam, seriously, my staff was directly picked by the president's personal security force within the Secret Service and by the national security advisor. These are not individuals with a mission of a mutiny. Their mission is to protect me and the citizens of Earth on this vessel if something goes wrong between us and the Proximan people." Charles wasn't certain that Crosby was buying the argument, but for the most part it was true.

For the most part.

"So, I'm asking you once again...how can I prevent your armed support team from mutiny?" Captain Crosby pressed.

"Okay, okay, I have an idea. You have a security force on the ship, right?" Charles leaned back in the guest chair of the captain's office and exhaled lightly.

"Yes, of course we do."

"Alright then, until we make it to Proxima or some other emergency were to occur, four of the five-person security detail will be under the command of your chief of security. You can lock up their weapons other than whatever you deem appropriate for onboard security. The fifth will have to be my shadow per her job description. She will relinquish all but her sidearm and body armor as per standard security detail equipment. The rest of my staff of nine persons will take on shipboard duties per your assignment and as per their skill sets."

"And what if we don't need those skill sets?" Crosby raised an eyebrow. "What then?"

"Captain, we'll stay out of the way, unless you need us for something. We are literally just hitching a ride here. Again, my team are not starship people. We'd end up crashing into an asteroid or something if we tried to fly this ship." Charles laughed lightly, hoping to relax the captain's mood.

"Alright then, Charles. We'll try it your way. Your people can come aboard. Please have them report to the XO for quarters and arrangements. Don't make me regret this. If I get so much as a whiff of mutiny, I'll either lock all your asses up in a hold down by the engine room or I'll toss you out the damned airlock. Does that copy?"

"Uh, yes. I'll have my people start loading on then." Charles stood to shake Crosby's hand.

"You want to help? Truly?" the captain asked.

"Of course we do."

"Well then, I have a bit of a sticky situation. Joaquin Luce, whom I think you've met before, is forcing his way onto the ship for a 'launch ceremony.' That son of a bitch couldn't care less if we launched or exploded," Crosby explained. "But until we're out of this system I have to pay lip service to the damned politicians."

"I know him well. He was the biggest opposition to even communicating with the Proximans from the start." Charles recalled Luce and they weren't nice memories. In fact, Charles recalled him as just a bureaucrat who had been the most outspoken voice against contact with the Proximans. His following was large enough that it propelled him into a seat within the European Parliament. "He's been meddling in the interstellar affairs since the original hearings on first contact with the Proximans. He's a political hack only concerned with his own growth of power. I'm not going to miss him at all once the star drive is kicked in."

"Good. We're on the same page, then. You're a politician. You take care of all that for me. I have too much to do to prepare for launch," Crosby said gruffly. "In fact, that'll be your ship duty. Keep politics away from me as best you can. Hell, we'll even call you the ship's political officer. Ain't that a hoot? Just like an old Cold War-era Soviet ICBM naval vessel. We have ourselves a political officer..."

"Captain, I'd be more than happy to oblige. I've had more than my share of days as an ambassador dealing with political situations that are absolutely no fun and for the most part useless, if not counterproductive." Charles showed a toothy grin. "I'll get right on that."

"Good, then. Now if you don't mind, I've got a lot of other things piling up that need my attention."

"Right. I'll get with the, uh, XO. Where do I find him?" Charles asked.

"Mr. Clemons brought you here to my office...oh hell..." Crosby got up from his desk and walked to the doorway. He tapped at the panel to the right of it and the hatch hissed open. "Artur!"

"*Aye?*" The man who had led Charles to the captain's office appeared almost immediately. Charles now vaguely recalled him introducing himself as Artur. "Show our new political officer here around and get his staff oriented and moved in. He'll fill you in on our conversation—and if you have further questions, don't bother me with them!"

"Aye, Captain!"

CHAPTER 14

July 15, 2089

"Right this way, Doctor." Artur led Joaquin Luce, MEP—Member of the European Parliament—and his somewhat appreciable entourage of staffers and a few press people down the main corridor that led toward the bridge. "The ship's political officer is waiting for you."

"Political officer?" Luce asked, surprised by the concept.

"Yes sir, the newly appointed ambassador from the White House. He and his staff started moving in a few days ago," Artur explained just as he had rehearsed with Mr. Jesus the day before. "Here he comes now."

"Dr. Luce, so good to see you again." Charles held out his hand as he approached. The MEP took it and looked at him squarely as if to size him up. Charles could tell that Luce did not at first recognize him, and then his expression changed as he did so—and not in an inviting way.

"Mr. Jesus, right?" Luce shook his hand cautiously. "From the UN hearings?"

"Yes sir. You have a good memory. I'm the political officer of the *Samaritan* and the ambassador for Earth-Proxima Commerce. Good to have you aboard, sir." Charles smiled a big fake grin while at the same time thinking of all the million things he would rather be doing—no, that he needed to be doing before leaving his home planet for . . . well, forever.

"What an amazing vehicle this is, Mr. Ambassador."

"Please, Doctor, call me Charles. And yes, it is. I'm no engineer,

105

so I can't tell you much about the wizardry it took to build and the magic within, but just imagine that where you're standing today in just a few weeks will be farther from our home world than anyone has ever traveled before. Mind-boggling, isn't it?"

"Yes, it is." Luce stepped between Artur and Charles and put his arms around them. "Let's get some pictures, shall we?"

Nobody pays attention to the press. Especially not the silent camerapersons or support staff. One extra tech guy here or there was essentially just a filler in the periphery of most people's attention. And at the moment, MEP Luce was making certain that all eyes were on him. He was good at that.

Raymond Simms—or at least that's who his visitor's badge and press pass said he was—had hung in the back with a bag that looked like any other press techie equipment bag slung over his shoulder. He stopped to dig through it as if he were looking for just that particular adapter or gadget he needed, giving just enough separation between the rest of the political dog and pony show and himself. Nobody had even noticed as he slid an ID badge different from the one he wore across a panel on a side hatch. The door opened and he slipped in, closing the door behind him.

Raymond waited about thirty seconds to see if anyone had noticed, but, thankfully, nobody came. He tapped at the monitor panel on his left forearm and a three-dimensional map appeared in front of him, projected on his contacts.

"Hmm, the contacts work great," he quietly said to himself. "Okay, this is the bridge here…yep…right there…astrogation. Down one level, back three."

CHAPTER 15

July 16, 2089

"...on this historic day one hundred twenty years ago, mankind embarked on its first mission to another heavenly body—the Moon. Just as those brave Apollo 11 astronauts faced the depths of space as never before, the brave crew of the *Samaritan* will engage the fusion drive and begin its departure from the Moon, sending man- and womankind on our most courageous journey yet. We will depart this, our home solar system, for the first time ever, reaching out a helping hand to our nearest stellar neighbors. Today humanity becomes a star-faring species..." The secretary general of the United Nations continued to speak in the most-watched live presentation feed in the history of mankind.

"...the *Samaritan* is firing its onboard fusion drive and has just now departed lunar orbit. I'm certain the mood in the space dock, as around the globe, must be jubilant. The scientists, engineers, and spacecraft technicians, and mission planners, and all other members of this multinational team, have managed to meet the ambitious schedule and we are now on this momentous day launching to the stars. The lower-powered engines are now sending the *Samaritan* out toward the orbit of Mars, where in a few short weeks it will engage its Samara Drive and be on its way to Proxima Centauri. On its way to meet our brothers and sisters across space..."

Roy Burbank was among those watching the ship depart with his own eyeballs from the space dock. He was one of the lucky few. The rest of the world watched it on video feeds around the planet and the Moon and throughout the solar system. He and his engineering team had installed, tested, troubleshot, and fixed no less than twenty-two of the major subsystems on the *Samaritan* and for that he was quite proud. They had done their job and done it well. He still had nagging concerns about the PINS and was not quite able to let go of the uneasy feeling that he had overlooked something despite having gone back over the equipment twice more after the initial installation and tests were completed. It was performing exactly as it should.

Burbank was planning to enjoy the day of celebration for as long as he could because he knew that tomorrow he was taking a weeklong cruise vacation with his wife to Mars and back, then it would be back to work. He'd been assigned to work on the next starship being assembled on the other side of the dock. He didn't yet know what he would be doing. He didn't even know the name of the ship. As far as he could tell, no one did. His employers had been quite stingy with the ship's technical specifications, insisting that he sign a comprehensive nondisclosure agreement before they would allow him to see or begin reviewing the specifications. And they would only allow him to begin preparing for the job on the day he reported to work. He suspected he would spend the first several days, perhaps even weeks, poring over design and detailed technical information about the ship before he would even begin hands-on engineering work. That was okay. He needed a break.

As the *Samaritan* faded from view, becoming a small, bright, moving speck in a sea of specks that was the stars, Burbank wondered what awaited the crew on their special relativistic journey and when they arrived. He did the math and figured out that nature was going to do weird things to the crew during their flight. The Samara Drive would allow the ship to accelerate at a constant one fifth of one Earth standard gravity, providing a comfortable onboard gravity roughly equivalent to that experienced by astronauts on the surface of the Moon. It was enough to keep the muscles from decaying too much when they were awake and moving around. While they were asleep, the electrostimulation of their muscles and bones would have the same effect, or better. The electrostim was designed to approximate one full Earth gravity.

But that wasn't the weird part. To optimize the trip time, the *Samaritan* would accelerate at two-tenths gravity until the halfway point, then turn around and begin decelerating until they slowed down enough for the onboard fusion drive to bring them safely into orbit around Proxima Centauri b. At that acceleration, the ship would eventually reach just over eighty-five percent the speed of light before the deceleration phase began. At those speeds, Einstein's special relativity would kick in and slow down their clocks—the rate at which time would pass for the crew. Taking into account the constantly changing speed due to continual acceleration and deceleration, the crew would age about seven years during the voyage while almost exactly ten years would pass here on Earth. If the crew could watch people on Earth during the trip, then they would see those left behind start moving, talking, and experiencing life faster and faster, like fast-forwarding through the latest VR sim.

Burbank knew that special relativity had been verified many, many times in different experiments, and even measured at relatively low speeds with high-precision clocks. But this was to be the first time that humans would experience time dilation on a scale that would be truly experiential. Burbank wondered what it would feel like for the crew. Would they notice any difference? He doubted it, but wondered, nonetheless.

He was extremely glad they were the ones going. He liked to think about things like relativistic travel and life on other worlds, but at the end of the day all he really wanted was an hour or so at the pub with his friends and coworkers, followed by dinner and an evening with his wife, Chloe. And when the weekend came around, bye-bye to all work thoughts and one hundred percent focus on Chloe. They were even starting to talk about having a family—well, once her last month was done at the ER. There was absolutely no way that he would sacrifice that for a trip to any world in the galaxy. No, his feet were firmly planted near Sol and preferably on Earth. His goal was to save enough money working at the space dock to afford a place in the Norwegian countryside where they could build a house, raise their family, and grow old together. He smiled at the thought and noticed that he had lost sight of the *Samaritan*'s exhaust among the other points of starlight. They were on their way—more power to *them*.

Of course, Roy knew that the *Samaritan* wouldn't engage the Samara Drive for quite some time to come. In fact, as modern-day spacecraft were concerned, the *Samaritan* was very average and maybe even on the low end as far as speed was concerned. The cruise ship that he and his wife were getting on tomorrow traveled a bit more than twice as fast. In fact, as part of the cruise package they hoped to see the *Samaritan* when they passed it going out and then coming back. Roy's boss had awarded him with the cruise as a bonus for all the late hours he'd put in while getting the ship ready.

The cruise ship was almost the same crew complement as the *Samaritan* but wasn't quite as big since there was no interstellar drive on the thing. Since the *Samaritan* was big and used modern nuclear fusion-based plasma propulsion for interplanetary travel, there was a lot more mass for the standard engines to push and therefore it was slower. It would take it several weeks to reach a point far enough from shipping lanes and other habitat regions within the Sol system before it could safely ignite the star drive. Perhaps, he thought, some of the crew might get cold feet and could still jump ship right up until a week before igniting the drive. It would take that long to get clear of the dangerous exhaust path of the interstellar engine—assuming there was a really fast ship nearby.

The ship had been underway for less than three hours when the chime sounded, indicating that dinner was being served in the mess hall. Rain, and about half of the thirty-six-person crew, moved from their stations to the mess to take dinner together. The remaining crew members would eat on the second shift. There simply wasn't room for everyone to gather in the same room at the same time.

Rain entered the mess hall and immediately noticed how small and cramped it was. It was the first meal post-departure and the first time that the crew was alone together without the technicians and engineers from the space dock intermingled with them. As she scanned the room, she saw some familiar faces and one in particular—Enrico Vulpetti, the aerospace engineer from Georgia Tech who had first told her of the *Samaritan*'s existence. He said he would make it as part of the crew and, true to his word, here he was. She hadn't seen him anywhere in the past few days and wondered where he'd been keeping himself before launch. He motioned for her to join him and three others around one of the tables in the corner of the room.

"Dr. Vulpetti, it's good to see you here," said Rain as she approached his table and sat down.

"Dr. Gilster—or should I say, Lorraine—it's good to see you also. And remember, you should call me Enrico. We're going to be spending a long time together and formalities can get very tedious," he replied, breaking into the same big smile she remembered from when she met him after her lecture over two years before. He was definitely a charmer.

"Fine, Enrico, and you should call me Rain. The only people who call me Lorraine are strangers and my parents," she said, breaking into her own smile.

"Rain. I'm glad you are here. Let me introduce you to Neil, Catherine, and Yoko. They are among the ship's biologists and we are just revisiting a discussion that I'm sure isn't new to you—the Proximans' humanity."

After exchanging pleasantries with the biologists and eating most of her lemon flounder, rice, and brussels sprouts freeze-dried meal (with a fresh green salad!), the conversation drifted back to the subject of biology.

"It just isn't possible for these two hugely different planetary ecosystems to have followed a path of parallel evolution to produce *Homo sapiens*, at roughly the same time, with roughly the same level of technological development. The probability of that occurring is zero," said Neil Polkingham. Neil was in his early forties, thin, and very Caucasian with pale skin and red hair. His British accent gave him away as one of the persistent upper class who had probably attended only the best universities in the United Kingdom.

"I agree with Neil," Yoko Pearl nodded. Yoko spoke English with what sounded to Rain like a Japanese accent. She was an attractive woman who looked to be in her thirties with long black hair and an intense gaze that bespoke of a passion for her subject matter expertise. She continued, "Proxima Centauri b has a year that is only eleven Earth days. It has virtually no axial tilt, so there aren't seasons. It orbits closer to its star than Mercury does to ours. That means it's bathed in Proxima Centauri's stellar wind that is three orders of magnitude more intense than that we experience at Earth. That alone should scour the planet clean of life, repeatedly, even if it did start to develop there. And if that isn't enough, Proxima Centauri is a flare star. Just a year before you heard those radio signals for the first time, astronomers cataloged a large solar storm there that, had it been our star, would have ripped away the Earth's ozone layer and killed us all. Not only should there be no humans there, but there also shouldn't be any life at all."

"Not to mention history," Neil added. "We know life first originated on Earth within a billion years of its formation, only to be wiped out, or nearly so, several times. We all know about the meteorite that killed off the dinosaurs and allowed our ancestors, the mammals, to survive, thrive, and evolve into the life-forms we see on Earth today. That meteorite was an accident of history that forced evolution in a very different direction from where it was headed pre-impact. It forced all that crap into the upper atmosphere that basically stopped photosynthesis and plunged the planet into the equivalent of a mini ice age. But that wasn't the first great extinction or the worst. Two hundred and fifty million years ago there was the Permian extinction that wiped out over ninety percent of the planet's species. It was caused by the eruption of a super volcano. That, too, was an accident of history. Did Proxima Centauri b have their own meteorite impact and super-volcano eruptions at the same times? With the same life-forms surviving and eventually becoming human? It is just impossible."

"But they are there. They *are* human," interjected Catherine Nkrumah. In their dinner conversation, Rain had learned that Catherine was from Guinea, had studied at Columbia in New York City, and, until the ship departed Earth, lived in Sydney, Australia. She was half of one of the few married couples on the ship. Her husband, Kieran, a doctor specializing in fertility, was responsible for the frozen embryos and their possible, future use with the Proximans. Until this point, Catherine had been quietly and politely listening to the discussion.

"Agreed. But there they are. The seemingly impossible appears to be possible—factual," said Yoko. "What about panspermia?"

"We've thought about that. Let's assume life evolved on Earth some time ago and then some big rock hit the planet and knocked pieces of it off into space. Let's also assume that these pieces contained Earth life. For that Earth life to get to Proxima Centauri b, the energy of the impact would have to have given the rock enough velocity to escape the Sun's gravity and reach interstellar space. It would then have to have crossed through over four light-years' deep space at nearly absolute zero temperatures, taking hundreds of thousands or millions of years to do so, and then land on Proxima, surviving the passage through its atmosphere and high-speed impact, to live and grow on a totally alien world. And then the parallel evolution and historical events we discussed earlier would have to happen. Simply preposterous," said Neil.

"Oh, not so preposterous, as you've got your physics all wrong," Rain disagreed. "There is no reason that an object the size of a rock had to be accelerated across the interstellar void. Simple dust particles or ice crystals barely large enough to see could still house millions of viruses, microbes, DNA, you name it. Such tiny particles could really be vastly accelerated well beyond the rock idea."

"Hmmm, hadn't considered that. Why had I not considered that?" Yoko mumbled to herself.

"It almost makes you believe in God. Directed evolution. Maybe all those Ancient Astronaut theorists were on to something." Enrico chuckled.

"Not sure why you laugh at that comment, Enrico," Rain replied matter-of-factly. "Nobody has any scientific proof one way or the other if any mystical gods from the past were real or not. Who knows? Advanced aliens might be just as plausible a hypothesis as any if they turned out to be real, but the problem is being able to falsify something that happened so long ago. Experimental verification of the hypothesis would prove to be extremely tough. Awfully hard to prove the negative too."

"Ah yes, prove that Santa Clause doesn't exist... very difficult," Yoko agreed.

"Or maybe the solution could be more like the old *Star Trek* 'Preservers,'" Rain said, offering another possibility. "When they made those early science fiction television shows they didn't have the money to create truly alien aliens, so they used people wearing makeup. To explain why many of the aliens their starship encountered looked so human, they invoked some ancient alien race that had planted humanlike life on multiple planets—the Preservers."

"This isn't an old television show and once we invoke God, we're basically giving up our search for scientific truth and accepting superstition, mysticism, or fantasy," said Neil dismissively if not arrogantly.

"Oh, I don't know about that, Neil. God can come in so many forms and one of them might be scientifically measurable and believable." Rain had never succumbed to the cliché that physicists were atheists. She wasn't sure what exactly to call herself, but she had no scientific evidence to rule God out and she knew several scientists who were able to be objective scientists and hold deep religious beliefs. It was very hard to prove or disprove something didn't exist and she did her best to stay out of such a faulty path of endeavor. In the end, she followed the scientific method in most things. That was sort of her religion.

"What other options are there?" asked Enrico.

Yoko squirmed, looking like she wanted to say something, but couldn't bring herself to interrupt and get it out.

"What is it, Yoko?" asked Rain.

"I am sure you are familiar with the story of Little Red Riding Hood. If you think of that story in the context of our current situation—look at the seeming impossibility of what we're discussing here and combine it with warnings of Stephen Hawking—then there is one other possible conclusion," Yoko said, her eyes moving from person to person until finally stopping on Rain's.

"That this whole 'Proximans are human and in dire need of our help' thing is all a ruse meant to lure us to Proxima Centauri so we can be eaten by the Big Bad Wolf?" Rain said.

"Or something like that," said Yoko.

The *Interstellarerforscher* spacecraft was robotic and designed to use its Samara Drive to go farther into the interstellar medium between the stars, at a faster speed, than any previous ship. It was ostensibly a German-funded science mission, equipped with high-power radar and sensors to measure the background radiation, the galactic cosmic ray flux, dust particle density, and magnetic field strength in the vastness of the space between Earth's star, Sol, and its neighbors. It was one thing to say that humans were going to build a crewed starship and send it on a journey across more than the four light-years separating Sol from Proxima Centauri and quite another to say that humans would send the starship and have it survive the journey. There were simply too many unknowns about the space between here and there. How many micrometeors and of what size, on average, will the ship encounter along the way? Hitting a dust grain while traveling at seven tenths the speed of light was one thing; hitting an object with the mass of a baseball was quite another. The ship's dust-charging magnetic shield could quite easily deflect one-to-two-gram interstellar dust grains but a chunk of rock the mass of a baseball would almost certainly get through the shielding and impact the ship with the explosive force equivalent to more than one million tons of TNT. Needless to say, that would be a mission-ending event. Fortunately, space is big and there aren't many chunks of rock between the stars that weigh as much as a baseball. But that didn't really help, because there were probably some that big out there and hitting just one would be catastrophic. One of the goals of the *Interstellarerforscher* was to measure the density of these particles to assess the probability of *Samaritan* hitting one on its much-longer journey.

The plan was for the *Interstellarerforscher* to launch a few days before the *Samaritan* and for it to fly just ahead of the crewed ship, searching the path for objects the *Samaritan* might encounter and relay the hazard information in time for a course correction to be made to avoid any sort of catastrophic event.

Deep within the fusion reactor onboard the *Interstellarerforscher*, enshrouded by intense magnetic fields generated by high-temperature superconducting electromagnets, hydrogen atoms were being forced closer and closer together by the combination of the magnetic fields and high-energy lasers until the electrostatic forces keeping the two like-charged nuclei apart were overcome by the nuclear force pulling them together, allowing them to fuse into helium, releasing energy. The fusion reaction increased in intensity, with more and more hydrogen being converted into helium and releasing yet more energy like in the interior of a main sequence star, ramping up the power available for the Samara Drive.

Once the minimum power threshold was achieved, the Samara Drive was activated. Within it, ultraviolet light as intense as any produced in nature lanced outward from the stern of the ship. From Newton's Law—for every action there is an equal and opposite reaction—the starship recoiled in the other direction as the light was emitted, accelerating it forward.

The beam of ultraviolet light, had it been close to and pointed toward the Earth, would have burned a hole through the atmosphere, scorching some of the planet's surface in the process.

But the ship's designers knew this, and, working with the United Nations, established a "keep out" region extending beyond the Moon in within which it was forbidden to activate Samara Drives of a certain power level. From that distance, the intense UV light beam diverged to an intensity that was not a threat to the Earth, the Moon or any of the many spacecraft now operating in near-Earth space. To minimize the risk to other spacecraft in the inner solar system, many of which could conceivably end up in the path of the light produced by a Samara Drive, a flight plan had to be approved that showed when and where the drive would be activated and by analysis show that none of the many registered operational spacecraft nearby were in harm's way. So far, there had never been an accident.

Glenn "Pops" Yenne was looking forward to the end of the journey. Despite his nickname, Yenne wasn't that old; at fifty-two he was just older than the rest of his small three-person crew and they never let him forget it. True, at the end of a run he would get paid a large sum of money and there would be the temptation to blow it all on gambling, booze, and drugs, and by paying for sex once he returned to Earth. Unlike his much-younger crew, he knew his days hauling contraband through deep space would soon have to come to an end and he needed to save some money to live on when that day came. Besides, his libido wasn't what it used to be, he never took drugs, and he really didn't like the hangovers that came from days-long drinking binges. Hence his fuddy-duddy nickname of "Pops." Instead of sex, drugs, and alcohol, he was thinking of the Caribbean beaches and days lounging by the seaside with nothing to do except admire the fine forms sunbathing all around him. Yes, the money was good, but there certainly wasn't much to spend it on out here.

Here was an interesting term to describe a location somewhere in the void between Mars and Earth. They had just dropped off contraband to two of the mining stations in the main belt, drugs and real-by-God Kentucky bourbon among it. Now they were taking some of the rare earth metals carefully skimmed from the mining company's operations back to the Moon where they were in high demand for the burgeoning lunar mining and manufacturing facilities. It was far cheaper for some of the smaller companies to buy their raw materials from him than to import them from Earth and pay the tariffs and taxes levied by the various transport and port authorities. When would the politicians realize that the confiscatory taxation only fostered black markets according to the universal economic laws of supply and demand? He hoped they wouldn't learn too soon. Having them get smart would be bad for business. And he was really looking forward to having enough business to afford his Caribbean dream.

He was, as usual, running his ship, the *Matador*, without a universal transponder and with minimal radio or laser communication with anyone else. The only thing nearby—and by considering solar system distances, it was virtually on top of the *Matador*—was some small robotic spacecraft outbound toward Mars. Looking at their relative trajectories, they would pass within about five hundred kilometers of each other at closest approach, which would be soon. If *Matador* were a passenger liner, then the Collision Alert warnings would already be going off. Yenne wasn't worried about collision with the spacecraft—five hundred kilometers was still a huge distance. He also wasn't worried about detection by it. If the spacecraft did have radar for tracking nearby objects, and if it did detect him, the likelihood of his ship being reported to the authorities was extremely small. Solar system traffic control out here, unlike in cis-lunar space, was virtually nonexistent. And if the spacecraft did send a message to anyone, no one would really be able to do anything at all about it. The *Matador* would be long gone, no one would know it was the *Matador* since his transponder was turned off, and no one would likely even care.

Yenne and his crew were breaking the law and advertising their location and trajectory would be just about the most stupid thing they could do. The emptiness of space virtually assured that he wouldn't be detected and stopped. And that meant success and payment. The risk was minimal and the profits high. After all, what could possibly go wrong out *here* in the middle of nowhere?

"Hey, Pops. Do you think those aliens out at Proxima would be in the market for some Captain Morgan?" The question came from Angelo Trabant, the youngest of the crew. Tall, rather gangly, and sporting a head full of black curly hair, Angelo wasn't the sharpest stick in the stack, but Yenne knew he could count on him in a pinch. Angelo was one of those people who didn't easily panic and could make quick, usually helpful, decisions when it mattered most. Yenne liked him.

"If they are as human as the newsies say they are, then I bet we couldn't get them enough rum even with a hundred ships like ours," Yenne replied, grinning. He knew it wasn't he and his crew who would be running rum to Proxima, but the mere thought brought a smile to his face.

"Hey, Angelo, are you stupid or what? Proxima is so far away that we'd all be dead before this piece-of-shit ship could get across four light-years—no offense, Pops." The soundbite was contributed by another of the crew, Addie Yang. Addie, the sole female on board, was also the toughest person on the ship. She knew her vulnerabilities and wasn't leaving her honor to chance. Any guy who moved the wrong way with her was likely to have his throat slit or his groin crushed—or both. Other than that, Addie was about as easy to work with as anyone Yenne had ever encountered. She always offered to do the extra job, never complained, and rarely screwed up.

Yes, Yenne had a good crew. Their line of work was shady, but otherwise they were quite respectable.

But none of that mattered in the least when the ultraviolet light from the *Interstellarerforscher*'s Samara Drive, traveling at 186,000 miles per second, sliced through the front of the *Matador*, vaporizing all four members of the crew and most of their cargo. Yenne didn't have time to be offended that his ship was being insulted nor did Angelo have time to even think of a smart-ass reply. They never even knew anything was wrong before their neurons, along with the rest of their bodies, were turned into vapor.

The coolant lines to the *Matador*'s fusion reactor were immediately severed, causing the reactor's sun-like heat to rapidly go from contained to completely uncontained, otherwise known as an explosion, in a fraction of second. It wasn't really a nuclear explosion, because that's not allowed by the physics of a fusion reactor losing coolant, but more of a rapid-heating explosion—one that was visible to naked eye on or near Mars and to any space telescope that happened to have it in the line of sight at the time.

A few seconds later, nothing remained of the *Matador* except an expanding ball of plasma, a few pieces of metal that were accelerated by the explosion, and the flash from the explosion radiating outward in all directions at the speed of light.

✧   ✧   ✧

For the *Interstellarerforscher* and the controllers at the German Space Operations Center near Oberpfaffenhofen who were responsible for it, the boost was perfect and proceeding according to plan. The ship was accelerating in the direction opposite to its ultraviolet-light lance and on its way to scout the path for the *Samaritan* on its soon-to-begin, decade-long journey. As was tradition when a new space mission started, the controllers stood and cheered, watching the telemetry stream indicate a picture-perfect engine start and as-predicted shipboard acceleration. Preceding the *Samaritan* by only a few days, the media attention was significant. After all, *Interstellarerforscher* was the first truly interstellar spacecraft built and launched by humans.

The radio telemetry from *Interstellarerforscher* took fourteen minutes to reach Oberpfaffenhofen. The light from the exploding *Matador* took the same amount of time to reach Earth-based and near-Earth space-based telescopes. It took almost a full twenty-four hours for the astronomers to see the explosion, understand it for what it was, notify the International Space Traffic Control Authority, and for them to then put two and two together to figure out that the unknown ship's demise was almost certainly linked to the departure of the *Interstellarerforscher* and its lethal ultraviolet exhaust.

For the scientists, engineers, and politicians, the danger posed by the Samara Drive suddenly moved from the theoretical to the real. For another group, or perhaps groups, it was merely a confirmation of what they already knew: The Samara Drive, what it enabled and how it was going to be used to contact aliens, was dangerous. Dangerous enough that *someone* had to do something about it.

CHAPTER 16

"What do you mean the PINS is showing something odd?" Crosby listened to the design engineer on the other end of the video feed repeating what he'd just told him.

"Dr. Burbank, if I knew that I wouldn't be calling for you while you're on vacation," Crosby replied. "Cindy, you want to explain it?"

"Sure." Dr. Cindy Mastrano, the chief engineer of the *Samaritan*, nodded from across the ready-room table. "Let me pull up the slides I just sent you, Captain."

"My chief engineer will explain." Crosby motioned to her while giving her the datapad he was looking at. Mastrano fiddled with the device for a brief moment and then nodded to herself with a smile.

"Yes. Here it is," she said. "Well, Dr. Burbank, several of the reference pulsars are in the wrong places. I mean, there are stars there but they are the wrong ones according to what the PINS is measuring. We did a routine precheck yesterday and for whatever reason, for example, while our closest pulsar, Geminga, is right where it is supposed to be and is pulsing at the right frequency, PSR J1748-2446ad isn't."

"What do you mean it isn't?" Burbank sounded sleepy as if he'd just been gotten out of bed for the video conference. Of course, that was exactly what had happened and exactly why he appeared that way.

"Well, the pulsar should be spinning at about seven hundred

sixteen times per second, right? But according to the PINS measurements we are detecting, it isn't doing that. In fact, it looks more like the pulsar B1919+21. At least it is according to the frequency and periodicity. It's like the database is right but the pulsars have been moved around."

"Wait, have you run the Doppler correction calibration sequence?" Roy rubbed at his eyes. "It might just be that the ship's acceleration has thrown the calibration off. The gamma ray spectrum analyzer we used in the original tests had an issue with that. That could cause some sort of seemingly random shuffling in the pulsar spectrum autorecognition software."

"That was the first thing we tried, Dr. Burbank. We have all of your design, build, and test notes with us and I've gone through them word for word, graphic by graphic. There's not a single byte of data in your files on this ship I haven't searched through ten times here. I think this is something new—that is, er, unless I misunderstood your notes." Mastrano paused and looked up from her pad. "That is very possible, this ship is very complex as you well know."

"Yeah, I don't envy you in your job at all. Tell you what, send me the diagnostics file and I'll dig into it right away." Roy groaned through the video monitor.

"We've sent it to you already. We really need you to look at it now," Dr. Mastrano told him.

"Alright, alright. I'm up now anyway. Let me look at it for about thirty minutes and then just call me back."

"Cindy, I'm not sure what to tell you. Something has corrupted the file addresses between the sensor data and the target recognition database. If you look here at the source files for the PINS reference coordinates stored on the backups back at the Luna shipyard and compare it to this, damn...they're like completely different files." Roy took a swig from a soft drink he'd taken from the minibar and was doing his best to keep his voice down so as to not awaken his wife. He waited as the drink slowly drained in the ship's low gravity, pausing long enough to take in the view through the porthole of an ever-increasing-in-size Mars. It no longer looked like a red dot in the sky. It actually was starting to look like a ball with a horizon.

"I was wondering about that," Cindy replied.

Roy turned his chair back from the window, swallowed down the caffeinated drink, and bumped his knee on the small desk muttering a profanity through his clenched teeth. "Shit!" He hoped he hadn't disturbed his wife. While the "estate room" on the cruise ship was the second from the largest offered, they were still smaller than a low-budget hotel room. He'd pulled the curtain between the bed and the "living area" but a mere few millimeters of polycarbonate material was truly all that separated them.

"I can't for the life of me figure out how that could happen. I mean, I've been playing it over and over in my head and I can't reproduce that. Weird data corruption." Roy shrugged.

"So, what, we reload and reboot?" the *Samaritan*'s chief engineer asked him through the small vid screen on his pad that he'd stuck to the magnetic device holder/charger above the tiny desk.

"Yes. I've already sent you a fresh set of nav database files that I want you to compare against the hard drive's files. I'd like to know how they were corrupted." Roy shrugged. "Like I said, I can't imagine how this happened. But at least you'll have the initial file system. You should take that and store it someplace safe."

"And you think this is the only issue here?"

"I'm not one hundred percent sure about it, no. Because I am not there to run a diagnostic." Roy could see the chief engineer's face light up suddenly and Roy would soon be sorry he'd ever let those words slip through his lips.

"What do you mean I'll have to make it home without you?" Roy's wife wasn't quite shouting, but she certainly wasn't whispering sweet nothings in his ear.

"Chloe, listen, my bosses said I have to go, *so*, I have to go!" His emphatic statement came across less as a direct statement and more as if he were pleading with her for forgiveness. "And I can't let all those people head off into interstellar space with a broken navigation system. They would be going to their doom for certain."

"Why *you*?" This time it was almost a shout. Chloe seldom raised her voice at him, but when she did, he knew she was angry. "We haven't had a vacation in . . . well, I don't remember the last one."

"Well, I'm the expert—wait, no, I'm the *only* expert on the

Pulsar Interstellar Navigation System." He continued pleading his case. "There isn't really somebody else to send. Look at it this way: The cruise ship is altering its course to meet up with the *Samaritan* tomorrow. I'll go onboard and fix things there and then get on a transport that is already on a rendezvous trajectory for the day after tomorrow. You'll at least get to see the *Samaritan* up really close like not many people ever have or will. And we will both still likely be in great viewing distance of her when she lights up the interstellar drive."

"I'd rather see you. Here, with me." Roy knew when to just shrug and accept a battle once it was won, or lost, depending upon the point of view.

"Sorry, honey." He didn't know what else to say. "I have to go."

CHAPTER 17

August 22, 2089

"We've been at this for hours and nothing seems to work right," Cindy Mastrano complained to Roy.

"Well, we need about ten graduate students in here running through every single line of code in this system to see what is going on. I have never seen anything like this at all!" Roy was flummoxed, exasperated, and a bit on edge. He was supposed to have finished the fix on the PINS hours ago. The cruise ship, and his wife, had already undocked with the *Samaritan* and were heading off toward a safe distance from the ship before it was ready to ignite the Samara Drive. A military cruiser was on its way out to take him as soon as he was finished. What that meant was, much to his chagrin, his wife, Chloe, was going to finish the last half of the cruise without him. That was going to take a lot of flowers to fix.

"Okay, we've reloaded the database twice and each time we still get the same issue." Roy scratched his head. "No matter that we know the datafile isn't corrupt and the pulsars are all in the right locations with the right frequency spectra, the PINS system is randomizing that data in such a way as to give the vehicle a correct current position, but no matter where we point the trajectory it will not reach that position."

"What does that mean physically?" Cindy looked up from her datapad and sighed. "I mean, I know what it means, but let's look at it from a very fundamental explanation or description. If we go back to the basics, then maybe we can figure out what is going on."

"Sure, that's exactly what we did in the test phase. Good idea," Roy agreed and paused long enough to think about the problem. The two of them were sitting in the Navigation Suite just off the engine room, a bit forward and beneath the main Samara Drive chamber.

The Nav Suite had several multimeter-wide transparent domes with optical telescopes viewing in every possible direction. There were other telescopes connected on the other side of the ship and ones on the forward and aft sections to give full optical imagery of the sky around them. There were several radio and microwave antenna feeds that were connected into the Nav Suite as well. In the center of the room was an instrument box that housed a gamma ray telescope and spectrum analyzer. There were clear polycarbonate walls around it and an air handler continuously keeping an overpressure in the small enclosure to keep any extraneous particulates, dust, or other contaminants out of the instrument. Electrical lines fed through a manifold in the polycarbonate to stations set up on all four walls surrounding the PINS instrument inside.

"You want to start?" Cindy asked.

"Uhm, okay, I guess." Roy turned and looked out the telescope dome nearest him and then back at the PINS. "We're in a spaceship in space. We're moving with a speed of roughly one AU per month, right now. We can use standard interplanetary navigation beacons, the sun, the planets, radar data from those planets and beacons to get our position and velocity vector precise to within a billionth of a meter and within a millionth of a meter per second, respectively. Using the PINS system, we should be at least that precise but we're not."

"Well, our current PINS position is accurate until the PINS operates on it with our velocity vector," Cindy added. "That means that the instruments are feeding the right position into the device. But the trajectory prediction filter is doing something with it to mess that up."

"Look at this graph here of our position state vector at time zero. It matches exactly to within instrument errors of the in-system position calibration. Then one calculation epoch away, we're still fine. But at about a hundred thousand or so calculation epochs, boom! We're off by thousands of kilometers in our position. By the time you do a few billion epochs we're off by light-years." Roy was frustrated with this. Trajectory calculation was simple state vectors, ephemeris data updates from sensors, and then injection of those updates into the trajectory prediction filter algorithms. It should be simple stuff.

"I'm about ready to pull my hair out on this." Cindy grunted. "If we don't get to the bottom of this, there's no way we can fire up the Samara Drive. This mission is over in four days if we don't figure this out."

"Are you going tell the captain that?" Roy asked.

"Are you gonna tell your boss that?" Cindy replied with the equally daunting question.

"Come on, Cindy. We're smarter than this. Could it be in the hardware somewhere?" Roy was grasping for straws. He felt like he was in a dark room playing darts and he had no clue which wall the dartboard was on.

"We've reinstalled the flight software for the PINS unit twice now. We've run all the diagnostics for the observation instruments. It's as if there's something in the computer system that clicks on after a thousand epochs." Cindy repeated again what they'd gone over and over for the past couple of days.

"Well, maybe it's in the computer system and not the PINS." Roy threw up his hands. "Who knows? Got an extra computer system lying around we could load all this up on?"

"Seriously?" Cindy asked. "That could take days to test."

"No. We don't build a new system for a flight unit. Let's just run the system with the hardware in the loop connected to the PINS software running on a different machine. Might run a bit slower, but so what?" Roy looked as though he was thinking about what he'd just said and then snapped his fingers. "We can use the environment control systems computer. It's powerful enough. We use a wireless input/output connection between the sensors and we'll run the software on that computer."

"How long will that take to set up?" Cindy asked herself out loud. "Hmm, a couple hours to rig the comm setup. I can do that while you load the software on a second terminal. We could try that in a few hours maybe?"

"Sounds like a plan. I think we should pull whatever techs you have in on this," Roy suggested.

"We have a small crew and there are only two techs, besides me." Cindy laughed. "We could get the scientists in the crew if you want, but I doubt they'd be up to speed enough to help much in short order. But if we're doing this, I'll have to run it by the captain first."

"Okay. Go run it by the captain." Roy yawned and stretched. "You, your two techs, and me. Let's get to work."

It took most of the rest of the afternoon. Connecting the environment systems computer to the PINS instrument suite required more troubleshooting than Cindy had expected. But in the end, she managed to make it happen. Roy had done his part and the PINS software was loaded, prepped, and ready to go. The plan was to run the PINS on the new computer system for the next four hours and determine if there were any mismatches in the trajectory measurements and predictions. At their current rate of speed, they would notice a position and velocity drift in that amount of time.

"We're all good on my end," Cindy said.

"Here goes nothing." Roy hit the execute command on his datapad interface and the PINS went to work. "Nothing to do now but to wait awhile."

"The PINS computer is bad. No doubt about it," Cindy agreed with Roy. After a few hours it was becoming clear that the PINS equipment being controlled via a different computer was functioning properly. "But what does that even mean?"

"This makes no sense. We tested and tested that thing. Computers don't just go 'bad.'" Roy was already pulling the covers off the panels on the computer rack. "Something doesn't pass the smell test here."

"I agree." Cindy looked at him shaking her head. "What are you going to do?"

"I built this goddamned thing. I've seen and still have images of every card, chip, board, wire, nut, bolt, and nook or cranny. If there's something broken or not supposed to be there, I'll find it."

"I'll go get some more coffee and send the techs for some flashlights," Cindy replied.

CHAPTER 18

August 24, 2089

"You found it where?" Captain Crosby looked at the little disk-shaped device in his hand. It was about the size of the button on a dress shirt with an adhesive backing on one side. As far as he could tell there were no other signs of electronics or microprocessors or anything. It was just a small, solid, and smooth gray disk.

"Well, that one and these two." Roy held up two more of the disks. "They were stuck right on top of the atomic clock circuits in the temporal calibration unit or TCU. I found them pretty quickly. Whoever put 'em in knew exactly where to place them to create the most havoc on our navigation system. And, by the way, the location was pretty easy to access without affecting anything else that would have alerted us to them being there."

"Three of them," Cindy added. "They must have even known the precise design of the clock system."

"You're right about that, Cindy." Roy sat slumped in the chair in front of the captain's desk. He turned and nodded to Cindy, who was standing against the door. "Cindy probably wouldn't have found it as quickly just because she didn't build the thing. Not her fault at all. As soon as I saw that first one, well, it stuck out like a sore thumb as they say. Then I certainly knew there would be two more."

"Wait a minute, Dr. Burbank." Crosby held up a hand to slow him down. "What does it do?"

"Oh, very simple, what you have in your hand right there is a little chunk of Cesium-137. It tosses out gamma rays very

129

regularly at six hundred and sixty-two kiloelectron volts. It was about a centimeter, give or take a millimeter or so, from one of the atomic clock axes inside the PINS. The others were aligned with the other two axes. Guess what each of those clocks uses as an atomic radioactive decay source?" Roy smiled.

"Let me guess. Cesium-137?" Captain Crosby frowned.

"Bingo! Give the captain a prize!" Roy leaned in closer and straightened himself in the chair a bit. "It was aligned just right by each of the clock axes that, as it decayed, the gamma rays from this little bugger injected spurious random clock pulses to the onboard clocks. Once the clocks were confused, the calculation epochs became damned near randomized."

"Wait, isn't there software or something to account for random gamma rays on a thing like that? I mean, we're in space. Gamma rays zip through all the time." Crosby was clearly puzzled and the look on his face showed it.

"You'd think so, but there are two safeguards against that," Cindy said while tapping at her datapad. She pulled up a three-dimensional schematic and projected it onto the screen in the captain's office. "See, here is the TCU. The first safeguard is this box. It's a combination of tungsten, silicone, bismuth, lead, and iron sintered as a ceramic. This is the best, most modern gamma ray shield known to man, but still some gamma rays get through it from time to time. So, note here how there is a one-centimeter polycarbonate cube with these chips connected on either side of the cube. These are chip-based atomic clocks and you have one on top and bottom for the y-axis, front and back for the z-axis, and either side for the x-axis. Roy, do you want to take it from here?"

"You were doing great, Cindy. But, uh, sure." He cleared his throat a bit. "The clocks on the same axis are synchronized with each other and if there is a spurious event in one x clock, for example say the one on the left that the one on the right doesn't see, then that means the gamma came from outside the clock and is likewise thrown out. The active area of each of the chip clocks is about a millimeter square. The odds of a gamma from space coming through this millimeter-square detector on this side and then traveling perfectly in line with the other is excruciatingly small."

"Okay, I understand that. You're talking about coincidence detection, right?" Crosby asked.

"Right again, Captain." Roy smiled at him while clapping his hands proudly. "But our saboteur was smart. He placed a fairly significant little gamma ray source right on top of one detector on each axis. Many times the gamma rays passed through both gamma detectors on the same axis creating a false time pulse. But not so many as to be obvious."

"Clever SOB, whoever did this," Cindy agreed with Roy. "And, as you can guess by now, the bottom line is devastatingly simple. When the clocks get screwed up, Captain, we have no idea what time the sensors made a measurement, or when our next data input was correlated, or even how long between calculations has passed. Early on the errors are small, but after tens of thousands of runs the big errors start to show up."

"How hard was this to do? I mean, did they need to be a PhD in interstellar navigation systems, atomic clocks, and such? Or could a clever person with some training do it?"

"Captain, that is not a part of the system that is just sticking out in the open for everyone to put their fingers on. At least four bolts on the outer instrument rack cover have to be removed, a handful of wiring harnesses unsnapped, and then the shielding plates have to be popped loose with a specific little tool in order to get access to this circuit board. There is no doubt that this was sabotage. But, if they had the design drawings and some time to practice, it could be done by a tech-savvy person in short order." Roy exhaled. "I put it all back together and had Cindy time me. I needed eleven minutes and thirty-one seconds to install the buttons and then close the PINS back up. I might could do it faster with practice."

"Somebody that knew what they were doing had access to the PINS for some period of time longer than that, maybe," Cindy agreed. "But, with all the visitors coming and going for the past few months, access to the PINS for an hour or two without being noticed might have been possible. I don't think we prepared for this kind of sabotage while in space dock around the Moon."

"There was security, but not extremely tight security. It takes a bit of resources to afford a trip to the Moon, then to the orbiting shipyard, and then atop that to get on board a ship without being noticed. But in the last months of final prep there were hundreds of people coming and going." Captain Crosby shook his head in wonder. "While we know who has been on this ship, we might never figure out specifically who did this. We'll start an investigation." Captain Crosby leaned back, nodding his head approvingly. "Great work, you two. So, am I to assume that the PINS is functional now?"

"Yes sir," Cindy answered. "There is no reason to scuttle the mission because of the PINS, Captain."

"I'll have to ask Mission Control about that. They're still in charge until we're out of the system," Crosby replied.

"While I am enjoying my stay and all, Captain, if you don't mind, I'll be ready to get off this thing as soon as possible," Roy said eagerly while trying his best to stifle a yawn.

"The Space Force cruiser from the US is on its way. I will ask the ship to be here first thing in the morning. It will stay long enough for a security detail to sweep the ship for other surprises. We need to think about what that might be. They are set to disembark no later than fifteen hundred ship normal tomorrow afternoon. Until then, Dr. Burbank, get yourself something to eat, maybe get cleaned up, and get some rest."

"Sure thing." Roy stood as the captain did, holding out a hand.

"Thank you, Roy." Crosby shook his hand. "I mean it. You probably just saved the mission and our lives. Great work. I wish you could come along with us."

"You're welcome, Captain, but there is no chance of that. I'm perfectly happy right here in the good ol' Sol system. And, if it's not too much of a burden, would you mind telling my wife about the 'saving the mission' part?" He laughed.

"I'd be happy to!" Crosby grinned back at him. "And I'm sure your bosses wouldn't mind hearing it from me either."

"Couldn't hurt."

"I'll see that Artur writes up some sort of commendation or whatever the protocol is for a non-crew member. Get some rest." Crosby waited for Roy to get to the door. "CHENG, would you mind staying with me for a few more minutes? I'd like to get your take on something."

"Yes, Captain." Cindy slapped Roy on the shoulder as he passed her at the door. "No rest for the wicked."

Roy sleepily wandered back toward his quarters hoping he'd make it there before he fell asleep while walking. Well, he didn't really consider it walking. The gee load was less than one fifth that of Earth gravity and it made walking more of a shuffle while trying to maintain your balance. The magnetic shoes helped with that a little. After several minutes of walking down the corridor, Roy realized that he must have taken a wrong turn because he was somewhere he hadn't yet been on the ship. There were only really three main corridors through the ship. He must have gotten on the wrong one somehow when he climbed down the stairwell from the captain's quarters.

He looked about, trying to get his bearings, but he was so tired he couldn't think straight. He shook his head, which then almost threw him off his feet. The nearest hatch was in front of him, opening toward what he thought was in the ship's inward direction. He turned there and was shocked at how confused his sense of direction must have been.

The hatch had clearly led him to an outer part of the ship. He was turned around a complete one hundred eighty degrees. He knew he was near the ship's exterior from the view through the windows in the large, long room. He could see one of the PINS gamma ray telescopes looming just outside the window to the aft of where he was. He was totally lost.

The room wasn't very deep, only five to seven meters or so. But it stretched out along the ship's travel axis in tens of meters both fore and aft. Along the exterior wall were rows and rows of dull gray metamaterial cylinders, each with multiple tubes and cables connecting them to various instrument panels on the bulkhead. Roy shuffled closer to the cylinder closest to him and suddenly realized where he was.

"Nigel?" he said to his data assistant sleepily. "Am I in the cryobed chamber?"

"Yes, Roy, you are. Can I help you?" the AI tattooed on his wrist asked him in a thick Scottish accent.

"Yes, give me a direction arrow back to my quarters, please. Somehow, I got lost."

"Right away, Roy."

A green arrow appeared in his lenses, showing him which direction to go in order to reach his quarters. He looked and realized the arrow was pointing directly through a bulkhead. That was no good.

"Nigel, I need actual directions not just *a direction*," Roy said as he fingered the screen on the cryobed he was standing next to.

"Aye, here you go, Roy."

"Great, thanks." He read the name on the screen to himself. "Thomas Pinkersly, Geneticist."

"Are ya okay, auld boy?" Nigel asked him.

"Just tired. Thanks for the map." Roy checked the map and backtracked it. He groaned once he realized where he'd made his wrong turn. He must have been completely sleepwalking to have missed his corridor. There were only three doors! "I am spent."

"Roy? Your wife has sent you several messages that just came in off the latest download. You want to hear them?" Nigel asked.

"Later. If I listen now, I will forget what she says. I don't know how she does it," he said.

"She's a lot younger than you, auld boy!" Nigel pointed out.

"Shut it, Nigel. How about some traveling music?" Roy shuffled himself out of the cryobay and down the corridor as very old classic rock sounded in his ears. It was a ballad about sailing by a famous Scottish rock star from, literally, a century past.

CHAPTER 19

August 25, 2089

"The absolute out-the-door time, Captain Jacobs, is August 27 at thirteen thirty-three ship normal time. If you are not undocked and engine engaged at max speed you will not get to the minimum safe distance zone before we have to ignite the Samara Drive at full power." Captain Crosby led the US Space Force captain down a corridor of the *Samaritan*. To Jacobs, the ship looked pretty much like any other large ship, just newer. The corridors were mostly spacecraft aluminum-titanium alloys with carbon composites here and there and the occasional dull white multilayer insulation material covering cabling and whatnot.

"Understood, Captain Crosby, but you also need to realize that if we don't do a sweep of this ship and clear it, the UN Security Council is never going to clear you to depart." Captain Alan Jacobs of the *Northcutt* watched the ship's captain closely for any reaction but got little. Jacobs had been in the Space Force for over twenty years and had sort of wished they'd have picked a military ship to go on the first mission to interstellar space. That was a job he would have certainly signed up for. He made a very subtle glance over his shoulder at the Quick Reaction Force, or QRF, with him as well as a few chief warrant officers who were experts in ship espionage and sabotage. If anybody could find something, then it would be his team.

"Ah, here we are," Crosby said as he cycled the hatch to the engine room. "We considered adding security to the doors here but we know everyone on board and decided against it." Captain

Crosby told the door to open on his authority and the voice and face recognition system cleared him.

"Hmm, I guess, but do you really *know* them?" Alan asked. "I can't imagine what the saboteur's motive might be, but that's not why I'm here. I'm here to make sure he, she, or they didn't hit you in more than one place."

"Captain Jacobs, I don't think there's anyone on this ship that wants to get lost in space and die. The saboteur must have been a visitor that has long since left us." Crosby motioned him and his team through the hatch and waited for them to step through. The way he flexed as he pulled the hinged white metal door closed behind them gave Jacobs the impression that the engine room door was pretty hefty. That made sense to Jacobs. He knew there was a fusion reactor somewhere within the room that could potentially spew out fissile materials and the doors were likely lined with heavy metamaterials for shielding. That would certainly help if there were a leak, but not if there were a total containment breach. Not much would help in a case like that.

"Wow! Very nice, Captain." Jacobs whistled as he took in the view.

"I am glad you approve."

The room was about fifteen meters on a side—cubic. In the center of the room was a solid-looking metal box about three meters on a side. Large, meter or so in diameter metal tubes entered into the cube on each of its faces with a large flange mooring each tube in place. Those tubes respectively led back through the bulkheads on either side of the room. Around each of the large metal tubes was a cylinder supported by struts between the outside of the main tube and the inside of the outer tube. The outer tubes had hundreds of thousands of turns of copper wiring around them with large high-voltage cables connecting them at each end. The cables snaked away in multiple directions to various control panels about the room. Captain Jacobs had seen Samara Drive engines before. Hell, he had one in his ship, but not like this one. To date, this was the most efficient Samara Drive built, at least until the second interstellar ship being built at the lunar shipyard was completed and came online.

Jacobs looked about the room like a kid in a toy store. He had studied propulsion as his main course of study at the Space Force Academy. During his first tour as a second lieutenant, he was a main propulsion engineer, but back then the engine rooms were mostly either nuclear thermal rockets or some form of electric rockets powered by fission reactors. The Samara Drive was something different entirely. He'd read everything there was to know about them as they were the main types of propulsion on all the Space Force vessels these days. He took a breath and turned back to Crosby, who was motioning toward others in the room.

"This is my chief engineer, Dr. Cindy Mastrano, my XO, Artur Clemons, our political officer, Ambassador Charles Jesus, our head of security, Mike Rialto, and our two ship techs: chief techs Xi Lin and Pankish Patel."

"It is nice to meet you all," Jacobs nodded. "I'm Captain Alan Jacobs, of the U.S. Space Force cruiser *Northcutt*. This is my Quick Response Force and forensics team. We are here to help you go through every millimeter of this ship before you ramp the Samara Drive up for interstellar levels. We hope to be able to give her a clean bill of health within the next ten to twelve hours. But make no mistake, we're here to make sure we aren't sending you brave folks off on a suicide mission to be lost in space beyond reach of any help from home."

"Captain Jacobs, when are you planning to leave?" one of the techs asked.

"Hopefully, by later tonight." Jacobs turned and nodded to his crew to start looking around. "However, we actually have a window, according to astrogation and Captain Crosby, that will close on us twenty-seven August at thirteen thirty-three ship normal. Either we are gone by then, the mission gets cancelled barring further investigations, or we are stuck along for the ride."

"Where would you like us to start, Captain Jacobs?" Cindy Mastrano, the CHENG, asked him.

"Why don't we start with you showing us exactly where the sabotage was." Jacobs paused and went through the mission objectives in his head. "I am supposed to pick up a Dr. Burbank who was brought here as an expert?"

"Yes," Crosby acknowledged. "He put in way too many hours without sleep. I ordered him to get some rest. He's in his guest quarters."

"Understood. CHENG?" Jacobs nodded to the engineer.

"Very well. This way." The engineer motioned him toward a hatch on the starboard wall.

"Hold on just a sec, Captain," the political officer interrupted. "Ambassador Jesus?"

"Call me Charles," the man said casually. "I was thinking you might want part of your team to question some of the crew, right?"

"Our first order is to do a technical forensics sweep of the ship. Interrogation really is not why this team is here. I suspect, and I think so does your captain, that whoever did this is already off the ship," Jacobs replied. "Do you think otherwise, Ambassador?"

"Oh no, not at all. But I was going to offer to take you around and introduce you to the crew if that is what you needed," Charles explained. "Just to, well, keep the panic and rumor mill to a minimum."

"Understood. And we anticipated that." Jacobs reached into a sleeve pocket and pulled out a data card. "I'd like you to contact Mr. Ray Gaines on my ship. He was sent here by the State Department and will discuss any details on the questioning of the crew. Introducing him was next on my agenda. State doesn't want any international friction from this."

"Thank you, Captain. I'll get right to that." Charles took the data card and looked at it closely.

"Captain Jacobs," Crosby interrupted.

"Yes?"

"If you have things under control here, I have lots to be doing to keep our mission moving forward. If you need me, Artur can find me." Crosby turned back toward the exit. "Good hunting."

"Thank you, Captain."

CHAPTER 20

August 25, 2089

The Space Force cruiser *Northcutt* had been docked to the *Samaritan* for several hours. Ray looked out the porthole of the guest quarters he'd acquired before the cruiser had left orbit at Mars. The ship looked bigger to him now than it did with the Moon hanging behind it. The large interstellar ship stretched beyond the limits of the porthole in all directions. Ray pulled the diplomatic pouch from his things and cycled the combination lock and the thumb-print scanner. The case clicked and he slid it open carefully.

He couldn't help but smile while shuffling through the various security badges, ID data cards, and other "tools of the trade" within it. He picked up one digital badge card with his picture on it that stated he was Raymond Simms from the Space Press Corps. He touched the back of the badge with his thumb and it shimmered slightly, giving off a digital blue and red flash. The card reconfigured into a blank white card with no information displayed on it.

"Mimi," he whispered to his AI data assistant. "Activate Ray Gaines ID."

"Identification for State Department Attaché Ray Gaines is activated," a soft female voice replied. The data card in his hand shimmered and showed an image of him in a blue suit and red tie wearing black horn-rimmed glasses.

"Ah yes," he said to himself. "The glasses. Almost forgot."

Ray rummaged through the things in the case until he found a small case of glasses. He mused at them. Nobody actually needed glasses for eyesight impairments any longer. Implants and various treatments had solved all of those problems. But many people wore glasses as interfaces, heads-up displays, and connectivity. Ray used these glasses for all of those, but mainly they made him look like a different person. He had contact lenses for other identity purposes.

He tapped the rim of the glasses on the right side, bringing up a virtual three-dimensional environment desktop in front of him. He shuffled through several icons until he found the folder he was looking for. He tapped the air before him effortlessly and the file opened up into a virtual diagram of the *Samaritan*.

"Mimi, find the most out-of-the-way path to the starboard gamma ray telescope," he said softly.

"There are several paths to the starboard gamma ray telescope."

"Can you open the ship's interior cameras for me and then identify paths with no other personnel in them?" He waited patiently.

"Yes, there are two. I have highlighted them for you."

"Thank you, Mimi. Now I'm going to take this path." He touched one of the ones before him and it lit up with a light purple hue. "Please hold the cameras as I pass. Stealth-mode algorithm."

"Understood, Ray, but note, there is someone approaching your door."

"Very well. Who?" He waited for Mimi to access the face recognition algorithms, AI ID tracking system, and other shipboard systems that would identify crew members.

"Ambassador Charles Jesus, the ship's political officer," Mimi replied.

"Well, I'm sure Ray Gaines isn't in the least reminiscent in appearance as Raymond Simms. And politicians shake a million hands all the time. I'm sure he will not recall me. Just in case, I'll be prepared to take actions."

"Yes, Mr. Gaines, this is really the first we've heard about this." Ray listened to the woman, a Dr. Lorraine Gilster according to Mimi, explain her whereabouts over the past few days. Of course, Ray knew who she was, everybody on Earth knew who she was, but he had to act the part of the curious investigator. The woman continued. "Captain Crosby mentioned there was a glitch with the PINS, but that he had it under control. Charles, what's this all about?"

"Rain, don't worry about it. The captain has authorized me to tell everyone what has happened and why we have had two vessels dock with us in the last few days," Charles Jesus started saying. Ray let him go. "A few days back the CHENG and one of the astrogation techs noticed there was a slight problem with the pulsar nav-system thing. At that point they reached out to the test engineer Dr. Roy Burbank, who just happened to be on a *Samaritan* fly-by cruise vacation so they brought him onboard to help. It turns out they found evidence of sabotage."

"*What?*" Rain and several of the other scientists Charles had gathered in the galley all gasped and started jabbering back and forth. Ray noted the chaos that could be instigated, but he wasn't sure if it were the right way to go—yet. So, he let them go on. But the ambassador didn't.

"Hold on! Hold on!" Charles held up his hands palms outward. "It's all under control and been fixed. There's a team of US Space Force experts here now sweeping the ship for anything else, and Mr. Gaines here has been asked to do interviews. None of you are suspects. In fact, it's pretty clear that whoever did this did it a long time ago. We're just collecting as much data as possible while we are still in the system and they can."

"So, as you were saying, Dr. Gilster," Ray interrupted. "Please, the first time you were on the ship was when?"

"A week or so before we left lunar dock," Gilster replied. "Like most of us that chose to stay awake for the first bit of the trip."

"Most of us?" Ray asked although he knew the answer.

"Mr. Gaines, if I may," Charles inserted himself back into the conversation.

"By all means, Ambassador."

"Only about ten or so of the crew chose to stay awake for the trip out toward Mars and then for the main step-up sequence of the Samara Drive," Charles explained. "The rest of the crew are already in cryosleep."

"I see." Ray nodded. "And once they are in sleep, how long does it take them to be awakened?"

"About ten minutes or so. Although I hear you still feel a bit hungover for the first day," one of the other scientists added. Ray looked at him and ENRICO VULPETTI appeared in his HUD view.

"I see."

Ray continued his investigation for about thirty more minutes or so and then decided that he'd done enough to fill his cover duties. Once during the conversation, Charles Jesus did make the comment that Ray seemed familiar to him and wondered if he'd ever been at the UN building. Ray brushed it off as if he just had one of those faces.

"I get that all the time," he said.

CHAPTER 21

August 25, 2089

Roy Burbank couldn't sleep. He was more than too damned tired. He was frustrated. Something kept nagging him. It was one of those just-out-of-the-corner-of-your-eye kinds of things that make you want to stop the car, turn around, and go take a look just one more time. He was having one of those "what the hell is going on" moments. The fact that there had been something acting up with the PINS months ago during the test phase that he never could put his finger on wouldn't leave his mind. It kept creeping into his thoughts. Sure, they'd found the gamma ray sources that were clearly not supposed to be there. But he'd never found the initial problem and then things just started working right.

"If it ain't broke don't fix it," he recalled telling the team. But that didn't rest well with him. To be honest, he hadn't really rested well since that test was conducted months back. But all the retests showed no problems. He'd gone over and over the data. He'd had Nigel run every algorithm, simulation variation, and every error check on the experiment, data, and analyses that he could think of. They found nothing wrong. But still, something nagged at him.

"What if I missed something then?" He raised up from the bunk and took a deep breath. "Lights on. What if the sabotage was there all along?"

He sat upright for a moment, rubbing at the sleep matter in the corners of his eyes. He glanced at the clock on the datapad screen and realized that he had slept longer than he'd expected

143

but not as long as he'd wanted. "That makes no sense. Oh hell, lights out."

Roy plopped lazily back against the pillow and sighed. The covers were warm and inviting and he was tired, dammit. He tugged at them, dragging the weak magnetically weighted blanket over him again. They'd been through the PINS front to back and couldn't find anything else wrong. Cindy and the techs would be all over it again and again. It would be fine. *But what if it wasn't fine? What if? The crew would be lost in space until they died of starvation, lack of something or other, or who knew what perils.*

He and Cindy and the techs had practically rebuilt the PINS main system down in the astrogation room. They'd tested it against simulated good data from the telescopes and it worked flawlessly. Roy thought about that again.

"We tested it with simulated good data and it worked flawlessly," he muttered into the darkened quarters. He thought about the original first test that went iffy months back. It actually had hardware in the loop, meaning the sensors were actually connected to the PINS box. It had worked...well, the second time.

"It worked the second time..." Roy yawned and tried to force the nagging thought from his head with hopes of going back to sleep for an hour or so. "We just had to insert the red/blue shift simulator algorithm to make the data from the telescopes look like the ship was moving on its way to Proxima. Easy stuff, Roy."

"Easy...stuff...Roy..." He had almost drifted back to sleep. "Easy...stuff..."

For a moment Roy was actually in that land between being awake and being asleep. He was at that moment where the brain often sends random leg-twitch signals that will either wake the body or not depending on how deeply tired the body is. Roy was tired, very tired. But his mind was twisted with doubt, a nagging doubt. His legs twitched.

"You wouldn't have to shift the clocks!"

Roy raised straight up, tossing the covers off so abruptly they flittered upward and billowed like a parachute in the low gee of the spaceship. The magnetic threads woven throughout them popped them back down in a wrinkled pile against the metal frame at the foot of the bed. Roy stumbled and almost rocketed himself into the bulkhead on the far side of his quarters before he could gain his composure and force his mind to wake up completely.

"We didn't check the data stream between the telescope with actual data from pulsars to the PINS. Each time we had to simulate our acceleration. There's a weak link in the chain." He rushed his clothes on and debated forgoing shaving and brushing his teeth until he took a deep breath and rubbed his tongue about his mouth a couple of times. He slowed down and decided a shower and general hygiene could come first.

CHAPTER 22

August 25, 2089

"Mimi, are you certain this is the panel?" Ray asked quietly.

"Yes, Ray," the AI instructed him via an image in his HUD view. "Remove the outer hasps on each side underneath the beveled edge here, here, and here."

"I feel it right there. Got it." Ray ran his fingers in behind the top of the panel until he felt the rest of the hasps and popped it free. He eased the panel down and stuck it to his tool case with a bit of hook-and-loop tape.

He shined a light down into the instrument box that was on the interior bulkhead just beneath the gamma ray telescope on the port aft section of the ship. The surface-mounted integrated nano-circuitry was so overwhelmingly complex that there would be no way to actually adjust the system at the component level. The components were beyond microscopic. But that was immaterial to Ray as he was more prepared than merely trying to hack into a system.

"Circuit board identified," Mimi said as a small card about three centimeters by two centimeters was highlighted in his view. Circles and arrows appeared, pointing out fasteners and two small screws.

"Yep. Got it." Ray reached into his little brown tool case and pulled a small tool about the size of an ink pen from within it. He carefully worked his hand through the box and placed the tip of the tool on the fasteners. As he depressed a small membrane on the side of the tool, there was a faint whirring sound as the magnetic tip backed out the screws. He set the screws against the magnetic plate in his toolbox and then carefully popped the

147

circuit card free and stowed it away amongst the other things in his kit. He then pulled a small translucent silver plastic bag from the kit and opened the ziplocked end. He looked at the card as he extracted it from the bag, noting that it looked just like the one he'd removed.

"There we go." He placed it into the slot and then reached for the tool and the screws stuck to the magnetic plate.

Roy Burbank shuffled swiftly down the corridor. He laughed at himself as he passed by the cryosleep room entrance that he'd gotten lost in the night before. He was following a map in his head to the gamma ray telescopes, starting with the one at the port aft of the ship. He had to make certain that the systems hadn't been monkeyed around with. He wasn't exactly sure how he would know, but he had seen every circuit board, every wire, and every screw of that system during testing. He just thought something, if anything were wrong, would stick out for him to see. At least, that was what he was hoping for.

He cycled the hatch on telescope instrument room and was immediately startled by the door being pulled open before he could grasp the lever. The light from inside the room silhouetted a man standing in the hatchway. At first glance Roy thought it was a man he knew, but that couldn't be.

"Patrick?" Roy rubbed at his eyes and blinked several times. "What the f—"

He didn't have time to finish his statement as the man pushed off the floor and bounded into him like a missile. Roy was still confused, and even more so, as he was slammed against another bulkhead just outside the doorway. His head *crack*ed against the metal wall with a thud and he saw stars. He hit hard enough to be concussed. He then felt a fist pound into his nose and then his eyes began to sting and tear up. He could feel blood rushing from his nostrils down his face and could taste the saltiness from it on his lips.

"P-Patrick, what are you doing here?" Roy stammered as he fought to get free from the man's grip. "Stop it!"

Roy flailed helplessly against his attacker, but he honestly had no idea how to fight. Roy realized that as far as he could recall, he'd never even been in a fight as a boy. He punched, slapped, and squirmed but he was overmatched and quickly overwhelmed.

He felt something press against his neck and then sting like a wasp had gotten him there.

"Patrick O'Hearn? When did you start wearing glasse..." Roy slurred as the light in the room tunneled out and he became indifferent to what was going on around him. He looked up, confused, as one of his old engineering team members stood over him doing... well, Roy wasn't sure what. His head rolled sideways and he could see through the hatchway of the telescope room to the windows. He looked at the stars visible through the window beyond the telescope aperture. His mind drifted. Roy was tired. Very tired. He just wanted to sleep.

"Dammit, now I have to deal with this." Ray Gaines looked at the now unconscious Dr. Burbank. "What the hell were you doing coming in here, Roy? Mimi, jam his AI. Deactivate it if you can."

"I've already deactivated it, Roy. It was a low-level data assistant," Mimi responded.

"Good."

Ray quickly ran through scenarios in his mind. How could he cover up this? If they found Burbank, then they would know something was up. If they didn't find Burbank, they'd know something was up. Somehow, they had to think Burbank left the ship as planned and all was well. That was going to be tough.

"I guess contingency plan B is now going to have to be plan A." Ray grabbed Roy under the arms and tossed him over his right shoulder. "Come on, Roy, we've got work to do."

Ray shuffled down the corridor a few meters to the entrance of the cryosleep room. He was his typically calm self even though his plans just had a major disruption. Mimi was keeping the cameras hacked and was watching all the tracking data for crew. The cryosleep room was very rarely visited and it was approaching lunchtime. He was likely to be uninterrupted for some time to come. There was time. He could manage the problem.

"Mimi, cycle the cryobed for Thomas Pinkersly."

"Wake cycle initiated."

"Good. Roy, I'm leaving you here for a moment. I have to finish up next door. Don't go away. I'll be right back." Ray chuckled lightly.

✧   ✧   ✧

"What the hell is going on?" Thomas Pinkersly blinked at the lights while holding his left hand to his forehead. "Why are you here?"

"There's been a complication, Pinkersly." Ray grunted. "Now get out of that thing and get your clothes off."

"We had a deal," Pinkersly protested. "My family..."

"Shut up and do what I said if you want your deal to continue." Ray began undressing Roy Burbank and tossing his clothes into a pile to the side. "Put those on and put your clothes on him—now."

"I think I'm gonna throw up," Pinkersly said. "Is he dead?"

"No, he's not dead. Now shut up and get moving." Ray cycled through various menus in his HUD, looking for the right instructions. "Here we go. Cryo initiation procedures. Mimi, can you identify the right sequence for this?"

"I am currently erasing the history of this bed and will have it ready in a moment," Mimi replied. "Be certain to remove any binding items of jewelry or clothing from him."

"Just get the bed ready." He paused for moment. "Mimi, rewrite Burbank's ID file for Pinkersly. And vice versa."

"Understood, Ray."

It took the better part of ten minutes, but Ray and Pinkersly managed to get Roy into the cryobed, seal it, and have Mimi cycle the sleep initiation sequence. Pinkersly followed closely behind Ray down the corridor.

The docking airlock was open and Ray ushered Pinkersly through with a smile while flashing their security data cards to the guards there. All he had to do was get him through security, into his private quarters, and keep Jacobs away from him until he could get Pinkersly up to speed on Burbank's identity.

"Ray Gaines, State Department. This is Dr. Roy Burbank." Ray held his data card to the scanner. The enlisted E-3 Space Force guard read the screen and then looked at them.

"Welcome aboard, Dr. Burbank. Good to see you again, Mr. Gaines." The soldier motioned them through.

CHAPTER 23

August 26, 2089

"Well, I'm glad you found nothing, Captain Jacobs." Ray stood at the end of the captain's ready-room table, nodding affirmatively. "I questioned the crew and there was little to learn there. Whoever did this must have done it during the test or even construction phase."

"Probably. Have you gotten Dr. Burbank squared away?" Captain Jacobs asked.

"Yes. He's eager to get to Mars and then to catch up with his wife," Gaines replied. "What is our current Mars orbit ETA?"

"Actually, we will rendezvous with another *Samaritan* sightseeing cruise in thirty-six hours and drop him off there. You're free to go with him if you like. We've been pulled to another mission and our trajectory will not take us back to Mars for a couple weeks. The cruise ship will be at Mars dock on four September about two in the morning. Is his wife there on Mars?"

"No, Captain Jacobs, she's not. She's on a transport back to the Moon and then to Earth. Any way you look at it, there's probably a two-week interlude before they rendezvous again." Gains chuckled a bit. "He made quite a sacrifice jumping on the *Samaritan* like he did. Good man."

"Good man. I agree."

"I'll book me a suite on that cruise as well. No need to hang out here with you space jockeys," Gaines said.

"Suit yourself, Gaines."

"If there's nothing else, Captain, then I need to go and get things lined up for our departure, then," Gaines said.

"By all means. Nice meeting you, Gaines."

"Likewise, Captain Jacobs. Likewise." Ray shook the Space Force captain's hand and began immediately cycling scenarios and egress path alternatives.

Once they were off the Space Force vessel and onto a private cruise ship, Pinkersly could assume Burbank's life for the week or so it would take to get to Mars. Ray would work out identities for him before Mars. Mars and the Moon for the most part were the new frontiers. Many people actually had moved to Mars to escape the prying life of civilization on Earth. It would be easy to vanish Pinkersly there.

"I'm so sorry, Chloe. I can't wait to get home either." Chloe listened and watched the video download from her husband, who was apparently on his way home via the Mars cruise docks. She was used to Roy traveling with his job and often he'd be gone for a couple of weeks or more at a time. That was the life of being married to a spacecraft design and test engineer. He did get paid really, really well on each of his off-world excursions.

"The Space Force ship *Northcutt* is dropping me off on the sightseeing cruiser *Bolivar*, and I'll transfer from it when we get to Mars in about five days. I'm already looking at my flight options that get me home soonest," Roy continued very matter-of-factly and all business. Chloe wondered if he had to make the video transmission recording while not in private. He'd done that before too.

"I miss you, darling, and will be home soonest. Love you." Roy waved goodbye into the camera and half frowned.

"I love you too, Roy," Chloe whispered and then gently touched the datapad touchscreen, shutting the image down. Then she mused over the message a bit. "Hmm, he's never called me 'darling' before."

"Very good, Thomas—or I guess for now, we'll always say 'Roy.'" Gaines watched the video a bit closer to make certain there were no tells. "We'll have to do another couple of these. Be careful about pet names and words of endearment as we don't really know how Burbank spoke to his wife."

"What do ya mean? I did pretty good," Pinkersly argued.

"You called her 'darling' in that one. Don't do that again." Gaines looked at him sternly and then let his expression relax a bit. "Look, I have my AI searching his emails, chats, and other media where his family is concerned. Soon, before we do the next one, the AI will write the script based on the most likely turns of phrase."

"You think the video rendering will keep her fooled?" Pinkersly asked. "I mean, do we really understand his facial expressions?"

"Don't worry about it. We have hours of video-conference data on Burbank. The imagery is good." Ray Gaines—at least that was his current identity—considered his next move. Did he simply toss Dr. Pinkersly out an airlock at some point once he no longer needed a live body walking around acting as Burbank, or did he just give him a new ID and tell him to get lost or else? He could tell by the way the man squirmed that he was probably considering the same things and was likely planning some weak attempt at escaping.

"Then what? Er, I mean, what about me?" Pinkersly asked.

"Thomas, Thomas, Thomas," Ray repeated. He diverted his gaze to the porthole in his quarters at the continually brightening light that was approaching them. The cruise ship was almost there. Another day or so and they'd be off the *Northcutt* and away from the Space Force. "What will we do with you indeed? You were going to die anyway on that ship."

"You're going to kill me?" Pinkersly began darting his eyes about the room and Ray could see the panic in his face. He looked to Ray as if he were going to hyperventilate.

"Settle down, Thomas. I'm not going to kill you, or even have you killed. I don't think. That's up to you." He paused and thought briefly and turned his gaze back from the star field on the other side of the porthole in the distance.

Ray knew that Pinkersly was a scientist not a survivor. And he was stupid because he had managed to get himself in very deep debt with some pretty serious gambling bookies. Thomas Pinkersly had a gambling problem that was quickly about to reach a crux. The only outcome of his situation would most likely have been his death, but before that, the death of his estranged wife and two teenaged daughters. That was before Ray had found him.

Ray's employers had very deep pockets. He basically bought and paid for Thomas Pinkersly's life with the deal that his family would be safe and taken care of well. The few hundred thousand Thomas owed his bookies was rounding error money to Ray's employers. They'd already paid billions to implement the plans they had put in motion. Paying off his debt and putting his family up with enough money to support them for years was miniscule in comparison.

But Thomas . . . well, he was now a problem. He was a loose end. Ray didn't like loose ends. He would have to find a place he could get lost in forever and become somebody else. Or that loose end would have to be tied up.

CHAPTER 24

August 31, 2089

"May I have your attention. This is the captain. As you are aware, today is the day we're supposed to engage the Samara Drive at full power and begin accelerating toward Proxima Centauri b. According to the chief engineer, our tech crews, and the ship's AI, the *Samaritan* is in perfect shape with all systems functioning as they should. As we planned, we'll start putting the crew in the cryobeds two weeks into the trip and awaken everyone when we're about two weeks from disengaging the drive at Proxima. This is it, folks. Once we enable the Samara Drive at full power, the acoustic resonator will stimulate the metamaterial matrix into the exotic-matter phase, which will in turn blue-shift the radio frequency electromagnetic radiation from the fusion plasma source to the ultraviolet in a super-radiant cavity of amplified stimulated emission. This process has a decay time of, as the CHENG and Dr. Vulpetti both tell me, over eight hundred days. Once we fire this thing up, there's no turning back. I'm starting a countdown clock now of thirty minutes. This is your absolute last chance to jump ship. In thirty minutes, barring any safety issues, we will press the go button and say goodbye to the Sol System forever. Also, as a final note, there's been a last-minute fifteen-minute hold placed on our departure by the UN—fallout from the recent destruction of the *Matador* by the *Interstellarerforscher*'s UV exhaust. We've been asked to use our shipboard collision avoidance radar to make sure there aren't any unregistered ships in the straight-line exhaust-cone angle from our Samara Drive. We

155

are also awaiting word from the US Space Force that they have cleared the engagement zone. We don't want a repeat of what happened as we engage our drive. I will keep you posted."

"That's not unexpected," said Enrico.

"Unexpected? Which one?" Rain asked.

"Um, the thirty-minute hold is on the schedule," Yoko added. "What would happen if one of us actually said, 'Wait let me off!'?"

"Like that's going to happen." Enrico laughed. "I mean the radar check hold. Too many folks probably got chewed out, maybe worse, for the *Matador* incident."

Enrico, Rain, and Yoko had become fast friends since lunar space dock departure and were in the rec room chatting when the captain's announcement was broadcast throughout the ship. As they waited on the approval to engage the Samara Drive, the ship's onboard fusion reactor was powering the Samara Drive propulsion system at a moderate rate and was continuing to accelerate them outward at an acceleration of two tenths of a gravity—the same as they would experience during the long-term cruise phase once the Samara Drive took over. It made shipboard life much easier to have just a little simulated gravity instead of no gravity. No one liked being nauseous, using zero-gee toilets, or encountering various body fluids floating around after a sneeze that went uncontained. Zero gravity was still a messy condition, despite all the technological advances. For the first two and a half years, Earth relative, the Samara Drive would accelerate at about eighty-five percent of Earth gravity. Then, the ship would drop back to twenty percent that of Earth for about five years. The reason had to do with the metamaterials inside the Weak Energy Condition Acoustic Violator—called the WECAV or "wee-cav"— that couldn't hold up to the stress of nearly a full-gee acceleration for much longer than that without serious degradation. The drive would be throttled back and repaired and then they would reverse thrust direction and throttle up again to start slowing down. The WECAV was never brought fully down because the phenomenon acted like a ringing bell and took months to ring down all the way to where it was safe to actually turn it off without damaging it. At least that was how Rain understood it. She was a radio astronomer not a breakthrough physics propulsion expert.

Rain was beginning to suspect that Enrico and Yoko were becoming *very* close friends. At first this caused her to feel...

jealous... and then, as she thought again about the age difference between her and the aerospace engineer from Georgia, she realized that what she really felt was her denial of growing older. She was old enough to be his mother and, of course, he saw her that way. He wasn't blind. Yoko, on the other hand, was a knockout beauty with brains—how could he not be attracted to her? She thought of her good friend, Hannah, who once relayed a story about when she realized that the hot young guys on the U-Bahn were no longer checking her out. It was just before her thirty-sixth birthday and she was so upset. Rain had been sympathetic and, at the time, sure she would not have the same reaction. Yet, here she was, twenty years older than Hannah, feeling exactly the same way. *Shit—growing older is not fun. And I've been alone too long...*

In true form, the whole feeling-sorry-for-herself train of thought lasted no more than a few seconds and she was quickly able to tune back in to the conversation around her. Enrico, having been part of the *Samaritan*'s mission since before there was either a ship or a mission and had had time to think about the capabilities of the Samara Drive and its implications, was speaking.

"Think about it. The Samara Drive efficiently converts gigawatts of power generated by the fusion reaction into a stream of ultraviolet light containing nearly all that energy. It's the ultimate death ray," he said.

"That's why we don't engage it until we're at the one and a half AU mark, near Mars orbit," Rain added, eager to cover her momentary "tune out" by jumping right into the conversation.

"Correct. But we're following the rules. In a war or terrorist attack, the bad guys don't follow the rules," Enrico replied. "As, I guess, was made clear by whoever our saboteur was."

"Or if they are smugglers running silent," Yoko agreed, referring to the *Matador* and her crew.

"The good thing is that the range is limited. The UV exhaust isn't like a laser. It's not collimated. The beam will spread out, diverge, with distance until the energy is so diffuse that it isn't a threat. But up close, it's deadly. It may not always be that way."

"Do we know if anyone is actually weaponizing it?" asked Yoko. "How likely is that? I'm a biologist, remember. Not sure I even understand how the Samara Drive works."

"You can bet they are," Rain said quickly. She was cynical

when it came to governments, technology, and secrets. Governments you couldn't trust, technology always advanced and someone would always find a way to turn it into a weapon, and she had always believed that secrets lasted only about as long as it took to classify them—at least when speaking about government secrets. There was always some government official's staffer who leaked information when it was politically advantageous to do so.

"I know they are," said Enrico, staring straight at Yoko. Rain got the impression that Enrico was showing off as if he knew about such classified things. On the other hand, he was the engineer who had led the team to develop the engine's design for interstellar travel. And, to top it off, the original development was all privately funded before the governments of the world got involved. Somebody most likely was developing a Samara Drive beam weapon—probably Enrico's employers. The implication of Enrico's statement remained unsaid, but certainly triggered unease in Rain.

Two hours later, the *Samaritan* began its journey to Proxima Centauri b.

CHAPTER 25

September 3, 2089

"...back on Mars finally. I'll catch a transport tomorrow evening that is headed for the lunar shipyard on the far side." Roy's face looked drained of expressions, Chloe thought. *He's tired. I hope he's not overworking himself.* She'd sent several messages to him while he was on the *Bolivar* cruise ship but now she had no idea how she'd contact him. She wasn't even sure he knew exactly which ship he would be taking to get home. He continued with an almost deadpan expression.

"...I have booked a flight from the far-side spaceport to get me back to Earth. I'm taking an extra few days off just to be home after all this. See you soon, Chloe. Love you."

Chloe tapped the datapad communication icon window closed and then tapped the light blue icon of a caduceus—two snakes intertwined around a staff with wings—and opened her personal medical app. The inbox had a red number one raised above it to alert her she had an unread message. She tapped it reluctantly and then opened the message.

Mrs. Burbank, your recent test activity is now complete. The test resulted in a 99.45% positive. We recommend you begin by setting up consultation with your personal health care professional for further follow-ups in order to maintain a healthy and complication-free pregnancy. Congratulations! For free pregnancy information please click the link below...

"Hurry back, Roy. I've got something to tell you." Chloe smiled warmly as tears formed in the corners of her eyes and rolled down her cheeks.

CHAPTER 26

December 5, 2089 (Earth timeline)
November 20, 2089 (Ship timeline)

Captain Crosby checked the AI and personally inspected the health and status displays of the crew members already in cryosleep. The ship had plenty of supplies and it was up to individual crew members as to when they would check themselves into cryosleep for the remainder of the nine year and eight month (ship time) voyage. The flight rules said that everyone, besides the three flight deck crew members on the three-month-awake rotation, had to be asleep by the end of December, but until then, sleep check-in was purely optional. Everyone held out for the first month or so. The novelty of being in deep space hadn't worn off, people were excited, and relationships were still forming. Crosby actually hoped that the crew was practicing the birth control protocols required or they would need pediatric care soon at the rate the relationships were progressing.

Finally, one by one, people came forward and put in their requests for entering cryosleep. Once a few people were asleep, the rest grew increasingly restless and bored, subsequently putting in their requests. There were now only six awake and the ship was extremely quiet. Even the requests for data bursts home were coming in fewer and farther between. Besides, they'd been accelerating at about eight tenths of a gee for a couple of months and were pushing the boundaries of the outer solar system. The ship was currently traveling far faster than anything mankind had ever done—that is, besides the *Interstellarerforscher*, which was following the same propulsion profile. But the *Samaritan* had people on and these people were traveling faster and farther away from their homes than any had ever before in the history of mankind.

Unlike the classic science fiction stories and movies, the body continued to age while in cryosleep. There were some scientific studies showing that cryosleep slowed the aging process down slightly, but there were few studies that had been conducted on extremely long-term cryosleep. For the most part, you were just spared the tedium and boredom of nearly a decade in a tin can zipping through black nothingness. For that, Crosby was grateful. He'd spent at least four of his forty-eight years in space as a military resupply pilot before being selected for the *Samaritan*. Most of those four years were extremely boring and tedious. He couldn't imagine being awake and occupying his time aboard ship for seven subjective years.

Crosby had about a month to go before he was to take his first rotation in cryosleep. As it worked out, the sleep cycle required two bridge crew trained in most ship's systems and one volunteer from the ship's compliment to be awake at all times in case of repair needs, navigation checks, and any other minor, or God forbid, major emergencies. There were enough bridge crew that they would get nine months out of the year in cryosleep while the other members only would do one rotation each for the entirety of the flight. There was also a scheduled all-hands one-week medical check and systems maintenance requirement at the midpoint.

CHAPTER 27

April 15, 2090 (Earth timeline)
February 23, 2090 (Ship timeline)

"XO, we have a message on the boards from the Space Force Command HQ. It says, 'Captain's Eyes Only.' You want to wake him up early?" Bob Roca stuck his head in the captain's mess where Artur, the current acting captain, was looking for the artificial sweetener that he'd squirreled away months back. He had his head almost all the way inside the dull gray metal cabinet and one arm reaching in all the way to the back, contorting him like an acrobat.

"Aha, there it is. Now who would have moved that damned package?" Artur Clemons retracted himself from within the cabinet and pulled out the container. At eighty-five percent of Earth's gravity, it poured almost as expected. After pouring the syrupy-looking clear liquid into his coffee cup he stirred it gently with a straw, only half listening to Roca. "From the damned Space Force? What's it say?"

"Uh, it says, 'Captain's Eyes Only.'" Roca repeated.

"Hell, I guess I'm the acting captain of this here ship and I ain't about to go wake up Crosby six months early on his rotation for just a message." Artur sipped the coffee and screwed up his face. "I hope they have better coffee on Proxima or I'm just going to give this shit up."

"So, um, what then?" Roca continued. "Send it to you?"

"Hell yes, send it to me, Bob. I'll read it and decide if it's worth waking the captain up or not." Artur he realized he sounded irritated and immediately regretted it. He wasn't really irritated

163

at Bob, or even the coffee. He knew that he was just getting stir crazy a bit and needed to keep an eye on that. Trying to change his tone, he chortled, "It's probably just that Space Force captain, what's-his-name, Jacobs, forgot his hat or something."

"Alright, then." Roca laughed. "You know, the machine will add sweetener to it for you, right?"

"Nobody likes a smart-ass, Bob."

"...and as of yet, nobody has been able to ascertain the whereabouts of Dr. Burbank. His wife has been calling the State Department, her congresspeople, the HR and Union reps for Interstellara, the company that employs Dr. Burbank. This is a strange situation, Captain Crosby, but we'd really like you to do a walkthrough of your ship and personnel just so we can appease Mrs. Burbank and the politicians..."

Artur shut off the feed. That was the fourth time he'd watched the message and was astounded by it even more each time he watched it. Burbank's wife was several months pregnant and now her husband was missing. To top that off he'd never returned home after being on the *Samaritan*. In fact, the *Samaritan* was the last place that any person who actually knew him could corroborate his whereabouts. Enrico Vulpetti had worked with him for years and knew him. But one thing was for certain: this wasn't something he needed to wake up Crosby for. Artur and the other two who were awake could handle this. Artur was a thousand percent certain that Burbank wasn't on the ship. If he were on the ship, then the mass-balance calculations would have been off by the mass of a person. Everything on the ship was measured and calculated down to a few kilograms.

"Well, even though he can't be here, I guess it will give the lady some peace of mind." Artur felt bad for Burbank's wife although he'd never met her. But from all that Artur had seen while he was on the ship, Burbank was a hard worker and appeared to be a good man. He hated the thought that something could have happened to him. But what? Artur had been a space jockey long enough to know that, every now and then, when a man hit the frontier and realized there were ways to disappear and start over, they sometimes did just that. They'd probably find him at a brothel or casino at Olympus Mons or somewhere similar, he thought.

✧   ✧   ✧

"The mass balance checks out, boss." Bob Roca had gone through the calculations multiple times on his data screen. The bridge of the *Samaritan* was typical of any spaceship—meaning it was nowhere near big enough for all the things crammed into it. Bob sat in his station chair, tapping away at virtual icons and adjusting various real ones on the touchscreen in front of him. Artur's face was on the screen next to the spreadsheet and graphs showing the ship's mass. Another face appeared below his: Yoko Pearl, the other crew member whose time it was to be awake.

"I've gone through every cubbyhole in Engineering and the PINS rooms and there's nobody there," Artur said. "Dr. Pearl, you find anything?"

"I've gone through the galley, all the quarters, and nothing out of the ordinary there," Yoko replied.

"Anything on any of the historical security feeds, Bob?" Artur asked him. "I mean, anyone coming into or out of this ship is recorded on video."

"I'm pulling those files now, XO," Bob said. "I'll let you know if I see anything unusual."

"This is a damn snipe hunt," Artur added.

"What's a snipe hunt?" Yoko Pearl asked.

"What do you mean there's no video of Burbank leaving the ship?" Artur grunted. The three of them had met in the galley for lunch and just to have exposure to other humans. Having the task of looking for Burbank had actually taken their minds off how isolated from the rest of humanity they were. Artur was happy to have something to do even if it was just a snipe hunt.

"Well, I've scanned through every camera for every second that Burbank was on this ship. There is no video of him leaving his quarters after this moment...here...when he goes into it the night before the Space Force arrived," Bob Roca explained. "He never came out of his quarters."

"That can't be," Artur looked over at Dr. Pearl and noted that she was being noticeably quiet. But she wasn't a big talker to start with. "Yoko, what are you thinking?"

"I don't know. This sounds like something out of a spy novel," she said softly over her bowl of ramen noodles. "I like spy novels. But I'm a biologist not an engineer. It seems to me like we need the CHENG or one of the techs."

"Well, I'm an engineer. Second CHENG to be exact." Roca sounded bemusedly hurt.

"I know, Bob. I mean, like, a systems tech or something," Yoko replied carefully.

"Oh hell, Yoko, quit worrying about hurting Bob's baby feelings and tell us what you're getting at." Artur didn't care for beating around the bush. Years in space took that ability right out of a person. Beating around the bush while in a spaceship might give some incident just enough time to get you killed dead.

"Uh, well, I mean, couldn't we look at some logs or something about when the mass changed on the ship, or doors that were given signals to open, or any other system that might have been turned on or off that wasn't typically supposed to be turned on or off? I mean, are there other records on the ship that might show an anomaly?" Yoko shrugged and went back to playing with the ramen noodles in her bowl as if she either was no longer hungry or didn't like them. Artur raised an eyebrow at her.

"Well, that isn't a bad idea." He turned to Roca. "Bob, we don't have records on hatch openings unless we're in an emergency status, so that wouldn't do it. But what about other systems like maybe the PINS, or the CO_2 scrubbers, or maybe the environmental controls?"

"Hmmm, well, let's see." Bob tapped at some virtual icons in front of him with his left hand and then shifted the peanut butter and jelly sandwich in his right to his mouth for a second so he could use both hands—after he'd taken the time to lick some grape jelly from his right thumb. He said muffled through the sandwich pursed between his lips, "Ffwwe might fe able foo..."

"For God's sake, Bob!" Artur growled at him. Bob spat the sandwich on a napkin.

"...take the data from the scrubbers and see which ones kicked on when. We have detailed records on those because we have to change the sofnalime matrix for recycling every so often." Bob then picked his sandwich back up and continued one-handing the icons.

"You're going to get jelly on the screen," Yoko laughed. "Can I help somehow?"

"You are damn right you can help him, Yoko." Artur grinned. "You can teach Bob some damned table manners."

"Here it is!" Bob finished off the last bite of the sandwich and made a face like his mouth was stuck together. He swigged at whatever was in the big blue mug he kept that claimed he was "The Greatest" and continued. "Look at this. Here's the video feed from Roy walking from the captain's office to his quarters the last time we saw him. It's actually kind of funny because he gets lost and wanders down the wrong corridor, ending up in the cryosleep room."

"Yeah, so? We saw that video already." Artur was getting impatient.

"It is funny, though, you have to admit it." Yoko nodded in agreement with Bob. "I've gotten turned around before, especially when the gravity was low."

"So what, Bob? The point, please."

"Watch this bar chart here. Each of these bars represent the CO_2 scrubbers' current draw and you can see them wiggle upward a bit by a few milliamps as Burbank passes through the ship, gets turned around, then makes his way back to his quarters, and it matches the video just fine." Bob pointed at each of the respective bar graphs as they grew slightly.

"Hey, a personnel tracker." Artur laughed and slapped the table. "Okay, good. Now what?"

"Well, so watch the video feed of the quarters corridor. The next morning at about nine fourteen, while we were all in engineering or dealing with the Space Force folks, Burbank was in bed, right?" Bob pointed at the CO_2 scrubber electrical current bars for that area of the ship. "But look here. The video doesn't change at all, but the scrubber starts wiggling upward here, then this one here, then this one here."

"Wait! He left the room but he's not in the video?" Yoko asked.

"I don't know. But the CO_2 scrubbers started working harder along this path here." Bob moved some icons about and then overlayed the path on the ship's interior map. A lime green highlighter line followed through the three-dimensional ship's map. "Looks like he ended up here in the PINS sensor room. Wait, now that's odd."

"What's odd?" Artur asked.

"The CO_2 scrubber was acting like it was working to support a person in that room already, but there's nobody in the video. Then it looks like two people must be in there," Bob explained.

"They stayed there for a while, maybe. Then they moved next door to the sleep room."

"What the hell?" Artur watched the bars as they moved but no video showed any change. All the rooms looked unoccupied. "Can this be right?"

"Well, the scrubbers are closely monitored, boss, so they're right." Bob continued to look and scan forward for changes. "Looks like several minutes go by with no change."

"Look what a spike!" Yoko pointed.

"Now there're three people in that room, it would appear." Bob looked perplexed. Artur was confused and he was getting a very bad feeling tingling up his neck.

"How long are there three people?" Artur watched. "Keep scrubbing forward."

"There! Look, it dropped," Yoko said.

"Two people in there now." Bob nodded. "Good eye."

"Wait a minute." Artur was working on something in the recesses of his mind that was dark or sinister or maybe both and he didn't like where it was going. "Why do the people in sleep beds not tax the scrubbers?"

"Oh, that's an easy one . . . You don't think . . . ?" Artur could tell by the look on Bob's face that he was suddenly having the same bad thoughts he was.

"Think what?" Yoko asked. She'd yet to figure it out.

"The beds are enclosed systems with their own environment controls and conditioning units. They don't affect the scrubbers external to them. But if somebody were to be awakened, well, that's a different story." Bob began swiping at virtual icons wildly.

"Check the beds, Bob!" Artur ordered him.

"Ahead of you, boss."

"No records show a bed was activated or deactivated." Bob continued to swipe away in the air at the virtual icons.

"So, we're stumped?"

"Nope!" Bob smiled. "The beds pull from the main liquid coolant supply in Engineering. There are valves and flow meters along the flow route. And . . . wait for it . . . boom! Gotcha!"

"Got what?" Artur was almost ready to just get up and head down to the cryosleep room as it was.

"A bed was deactivated and then reactivated," Bob said.

"*Which one?*" Artur and Yoko exclaimed simultaneously.

"Bed twenty-eight. Dr. Thomas Pinkersly." Bob hadn't even finished the statement before the three of them were already on their feet and on their way out of the galley.

"Dr. Burbank, can you hear me?" Artur gently slapped both sides of Burbank's face while shining a light in his eyes. He was responding sluggishly, but coming around.

"My head hurts...I'm thirsty..." Burbank whispered.

"Here, drink this." Yoko handed him an electrolyte cup that was part of the rehydration and waking process. "Maybe we should wake up one of the doctors."

"There was someone else...I knew him..." Burbank continued to mutter incoherently.

"Roy, just relax and let the meds kick in," Artur said.

"I have...to catch my ride...Space Force..."

"We'll take care of all that, Roy." Artur's heart sank for the man. It was too soon to tell him where he was and what was going on. Besides, Artur wanted an untainted recount of what happened. "Just relax and we'll talk in a few minutes."

"Jesus." Bob shook his head and looked at Yoko and the XO.

"Later, Bob. Yoko, just get him stable and awake." Artur stood up from the cryobed. "Bob, let's wake up Crosby and the doctor."

CHAPTER 28

April 16, 2090 (Earth timeline)
February 24, 2090 (Ship timeline)

"I would like to have sedated him, but after being in cryo with a concussion, I just didn't think it was a good thing. So, before he got completely awake, I had him restrained to the bed," Dr. Maksim Kopylova explained to the captain.

"You haven't told him yet?"

"I think that's a captain's job, don't you?" Maksim said rhetorically. "But if you want me to..."

"Aw hell, he needs to know." Crosby slid back the curtain.

"How you feeling, Roy?" Captain Sam Crosby asked as he stepped into the curtained-off area of sickbay housing Roy's bed. There were a couple of wireless sensors on his forehead and one on his wrist as well as an I.V. connected to him. His arms and legs were restrained to keep him from tearing himself free and hurting himself.

"Captain Crosby." Roy looked up at him and Sam could tell he was very confused. "I have to get to my ride."

"Roy, stay calm. Dr. Kopylova says you need to take it easy. Looks like you had a concussion before you were put in the cryobed..." Crosby was interrupted.

"The doc told me all that! I need to get off this ship!" Roy exclaimed. "Why am I restrained to this bed?!"

"You had a bad bump on the head and the cryosleep caused some aftereffects. We just didn't want you getting up and hurting yourself worse. We can take those off if you promise to relax

171

and stay calm. You are perfectly safe where you are," Crosby said carefully.

"Okay, okay. Just get these things off me," Roy begged.

"Alright." Crosby reached down and started unfastening the restraints. "Roy, you need to listen to me carefully. You were knocked out and put in a cryobed on August twenty-fifth, ship's timeline. Right now, today, is February twenty-fourth, ship's timeline. It's like April on Earth. Roy, you've been on the ship for six months our time and almost nine Earth-wise. We're in deep interstellar space on the way to Proxima already and have been for some time."

"What? That can't be!" Roy shouted. "I've got to get off this ship and go home!"

"Roy, calm down." Crosby really didn't know what else to say. The poor man had just had his life forever changed and there was more.

"Calm down? I have to get off this bloody damned ship!"

"You can't, Roy." Crosby's head sank. "The Samara Drive has been at full power for months. Even if we turned it off now it would take months for the metamaterial to return to normal without damaging it. Then we'd have to slow down for a long time just to turn around. Roy, I'm sorry, but...there's no going home."

"No! Turn the ship around and take me home! I'm not supposed to be here!" Roy shouted. Tears formed on the corners of his eyes. Roy tried to rise up but fell back into the bed almost immediately, grabbing at his head. "My wife! I have a wife at home. I have to see her!"

"Doctor!" Crosby no sooner than shouted before Maksim appeared through the curtains with a sedative gun.

"Roy, I'm going to give you a mood stabilizer to help calm you down," Dr. Kopylova told him as he then pressed the injection gun to his neck. There was a *swoosh* and a *click* sound. Roy cringed slightly from the injection. "You need to quit moving about. Cryo slowed the healing process down and you are still recovering from a concussion."

"Roy, you need to calm down and listen to me." Crosby put a hand on his shoulder. "Doc?"

"Tell him, Sam. He has to know."

"Tell me *what*?"

"Roy, your wife has been looking everywhere for you. You never came home. It's been a bit more than nine months for her since she's seen you," Crosby explained. "She was afraid you had disappeared or even been killed. Fortunately, you are alive and will be well soon."

"So what? If I can't go home..." Roy started calming down. Crosby assumed the drugs were kicking in.

"Roy, your wife is pregnant. She never got to tell you. She's due, probably any day now if we've figured our time dilation deltas correctly, and it is a girl. She still has no idea where you are," Crosby told him. "We immediately sent a message back toward Earth that you are here—alive and well. It will be a couple of months before they get it. But she'll know you're okay. As soon as you are ready, you can compile videos for her and we'll send them with top priority."

"Okay? I...I...will never get to see my baby girl..."

"I'm sorry, Roy."

"She'll be, what..." Crosby could tell Roy was doing math in his head. "Eighteen before we even get to Proxima. You bastards *had* to bring me here!"

"I know, but, Roy, you need to tell us how you got in the cryobed. What happened?"

"What does it matter? I'm stuck here. I might as well be dead."

"Enough of that. You are still alive. We are still alive. But something happened that was nefarious and wrong and we need to know if it has put us all in danger." Crosby spoke sternly with his voice of command, hoping it would snap Roy out of his fervor, but he wasn't overly optimistic about the odds. Had he been on the other end of this conversation, Crosby wasn't so certain how he'd react. "Roy, tell us what happened the night after you left my office."

"Artur, wake up the CHENG, and all the flight crew, including the political officer. Plus, I want Vulpetti, the computer guy, um, Dr. Renaud, and that cyber-warfare Russian guy from the UN Landing Party team. Get them awake, alert, and in the galley by oh-nine-hundred," Crosby ordered his XO.

"Aye, Captain. To what end, if you don't mind me asking?" the XO asked cautiously.

"No, I don't mind, Artur. We're going to sweep this ship

from bow to stern, top to bottom, and port to starboard. Every system. Whoever this Gaines or O'Hearn character was understood the ship's design and was here for some reason." Crosby opened a drawer in his desk and depressed a thumbprint reader mechanism. A panel opened, revealing two 9mm semiautomatic pistols and multiple magazines. He looked at them briefly and thought that it was too late for that. He reached to the side of the pistols and pulled out a bottle of bourbon that he kept hidden there. There were two small unbreakable tumblers stacked together as well. He sat them on his desk and pulled them apart. "As soon as Burbank is able, I'm ordering him to have a snort. In the meantime, fancy one?"

"Helluva mess, Cap'n." Artur sat down and nodded in the affirmative.

CHAPTER 29

August 16, 2090 (Earth timeline)
April 30, 2090 (Ship timeline)

"Your daughter is beautiful. Roy, you should be here. She looks like you." Chloe's face was streaming with tears. She held their little girl up, completely naked except for a newborn diaper and a pink-and-blue-striped baby toboggan so he could get a full view of her. Roy was amazed at how beautiful she was with the little bits of bright red hair sticking out underneath the little hat. "She's three full days old today! Her birthday was June thirteenth, 2090. There were zero complications. Your mother was a nervous wreck the entire time, but your father, he held my hand and took all the verbal abuse I could muster..."

Roy always laughed at that part. Then cried some more. Chloe kissed the baby on top of a full head of red hair. The little girl just looked indifferent to the world, but then she started to cry a little.

"I wish my parents could have seen her... I wish you could be here, Roy... There, there, Sammie, it will be okay." Chloe held the infant to her breast and let her start breastfeeding. She quit crying and took to the breastfeeding quickly. "Oh my God, Roy, what are we going to do?"

Chloe continued to cry. Roy continued to cry.

"I don't know, baby..." he whispered to himself as he cried along. "She's beautiful, like her mother."

"I wish you could be here. I miss you so much," Chloe continued. "I named her *Samaritan* Ro Burbank. Thought we could call her Samari or Sammie. I want her to always know who her father was...I just wanted her to...Oh God, Roy!"

They both wept so hard...

Roy had played the video over and over and over and over. Had it been possible to wear out a digital file, he was doing his best to do so. And he had cried every single time. He couldn't just call back or talk to her on the comm feeds or over the internet—there was just no technology that allowed that. The *Samaritan* was about three light-months away from Earth and the signal he'd gotten from Chloe had been three months old. His daughter was probably now sleeping through the night and cooing. She might even be starting to eat soft baby food. Roy didn't know for sure. He'd never had a child. And now he had one, but he couldn't do a damned thing to help raise her—little Samari. He thought he'd call her Samari using the second A and R in the long sense like in the word "are" or "Sam-R-ee." That way, he thought, it wouldn't just sound like the ship's name. He wanted off the godforsaken vessel. He wanted to find Patrick O'Hearn or Ray Gaines or whatever that asshole's name was and dump him out an airlock. Roy just wanted to go home. He wanted to hug his wife and hold his little girl next to him.

But that just wasn't going to happen. Ever.

Roy had to come to grips with the fact that he was never going to hold his daughter in his arms and kiss her head. He was never going to help her learn to walk or to ride a bicycle. He'd never get to fix the scrapes on her knees with a dermasealer. Roy was not going to see her first day of school or her last day of school. He'd never get to see her find someone and fall in love. He'd never see his grandchildren.

And on top of all that, he was never going to get to hold his wife again and tell her that everything was going to be okay. Roy felt like dying. There was nothing else for him to do. He'd found the woman he loved. He'd started a family—albeit a bit late in life—but that was quite common in modern times. People from Earth often didn't have children up into their late forties or fifties, or sometimes even up into their late seventies. Folks from the Moon and Mars sometimes had children even later than that.

Roy had been set to retire in a few years and he'd planned to do nothing but play with his wife and hopefully children from then on. Now, well, that just wasn't going to happen. But he was getting videos from his wife almost every day by Earth standards. From his standpoint, he received them in a constant stream of many per day. The time dilation was odd and would get even more odd the faster they traveled. The current projections had them hitting about zero point eight five times the speed of light or eight-five percent. At that speed, time crawled at about half the pace it would on Earth. To Roy, the trip would last just under seven years.

To Chloe and Samari it would take about ten. Roy couldn't fathom how complex the data compression schemes must be to allow for special relativistic red shifting of the comm signals to and from Earth. He let his mind wander from thoughts of walking out an airlock briefly to think on the technical problem. Technology was always a good distraction. Finally, his drifting mind was prodded by a buzzing at his door. He paid it little attention at first. Then...

There was a *buzz* at Roy's door again. Then again. Roy snapped himself out of his trance long enough to realize that the buzzing wasn't going to stop. Whoever was at the door was very persistent.

"Just a sec." He paused the video and wiped at his eyes and cheeks. He gave himself a second or two to gain his composure. And then in a rough hoarse voice said, "Come in."

"Hello, Roy." Dr. Maksim Kopylova's large, almost two-meter-tall Russian frame was silhouetted in the hatchway as it opened. The man had all the typical features of the big "Russian Bear" of stereotypical descriptions. He had dark graying black hair accentuated by his dark eyes and burly goatee. It wasn't an unruly beard; on the contrary, it was quite well kept. The ship's doctor, while a large man, wasn't overbearing in personality. In fact, Roy found something soothing and even comforting about the man. He was like a big Russian teddy bear.

"Doc. What can I do for you?" Roy asked.

"Nothing, really. I just wanted to stop by and check on you," the doctor said softly in his deep voice. "Are you doing okay?"

"Um, I don't know. I—I mean, my life is over ... I'm done with it ... I, uh, I dunno, you know?" Roy had trouble stringing his thoughts together into a coherent statement. He unconsciously wiped more tears from his face and sniffled a bit.

"Sorry, Roy, I can't imagine how you must feel." The doctor came in and sat beside him. "I brought you this." He handed Roy a dermapatch that had a microcircuit pattern printed on it.

"What is that?" Roy asked.

"It is a mood stabilizer." Dr. Kopylova explained. He peeled the backing off the centimeter square patch and depressed it to Roy's inner wrist. Roy felt it burn for a brief second and then it was on him like a tattoo. "I want you to wear this until we get you straightened out from all this. Something like this...well, it can make a man start thinking really dangerous things. Like giving up. Like stepping out an airlock while in deep space. All of these things are no good for you. No good for your wife and daughter. And they are no good for us or the Proximans."

"I don't give two shits about the damned Proximans! I want to go home," Roy spat angrily.

"Yes, I understand." Maksim sighed. "Are you religious, Roy?"

"No. Not really." Roy thought about it briefly. He wasn't even sure what he'd say his religion was. Maybe some version of Christianity. His grandparents were and he could recall going to church with them when he was a child. He and Chloe had gotten married in a secular Christian church in Maryland where they had lived at the time. "I don't know. Not much."

"Me neither. But, as the ship's doctor, I'm sort of the only spiritual aid we have here. Maybe you could talk to one of the science team when they wake up. There are two that are metaphysics and/or theology experts among them. But, for now, I'm all you've got." Kopylova half smiled at him.

"No offense, Doc, but I don't really care to hear any sermons right now."

"Great! Because I don't know any, uh, sermons as you say," he replied. "What I do know is that you are here with us. While you are still alive, your family must know it, feel it. They are a part of you and you are a part of them. From a quantum mechanical standpoint, you are most certainly entangled with their reality."

"So what?"

"Well, hang on to that. *That* is 'what.' As long as you are alive, they will feel it too. You will at least be a part of them in that regard." Kopylova paused and then slapped Roy on the shoulder. Roy was almost startled by the contact, but it felt good to have some contact with a human, even if it was just a slap on the shoulder.

"Uh, okay. I'll try that."

"I'd like you do something else for me, too," Kopylova said. "Three things, actually."

"Okay," Roy said hesitantly.

"Number one, you are an expert engineer. Be one! Become part of this crew. There's a Russian proverb that goes something like, 'Work is afraid of a master.' It means tasks come easy to experts or something similar."

"Hmmm, never heard that."

"Well, you are a master. Be one. It will give you daily purpose and distraction. I don't want you going back into cryo for the next two months at least. You need something to do." Maksim ticked off with his left pointer finger and then ticked his middle one. "Two, I want you to make a video to your wife and daughter once per day, every day, at the end of each day. No more and no less. This will give you a daily connection with them and it will give you a time to reflect on your day. And, only once per day will keep you from consuming yourself with it."

"Can I only watch the videos from home once a day, too?" Roy didn't like that thought.

"Oh no. Do that as often as you like as long as you do your other things. I have a picture of my long-dead wife that I see many times a day. Makes me feel her still." Kopylova stammered slightly and Roy could see that there was some pain there. Then the man pointed at his heart. "In here."

"Okay. What's number three? You said three things."

"Yes, I did." He grinned a bit and the goatee accentuated his features as he did so. Roy was a bit amused by it. He had never been able to grow a beard. He'd tried once before but with little luck. It had grown in patchy, red, and had gray splotches throughout it.

"One and two are easy enough, I guess." Roy nodded.

"Finally, three, I want you to read a story from the Bible."

"Thought you weren't going to give me a sermon, Doc," Roy protested.

"No sermon. Well, um, other than saying another Russian proverb, '...from mangy sheep at least take lock of wool.' And tell you to read the story of Job."

"A mangy sheep? What the hell does that have to do with jack?" Roy asked.

"I don't know Jack," Maksim looked puzzled.

"Just an expression, as in, jack shit."

"Aha, yes, I've heard this before. Often wondered if it was

connected to the jackass." Maksim chuckled. "Just think of the proverb. Read the book of Job for entertainment."

"I have never have much enjoyed reading the Bible."

"Me neither. It puts me to sleep with all the prose, but it sometimes gives profound insight into the human condition. If you'd rather, there was an old novel that retold the book of Job from a science fiction perspective. I forget the title, but I'm sure you could look it up."

"Are these doctor's orders, Doc?" Roy wasn't sure he wanted to read anything. And what the hell did that have to do with a "mangy sheep"?

"I guess they are, Roy. Doctor's orders. And come see me anytime you like if I'm awake. Or just go be with other people. Make some friends here." Maksim stood and slapped his shoulder again. Roy was wondering if that was a Russian thing or just a Dr. Kopylova thing.

"Okay, Doc. Whatever you say."

CHAPTER 30

August 26, 2090 (Earth timeline)
May 3, 2090 (Ship timeline)

"We've searched this ship from top to bottom, Captain, and found nothing out of the ordinary." Cindy Mastrano rubbed at a scrape on her forearm she'd gotten while crawling in one of the equipment tubes in the engine room. She needed to clean the cut and put some dermaseal on it before it got infected. "Whatever Gaines was doing, we can't put a finger on it."

"He was in the PINS sensor room," Roy added. "I finally figured it out once I realized that the testing we'd done back at lunar dock was using simulated sensor data because it wouldn't be red or blue shifted from acceleration as we were effectively sitting still. I had gotten out of bed to go check the path between the PINS and the telescopes when..."

"So, we tore everything apart in there between the telescopes and the main PINS boxes and found nothing out of the ordinary," Cindy interrupted, so Roy wouldn't have to go into his traumatic experience. Roy was trying, she could tell. But the poor guy was just a shell of the man he was when she'd first met him. Right now, he acted as if he were running on fumes. She was concerned what would happen when he ran out of those fumes.

"Dr. Renaud has gone over all the code and found nothing?" Bob Roca asked her.

"As far as we can tell, all the flight software seems normal, Bob," Roy added. "At least down here it does. Have you found anything anomalous on the bridge?"

181

"Not yet. Zhao and Mr. Tarasenko have looked for any signs of hacks and we've yet to find anything from top down. Whoever the Gaines guy was, he was good," Roca said. "Or at least he was better than us."

The flight crew, Roy, Dr. Renaud, and the cyber-warfare expert, Victor Tarasenko, had been taking the ship apart and putting it back together one piece at a time looking for signs of intrusion, hacking, malicious or nefarious intent, but they had found nothing. Captain Crosby had called the senior flight team and Roy into his ready room to discuss the possible scenarios. Cindy had been working herself ragged to find what Gaines had done, while at the same time she was handholding Roy, trying to get him back into the game. Roy just looked checked out. Currently, he looked like he was paying attention, but she could see he was millions of miles, almost a light-year, away.

"CHENG, are you telling me that nothing was done? Maybe Roy interrupted him before he could finish or even get started? Or are you telling me you just can't find it?" the captain asked. "We need to know either way."

"There is just no way to tell, Captain. At least, not until we see some type of perturbation in our navigation or something. We've checked, and right now as far as we can tell we're on trajectory for Proxima. But a tiny error right now might not show up for a year or more in our flight data. It could be just like with the atomic clock chips that Roy discovered back before we left Sol," Cindy explained. "I suggest we increase our verification testing rate on our navigation."

"So, you want eyeball and hand calculations? How often?" Roca whistled. "That's going to be hairy math."

"Not really," Roy nonchalantly replied. "Take the images from the six telescopes with the atomic clock timestamps on each measurement. We correlate those with a stand-alone computer and compare it to the PINS output two-line-element arrays. We could actually set them up to compare to each other regularly, but I'm not sure connecting them to each other is smart from a hacking standpoint. Hacking isn't my expertise."

"Right." Roca nodded his head in agreement. "I see that. The computer does most of the work. We'd need to pick a computer and strip it down from any outside software and connectivity to other ship's systems so we know it isn't hacked or compromised in any way. Maybe we even shut off the wireless just in case Gaines left some sort of malware floating about that we've yet to find."

"Get on that, Bob," Crosby ordered. "XO, once we have decided that the ship is in order, we need to get our sleep schedules realigned. I want to make certain that there is always somebody up that has knowledge and is trained on the stand-alone nav system."

"I'm on it, Captain," Artur replied. "Maybe we should start training the other awake parties during their awakened cycle as well?"

"Good idea. Do that, Artur. Dr. Burbank, I have one more request, if you would oblige?" Crosby asked.

"Certainly, Captain." Roy shrugged uncaringly.

"We've all heard the great news. And we want to see some pictures of this pretty girl of yours." Captain Crosby turned and looked knowingly to Cindy.

"Aha! Yes, we also have something for you." Cindy clapped her hands eagerly and then pulled something from her backpack that was typically filled with data pads, tools, and various CHENG things. She intentionally fumbled a bit as if she couldn't quite find what it was she was looking for, and then finally, she sat a small package on the conference table in front of Roy. She smiled at him with a large toothy grin.

"What's this?" Roy asked uncomfortably.

"It's a little something from all of us," Cindy answered. "Go on. Open it."

Cindy watched as Roy looked at the little package in front of him. It was a small box about six to eight centimeters on a side. It was in pink wrapping paper with a rose-colored ribbon holding it together. Roy rolled it over in his hands several times. Cindy grew impatient.

"Go on, Roy. Open it!" she urged.

"Okay, okay." Roy tugged on the ribbon and released it from the box and then opened it. Inside was a small data-cube projector. By his continued fumbling, she could tell Roy was having trouble finding the switch to turn it on.

"For God's sake, Roy, press the button on the bottom and then set it down," she said.

Roy found the switch and turned the device on. Then there was an audible *ding* and a voice asked, "Please approve database access."

"Access to what?" Roy asked.

"Oh, it needs permissions to look at your imagery and videos you have on file," Cindy explained.

"Okay. Nigel?"

"Yes, auld boy?" The Scottish accented AI's voice filled the room. Cindy almost laughed.

"Handshake with this thing," Roy told the AI.

"Done."

PROCESSING DATA. PLEASE STAND BY. appeared in solid three-dimensional letters above the cube. Then suddenly a three-dimensional image of Samaritan Ro Burbank appeared in front of them above the cube looking back at them. Roy peered through the hologram for a moment silently and Cindy could see in his eyes that he was going to break down again. So, she quickly got his attention by explaining what the device did.

"It's not just a single image, Roy. Zhao, Bob, and I created a rendering program that will take data from each video you get and update the image in real-time, assuming you give the program permission to intercept your mail, and you will have a day-to-day live growing image render of your daughter. You'll be able to see how she grows from video to video this way."

"I uh, well, thanks," Roy said sheepishly, doing his best to hold back the tears.

"You're welcome."

CHAPTER 31

December 1, 2090 (Earth timeline)
March 13, 2090 (Ship timeline)
approximately 6 light-months from Earth
3.64 light-years from Proxima

Captain Crosby was taking his turn at being awake. To pass the day he was at the desk in his ready room, checking the cryo tubes and sleep requests for all the crew on board. Roy, the unplanned crew member, had no specific requests other than wanting to be awake to view any messages from home. Doctor Kopylova had ordered that he be awakened every month for the first eight months since they'd found him in order to do concussion protocols and reassessments on him. Roy was currently in cryo and wouldn't need to be awakened for a few more weeks. Crosby looked at the data piling up in his personal folder and could see that there must be many videos of his family being stored there. Roy would have a lot of "letters from home" to go through once he woke up.

As Crosby checked Enrico Vulpetti's status, he noticed Vulpetti's personal request to be awakened at the halfway point of the voyage. When Enrico had first made the request, Crosby denied it. There was no health reason for the denial—cryosleep was extremely safe and there had never been a case of adverse effects from either going into or being awakened from it. Flight rules said that no one was allowed to be awake and alone on the ship. In fact, the requirement was for either no one to be awake or a minimum of three people at any given time and at least two of them had to be members of the flight crew. Then Crosby told him why he wanted to wake up and the next thing he knew, seven others, including both Roca and Zhao, wanted to join him for his three-day, mid-flight awakening. Crosby was yet undecided. Since he, Roca, and Zhao would be the last to enter cryosleep, he still had time to decide. Vulpetti's status was one hundred percent normal for someone in cryosleep, as had been all the rest.

"Captain Crosby, please come to the flight deck." The announcement came over the intercom from a voice that Crosby knew to be Ming Zhao's. Zhao was a meticulous pilot and engineer, and unbeatable at Scrabble. For a nonnative English speaker, Zhao's vocabulary was amazing. He attributed it to being a nonnative speaker. He had to learn English as a second language, and, being an engineer, he took an engineer's approach to doing so—memorizing a vast number of vocabulary words before he ever began to learn the mechanics of the actual language and sentence construction. Scrabble was the game of choice on many deep-space trips and just about everyone in the business took part. Until playing Zhao, Crosby considered himself to be a rather good Scrabble player, but he'd met his match.

The flight deck was two levels up, and Crosby quickly ascended the ladders to answer the call. The ship designers hadn't installed a lift because they knew that the crew would need the exercise and that going up and down ladders provided sensory stimulation that would otherwise become lacking on the long voyage. Every little bit of stimulation helped. Besides, elevators could break down and that would be just one more thing to worry about. Ladders were pretty stable as far as maintenance was concerned.

Zhao looked grim as he turned to address Crosby upon his arrival. "Captain, the latest telemetry update from Earth just arrived and they're telling us we're off course."

"How bad? Hell, that message is six months old by now!" Crosby had been worried about this very problem. He knew that even a small deviation in their trajectory this early in the mission would lead to missing the planetary rendezvous by a large margin. It could be a serious problem. And even though they'd never figured out what Ray Gaines had been trying to do to the PINS, or why, it was pretty clear that the asshole hadn't wanted them to make it to Proxima for whatever reason. Crosby also knew that the engineers, scientists, and flight crew had worked diligently to build a back work-around navigation fix so they wouldn't be in this very predicament. Apparently, the work-around wasn't working around whatever problem Gaines had created for them.

Instead of answering, Zhao handed him his datapad containing a string of numbers. It showed what their predicted location should be versus their actual location. For the first few months, they were aligned as best anybody could tell. The "should be" were exactly the same as the "actual," but sometime within the last year the numbers began to diverge, and the rate of divergence was increasing.

"Shit. Unless we fix the problem, we'll miss the Proxima Centauri star system altogether," Crosby said.

"I checked the PINS and it says we aren't off course. According to our onboard navigation system, we are exactly where we should be," said Zhao.

"Of course it did." Crosby frowned and shook his head left and right with a sigh. "Wake the CHENG and Burbank up."

By this time, Roca entered the room and was listening from near the top of the ladder.

"Bob, I'm glad you're here. Can you double-check the PINS to make sure it's working properly?" asked Crosby. "And I want you to double-check the backup stand-alone system for errors."

"I haven't received any alerts or any other indication of a problem, but I'll check," Roca replied, moving toward the ladder as he spoke. Roca was definitely an action-oriented person. Crosby had worked with Roca before and personally recruited him for the one-way trip to Proxima Centauri. It hadn't taken much convincing. Roca, like himself, really didn't have any family to speak of. Wives and kids weren't usually compatible with the career of deep-space pilots and engineers. Too much time away from home port didn't make for good relationships. He thought about poor Burbank and his situation. Family wouldn't be a benefit to the deep-space traveler.

"Do we have any other options for astronavigation?" asked Crosby.

"No good ones. Radio tracking from Earth and the other antennas in the inner solar system aren't a lot of help to us now since we are traveling a significant fraction of c and we're so dang far from home. From our radio signals they can easily tell how far away we are and our speed. With multiple antennas they can even triangulate and give us a pretty good location fix. But that will get less accurate the farther out we go and then it will get even more complicated by the time-of-flight delay in getting updates. Hell, we're already to the point that this update is so old it doesn't do us a lot of good. Traveling at pushing forty percent of c now will allow us to go a long way in the wrong direction in between updates," Zhao replied. "And once we have reached full speed at about eight five percent lightspeed, who knows how difficult it's going to become to stay on track."

"But with enough updates, we could make it work?" Crosby thought rhetorically. He knew that was not going to work.

"Uh, maybe, Captain . . . but, umm . . ."

"That was sarcasm, Zhao. I know that isn't going to work."

"I see. Well, Captain, any fix we can do really depends upon how far off course we are between each update. And it's a problem I wouldn't want to leave solely up to the AI," said Zhao. "We might want to rethink all of us going to sleep at the same time."

Crosby had thought of that. If they were to go that route, then someone, or three someones, had to remain awake to oversee the constant course corrections. From personal experience and the psych briefings, he knew that was a recipe for disaster. He would mark this option as the last resort.

"Any other ideas?" Crosby asked. "We're pushing that year in space. While most of us have had a month-long nap here and there, I don't want to take chances on somebody going nuts on us. We need a plan B."

"I have none that I can think of right now."

"Let's see what the CHENG and Roy can come up with. We'd better go wake them up. Might as well get Lin and Patel too."

Three hours later, Captain Crosby, Ming Zhao, Bob Roca, Xi Lin, Pankish Patel, the CHENG, and Roy Burbank were gathered around a table in the mess hall. The captain had decided to let the XO stay in cryosleep. The scientists who had been awakened when they had found Roy had long since gone back to cryo. The captain had decided there was no need for any of them to be awake if they couldn't find a problem to fix. And Dr. Kopy-lova wanted Roy in cryo as much as possible with the fear that he might be a suicide risk. They had already gone back to the standard three-person awake rotations and were almost to the point of deciding it was safe for everyone to go into cryo until they reached designated wake points of the trip.

"The PINS appears to be functioning correctly. I checked each of the imaging telescopes—they're all tracking the pulsars as they should. The onboard data processor is working at its rated capacity and there aren't any error codes coming through. I reran the calibration code and reset the system. Nothing changed. As far as I can tell, the PINS is working just fine," Roca said, completing his update. "And the backup system is doing just what we set it up to do. Both systems are independently in agreement with each other. We're on course according to them.

"If you extrapolate the two-line-element data backward from where we currently are to where we would have been six months, three days, four hours, nine minutes, and seventeen seconds, and counting, ago and then re-extrapolate that forward, we can see the difference in the trajectories." Bob Roca spun a three-dimensional map in front of them and overlayed their current trajectory in blue versus the correct trajectory in green on it. The two curves were for the most part straightening out and would look like straight lines before long, but, unfortunately for them, their current blue line was veering away from the required green line. "We're significantly off here. If we don't correct it, we'll miss Proxima."

"Looking through the telescopes at Proxima, the bow still appears to be pointed right at it," Crosby noted. "But we're too far away to just point and shoot. Interstellar navigation is a lot trickier than going to the Moon, Mars, or even the outer solar system."

"I say we make corrections," Roca said.

"The problem is that whatever we do now, Earth will not know it for months to come. Folks, we are reaching that point where we are mostly on our own," Lin added. The tech was tapping away at some virtual icons in midair that only he could see before he looked up. "We need our own true nav system that doesn't use any of the PINS equipment. Maybe we could print or rig from spares or dismantle one of the science telescopes and try to build a point-and-shoot system."

"That would get really complex, Lin." Burbank rocked slowly back and forth in his chair. "The stars are all crazy shifted in spectrum right now. The pattern recognition software alone to filter the stars to the spectra we know is extremely calculation intense. Also, if we slightly overcorrect and the point star goes out of view, then what type of control algorithm is going to steer you back to it?"

"Well, we can't sit on our hands and just do nothing!" Patel blurted out. Clearly, he was starting to get nervous about the likelihood they were all going to be stranded in deep space. "*You* might not care if we all die out here, but I don't want to be lost in space until we freeze to death, suffocate, or starve!"

"Stow that shit away!" Crosby almost shouted at the crew tech. "Another outburst like that, Mr. Patel, and you'll be confined to cryo for the duration."

"No, Captain, it's alright." Burbank held up a hand. "I can understand what some of you might think about me..."

"Roy, you don't owe anybody an explanation," Cindy Mastrano told him and then glared at Patel like she was a lioness about to pounce on a gazelle.

"No, no, it's okay," Roy continued. "I don't want to be here. My life, the one I had, is over. I understand that now. But I'm still alive. For a bit I thought maybe I didn't care if I lived or died. But, no, I don't want to die. And I don't want to be stuck in deep space to that end."

"Any ideas then, Roy?" Captain Crosby asked him.

"Not yet."

"Well, I've entered the trajectory correction maneuver most likely to keep us on target based on the data from back home, our best current estimations of our whereabouts, and the best bet on where Proxima is from non-PINS camera observations and extrapolations. My hopes are that this maneuver should put us mostly back on course. I'll engage it with your permission, Captain. This should reset everything and, with the PINS being reset, maybe the problem will be solved," said Zhao.

"Very well, I guess the prudent thing to do is wait for the next update from both systems tomorrow and see if the problem is fixed. The thing that worries me is that we couldn't find any issues with the PINS that had to be fixed. It looked like it was working correctly before and after the reset. Which means that nothing has really changed," Crosby said.

"At least we have a lifeline home. Being out here with a

shaky nav system makes me think of all the ships lost at sea and never found, like the *Waratah*. She was a steamship that operated between Europe and Australia. In 1909, she was on her second voyage going from Durban to Cape Town, South Africa, when she disappeared with two hundred eleven people aboard. No trace of her was ever found," Roca told them.

"I don't know that that story was very uplifting, Bob." Cindy scowled at him. "It's true that if we become lost out here, no one will ever find us. But we're a long way away from being lost, so please hold on to your 'lost forever at sea' stories. Are you a history buff, Chief?"

"Only nautical history. If you ever want to know about the life of Sir Charles Wager, First Lord of the Admiralty in 1733, then just let me know."

"Maybe if we have to pass the time waiting on daily navigation updates," Captain Crosby interrupted. "Listen, there's no trying to make light of this situation. We're in it deep out here, folks. We will either trek forward or make an all-stop, figure out how to abort, and return home. As it stands for now, we're moving forward."

CHAPTER 32

December 20, 2090 (Earth timeline)
March 13, 2090 (Ship timeline)
approximately 6 light-months from Earth
3.64 light-years from Proxima

"Damn. Still off course," Crosby grunted. Twenty-three hours had passed since they reset the PINS and performed their first trajectory correction maneuver and now Crosby knew there would have to be another. The same group was gathered again in the mess hall, which was, to no one's surprise, the most likely location aboard ship to congregate. Even in deep space, breaking bread together was still among the most social of activities for humans. They had just finished their lunch when the latest navigation status data was calculated. Good food even helps to assuage bad news.

"The correction we made yesterday should put us back on course at least for the next six months or so. The problem is that we are going faster and faster and the errors grow more quickly. We really need a better way because I'm not excited about going to cryo with an unproven nav computer steering our way," said Roca, moving toward his datapad. He could control most ship systems from his datapad. The entire *Samaritan* network was accessible if you had the proper codes and hardware. Roca had set up a routine to take the new navigation data and feed it directly into the AI for the appropriate course correction.

"Did we have any clues as to what's wrong with the PINS?" asked Zhao. "I mean, Roy, Cindy, there has to be some way to find out what Gaines did to it."

"I still say we build a completely new system," Lin added.

"No way to really test anything out here other than just do it for real and keep correcting everything. We've run our input data through the PINS, through the backup system, and even through the system simulator and it appears to be working fine. The problem appears to be local. The fact that the data going into the PINS is good rules out any problems with the pulsar telescopes. The issue has to be in the PINS hardware itself or its programming," said Burbank.

"I say we reload the PINS software one more time. I can delete the current load and replace it with the code we know works back home that Roy brought us. Maybe something is wrong with the software we're running," Cindy Mastrano said. "If that doesn't work, Lin, you might be right about building a new system of some sort."

"I'll keep thinking on a new nav concept with tech that is in our inventory or can be printed," Patel offered in agreement with Lin.

"Me too," Roy agreed.

"Okay CHENG, reload the software. It's worth a try. I will want a plan B. We should all be thinking about that." Crosby looked about the table at all of them to see if there were any further questions or comments. Hearing none, he was ready to adjourn. He waited for a brief moment before rising and turning to the door. "In the meantime, I'm going to get some rack time."

"None of us want to go into cryo until the problem is resolved. It's completely understandable to me. I want to know that I can trust what's driving this ship," Crosby said to the CHENG as they entered the galley. Burbank, Zhao, and Roca were sitting about a table in the middle of a heated game of Scrabble. From the looks of it, there were only a few letters left and the game was nearing completion. They'd all been focusing on the navigation issue for so long that the captain had ordered everyone who was still up to take a two-hour break from all things PINS related. They needed to rest and reset their minds. They were all too close to the problem and most certainly too emotionally connected to it.

"It's been a week since we got the message from home and found out about the problem and nothing has fixed it. We've had to perform a correction maneuver every day based on handmade observations with the digital sextant system on the bridge. That will get incredibly old really quick and it looks like we'll have to continue to do this or we will never arrive anywhere. With the replacement software still giving us bad data, I'm out of ideas," Crosby told Mastrano as they took a seat around the table. The other three looked up from their game.

"Where's Lin and Patel?" Crosby asked.

"Sack time," Roca responded without looking up from his letter tiles.

"I guess we're going to be awake for the duration, then?" Zhao asked. "I mean, in three-person shifts?"

"I ran that by the AI psychologist and it said that would be a recipe for disaster. The AI gives it an eighty-nine percent chance one of us will lose it, perhaps even become violent, if we try. Seven years is a long time to be stuck with only each other for company. However, it did give us a good chance of staying awake a few months at a time, each in cycles. Not as easy as closing your eyes and waking up at the destination point, I must admit!"

"There's got to be something we're missing." Zhao shrugged. "Some bit of data that we can get from another system. The optical telescopes, the radar, something. There has to be a way to automate a new completely trustworthy system?"

"We've been through all that before. The optical telescopes will help us refine our trajectory when we get close to Proxima Centauri because they'll have several things to see and use as reference points—three close stars, multiple planets whose locations are well known, etcetera. But that's only when we get close. Out here, the radar can only see things that are relatively close and there isn't much. Just the occasional pebble and the *Interstellarerforscher* out there in front of us by a few light months," replied Crosby.

"The *Interstellarerforscher*. Hmm, how well can we see it in the forward cam sensors?" Roy Burbank stopped paying attention to the Scrabble game and looked up at the captain.

"I don't know. It's one helluva bright UV beacon so all of our systems are filtered for it," Crosby replied and then turned to Cindy Mastrano. "CHENG?"

"Yeah, we can see it a bit with the larger observation scopes but it's mostly filtered out," Cindy explained. "Roy, you could spell something with your Q and that A right over here." She pointed at the board.

"Not my turn." Roy pushed back from the table, causing the chair legs to squeal against the deck plates like fingers on chalkboard. "Are the filters on a wheel, in software, or what?"

"Filters?" Roca stopped paying attention to the Scrabble game and made eye contact with Burbank. "What're you gettin' at, Roy?"

"The *Interstellarerforscher.* I don't know why none of us thought of it before. I can't believe I didn't think of it before." Roy was disgusted with how dull, tired, and depressed he'd become. He thought he was beginning to get himself right, and then he'd think about never being able to meet his little girl. He thought about never seeing his wife again. He'd cry. He'd get angry at Gaines and want to kill the bastard. Then he'd get angrier. Then start the cycle over. He'd take his mind off all that by staying busy. But the busy he stayed wasn't creative busy, it was one foot in front of the other shell-shocked busy. That shit had to change or he might as well just jump out an airlock. And he wasn't going to do that.

"What? How can the *Interstellarerforscher* help us?" Captain Crosby asked.

"Because she's close, running only a few light-months ahead of us, making sure the path is relatively clear, and she has a functional PINS that appears to be working correctly or we'd have been told about it. Simple enough to take our trajectory and lay it over hers and see, but I suspect Gaines never had any reason to mess with the probe. That probe is on target," Roy explained. "We just need to be able to see it better."

"A big, bright, ultraviolet beacon in the sky leading the way," Zhao added. "That could work, but the filters are in the housing of the instrument box behind the Optical Tube Assembly, if I recall. Hold on and I'll pull up some drawings."

Roy and the others waited while Zhao tapped at his imaginary keys in the virtual heads-up display his contacts were showing him. And then he made a throwing motion at the table and the datapad in the center of the table changed from showing a Scrabble board to a three-dimensional diagram of the Forward-Looking Optical Telescope Assembly, or FLOTA (they all called it the "flo-tah").

"Dammit, Zhao, you better have saved that game. I was winning!" Roca growled at him. Roy didn't really care, but he did at least feel a flutter of laughter pass through his body.

"Relax, Bob, I saved it. Besides, I was about to lower the boom with a triple word score." Zhao chuckled lightly.

"Gentlemen?" Captain Crosby looked across the table at them with a raised eyebrow. "Can we get to work here?"

"Sorry, Cap'n," Roca replied sheepishly. "Go ahead, Zhao."

"Oh, no, not me. Here's the drawing. Roy, Cindy? The filters are in this box here." Zhao pointed. "I have no idea how we'd modify the thing without breaking it."

"Only one way to make an omelet. Right, Roy?" Cindy said. Roy watched as she tapped at the icons floating in front of them and then a virtual toolbox appeared. She reached in, extracted the electric socket driver, and handed it to Roy. "You go first."

"Uh, mmm, okay. How hard can it be?"

Roy took the virtual tool from her and started tracing the virtual version of the telescope in front of him for modular connectors. He followed the edge of the box to a corner where there were several space-rated exterior bolt fasteners. He pointed the tool at them and the bolts backed out and vanished. He peeled away the panel that in reality would have been about a meter in length and half that tall. The material was labeled as spacecraft aluminum, titanium, zinc alloy. He dropped the panel in the storage file and then reached into the virtual world with both hands together, separating them so to zoom in on the drawing.

"Ha! I bet that little bugger is it right there. You see how the optical tube here comes out the back of the telescope Optical Tube Assembly here and then there's this box, right here, about ten centimeters across on either side?" Roy asked to nobody in particular. He did hear Cindy and Roca making affirmative sounds. "Then look here at this box with the tubing going in and out of it. Here, this one is labeled LN2, liquid nitrogen. That must be the focal plane array."

"Yeah, I see that, Roy," Cindy agreed. "The trick will be to pull the filter wheel out, the box just before it, replace it with a spacer box we'll have to build, and all without knocking this thing out of alignment."

"Sounds like a pain," Roca added.

"Hold on a minute. Look here." Roy zoomed in on the filter box. "See this?"

Roy pointed.

"What am I looking at, Roy?" Cindy asked. "Zoom in."

"Sure. Here." Roy spread his hands again zooming in a bit more. Then he put his finger on a little stud sticking out of the filter wheel box. "That is an electrical install-before-flight terminator."

"I'll be damned!" Roca nodded. "I'd have missed that."

"Because you're not a ship builder and tester." Roy smiled. He tapped the little stud with the information wand and a datasheet window popped open near it. "Let's see . . . filter wheel test port A3 . . . pinouts see Appendix F9, page 341 . . . There we go."

"Rachael, open Appendix F9, page 341 of the Ship Design Manual Drawings Package," Cindy told her AI assistant. Her datapad quickly shook hands with the table and displayed the manual.

"All we need is right here. This connector was put in place by the instrument builders to test the filter wheel and for internal alignments after installation. Then they locked it all down and sealed it up and terminated it. I'll bet you there's a hundred thousand of these little connector ports throughout this ship." Roy nodded knowingly as he explained. "All we have to do is pull this panel, connect a cable to that connector, run the internal component test software from the vendor, which should be somewhere in the database here, and tell it to rotate the UV filter out of the way."

"Roy! That might work!" Cindy slapped him on the back. "That might work."

"Who's doing the EVA?" Crosby asked.

"Shit. Somebody's gotta go out there and rig that thing," Roca said. "I hate EVAs."

"Two-man job," Cindy said. "I'll go."

"I've done plenty of them at lunar dock," Roy added. "I'll go."

"CHENG, you'll stay put and monitor from inside," Crosby interrupted them. "Patel is our best EVA astronaut. Roy, if you are up for it, fine. Zhao, go wake up Patel and Lin and let's walk through this several times and make certain this is the right path to take."

"In the meantime, Captain," Roca said, "I'll get started on a nav software package to follow the *Interstellarerforscher*."

"Right. Get to work, everyone."

CHAPTER 33

January 11, 2091 (Earth timeline)
March 18, 2090 (Ship timeline)
approximately 6 light-months from Earth
3.64 light-years from Proxima

Roy sat in his quarters watching the latest videos that had been processed, correcting for the speed-of-light red shifting and other data error corrections. He was getting between two to five per day, depending on how long they were, how much post-processing was required, and how busy his wife must have been at the time with the newborn, who by Earth time now was almost eleven months old. He watched as the holographic projector rendered his daughter's newest form. In the video, Roy estimated her to be about six months or so old and she was standing upright with one hand in the air, clearly holding on to something, probably her mother's hand. She was trying to pull herself up and it looked like she was starting to scoot by herself. Roy wouldn't have called it a crawl yet.

Samari's red hair was getting curly like his had been as a young boy. She was wearing a onesie that was light pink with a large cartoonish Bengal tiger standing and nuzzling a little tiger cub. The words DADDY'S LITTLE TIGER curved over the top. Roy couldn't help but smile and cry at the same time. He wondered what she must smell like and what her different crying and cooing voices must really sound like in person. The video was great quality sound, but a recreation of a person just wasn't the same as the actual person. There was nothing tangible or warm about hugging a hologram.

199

Roy finished watching the last video that had been processed and then clicked it off. He looked out the porthole of his quarters that gave him a forward-looking view. He could not see much, just a few blue dots in the distance. From his view, he realized, he couldn't see Proxima or Earth. He was stuck in the middle and couldn't see where he was going or where he'd been. That was exactly how he felt. Roy tapped a few virtual icons and opened up the camera and set it to record.

"Hi, Chloe. Hi, baby doll! Hi, Samari! This is your daddy." He wiped the tears from his eyes and smiled. "We're about a year in for you at the time of this video. You'll get it in another six months or so from now. I think our date is March seventeenth or... no... the eighteenth of 2090. My estimations are that Earth is sometime in January of the next year, 2091. I'm so sorry that Daddy missed your first Christmas and New Year's. I can't wait to see how Mommy and the grandparents spoiled you. Samari, you must be trying to crawl by now and maybe even jabbering a lot. I can't wait to see those videos. You be really good for your mommy and let her get some rest every now and then. Know that I love you, sweetheart, in anything you do all your life. I may not be there on Earth with you physically, but I'm thinking of you every moment..."

Roy paused briefly and sniffled a bit. His nose had gotten sore on the end and was slightly red and scabbed on one nostril from all the crying, sniffling, and rubbing his nose, to either clear it or cover up the fact that he'd been crying from the others in the crew. He took a long, deep breath and then let it out.

"...Hi, Chloe. I miss you so much. I am getting a little better with the aching for you two. But I don't think I'll ever be right again. I miss you two so much. Please don't ever stop sending me the updates. So, uh, today we have to fix the ship with a new navigation system. O'Hearn, as we knew him, messed up our nav systems so badly we're pointed way off track. We correct and then within a few days we're right back off track again. I hope they catch that guy and put him under a jail somewhere. Anyway, I'm sorry, I'm just so angry at that asshole. I love you. I said that already. I don't know what else to say...

"I, uh, was telling you about today. One of the flight crew engineering techs, Pankish Patel, and I are going outside for an extravehicular activity, or EVA as we call it in the business, LOL. This won't be like any other EVA anybody has ever done ever. We have to stay tethered because the ship is accelerating so abruptly and at about eight-five percent of one Earth gravity. If we slip off the ship we'll fall off and be left behind in the middle of deep space. It's kind of like mountain climbing. We'll have all sorts of safety gear, so it really isn't as scary as it sounds. I'll send you a message tomorrow and let you know how it went..."

Roy paused again and swallowed the lump in his throat. There were so many thoughts going through his mind right at that moment. He'd even considered how hard it would be for him to just disconnect a carabiner and float away and die. Then Chloe wouldn't be burdened with a long-lost husband that she'd never see again. He tried to put thoughts like that out of his mind, but every single time he thought about the burden on his wife and daughter because of him being where he was, he couldn't help himself but to almost fall off into that pit of despair.

"Love you two. Give Mom and Dad and my sister my love for me." Roy stopped the recorder and hit the send button. It was now streaming in bits across the void of space and would reach his wife and daughter sometime in about six months or so.

He sat there quiet for the next ten, or maybe it was thirty, minutes; he wasn't sure. He didn't care. He looked at the hologram of his growing little girl once again and then reached over and turned it off. Roy let out a long sigh as he rolled his head from side to side, stretching his neck. Slowly, he placed his hands on the forearms of his desk chair and rose. He unzipped his coveralls and tossed them aside. At eighty-five percent of one gravity, they draped across the bed and stayed put. He dropped his underwear to the floor and slid on the Excreted Fluids and Solids Compression Under Garment, or EFaSCUG (pronounced "ee-fa-scug"), It took him a moment to get his private anatomy in just the right comfortable position.

Carefully, he slipped on the Liquid-Cooled Ventilation and Compression Garment, or the LCVCG. The microfiber garment slipped over his body like a pair of spandex tights—very tight and form fitting! First, he slipped his legs through the zippered open-front torso of the suit, working his feet down into place. He had to carefully work each toe into the "toe-boots," making sure not to miss one of the toe sockets in them. He slipped his heels into the heel cups and then worked the tight spandex-like carbon suit up past his ankles, over his knees, and then into place on his hips.

He had to stand at that point and work the outflow tube from the EFaSCUG into the right port on the LCVCG and test it for good seal.

Once he got the tube into place he reached under his crotch and grabbed the fastener pull and zipped it up to his belly button. He stretched his shoulders back as far as he could, pulling the sleeves up over his shoulders while forcing his hands down through the armholes. *Anyone who's ever put on coveralls, especially very tight ones,* Roy thought, *knows how this must feel.* He wiggled, squirmed, hopped up and down a couple times while puffing out his chest and flexing his shoulders until the garment felt in place. Roy worked the wrinkles out of the sleeves down to the wrists and then he zipped the suit up all the way to just below his neck, leaving it open for the neck seal on the helmet, which was down by the airlock.

"That's tight," he said aloud. "Nigel, handshake with the LCVCG."

"Handshaking, Roy," Nigel told him. He could feel the suit suddenly get warmer and then a display appeared in front of him via his contact lenses, saying the LCVCG was online and ready to connect to the EVA system. "I think you are good to go, auld boy."

"Thank you, Nigel. Now do a EFaSCUG flow-tube check." Roy waited nervously, bouncing up and down on the toe-boots, getting used to them.

"Flow-tube shows negative pressure to reservoir," Nigel responded, which was exactly what the tube was supposed to do. There was a slight vacuum between the reservoir—the LCVCG capillaries—and the flow-tube so that any excreted materials would be sucked into the LCVCG and away from the body. Roy recalled that it was a lot like a suit that one character in one of his favorite twentieth-century science fiction novels wore—Fremen stillsuits, as he recalled—but they didn't have toe-boots and they didn't use them to walk in space.

"Good. Thank you, Nigel." Roy cycled the door to his quarters open.

"You are quite welcome, chum. When you are scared..." Nigel added the front part of an old Scottish friendship saying that Roy had programmed into him years ago. Nigel threw things like that into the conversation from time to time.

"I'll shake the piss out of ye until you're not," Roy finished, almost laughing. "Well, let's go walk in space at sixty-something percent the speed of light."

CHAPTER 34

January 12, 2091 (Earth timeline)
March 18, 2090 (Ship timeline)
approximately 6 light-months from Earth
3.64 light-years from Proxima

"Pankish, you ready in there?" Cindy Mastrano's voice sounded in Roy's helmet. He had to squint each time the red flashing light by the airlock egress illuminated because of the glare it made inside his bubble. "My screens show you are all in the green and good to go."

"Copy, CHENG. My suit is good. Dr. Burbank has given me the second-party inspection. Seals are green. I'm good to go," Patel replied. He turned and looked at Roy with a grin and a thumbs-up. Roy scanned the small light-emitting diodes at each seal once again to make certain they were green. All was good as far as he could tell.

"Roy, you ready?" Cindy asked him through the suit comms. It had taken him several attempts to have Nigel adjust the volume settings just right so that Cindy's voice didn't rupture an eardrum when she spoke. She was the type of personality that spoke loudly, always, so Roy had his AI put a filter on her voice. "Pankish is second-party checking my seals and systems right now. My suit shows all greens, Cindy. I am good to go as soon as Pank gives the thumbs-up."

Patel patted the backpack of his suit twice and gave the thumbs-up as Roy turned around to face him. They both nodded to each other and held out a shiny metal carabiner in their left hands. They each pulled cable from the box harnessed to their suits and then snapped the fastener to the two-centimeter-diameter metal bar fashioned into a half loop moored to the inner bulkhead of the airlock. The fasteners snapped and then clicked, locking the connector mechanism into place. To remove it required depressing two spring-loaded hasps at the same time—it wasn't easy to undo on purpose.

"Burbank, tether number one in place." Roy tugged at it a couple times just to make certain.

"Patel, tether number one in place." Roy watched as Pankish did the same.

They both then started pulling a second tether with a red carabiner on the end. Roy started working out the cable to give him a bit of slack and then he snapped it onto the metal half loop about twenty centimeters below the first one. Patel quickly repeated the same process.

"Burbank here, tether number two is in place and secured." Roy stood still and waited. His mind was racing with all the things that could go wrong on an EVA like the one they were about to do. No human, as far as they knew, had ever attempted such an EVA that had such severe consequences for becoming detached from the ship. Back home in-system, if an astronaut fell off during an EVA, then they could use the EVA jets to pull back to the ship or a ship or shuttle could drop back and pick them up. There was no chance of a rescue here. No clever release of toolbelts, oxygen, or anything other than divine intervention would catch them back up to a nearly one-gravity accelerating ship if they fell off it in very deep space.

"Patel here, tether number two is in place and secured."

Roy stood and waited and waited. It seemed like a while, almost too long, and just as he was about to say something over the comm network, Cindy's voice broke the silence. She seemed all business and professional. Roy was glad for that.

"EVA Astronaut Roy Burbank, EVA Astronaut Pankish Patel, be alerted that Captain Crosby has given the authority to cycle the airlock," she told them in a nearly monotonal voice. Roy thought an AI couldn't have been more to the point. He suspected that it was more for the legal recording of the orders rather than pure professionalism. Roy had done EVAs before and this seemed pretty much standard as far as he could tell. That is, standard other than the fact that they were cruising through open very deep space and pushing the speed of light. "Depressurization will begin in ten, nine, eight, seven, six, five, four, three, two, one, depressurization sequence activated."

There was no hissing that Roy had expected to hear at first. But then, he could feel a high-frequency vibration through the floor that was a high enough frequency that it actually tickled his feet within his EVA toe-boots. Then he could hear it—an air-handler pump was humming loudly. A pressure number appeared in his virtual view displayed through his smart contacts. It started at "1.00 ATM" and then started dropping at the second decimal point. Each time the number dropped by a tenth of an atmosphere Roy could feel his LCVCG squeeze his body just a bit tighter as the power source in his backpack excited the metamaterial carbon nanotube filaments with an electromagnetic field, making them tighten like a boa constrictor.

The suit constricted and kept the body from expanding and swelling in the low pressure. Modern suits worked through compression, not like the suits of the last century where the astronaut was actually inside an inflated body suit. Those were too clunky, cumbersome, and motion constricting. The modern compression spacesuits enabled astronauts to pretty much move about as well as they could while not wearing it. In fact, the compression suits worked so well in body function that there was an entire line of them sold to the fitness industry to remove body soreness, protect weak joints, and enhance athletic performance. All the Olympic and professional athletes wore them across almost every sport that required high stress and elite performance. The military had also implemented them as the undergarments for combat uniforms. The days of the "Michelin Man astronaut suits" were long gone. The only inflated space in the suit was the transparent bubble around the head.

By the time the number got to "0.35 ATM," Roy could still feel the vibrations in the floor, but he could no longer hear the pump cycling the air out of the lock. While the suit continued to constrict him, his body got used to it. A few minutes into the process and Roy just felt like he was wearing a really tight pair of stretchy pants. After about ten minutes the airlock pressure showed that there was no atmosphere and they were at the point of opening the exterior hatch.

"Okay, guys, lock systems show that you are at zero-pressure differential on either side of the hatch. You are cleared to disengage the locking mechanism," Cindy's voice instructed them.

"Roger that, Cindy. The airlock-to-ingress light is red showing a one-atmosphere pressure delta. The airlock-to-egress light is green for zero delta pressure. Airlock shows we are clear to disengage the hatch locking mechanism," Patel stated. "Dr. Burbank, do you concur?"

Per union rules of any shipping company back in the Sol system all members of an EVA party exiting a craft had to concur on opening an airlock door. It was and had been standard procedure pretty much since the beginning of commercial space travel. Roy wasn't sure how he felt about union gigs, but as far as safety regs went, he didn't mind so much.

"This is Burbank. I concur." Roy watched as Pankish grasped the metal wheel of the door locking mechanism with both hands. His right on top of the wheel with an overhand grip and his left at the bottom with an underhand grip, he turned the wheel three complete revolutions until there was a clanking vibration through the door that translated across the floor and into Roy's feet. Then there was another vibration as if some spring-loaded or electromechanical device had cycled. Patel pushed the door and it popped outward quickly and then cycled out of the way to the outside of the ship. It happened so quickly that Roy almost flinched.

"Hatch is open, we're staring at space," Patel said as he turned and gave Roy a big toothy grin. "Come on, Roy, it's time to earn our pay today."

"We get paid for this?" Roy chuckled.

CHAPTER 35

January 12, 2091 (Earth timeline)
March 18, 2090 (Ship timeline)
approximately 6 light-months from Earth
3.64 light-years from Proxima

"The FLOTA is just beyond us now," Pankish told Roy. Roy watched as he scaled the *Samaritan* like it was El Capitan in California back on Earth. Roy wasn't much for mountain climbing. In fact, he'd never been mountain climbing, but he had been on the outside of spacecraft before—just not while they were accelerating as fast as this one was. "Once we get there, Roy, we will need to anchor again."

"Copy that, Pank." Roy took a short swig of water from the tube in front of his face. For a brief moment his nose started to itch and he wanted to scratch it, but the mood-enhancement patch kicked in and calmed the nerve endings on his skin to reduce that urge. "Everything is dandy back here."

"Good." Pankish paused his climb for a second, standing steady on the exterior ladder hooks. Roy could see he was looking back at him. "Need a breather yet?"

"I'm good, Pank. We can keep going if you want," Roy said, not quite breathing too heavily to carry on a conversation.

"Well, dammit, Roy. You are going to make me look bad." Pankish stopped, extracted a small half-meter-long tether, and clipped himself onto the ladder. Once he checked that it was good and secure, he let go with his hands and leaned back into his harness, shaking his arms out. "I suggest we take a moment, Roy. Lock in and rest."

"Hahaha!" Roy laughed at himself and then pulled the safety cable out and clipped it onto the ladder handle. "No problem."

"Think we can see Proxima, Doc?" Pankish asked.

"I think we're too far behind the bridge dome. We'd need to be outward radially another couple meters or more."

"Yeah, what I was thinking too." Pankish shook his arms out again and then put one hand on the ladder above him. "I'm good to go if you are."

"Go."

It had taken about fifteen minutes for the two of them to reach the spot on the ladder about five meters above the Forward-Looking Optical Telescope. Once they had gotten there the two of them immediately strapped in safety harnesses and did their best to catch their breath. It had been a long forty-meter or so climb. Roy had been telling himself to keep putting hand over hand and foot over foot until they'd reached the peak nearest and just above the telescope.

The five meters laterally from the ladder to the telescope were the more frightening to Roy. They were going to have to strap to the ladder and then descend back down below the telescope level. At that point they would use pendulum motion to swing themselves up to the assembly.

"The next time we design a starship, we need to put magnetic pathways to all the pertinent spots!" Roy grunted sarcastically. "Why we didn't think that through is beyond me."

"I know you are saying that with sarcasm right, Doc?" Pankish laughed. "If not, I'm sure the CHENG would love to spend a couple hours lecturing you on the MLIMPRoSS if you want her to. Believe me, I made that mistake once."

"You two know I'm listening, right?" the CHENG said over the comm channel.

"That will be okay, Cindy. I know all about the Multi-Layer Insulating Metamaterial Particle and Radiation Shielding System. But would it have destroyed the diamagnetism of the metamaterial to put little ferromagnetic walkways about the circumference of the ship here and there?" Roy said. The idle chatting kept his mind from going into the fear zone of what they were about to be doing.

"You volunteered, Roy," Cindy added. "Having second thoughts? Regrets?"

"Not on your life." Roy dropped down about two meters behind Pankish to get out of his way. "I'm clear if you are ready, Pank."

"Affirmative," Patel said. "Do your best to hold your cable down against the ladder if I don't catch on the first swing. I don't want to get tripped up on it."

"Maybe we should've gone up one at a time?" Roy noted. "You can't get tripped on my wire if my wire isn't there."

"That is against regs," Pankish rebutted. "Have to have a safety backup ready and enabled to take action if something happens to the first jumper."

"That makes sense. Not sure I've read that reg before." Roy was beginning to wonder if he was qualified for this particular EVA. But he was fairly sure that nobody truly was. He'd have to be careful and absorb as much on-the-job-training as he could manage. "I'm out of your way. Good to go whenever you see fit."

"Alright, here goes nothing."

Roy watched closely, just in case he had to act, but more to the point, so he would learn how to do what they were about to do. Pankish placed his feet firmly against the hull of the ship and let slack out on his line until he was standing perpendicular to it. He was in the classic climbing/rappelling position. He tested his balance a couple of times by jumping outward from the ship a few tens of centimeters and then landing in place with his knees bending softly as shock absorbers. Once he appeared to have his balance and bearings, Roy could see him turning his head toward the target.

"Roy, pick yourself a target. Mine is the portside-most hand-hold. I'm going for that," Pankish told him. He adjusted the electromagnetic grips on his glove and then started running hard away from the ladder in the direction of the telescope.

Pankish reached the point where the acceleration of the ship, their artificial gravity well, was more of a force pulling at him than the friction of his toe-boots could overcome and his feet slipped free of the hull—but not before he gave one last kick off. He let the pendulum swing carry him through the arch, and as he bounced back toward the hull, he managed to kick once more giving him just enough angular momentum to reach the FLOTA and his targeted handhold. Pankish reached out, grabbed the handhold, and came to a stop. He quickly snapped a cable in place and Roy could hear him sighing in relief.

"Easy as that," Pankish said. He rested in the rappelling position and turned to Roy. "Alright, now for the easier part."

"Good job, Pank. CHENG, Patel is in position at the FLOTA." Roy radioed in. "I'm now making the egress from the ladder to join him."

As with any such climbing maneuver, Roy and Pankish were not just tethered to the ship's hull in various places along their path, they were also tethered to each other. Once Pankish had made the leap across to the FLOTA, he merely needed to lock in and then reel Roy over to him.

"Start the line, Pankish," Roy told him as he worked himself into rappelling position. "I'm ready."

"Line reel on."

Roy felt the tug at his waist where the line was snapped to his harness. As it tightened, he was pulled toward Pankish and the FLOTA. He bounced off the hull a few tens of centimeters and was pulled through the pendulum arch. He continued to bounce as the cable tightened each time. He picked a target safety loop on the starboard side of the FLOTA and as he got close enough, bounced himself in that direction, reaching out with his left hand stretching as far as he could.

"Dammit!" he exclaimed, just missing the handhold and falling backward by a couple of meters. His feet slipped out from under him and he fell over sideways, slamming his left shoulder against the hull. "Shit!"

"You alright, Roy?" Pankish asked. "Stopping the line."

Roy hung upside down about a meter and a half away from the spot he'd targeted. He wasn't tangled up in the cables and he wasn't hurt. He just needed to work himself back over to his feet. Struggling to get friction between his knees and the hull he managed to squirm himself to an all-fours posture.

"Reel me in like this," Roy said. "I'm okay. Just a bit embarrassed."

"Reeling," Pankish replied. "There is nothing to be embarrassed about. We've all been there and done that."

"Have you really?"

"Anybody who has done long hauls to the Belt or Mars has absolutely had to go out and do something on a tether that ended up, well, upside down. No shame," Pankish said. Roy wasn't sure if was just trying to make him feel better or not. He honestly didn't care.

"Reeling."

The cable pulled snug and Roy began crawling with the tether's tension as best he could. Finally, he reached the handhold and pulled himself up, locking a safety cable into position. He caught his breath briefly and then nodded a thank-you to Patel.

"CHENG, EVA team is in position. We are ready to start with step one of the disassembly," Patel said. "Roy, let's get started."

"Damned good work, Roy!" Captain Crosby poured some more of the scotch into the glasses around the galley table. "From what the CHENG tells me, it looks like we can lock onto the *Interstellarerforscher* and stay that way. As long as it goes in the right direction, we'll be going in the right direction."

"That's right, Cap'n!" Bob Roca slapped Roy on the shoulder. "Had you not been here, Roy, we'd all have gotten lost at sea."

"I don't know about that, Bob," Roy responded sheepishly. He was tired, but only physically. Emotionally, he was on a high he hadn't felt since he was awakened from cryosleep. "But I do agree that this nav system should work. It needs a new snazzy acronym or something."

"How about the Burbank System. We can call it BS for short?" Patel said, grinning across the top of his snifter full of alcohol. "Nav officer, how do we know where we are?"

"BS, Cap'n!" Bob Roca affirmed.

"What happens at the halfway point, though?" Zhao asked. "I mean, the probe is a flyby probe. It plans to keep on accelerating right on past Proxima and on out into deeper space. We're going to start slowing down in a few years."

"We'll still be able to see the probe just fine. Its exhaust will be visible at quite a distance. We have our very own guide star," Cindy Mastrano answered as she held up her glass. "To Dr. Roy Burbank, truly a good Samaritan."

"To Roy!" They all clinked their glasses together and took deep draws. Roy drank, but he wasn't so sure he'd done anything that Cindy or Roca or even Patel wouldn't have figured out eventually.

"To me, I guess," Roy said, finishing off his drink. The captain immediately refilled it. Roy held out his hand in protest. "Not sure I should—"

"Roy." Crosby moved his hand away. "If anybody deserves to tie one on, it's you. Besides, we can't do anything but watch how the system works over the next couple of days anyway. Now drink up."

Roy did. He finished his glass and then another. By the time he started on the fourth one, only Patel and Mastrano were still in the galley with him. There were several half-eaten bags of microwave popcorn spread about the table as well as a nearly empty fifth of scotch. Roy was reaching the point where if he had one more he would either throw up and have a really bad headache in the morning, or he would pass out and have a really bad headache in the morning.

"The ship is quiet, you know?" he said slurring the words a bit. "I mean, it's *quiet*."

"Nah, it ain't quiet at all, Roy." Pankish slurred even worse than Roy around a handful of popcorn he was shoving into his mouth. "The damned bulkheads pop and creak with temp changes and every single damned time a scrubber kicks in I can hear my bones rattle."

"That's because it is so quiet, Pank." Roy lightly sipped his drink. He'd made a point to add extra ice and soda this go around. They'd run out of the scotch and were on bourbon. He didn't feel sacrilegious about mixing that.

"Hell, even in the airlock with all the air gone you could still feel the ship vibrating. Then there is that weird feeling you get as you approach the propulsion system. That ultra-high frequency sound in there makes my skin crawl," Cindy told them. "I agree with Pank. Not quiet at all."

"I don't mean mechanically quiet." Roy took another sip and debated on eating some of the popcorn. The salt would be nice but then again, there would be food in his stomach that could cause problems later when he expected to start throwing up. He decided against it. "I mean . . . people. There're not enough people. No background noise of conversations, work going on, media vids, kids jabbering . . ."

He paused mid-sentence and almost immediately fell off the cliff of his emotional high. He fell a very long way into a pit and tears formed in his eyes.

"There are no kids." He sat his glass down as tears started running down his cheeks. "I'm sorry, guys. I don't know why I can't stop this."

"Stop wha—" Patel had dropped some of the popcorn on the

deck and was picking it up with his head below table height. He had been looking away, but when he turned back to face Roy and Cindy he just stopped talking. Roy was embarrassed.

"Roy, there is nothing to be sorry for," Cindy said softly, at least as softly as her loud demeanor and four very stiff drinks would allow, which wasn't very soft. "Hell, first, you're lucky that bastard didn't kill you outright. Second, you're lucky that you've got to at least have some communications with your family."

"Doesn't sound like luck, Cindy."

"Roy, I don't know about how lucky you are, but your misfortune has saved our collective asses," Patel said, slapping the table a little too vigorously.

"How's that, Pankish?" Roy continued wallow. "I don't see how."

"I don't believe in coincidences or serendipity," Pankish argued. "I believe that shit happens because it is supposed to happen."

"Fate?" Roy muttered.

"Call it programming in the Simulation, God's will, or Fate. I don't really give a damn. If all the things don't happen the way they happen then what happens can't happen." He stopped himself and repeated what he'd just said under his breath. Roy watched as his lips continued moving. "Yeah, that's right. What I just said."

"What in the hell are you babbling about, Pank?" Cindy asked. "That didn't make one lick of sense."

"Of course it did!" Pankish sounded hurt and straightened himself up like a defense attorney about to save someone from death row. "We'd be dead if it weren't for Roy! All of us, D-E-A-D with capital letters, dead!"

"I don't know, Pank. You folks aren't total dafties," Roy said. "In fact, I suspect you all would have figured out the problems along the way and fixed them yourselves. Me being here just sped you along."

"I don't know, Roy." Cindy raised an eyebrow. "You found the original sabotage."

"Did you ever stop to wonder if maybe you *had* to be here, Roy?" Pankish kept on with it. "That's right. You, Dr. Roy Burbank, had to be here. Otherwise, the *Samaritan* and her crew were toast, and maybe even all of Proxima with it."

"I don't see that," Roy argued, starting to feel a bit dizzy.

"Think it through. Maybe, maybe, just maybe... oh hell, not

maybe, for damned certain. Had we not called for the expert's advice on how to test the PINS, and had that expert not just happened to be nearby on a vacation cruise ship, and had that expert not come aboard, and had that expert not stumbled across an asshole attempting to sabotage the ship, that expert would not have been at the wrong place at the wrong time, and all of us here on the ship would have been asleep and not even realized the PINS had been sabotaged. We would have been long gone and too far off course by the time anyone figured it out and woke somebody up to fix it. We might have come up with a fix like following the interstellar probe or we might not have, but by then it would have been far too late."

"Damn, Pankish, you might be right there," Cindy added. "Had your wife not got us looking for you, we wouldn't have even woken you up until the midpoint med checks. By then we'd have been so far off course..."

"That is absolutely right, CHENG!" Pankish slapped the table again. "You had to be here, Roy. While I'm so sorry for what has happened to your life being upturned and all, and I'm sorry about not getting to be there with your family—that's awful—but, selfishly, for myself, the crew, and hell, Proxima, I'm damned glad you are here!"

Roy turned and looked Pankish right in the eyes. He wiped the tears from his cheeks. Then he promptly vomited across the table.

CHAPTER 36

January 16, 2091 (Earth timeline)
March 19, 2090 (Ship timeline)
approximately 6 light-months from Earth
3.64 light-years from Proxima

Roy had about the worst hangover he remembered ever having, ever, in his life. Once Cindy and Pankish had dragged him to his room, he was still nauseous. He had kept one leg off the bed touching the floor with the hope that connecting to the floor would help keep the ceiling from spinning. It hadn't. Finally, Roy had just taken his blanket to the bathroom and slept there. The air toilet looked similar to normal ones, but there was no water flow; instead there was an air-sleeve that activated once the lid was opened. Roy hadn't been certain how it would respond to projectile vomiting, but after about the third time he realized that the design was quite capable of handling anything he could throw at it—or more to the point, throw up at it.

Midway through the next morning his brain was becoming almost coherent enough to realize that he was curled up into fetal position on the bathroom floor shivering against the cold metal deck plating. His body being in direct contact with the very efficient heat sink was sapping all the heat his body could generate and was bringing him close to hypothermia. The loss of body heat actually had probably helped his hangover, acting somewhat like an icepack on his pounding head. But, in reality, Roy wasn't sure that anything could help.

Roy wanted to die. Flat out, all he wanted at the moment was

Travis S. Taylor & Les Johnson

for his head to quit throbbing, the uneasiness in his stomach to go away, the scratchy sore throat to heal, and most of all, the lingering depression from the knowledge that he couldn't go home to fade. Drinking might not have been the best idea as he was already fighting that severe depression as it was. He was on antidepression meds the doctor had given him and then he had mixed them with alcohol, lots of alcohol. The knowledge of being lost in space from his wife and the daughter he'd never meet or even get to speak to in real-time was just too much for him without the added toxins to his brain.

Roy crawled to the bed and pulled the weighted magnetic blanket up over him. He lay shivering for what seemed like an eternity, but the heater coils in the sleep unit, combined with the thermal sensors and the feedback control loop, finally brought his body temperature back to normal. He drifted in and out of sleep. Recurring nightmares of not being there for his family made what sleep he managed to be unrestful. Once, he thought he was going to have to get back up to go to the toilet and heave, but he managed to choke the throat-burning bile back down and mentally force himself to keep his mouth clenched.

A few hours later, he managed to get up and drink some electrolytes and brush his teeth. He thought, very briefly, that a slow walk about the ship might do him some good. Then he thought less of that idea and crawled back into his bunk. After another thirty or forty minutes of lying sleepless in bed, he rolled over and reached out to switch on the light nearest the bed, knocking over the holoprojection of his rapidly growing daughter. He froze motionless and took a deep breath. He picked up the little silver-and-pink cube, rolled up onto his back, placing the cube on his stomach. Roy depressed the on switch and the data cube updated. It seemed to him that his daughter had grown an inch since he'd looked at the cube just hours before.

"Nigel?"

"Yes, Roy?"

"Are there any new letters from home?"

"Not yet, Roy."

"Damn. Okay. Play the latest one."

"Okay, Roy."

"I think we're going to have a hard time getting Roy to go to long-term cryo," Cindy told Captain Crosby. She wasn't as hungover as Roy and Pankish because she'd more or less sipped at her drinks, knowing that somebody was going to have to make sure they had gotten to bed safely. "He is afraid he'll miss a video from home, I think."

"If I have to do something, you're right. I'll make it an order. Or I'll wake up the doctor and let him do it," Crosby replied. "This is just a damned mess. If we hadn't already gotten into the no-return level with the Samara Drive, then I would say to hell with the Proximans and turn this ship around."

"Well, by the time we did that...I'm not sure we even could." Cindy had thought about that already and wasn't sure about their ability to go anywhere due to the astronavigation problems. "With the PINS being done for, I don't think we could go full speed home without getting lost."

"I've thought about that too. I think you are right about that. Roca and I talked it through a couple days ago," Crosby said. "We'd have to go at a slower speed and make nav measurements by hand and do trajectory mods continuously. We're in one helluva bad spot right now. And poor Roy is just stuck with us."

"I think it would be better for him to go to cryo as soon as the doc said he could. That's in a couple weeks, right?"

"Mak said that he wanted him to avoid deep cryo for the first six to eight months. We picked mid-March as a generic time in that window to assess him. I'd say if he's not showing physical symptoms of his concussion, then we need to talk him into napping as soon as we can." Crosby spun about in his desk chair so he could look out the forward-view window in the ready room. Cindy followed his gaze and could see him looking for Proxima. It was hard to miss as it was dead center straight ahead. "It is hard to believe it is so difficult to navigate to a bright shiny beacon like that."

"It is a great deal harder than it looks for sure," Cindy agreed. "I'll talk Roy into letting us have the autodoc do a concussion assessment on him and then I'll try to get him to cryo. I'm pretty sure if the damned thing cleared him for EVA, then it should clear him for cryosleep."

"Don't bet it on. I thought so too, but Mak said the system used different protocols and algorithms for the two different things," Crosby said. "If you need me to come make it an order just let me know, subtly and privately."

"Yes sir. I'll get right on that."

CHAPTER 37

January 16, 2091 (Earth timeline)
March 19, 2090 (Ship timeline)
approximately 6 light-months from Earth
3.64 light-years from Proxima

Chloe juggled the little redheaded infant about in the baby pouch strapped across her chest in order to adjust the backpack she had on her back. She did her best to hold the bottle in place for Samari with her left hand while she opened the glass door to the training building with her right. Once she got the door wedged open with her foot, Chloe kicked it wide enough to slide through and push it the rest of the way open with her backpack by leaning backward into it. Just as it looked like she was going to make it through, one of the straps on the backpack looped around the L-shaped angle aluminum door pull, fixing her to it as it swung wider with the sharp gust of north Alabama winter wind that nearly knocked her off her feet.

It was getting cold and looked like it was going to rain. The last thing Chloe needed at that moment was to have her back stuck to a door while there was a baby on her chest. The only upside to getting caught on the door was that being hung up with it actually kept her from losing her balance, but had she not been hung on the door she would have already been inside and the wind wouldn't have been an issue.

Then the rain started.

"Shit!" she muttered to herself as she grasped outward for handholds in any direction. The bottle flew from her left hand

and Samari promptly let her know by screaming her lungs out. "It's okay, baby. Mommy will get it together."

Chloe reached with her left hand for the bottle but was so affixed to the door handle that she couldn't reach it either. Samari continued to cry for the bottle with her little hands outstretched, reaching, and the fact that she was now being pelted by raindrops didn't help matters. Chloe was suddenly overwhelmed by the fact that she'd been trying to do everything as a single parent for the last year, while at the same time working mostly around the clock training for her new job. The training was intense and took every waking second of her day. At the same time, taking care of an infant by herself mostly took every waking second of her day as well. Roy's parents helped as much as they could and she had considered hiring a full-time nanny, but she didn't want to deprive Samari of both parents.

She was the primary bread winner now, although the company had taken good care of them due to what happened with Roy, but she was not just going to sit idly by on that money. No, Chloe had a plan. She had a plan to fix things as best they could be fixed. But at the moment, that plan was wearing her down. No, it was literally beating her down and she was almost to the breaking point and ready to tap out. She started crying uncontrollably and just couldn't stop it. Being a medical doctor, she understood that she was having post-partum hormone imbalances. She made a mental note to see an endocrinologist to get that straightened out as soon as possible. She continued to cry but there was just enough rain to cover the tears.

"Here, ma'am, let me help you with that." A young Space Force major grabbed the bottle from the ground and handed it to her. Chloe accepted it and quickly shoved it in the baby's mouth. Samari went right to it and stopped crying immediately.

"Thank you."

"Hold on a minute. You're really strapped into this thing back here."

"I can manage..." she started to say through sniffles. She wiped the tears and rain from her eyes as best she could and tried to straighten herself.

"No worries, ma'am. Just one more second—aha! Got it. There you go. All free." The soldier smiled at her and helped her get her balance. "I've seen you around the base a bit. I'm Malcolm Reyes."

"Thank you, Malcolm." She continued to cry. "I'm, Chloe, Chloe Burbank. Space medical."

"Ma'am, are you okay?" the major asked her. Chloe nodded her head in the affirmative even though it was clearly a lie.

"I, uh, well, I am just tired," Chloe lied verbally to go along with the opposing body language. She was more than tired. She was worn ragged and fighting depression on top of that. But she wasn't going to quit. "Thanks again...but...I'll be fine. I have to get to class."

"Where're you headed?"

"Trauma Care in Microgravity. Third floor, um, conference room three-oh-one." The major looked at her and then the baby. "I know, I know, but I couldn't get a babysitter because the damned instructor changed the class time on me. And I emailed him to get a VR link but he never responded. And I can't miss the class or I can't get into the second part in Boulder next month. And dammit, this is the last time this one is offered in time. I can't miss these classes. I have to get certified. And I think I'm going to be late."

"Fancy, that. I'm going to the third floor, also. Let me give you a hand with your bag." He reached to take the bag but Chloe stopped him.

"No thanks, Malcom. I can handle it." Chloe straightened her posture and wiped her face with the sleeve of her jacket. The Alabama winters got cold every now and then, but it was nothing like Colorado was going to be next month when she got there. Either way, she was glad to get inside and out of the weather. She was sure Samari was too.

"Really, ma'am. No bother." Major Reyes took her backpack and ushered her toward the elevator. "I'm going that way."

"Again, thank you." Chloe had to sometimes just accept help. It was not there often and she needed to force herself to take every little hand-up and break offered. Being the one needing help was atypical for her.

"Yes ma'am. And who's this little beauty?"

"This is Samari." Chloe held one of her baby's hands and waved it at the major. Samari didn't seem to care. She cooed around the nipple from the bottle in her mouth and swatted her free hand back and forth and then grasped the bottle with both hands. "Say hi, baby."

"Hello, Samari."

After the elevator, Major Reyes led them down the hallway past several light tan faux-wood doors. Finally, they reached the door marked 301 and he opened it for her. Chloe nodded a thank-you but he motioned her to go on in.

"Go ahead. I've got this." He held up the bag and followed her to an empty seat on the second row behind the main conference table. Chloe looked at her watch.

"I think we're a few minutes late."

"No worries," Major Reyes said.

Chloe shuffled her stuff around and then made herself comfortable in her seat. She checked to make certain Samari's bottle was filled and she prayed that after that, she'd be sleepy. If there were a bowel movement, she'd just have to slip out the back of the room and find the bathroom. She kissed Samari on the head. "You are being good for Mommy, right?"

"Major Reyes, I have the simulator ready to go, sir." A civilian that Chloe didn't know approached them. "We're ready when you are."

Chloe gulped and quickly panicked. She tapped at her datapad, bringing up the roster for the short course training. It listed the instructor as Dr. M. R. Reyes, Major USSF Reserve. Chloe was so embarrassed.

"Here's your bag, Dr. Burbank. And don't worry, if things get stressful with young Samari here"—he patted her on the head and baby-talked a bit with her—"just slip out. If you miss something today, I'll make sure you can get caught up. You know we have a day care on the first floor?"

"I thought that was for military only." Chloe was still embarrassed.

"Military, yes, but it's also for flight crews in training."

CHAPTER 38

February 11, 2091 (Earth timeline)
April 7, 2090 (Ship timeline)
approximately 7 light-months from Earth
3.54 light-years from Proxima

"Not that it really matters, Captain, but I'd like to stay up a few more weeks," Roy pleaded with Captain Crosby. "I like keeping up with my daughter's growth."

"I get it Roy. I really do," Crosby replied, "but we can't have one person up by protocol. There has to be three at a time, all the time. And if we have more than that up for long periods of time, we will start taxing the environment systems and the food and water stores more than planned. We wouldn't run out, but it would eat into our contingency percentages more than I'd like. We've had this discussion."

"Well, you didn't plan a contingency for having me on this ship for the duration either!" Roy exclaimed. He'd looked at the statistics for the ship supply stores and environment systems. He didn't believe that his being up would cause any problems.

"Roy, you need to calm yourself down." Crosby exhaled and looked to Roy to be counting underneath his breath. "If you like, I will put you in every fourth rotation. You will be part of the awake team once per year for three months. That's the most I'm willing to do. You can spend that time catching up on videos and helping check the nav system."

"Nothing more than that?" Roy was defeated. He knew that the captain could have him restrained and put in cryo for the next nine years if he wanted other than the mandatory midflight week for medical exams. He decided to take what he could. "Very well. Sorry for my outburst, Captain. This is very...difficult for me."

"Roy, this is difficult for all of us. This is ridiculously horrible for you. I understand your frustration, your anger, your sadness, and any other emotions that might run away with you." Crosby nodded knowingly as he was choosing his words slowly. "Dr. Kopylova and I spoke at length about your situation and here is the issue. I'm just going to be point blank and blunt with you."

"Please do, Captain."

"Roy, anytime you are awake, we have you on suicide watch."

"What?"

"Use that brain of yours to figure it out," Crosby said. "You are a risk of deep depression and therefore suicide. While the doc has given you various treatments to prevent that, treatment never is perfect." Crosby paused and Roy wasn't sure if he was done or pausing for some effect. "Now Roy, I want you to explain to me why I don't want you awake as part of the three-man awake team."

"Me, explain?"

"Yes. You need to come to that realization yourself."

Roy thought about what Crosby was getting at and didn't really understand where he was going. Why did it matter? Hell, even if he did commit suicide, and he wasn't sure he was a risk for that, it would be one less person sucking in air, using food and water, and needing power. Seemed like a positive to him.

"Well? I want to hear your thoughts, Roy," Crosby insisted.

"Um, well, if I am on suicide watch, um, I don't really understand why it matters. Why watch? If I jumped out an airlock, who would care? Your resources would be spared by the needs of one person," Roy said very matter-of-factly. He didn't really see why anyone should care.

"If you were to jump out an airlock, what if you bounced into a sensitive component of the spacecraft, causing damage and maybe putting the mission or the crew at risk?" Crosby frowned. "What if, Roy? What if?"

"Okay, I'd be more cautious, then." Roy shrugged and realized that he chuckled, which was kind of weird. Talking about how he would commit suicide seemed too unemotional to him.

"Maybe I'd just take some pills or something in my quarters. Or...I don't know, whatever."

"Roy, do you want us to have to report home to your daughter that you have died?" Crosby asked.

"I, uh, well..." Roy had not really thought about that. If he killed himself because he couldn't be with his wife and daughter what type of burden might that place on them? Sheepishly he had to admit that he didn't want that.

"I guess not," Roy admitted. He actually wasn't sure he'd ever contemplated suicide, although he'd felt like his life was over and dying didn't matter.

"Well, I'm glad to hear that," Crosby said. "Roy, many times when someone commits suicide on deep-space missions it is not premeditated and thought through. It is just done. You are on suicide watch until such time as we reach Proxima. That means that the crew that is awake with you must check your where-abouts and status hourly. That is an extra burden on them. That means that somebody must have an opposite sleep cycle or have sleepless nights getting up to check on you all the time. That is a lot to ask of someone for ninety days."

"I never thought of that." Roy honestly hadn't even considered that he was burdening the crew with his moods and depression. Maybe he would be better off just going into cryo for the dura-tion of the mission. "I guess, if I were you, well, I'd put me in a cryobed and only wake me up when I had to."

"Now you are getting it, Roy." Crosby nodded his head up and down slowly. "So, you can stay up once a year for three months, but that puts a burden on the crew with you."

"I won't commit suicide," Roy said as sincerely as he could. "I just won't."

"While I'm glad to hear you say that, I can't, in good con-science, believe it."

"I can't impose on the crew to have to watch me every hour through the day. What if I wear a health status monitor or something?" Roy offered. "Have it only accessible by them and not me so I can't turn it off, unlock it, or take it off?" Roy truly didn't want to burden the crew with this crazy "suicide watch."

"We don't have any such device, Roy. We have health moni-tors but none we can lock you out of."

"I see."

"For now, it's time for your rotation in the cryobed. We'll wake you on your next planned rotation," Crosby said with an inflection in his voice and an expression on his face that told Roy he was done discussing it.

"I understand, Captain."

CHAPTER 39

December 25, 2094 (Earth timeline)
July 24, 2092 (Ship timeline)
approximately 2.122 light-years from Earth
2.122 light-years from Proxima

Enrico Vulpetti groaned. It wasn't exactly a painful groan, more of a "I'm waking up from a deep, deep sleep and don't want to wake up" groan. He was, in fact, waking up from a very deep sleep. He was also cold. In his half-awake state, he couldn't figure out why he was so cold. *Where are the blankets? Who pulled off all the blankets?* He couldn't quite figure out where he was or why he was having such trouble waking up. He had been dreaming, but for the life of him he couldn't remember about what. It hadn't been a nightmare, that he was sure. Maybe something about horses? The memory wouldn't come.

Then he remembered. He was aboard the *Samaritan* bound for Proxima Centauri b. He was probably waking up from the cryosleep and the reason he groaned was probably because his muscles were sore from having only chemical and electrical stimulation for weeks. Or was it months? *Years?* Hopefully, this was the wakeup he'd requested before going into cryosleep. His excitement level jumped at the thought. His throat was dry, as were his sinuses. As he tried to move, he became aware of the catheter and biobags attached to his lower body. He was trying to remember if he were the one who was supposed to remove them or if someone else would help him.

Slowly, his level of consciousness rose, along with his mobility.

Finally, he felt hands on his legs and the sensation of the catheter being removed. He opened his eyes and was greeted by none other than Captain Crosby.

"Welcome to the land of the awake, Enrico. How do you feel?" Crosby asked.

"Sore. And my throat is parched. May I have some water?" he asked.

"Absolutely. Let's just get you out of the cryobed and then you can have whatever you want to eat and drink," said Crosby as he extended a hand to help Enrico out of the bed and onto his feet. "How you feeling?"

"You just asked me that," Enrico replied. The captain had just asked him, right? Was he still dreaming? No, Enrico was pretty certain he was awake.

"Yes, I did. But we have to ask." Crosby laughed. "Everyone always responds the same way even though we have been trained on how this goes. So, here goes the next one. Are you awake or are you dreaming?"

"Yes, I get it. I am awake," Enrico replied.

"Good. You know, I've always wondered how we really know the answer to that one."

"Right. Uh, where are we, Captain? Is this it? Did you wake me up for the starbow? Or did I draw the random straw for a shift? Or are we at Proxima?"

"We're not at Proxima, but I'm extremely pleased to report that we are still on course," Crosby told him. "As you requested, we woke you up to see the starbow."

Enrico didn't understand the last comment. *Why wouldn't we be on course?* But he was pleased to learn that they were. He hadn't given a single thought to the possibility that they might not be. He looked around the cryosleep chamber and saw that his was one of six beds now open. Everyone else was still asleep, but he also knew that from protocol everyone would be awakened over the next few days for medical checks and for some actual time out of the beds. For now, all he wanted to do was get out of this room and into some other part of the ship with living, breathing, *awake* people. The sight of all those bodies being asleep was, for some reason, more disconcerting now than when he entered cryosleep. They'd all soon be awake.

Enrico was just a little unsteady on his feet, which wasn't

surprising given that he probably hadn't stood up in years. He was a little surprised that he was able to stand at all. He knew the electrostim technology used to keep the bodies in shape while asleep had been used many, many times, but this was his first time to experience it. And, like most human beings, something wasn't *real* until he had lived it. He moved, with Crosby's help, to the small changing room into which he had put on the tunic he was now wearing just before he entered cryosleep. By the time he reached the changing room, he was steady enough to wave off Crosby's help.

"I'll see you in the mess hall after you change. You're the last to wake up today and if you are as ravenous as me, then you will probably consume twice our normal rations," Crosby said.

"I'm starving," Enrico agreed.

Enrico removed the tunic and put on his blue one-piece body suit. Affectionately called *onesies* by the crew, the easy-to-clean outfits were worn by everyone while in space. The only differences between each person's onesie, other than their size, were the colors. Each of them had been provided red, orange, yellow, green, blue, and violet onesies, the colors of the rainbow, that each could wear at their own discretion. It wasn't much variety, but it was better than it would have been had each crew member worn the same color as everyone else, day after day.

He didn't have any trouble walking out of the changing room and rather enjoyed exercising his leg muscles for real as he climbed the ladder to the mess hall. He entered the room and saw his five colleagues gathered around one table, each with a bottle of water and a steaming plate of hot food.

"Merry Christmas!" said all five in unison as Enrico approached the table.

"Christmas?" he asked.

"Today's December twenty-fifth—Earth time. It's July twenty-fourth here on the ship. It's up to you, I guess, which day you want it to be," Bob Roca told him as he shoveled a heaping spoonful of rice into his mouth. "Better eat now while we have gravity. We have the planned cycle-down of the drive in a few hours and then will reverse the ship's orientation."

"So, we're at max velocity?" asked Enrico. "How fast did we reach?"

"Yep. Looks like we're somewhere around point eight five c,

or thereabouts Earth relative. We'll cruise here for a few more hours and then the ship will turn around and begin decelerating," Ming Zhao explained, spooning another helping of the hot meal before him. "Everything aboard looks good and is working as it should, thank God."

"When can we see the starbow?" asked Enrico.

"We're all set up to display the view from the front camera whenever we want. We were so hungry from being asleep we decided to wait until after we'd had some food," Zhao said.

"That's fine with me. I'll get my meal and be right back."

As Enrico went to the food locker and picked out his dinner to microwave, he overheard someone at the table ask if there was any news from Earth. He hurried to not miss too much of the update.

"Not much, really. The AI logged all the personal messages and queued them up in everyone's inboxes. There's a new UN director general, and Chinese president, and some major cyclone hit Japan last year, causing a boatload of damage. Fortunately, Yoko's extended family is okay," Roca said.

"And then there's the priority dispatch," said Crosby as he entered the room with Dr. Kopylova.

"May I ask what that is about?" Dr. Maggie Oliveira-Santos asked. She was the ship's linguist and probably the world's expert on the Proximan language. They were lucky to get her as part of the crew. Not many would sacrifice such a promising career. At forty-five, Maggie Oliveira-Santos could have had an appointment at any major world university to teach and study the Proximan language, and she'd chosen instead to go to converse with the Proximans in person.

"I don't know," Crosby said. "The instructions were to read it only when we enter the Proximan system and before we make orbit; not before. That's pretty unusual."

"And you are really going to wait? There's nothing they can do if you read it early," Roca said around a mouthful. The look on his face gave away his true feelings—no one doubted that had the message come to him, he would have read it as soon as it arrived.

"I'm going to wait. They have their reasons and I'll explain them when I can. If I can," Crosby added.

"Well, let's not worry about that until we have to. Turn on

the forward viewer. Let's see what we woke up to see," Enrico said eagerly as he rejoined the group with his rehydrated ham, green beans, and sweet potato dinner.

The primary mess hall viewscreen was curved, covering a full 130 degrees, nearly a half circle. With cameras located all around the exterior of the ship, they could set the center of the screen at any point and see a large fraction of the starfield. For now, the center of the screen was set for the direction they were moving, and the view was not what they saw when they departed Earth. Instead of a fairly uniform field of stars covering the entire view, they instead saw a cluster of stars near the center with noticeably fewer toward the right and left edges. The starbow.

"Okay, when Enrico told me about this, he got me excited and it certainly looks cool, but what am I looking at?" asked Maggie, staring at the viewscreen.

"It's called the relativistic starbow, but it's not what the name implies. When relativity was first proposed, some calculations showed that there would be a shifting of starlight, creating a multicolor rainbow effect. The name stuck but what we're actually seeing is much different. Because we're traveling at about eighty-five percent the speed of light, the light coming from stars in front of us is blue-shifted to higher energies, and since our eyes are more sensitive to blue light than longer wavelength red light, the stars in front of us appear brighter and the ones at the side or behind us are not as bright," Yoko explained.

"Remember that when Einstein was around, their version of quantum mechanics said that light can be described as both a particle and a wave. We don't use that version of quantum theory any longer but it was or is like a Newtonian version of modern theory. I've just explained what happens to the photon as a wave. Now, thinking as Einstein would have, of photons as particles traveling with a finite velocity, c. When the *Samaritan* moves, the photons get a velocity component added in the opposite direction to the spaceship movement. That makes them seem to come from a direction closer to our forward direction, even though they're not. Now, if we were moving really fast, say over ninety-nine percent the speed of light, all the stars from every direction would appear to be in front of us and take up no more than ten percent of the sky," she continued.

"So not only is time passing slower for us, we are actually

seeing the universe in an altered state due to our velocity. Reality is pretty strange," Enrico said and all the while continued staring at the viewscreen.

"That's an understatement," Crosby said, as he also stared at the screen.

"It's probably the most spectacular Christmas sky since the first one. You know, that Star of Bethlehem and all that." Maggie laughed.

CHAPTER 40

December 31, 2094 (Earth timeline)
July 26, 2092 (Ship timeline)
approximately 2.122 light-years from Earth
2.122 light-years from Proxima

"At this point, we are far enough away from Earth that the information lag is probably three or more years behind." Rain rolled her neck back and forth to get the kinks out. Her shoulders felt pretty stiff too. "Doc, how long before I feel normal here?"

"You've been lying down for several years, Dr. Gilster. It'll probably take some time," Dr. Maksim Kopylova told her. "My own neck and back both feel like I've been through twelve rounds of wrestling with a bear."

"The electrostim didn't keep us in as good of shape as they claim, huh?" Rain asked rhetorically. "Maybe I need to do some yoga or something."

"Yoga would be good. At least do some walking and stretching. And make certain to hydrate well." Kopylova shined a light in her eyes, checking her pupillary response. And then motioned to her that she was done. "You are as healthy as can be and seem steady enough on your feet. Get dressed and enjoy your week awake."

"Thank you, Mak." Rain slid off the examination table and started mingling through her articles of clothing laid across a cart at the foot of the table. "Anything else?"

"Well, not really. Just be prepared for the 'all hands' briefing at eleven hundred hours," Maksim told her.

"What's it about?"

"Captain's update. I'd say that it is probably a typical thing for this point in a long-duration mission like this, but there's never been a long-duration mission like this." The doctor chuckled and grinned, causing his mustache and goatee to look even more overstated of a facial feature than usual. Rain liked it. The doctor was handsome and probably closer to her age than most on the ship, besides the captain.

"Alright, I'll see you then," Rain said awkwardly. After all, she was standing there in front of him mostly naked in a very clinical setting. Maksim was so professional he only nodded at her and let himself through the curtains of the examination room.

"See you then, Dr. Gilster," he said from behind the curtain.

"Rain!" Enrico Vulpetti held out a hand to greet her. "Have you met Commander Rogers here? Mike, this is Dr. Lorraine Gilster. She's the one who found the signal from Proxima in the first place." Enrico introduced the man sitting next to him. The man stood up stiffly and held out a hand. Rain was surprised that he was not wearing the typical flight coveralls that the others onboard typically wore. Instead, he was wearing black tactical pants, a dark navy-blue T-shirt, and sneakers.

"Ma'am, it is my honor." Rain shook the man's hand. It was firm and strong but gentle. The man looked to be in his early thirties with dark closely cut straight hair, brown eyes that were bright and serious, and a solid, extremely athletic frame of nearly a hundred and eighty-three centimeters tall. As solid as he looked, Rain approximated his body weight to be over ninety kilograms, maybe more.

"Commander of what?" Rain asked.

"Hahaha! Rain, you're funny." Enrico laughed at her. "You've not spent much time with military, have you?"

"No, not really. I don't really know much about it. Commander implies navy, right?" She asked politely.

"Yes ma'am, I'm in the navy." Rogers smiled.

"Dammit, Mike, don't be so humble." Enrico slapped him on the shoulder. "Mike here is the leader of the US Navy SEAL team that has been appointed as security for our first embassy with Proxima. He's here to protect us."

"All by yourself, Commander?"

"No ma'am. There is a team of us here on security detail."

"Where's the team, then?" Rain asked. "And how did we not meet before we left Earth?"

"Well, ma'am, my team is over there at that table. We were brought on quickly and all of us went down to cryo almost immediately. That was done for, um, diplomatic reasons," Rogers explained.

"Diplomatic reasons?" Rain didn't understand what that meant. Why would a security team on the crew be kept from the rest of the crew? That made no sense to her.

"Rain, Rain, there was an entire multinational security force that was brought on quietly." Enrico laughed. Rain wasn't sure if he was laughing at her naivety or her lack of knowledge or what in particular was so funny.

"Dr. Gilster," Commander Rogers interrupted. "It was done quietly, in order to keep any last-minute diplomatic disagreements from being stirred up within the crew."

"Charles did this at the order of the UN Security Council and the White House," Enrico said, motioning across the room at Charles Jesus. Both he and Rain had known him pretty much since the beginning of the entire Proxima affair. "While it is a multinational team, it isn't uniformly spread and there isn't complete representation from every nation that might have wanted it. So, it was done quietly, quickly, and before anyone could object."

"Well, I still don't know what that means, but Commander, it is nice to meet you." Rain looked around the galley that was filling up. "How many are in this security force?"

"There are thirteen of us, ma'am. Not quite enough to protect you against an entire planet if it came to that, but we'll do our best to keep you and the rest of the *Samaritan*'s crew safe," Rogers said humbly.

"So, a baker's dozen of you, ten of the flight crew including Captain Crosby, and um, let me see, eighteen of the science team . . . forty-one? Yes, forty-one total of us. That's a considerable crew for a first interstellar mission. I hope they didn't give any of you red shirts." Rain laughed. Enrico and the commander didn't seem to get her joke. "I refuse to wear the damned red coveralls."

"Red shirts, ma'am?" Rogers inquired. "We do have some red coveralls, but most of us will stick to our uniform requirements."

"Hahaha! Now who's funny?" Rain asked. "I suggest you two go watch some late-last century space exploration science fiction entertainment. The guys wearing red shirts were always the expendable security teams and whatnot. They were the extras in the movies like 'Crewman Jones' that nobody ever knew more about and as soon as things went bad, they were the ones that got vaporized by the alien ray guns."

"I see, ma'am." Rogers grinned at her. "I'll make a standing order for none of my team to wear red, then."

"If any of them are named Jones or Smith, you might consider getting that changed as well." She chortled.

"Can I have your attention, please?" Executive Officer Artur Clemons said in a loud but calm voice that was barely audible over the multiple conversations throughout the galley. He stood at the front of the room where the assembly stage was. The ship's chief of security, Mike Rialto, stood next to him at the ready. Ready for what, Rain wasn't so sure.

"Is it eleven hundred already?" Rain said in a normal voice. The commander had immediately quieted down and said softly to her that they would speak again soon. He filtered toward a table that had several other younger multinational people that she didn't recognize. A quick head count tallied up to thirteen. Rain figured that was the security team. "Enrico, mind if I join you?"

"Please." He pointed to the seat next to him. Rain caught a glimpse of Dr. Kopylova slipping in the back entrance to the galley, scanning for a place to sit. She smiled and nodded him in their direction.

"Thank you," she told Enrico. "Do you mind if the doctor joins us?"

"Not at all."

"*Can I have your attention, please?*" the XO shouted this time. The chatter in the galley dropped to almost silence, but not quite.

"Doc," Enrico whispered to Kopylova as he sat next to them.

"Alright, now that I have everyone's attention, the captain has a few things to go over with you." Artur turned and nodded to the door and Captain Crosby entered.

"Hey everyone…" Crosby's voice trailed off for a second as he shuffled through some things on his datapad and then set it aside. Finally, a briefing appeared on the data screen behind him. "Sorry about that. A captain's job is never done."

"Any idea what all this is about?" Rain whispered to Enrico.

"None."

A graphic displaying the ship's trajectory with Earth on the left side and Proxima marked on the right appeared on the screen. The ship flashed in light blue with a solid gray line behind it showing where they had been and a dotted one in front of it showing the path ahead.

"According to astronavigation, we are officially two point one two two light-years from Earth today. All estimates show us at halfway to Proxima. Our current relative speed with Earth and Proxima is about zero point eight five c. We're moving faster than anybody ever has before—at least anybody from Earth that is. The doctor has reported in that *all* of the complement of the *Samaritan* is in good health and with no symptoms from long-duration cryo. To me, that is great news—best news I could have hoped for. Also, it is likely that sometime about now, the signal sent from Earth telling the Proximans that the *Samaritan* is on its way there should be reaching them. In other words, from this day forward we can assume that they know we're on our way to them.

"We have the latest news from Earth. All the latest news feeds have been downloaded; just keep in mind they are almost three years behind due to the speed of light lag. Also note that you have all received personal data from home. I'll let you folks filter through that as you desire. The highlights that are pertinent to us are as follows. One, construction of the *Emissary* is ongoing and crew choices are being made." The latest video of the next interstellar ship to be built by humanity started. It was from what appeared to be a survey drone's point of view. Rain guessed it must have been flying around it, making three-dimensional maps and historical records of the building process. The Moon in the background was a familiar and comforting sight to her. There were many audible approvals muttered throughout the crew.

"Initial design testing of the propulsion system suggests the Samara Drive for that ship will be much more efficient than ours and the speeds available might approach ninety-nine percent the speed of light. There is no scheduled launch date as of yet.

"Two, the Solar Gravity Lens Telescope has gone through initial checkout and is now fully operational. The first available images of the Proxima system are in the data download. I'm sure you will find them to be very interesting. I've looked at a couple of them and the images of Proxima b are absolutely stunning.

Since the Proximans don't have satellites yet, I suspect that these are better aerial images of their home planet than they have."

The display screen switched to several views of Proxima b from the SGLT that caused quite the reaction throughout. The planet looked like Earth. The continents were all wrong, of course, but it looked blue and green and white just like Earth. There were two small moons that were clear in one of the images. Rain was amazed at the resolution the telescope was able to achieve. The images were beautiful. She was even more invigorated to see the planet and do what she could to save the Proximans from their genetic downward spiral—even though she wasn't a geneticist.

"Three, as of yet there is no change on the status of birthrate on Proxima, which I guess none of us expected there to be. By this point, they've likely been able to absorb the data dump on genetics that we sent them but their technology level is still way too low to do much about it. We'll just have to wait and see when we get there.

"Four, the whereabouts of Dr. Thomas Pinkersly are still unclear and nobody has been able to identify this man..." An image of a man appeared on screen in multiple angles. One image set listed him as Patrick O'Hearn and the other as Ray Gaines. The images were clearly of the same man although the hair color was slightly different between them and the latter images showed the person wearing glasses. "Nobody knows who this man is or who he is affiliated with, but we do think he is key to understanding what happened to Dr. Pinkersly, Dr. Burbank, and the sabotage of the *Samaritan*. Anybody with any clues of this man's identity please come see me, Artur, or Mike."

"Enrico, doesn't he look familiar to you?" Rain whispered. Then it hit her. Captain Crosby had just said sabotage of the *Samaritan*. Sabotage! She could see the same reaction spreading like wildfire across the galley.

"Please, please, hold it down. I plan to go into much more detail here." Crosby held up a hand and was trying to calm the crowd as best Rain could tell. "We are currently out of danger. And that is mostly due to Dr. Roy Burbank of the design team at Interstellara, Incorporated. This man, Ray Gaines, or whoever the hell he is, actually managed to get onboard the ship, perform various types of sabotage to the PINS, and left us flying blind across the void. It was clear that the intent of the sabotage was

SAVING PROXIMA   239

to keep us from ever reaching Proxima. During the process of the sabotage Dr. Burbank, who just so happened to be near the *Samaritan* on a sightseeing cruise ship, came onboard and found the first bit of sabotage and fixed it for us. At the time, we believed that Dr. Burbank had then left with a fast Space Force vessel and was on his way to be safe and sound at home while we ramped up the Samara Drive to full power."

"Did you two know any of this?" Enrico asked them. Rain shrugged. She was bewildered. It was all news to her. But something about that Gaines fellow was bothering her. Something way back years ago, deep in her memories.

"Pay attention." Kopylova grunted.

"We were several months into the mission. The Samara Drive was running at full power on the Weak Energy Condition Acoustic Violator. In other words, we were on our way with no turning back. We then received a message from home explaining that Dr. Burbank had not reported home and was missing. Upon further investigation, we found Dr. Burbank here on the ship in the cryobed slated for Dr. Thomas Pinkersly. Dr. Burbank had a serious head trauma but was alive."

Captain Crosby waited after that and Rain could tell he was letting the news sink in on the crew as to what had happened. Rain realized that the poor man was stuck in the cryobed on the starship against his will by this Gaines person. And it was highly likely that Dr. Pinkersly was in on this. It was all so crazy and almost unbelievable. Why would anybody want to keep the *Samaritan* from reaching Proxima so badly that they would do such a thing? Who didn't want the ship making the trip anyway? There were only a few groups of isolationists across the Sol system that argued deeply against the mission, but there wasn't that many of them. The only real opposition had been early on, by that jerk at the UN hearings she'd originally attended years prior. That jerk had parleyed the opposition into a political career. Rain was trying to recall the politician's name. She made a note to discuss it with Charles. He had been there as well.

"We've yet to wake Dr. Burbank up to greet you all because there is more. Once we found Roy, well, we also learned from home that his wife was pregnant with their first child. Roy's wife gave birth to a baby girl. She is, I think, about three years old or so by now. Folks, this is a seriously sad state of affairs for Dr.

Burbank. On the one hand, we'd all be lost in space or maybe even dead by now, which is highly likely, had he not been here. We owe Roy for what he has done. He also came up with the solution to the sabotaged navigation system that is guiding us on our way currently. More that we owe him.

"But on the other hand, Roy is devastated emotionally. We've had him on suicide watch continuously since we found him. Imagine what he's going through. He will never see his wife again. He will never get to meet his child. This has been a horrific and bizarre string of events."

Rain was floored by the story. Just hearing it brought tears to her eyes. She could hear gasps and whispers, and people saying their own versions of "oh my God" under their breath. The general idea that somebody had done this to the ship and to this poor man was startling and unnerving. It still bothered Rain that she couldn't remember that politician fellow's name. She recalled mostly that he had been a total ass.

"We plan to wake Roy tomorrow morning. I'd ask that you all get to know him and do your best to make him feel like a part of the crew and the mission. He needs something to give him purpose. I'm sending all of you a datafile on Roy's credentials and standard crew information. Get to know it and help this man out. He deserves better than we can give him.

"Alright, that was the hard part. Finally, I guess by now you have all noticed that there are about thirteen more people onboard the ship than when you were briefed before we launched. I'm going to go through the personnel information for each of these crew members one by one and I want you all to meet them today. These brave souls are here to act as our security team once we reach Proxima and set up an embassy there. They will be there to protect you on the ground. In a moment I will have Dr. Jesus brief us on their diplomatic status and mission. Before that, I want to make abundantly clear to all of you on this ship that I am the captain of this ship and Chief Mike Rialto is the top cop on the ship. Mike has top security authority over all matters on the ship. The security crew has no jurisdiction on the ship other than as passengers. I'm making this point to all of you, not the security force; they understand their mission orders. Commander Rogers, the leader of the security detail, has subordinated himself and the security force to Chief Rialto at all times while on the ship. Any matters of security while here, please bring them to Mike. Hopefully, we won't have any such issues. God knows we've had enough trouble already with Gaines and the sabotage.

"Ambassador Jesus, please come up now and brief us on your mission orders," Crosby said. He stepped podium right as Charles approached.

"Thank you, Captain Crosby," Charles started. Rain watched and listened with fascination. So many things had happened while she was asleep. She couldn't believe all that she'd missed.

CHAPTER 41

January 3, 2094 (Earth timeline)
July 28, 2092 (Ship timeline)
approximately 2.122 light-years from Earth
2.122 light-years from Proxima

"Charles, I was thinking about this and I cannot seem to get it out of my head." Rain pointed at the image of the saboteur, Ray Gaines, on the screen in front of them. Rain had a thought in the back of her mind that she had seen that man before. She wasn't sure exactly where, but she knew she had. "So, I went through a lot of video to find this."

"What is this about, Rain?" He sipped at a beverage in his hand as he watched her excitedly flipping through files in front of them on the big screen in the galley.

"That Gaines fellow. We've both seen him before. Many times, actually," Rain said.

"We what?"

"Look here." Rain tapped at some icons in the air around her that only she could see. Then she tossed one of them toward the big screen. "You remember that day that Dr. Luce came on board the *Samaritan* while we were getting ready to leave from lunar dock?"

"I do," Charles Jesus replied.

"Well, I went back and got the video feeds from security at the dock entrance. Look here." She pointed with an arrow icon on the screen. "You see this guy here in the back of Luce's entourage?"

"Yeah, from the looks of it he's wearing a press badge."

"He was. Records show him as Raymond Simms." Rain tapped at the air a bit and then turned back to Charles. "Look, here are the dock airlock records showing his credentials."

"Okay. He was a press guy. So, uh, where are you going with this, Rain?"

"He only appears in this video. Any other video where Luce is on the ship, he's not there. Either he's been edited out, or he wasn't there. He came on the ship but didn't stay with the MEP's tour," Rain said excitedly. "So, I took this picture here from the dock video and enhanced it using some planetary imagery astronomy software on my pad. And voilà!"

"It's Gaines…" Charles said quietly and leaned forward for a closer look, setting his cup down suddenly appearing to lose interest in the drink. "Holy…"

"Ha! I was wondering if you'd say 'Jesus' like the rest of us," Rain joked with him.

"You're not funny, Rain." Still, Charles laughed.

"But you'd be right to have said it. And there's more." Rain tapped some more in the air. "I got to thinking about Luce. You remember how he was such an ass during the UN hearings on whether or not to communicate with Proxima?"

"I do. And he was an ass," Charles agreed.

"Well, I was thinking that the reason I recognized Gaines wasn't because of the tour that Luce did on the ship. No, I recalled it from sometime before that. And I finally figured it out."

"Go on."

"Gaines, or Simms, or whoever he is, was there at the UN summit with Luce. I found him in the background of this press briefing here." She tossed another video on the screen and drew a little red circle around a man in the background behind Luce. "See?"

"I would be hard-pressed to say 'exactly' from this video." Charles sounded apprehensive.

"Well, watch this. Same enhancement algorithm." Rain hit an icon floating before her again and the image zoomed in and enhanced. She then pulled all three images up. "Here's Gaines, Simms, and this person. All three match to be the same face to a ninety-nine point nine eight correlation percentage. It was him."

"I see, Rain. Jesus," Charles said with a raised eyebrow. Rain chuckled.

"Now you're just patronizing me." She laughed. "But it's him. And he was with Luce. I remember seeing Luce talking to him."

"You know. Now that you mention it, I think I do too." Charles sat up straight and turned to face Rain. "We need to show this to the captain and get it sent back home to the right authorities."

"Alright. I'm sending this to you and Crosby."

CHAPTER 42

May 3, 2094 (Earth timeline)
February 2, 2093 (Ship timeline)
approximately 2.25 light-years from Earth
1.87 light-years from Proxima

"Why is it that you're waking me up, CHENG?"

"Sorry, sir." Cindy Mastrano had hated having to wake the captain up again out of cycle. But this required it. She got straight to the point. "Captain, Gaines left us another present."

"What the hell is it this time?" Crosby growled over his orange juice. From the looks of his skin color and the way he attacked the drink, Cindy figured his electrolytes and blood sugar were still extremely low from the cryo.

"The comms from home, well, something is scrambling them," the CHENG explained. "We've tracked it down from antenna-to-screen and can't figure out how and where it is happening."

"Wait, you mean our communications from home are scrambled?" Crosby asked.

"Yes. We've spent two weeks trying to isolate and repair the problem. We even replaced all the modules with the spares," Cindy said. "Nothing is working. We can see the signal plain as day on the spectrum analyzer, but it is encrypted to hell and gone. Without a key, I doubt we ever decrypt it."

"When was the last data that we could read?"

"Just after the midpoint physicals. It's like he knew when we'd all be asleep and not looking," Cindy said. "If he somehow got this embedded in all the spares and components, which it looks like he did, we'd have to build a completely new comm system to fix this."

"Do we have the materials to fix it?" Crosby asked.

"I don't know, maybe, but..."

"Well, spit it out, Cindy."

"I don't think so."

"Son of a bitch!"

"Yes, sir. I agree."

CHAPTER 43

November 28, 2099 (Earth timeline)
November 26, 2096 (Ship timeline)
approximately 4.14 light-years from Earth
0.1 light-years from Proxima

Captain Crosby had been awake for the last three months. It had been his plan all along to be on the last awake team as they made their final approach to the Proxima system. For those three months he and Bob Roca had been studying over the last unscrambled data from the SGLT and from the telescope and sensor systems onboard the *Samaritan*. All of the imagery of the system and data from astronomers from Proxima led them to the conclusion that there were at least seven planets there of appreciable size. There were no gas giants, as was expected from the red dwarf star. Proxima b was right where it was supposed to be at about 7.5 million kilometers from the star. It looked to be right at 1.17 times the mass of the Earth and it was slightly inclined in its orbit about the star by a little more than a couple of degrees. The eccentricity of the planet's orbit was about 0.3, causing it to be in what was known as a spin-resonance orbit. The planet took about eleven days to orbit its star and had a day that lasted about twenty-two Earth days, which was confusing because the planet actually rotated about its axis once every seven and a half days.

Crosby focused on the details that were important, not the orbital mechanics per se, but more of the practical knowledge. Day and night on Proxima b were about twenty-two Earth days each. A Proxima b solar year was about eleven Earth days long. There was more. There were two small moons orbiting Proxima b that were roughly the size of Phobos and Deimos orbiting Mars back home. The nearest planet, Proxima d, was actually about half the distance closer to Proxima and was small and rocky, about a third the mass of Earth. Farther out, at about one and a half the distance of the Earth from Sol, was a very large super Earth-type planet astronomers had called Proxima c. It was about seven times the mass of Earth. It had several moons.

"Captain Crosby, medical here." Crosby tapped at a control on his chair. He looked out the viewscreen as they approached through the system from its Oort Cloud. They had actually done it. They were literally entering another star system far away from home. 4.244 light-years away from home.

"Crosby here, Doc. Go ahead," he said.

"The last of the cryobeds has been cycled," Kopylova told him over the comm net.

"Understood, Doc. When Dr. Burbank is able, tell him to report to the bridge."

"Affirmative, Captain. Medical out."

"Bob, is there liquid water anywhere else in the system?" Crosby watched as Roca zoomed through various spectrographs, images, and particle sensors. "What about methane ices or carbon dioxide ices?"

"This is a fairly rocky system, Captain. I think we'll be better off mining for gold than for water," Roca replied. "But there might be some water in places on the Proxima c or its moons. If it is tidally active there might be volcanic activity under the surface heating some of the ice."

"Maybe we should get Gilster and Shavers doing some astronomy and analysis on the system once we get settled in. Maybe they can help us with that," Crosby thought aloud. "How about the other rocky planets farther out? Anything useful?"

"Without doing magnetometry and/or ground penetrating radar, Cap'n, I couldn't really say. Maybe as we fly closer in, we might use the four Earth masses planet way out here as a fly-by to bleed off some of our velocity vector. We could do some radar analysis then."

"How long will that take, Bob?"

"Probably like a day?"

"Let's do that. In fact, let's do a complete system survey of every planet from the seventh one in. We'll take this next two weeks getting to know the system. Also, we'll start an open near-real-time dialogue with the Proximans before we just show up in orbit around their planet saying, 'Take us to your leader.'" Crosby laughed. "I'd rather take this slow."

"As you wish, Captain. I'll work up the best trajectory for maximum survey."

"Get Gilster and Shavers on that too. They're the two astrophysics experts on the team," Crosby ordered. "What's the use in having a science team if we don't put them to work?"

"On it, sir."

"Captain Crosby to Dr. Maggie Oliveira-Santos." Crosby tapped the icons for ship-wide communication.

"Hello, Captain. Maggie here."

"Could you please report to the bridge, Doctor?"

"Certainly, sir. Is it urgent or can I finish up with lunch?" Crosby muttered under his breath how the damned scientists didn't understand ship protocols. When a captain asked for something done, dammit, he wanted something done. But, hell, Crosby had a crew of eggheads who weren't space vets. He had to recall that almost every single time he dealt with them. He was beginning to recall why he had them all sleep most of the way there.

"Dr. Oliveira-Santos, finish your lunch, but report to the bridge as soon as you can following that," he said begrudgingly.

"Aye aye, Captain," the linguistics expert responded jovially.

"Crosby out." He looked up and noticed Roca staring at him bewildered. "You have something to add, Mr. Roca?"

"Um, no, Cap'n, nothing at all." Roca turned and kept his mouth shut.

"Bob, as soon as Santos gets here, have her wait ten minutes. I'll be in my ready room twiddling my damned thumbs. Then come get me," Crosby said. "See if she gets the damned point."

CHAPTER 44

December 8, 2099 (Earth timeline)
December 8, 2099 (Ship timeline reset to Earth)
approximately 4.24 light-years from Earth
0 light-years from Proxima

"Captain Crosby of Earth!" the face of a very old female Proximan said. The video was very primitive and low resolution. "It is so wonderful to make your acquaintance. I am Secretary General Balfine Arctinier, the chief executive of Fintidier, which you call Proxima b. The representative governors of our lands have appointed me to make first real-time contacts with our brethren from the stars. Our astronomers tell us you are approximately twenty-five of your minutes away by signal speed. While we appreciate your first communication being in our primary language, that will not be necessary.

"In the ten years that you have been along your way to us, we have mandated worldwide training in your language. You call it English. We welcome you to our system and await further communications with you and your great ship. We are calling upon all of our governors to meet at our preplanned landing facility. We have been anxiously awaiting your arrival for a very long time and cannot wait to meet you in person. Attached to this communication are safety and quarantine protocols our various communities have agreed to. Please familiarize yourself with these protocols. We have time to discuss before your arrival. We look forward to hearing your next communication."

✧   ✧   ✧

"Alright, Zhao. Bring us to an orbit geostationary with the prescribed landing spot," Crosby ordered. Ming Zhao sat in the pilot's seat and was literally driving the *Samaritan*. Crosby waited as the ship slowed into geosynchronous orbit about forty thousand kilometers above the planet. "XO, sound the microgravity alert."

"Aye!" the XO replied. "All hands, all hands. Prepare for acceleration all-stop and microgravity. Take microgravity stations now. Repeat. All hands, all hands, prepare for microgravity now, now, now."

"Alright, Zhao, start a five-minute countdown to all-stop and make it happen," Crosby said.

"Aye sir," Zhao replied. "Roger, Captain. We are approaching forty-one-thousand-kilometer altitude over the landing spot. I have us slowing in a spiral that will end in five minutes with a final orbital relative velocity of about three point five kilometers per second. Countdown clock is ticking and trajectory course is laid in and activated."

"Good, Zhao. I guess now we just ride it down. Hope none of you ate a big breakfast this morning." Crosby could already feel the effects of the lower gravity. The ship had been at very low acceleration for a couple of weeks now and they were about to drop to no acceleration to speak of. The ship would be as "weightless" as they were in lunar dock. They hadn't been weightless for a long while now and that was going to take a bit of adjustment. He half expected the scientist crew to be deathly sick by the end of the afternoon.

"Captain, I have the landing zone on high-resolution imagery if you want to see it," Roca said from the astronav station.

"On viewer, Bob."

"Aye." Bob grabbed at something in the air before him and made a tossing motion toward the front and main data screen.

The screen in front of the bridge dome switched to an area on a small continent at the equator of the planet Fintidier. Crosby guessed that the continent was not much larger than Iceland or the United Kingdom and it appeared to be, for the most part, uninhabited. The land looked green with a large peak in the middle that suggested volcanic activity. The only inhabited area was the pinpoint marked as the landing zone. Over the past ten or so years since they had left Earth the Proximans had been building up a safe uninhabited location for the Earthlings to land with minimal exposure to the Proximans. Crosby realized that now that they were there and that the Proximans had started speaking English, it was only right for Earthlings to start referring to Proxima b as Fintidier. He wasn't quite sure how the Proximans, or Fintidierians, decided to spell the name of their planet. To him, when he heard the aliens pronounce the name, it sounded more French than English. Had he been asked to spell it he might have spelled more like Fintideeyay. Maybe it was Cajun, he thought, and the people were Fintidayans. He wasn't a linguist and he didn't really give a damn.

There were a few buildings and lights about. It was nighttime currently over the landing zone and would be for another eleven days or so. Not that it really mattered since the star Proxima—which the locals called Finti, according to their protocols package—was a red dwarf and the peak of the light spectrum was in the infrared not the visible. Even during midday on Fintidier the light level was about that of twenty minutes before dusk or after dawn—in other words, very low visible light. In expectation of this, multiple types of starlight, low light, and infrared vision enhancement systems had been brought along. All of the landing party teams would have special low-light contact lenses issued to them as well as infrared glasses.

"Captain, we're in position and cutting the engine in thirty seconds," Zhao alerted him.

"Good. Bob, as soon as Zhao can take his hands off the wheel, you two work us out a landing party deorbit plan," Crosby said.

"Roger that," Roca replied.

"Captain." Victor Tarasenko entered the stoop of the bridge just outside the main door, but inside the security door by the down ladder. "Permission to enter the bridge?"

"Yes Mr. Tarasenko, please." Crosby waved him in. "How can I help you?"

"Captain, I've been conducting intelligence, surveillance, and reconnaissance as we approached—all using our passive instrumentation. I'd like to suggest an active radar mapping of the planet as well as using the particle counters to look for terrestrial gamma ray sources." Tarasenko shuffled the magnetic sneakers against the deck plates to keep his balance in the ever-decreasing microgravity. He stopped about a meter from the captain's chair and kept his shoes locked onto the floor.

"I'm not sure how the, Prox...uh, Fintidierians will like us actively pinging their planet without asking," Crosby replied to the Russian signal intelligence expert.

"They will not detect our digital radar, Captain Crosby. I have been paying very close attention to the signals-technology levels on the planet. They do not have digital capabilities and have yet to understand spread spectrum. If we use our modern low-power digital spectrum hopping radar systems with multipass filters they'll never even know we had them on. And I think we should verify that they have been telling us the truth about themselves."

"Very well, do what you need to do, but don't get me into some interstellar diplomatic concern. Hell, Ambassador Jesus should be here and involved in all this. XO!" He turned to Artur's station.

"On it, sir!" The XO switched about some virtual icons. "Ambassador Jesus to the bridge. Ambassador Jesus to the bridge."

"While you're at it, Artur, get Commander Rogers up here too."

"Aye sir!"

"Captain! Engine all-stop in six, five, four, three, two, one, all stop," Zhao reported. Crosby suddenly felt his stomach floating. He choked it back down.

"Great work, Zhao." Crosby flipped a channel open. "CHENG, this is Crosby."

"Aye, Captain?" Cindy Mastrano replied over the comm channel.

"Pilot says we're all-stop and no more corrections needed. You are free to begin Samara Drive all-stop protocols and repairs. I want this ship ready to move as soon as you can get it so."

"I'm on it, Captain. Anything else?"

"Nope. Crosby out."

"The first thing we need to do, Captain, is to have Chief Walker and Colonel Ping take the OSAMs and drop our ISR"—intelligence, surveillance, and reconnaisance devices—"our comm relay, and global positioning satellites into low Earth—uh, Fintidier?—orbit. I guess that's a new acronym, LFO instead of LEO; doesn't roll off the tongue as well, sir." Rogers walked through the steps they needed to follow before making first contact with the Fintidierian people in person. Landing with an entire complement of civilians on an alien planet was all new to everyone. Rogers had been given the mission of making it happen safely and without creating an interstellar incident—honestly, it was Ambassador Jesus's job to keep diplomatic incidents from happening. Rogers just had to keep them safe so they could do it.

"Right. LFO." Crosby thought it was in good humor. "Walker and Ping, take the Orbit and Surface Access Modules. Are the payloads prepared and ready for deployment?"

"We've been awake for a month, Captain. SEALs don't like boredom."

"Good. I guess." Crosby laughed. He wasn't actually used to military on his ships. He was a corporate spaceman. "Okay. You deploy the satellites. Then what?"

"We bring the sats online and collect data for several orbits. We have thirty-two birds so a day should be enough to give us a good mapping and topography data as well as all the signals intel that Tarasenko could ever want. It will take a couple of days for the global positioning systems to settle in to high resolution, but we should get meter resolution within a few hours." Rogers was starting to feel a bit queasy from the microgravity and was doing his best to clench his abdominal muscles and work his jaw to help. He'd been on naval ships at sea thousands of hours and never had problems. He'd only had a few hundred hours in microgravity and they were never his favorite. "Then, we can make our planetary descent to the designated location. Once we are certain it is safe and secure, the scientists and other crew can start settling in."

"Alright. Let's make this happen. Get your first landing party ready to drop first thing day after tomorrow." Crosby moved a couple icons about in front of him. Rogers just stood at ease with his magnetic shoes holding him in place. He continued to clench his jaw as he thought he was on the verge of getting space sick. "Are Walker and Ping ready to go?"

"Yes sir."

"Then don't wait on me to tell you to go. Go," Crosby told him. "And Mike..."

"Captain?"

"Go get a micrograv patch from medical. We can't have you tossing your cookies all over the ship."

"Yes, Captain."

"In fact, have your whole team do it."

"On it."

"Go."

CHAPTER 45

December 10, 2099 (Earth timeline)
December 10, 2099 (Ship timeline reset to Earth)
approximately 4.24 light-years from Earth
0 light-years from Proxima, aka Fintidier

"As soon as we land, everybody exits the shuttle as quickly as possible. Ingress and egress are the most vulnerable points of operations. While we don't expect hostilities, we've also never been here before. So, we're going to move forward with each step, expecting hostilities until further notice. I want the drones immediately deployed the second we crack the door. Our first footpaths will be checked by the drones for anything unusual: booby traps, tripwires, and so on. While we don't expect to have issues here and this is expected to be a cordial invitation, we're not taking any chances. We are doing a complete sweep before letting the rest of the crew drop down."

Commander Rogers swiped to the next image. A path was highlighted in light green from the landing zone, marked LZ, toward the objective location for the Tactical Operations Center, marked TOC. He marked several positions with red X's and continued talking.

"You will take cover at this point here by the entrance to the quarantine housing unit. We move to this specific building here in the quarantine quarters at full pace. Intel and Ord teams will all sit tight right there until my team completes sweep and clear. At that point, we'll call in you specialists to sweep the quarters for transmitters, CBRN"—chemical, biological, radiological, or nuclear hazards—"of any sort, and any other forms of INTs"—intelligence collection devices—"or hidden surprises. We're doing this with Mission-Oriented Protective Posture Environment suits until the bio teams approve the atmosphere for standard uniform. Nobody removes the MOPP-E—and I mean nobody—or cracks a face shield until bio gives the all clear." Commander Rogers paused and scanned the hangar bay. All eyes were on him and paying close attention.

His plans all along had been to drop in, sweep the area, check it for hazards and eavesdropping, and then bring in the first wave of crew. He knew that the scientists were all very eager to get off the spaceship as soon as possible, but he had been sent there to keep them safe and he figured if all those people waited seven effective years to get here, a few hours more wouldn't kill them. If he skipped those few hours it might get them killed. And he wasn't going to let that happen on his watch.

"Victor, you have any details from the ISR you want to fill us in on?" Rogers turned to the Russian intelligence expert.

"Nothing particularly interesting, Commander Rogers. Being at nighttime here is best for infrared sweeps and we have identified zero persons thus far on this continent as has been expressed by their leadership. There are some local animals we've detected, only one of which seems large enough to be of predatorial concern," Tarasenko explained. He switched the data-screen view to show a different area of the map. "Also, there are no signals here either. The area is completely radio silent unless the Fintidierians make contact. The area is fairly quiet from ambient radio. We might pick up some of their old amplitude modulation radio broadcasts as they do have an ample ionosphere. Which reminds me, the planet has a strong magnetic pole oriented even closer to geographical north than on Earth. Old-school compasses will work well here."

Tarasenko swiped the slide to the next one and pointed out a couple of locations. One in particular he circled and spent more time on.

"All the power for the facility appears to be coming from this location, here. It is the only main heat source anywhere. It appears to be a geothermal vent that is running three turbines. By my estimation, the thermal vents are supplying roughly twenty kilowatts of power, which is being transferred via these large power lines here leading to this building. I suspect those lines are carrying power from the geothermal turbines to charge a battery bank that must be inside. Multiple lines then run from this building underground across the complex. I am guessing that this is how all the lighting and other systems here are powered. What you might have noticed from the images is that the lighting is very dim."

"I caught that, Vic." Rogers nodded.

"The Fintidierians have different eyesight, I believe. Having evolved in predominantly infrared light, they must see farther into the IR than we do and less of the visible. Contact lenses will be required until we get some of our own lighting in place," Victor added. "And I would recommend that security teams maintain their IR contacts while on duty."

"Understood," Rogers said. "Anything else?"

"Nyet."

"Very good. Dr. Ash, as soon as we get in place, you start the electric infrastructure. I say we take down a couple of our own generators so we aren't dependent on the Fintidierians."

"I have three one-hundred-kilowatt fission generators loaded and ready. Also, we've got a complete tactical operations center compliment of Wi-Fi, uplink/downlink equipment, Vic and I have put a package of sensors together, and Chief Jones and I have a bag of goodies with us in case things go sideways," replied Dr. Carol Ash, the New Zealand Special Forces war machine subject matter expert.

"Master Chief Jones, what about medical?"

"We have a full combat field kit packed as well as about three pallets' worth of gear that Doctors Kopylova and Thomaskutty had prepackaged as the first field hospital gear. We'll take it and find a place to set it up. The map that the Fintidierians sent us show this building here on the southwestern side of the runway to be a hospital ward. We'll check it and see if it makes sense to be a hospital or not."

"Petty Officer Third Class Visser?"

"Aye?"

"Once we're down and unloading, you and PO1 Slater will take the ATVs and the drones and maintain perimeter. Understood?"

"Hooyay!"

"Alright, then. We're good to go. Let's move out."

CHAPTER 46

December 10, 2099 (Earth timeline)
Proxima b, aka Fintidier

"Air quality is clean." Master Chief Petty Officer Havier Jones looked at the air-quality device and pointed out the all-green indicators. "All greens. No CBRN, nothing. Little less nitrogen than Earth but not much. Trace gasses about the same. There are some pollen spores and other biologicals, but they seem to be inert according to the instruments."

"Great, Chief. So, we can remove MOPP-E?" Commander Mike Rogers asked.

"Yep."

"Alright." Mike used some eye movements to click on the open comm channel. "Away team, Master Chief Jones has cleared us to breathe the air. MOPP-E can be removed. Standard combat-ready uniforms, and civilian away team is authorized from here on. Anything else, Chief?"

"Nope. If we're good here, Mike, I'm going to start setting up the hospital."

"Good idea." Mike switched channels. "Visser, anything to report on the perimeter?"

"No, Mike. Drones should be sending you feeds now. Zeke and I have it covered by patrolling on the ATVs, but this complex is pretty big. We need to put up some fences or get some more guys," PO3 Daniel Visser replied.

"Copy that. Keep the drones on it. We'll start pulling the feeds here at the TOC." Mike turned to Lieutenant Commander

Geni Holland, who was on her back underneath a table they'd moved into place and was routing cables between instrument panels. "Geni, as soon as you get that done, pull up the drones."

"Sure thing, Mike. Hey, could you hand me that wire stripper on the end of the table...no, the one on the right side," she replied.

"Here." Mike dropped it down to her and then slipped off his MOPP-E headgear. "I might have to break out a jacket. What do you think it is, ten or twelve degrees C?"

"My AI says it's eleven point five." Geni crawled out from underneath the table. Her muscular frame moved fluidly. She pulled the MOPP-E headgear and dropped it beside her, running a fingerless gloved hand through her three-centimeter-long bleached blond hair. "Don't be such a wuss. It isn't that cold."

"Let's run the list." Mike sat down in a metal chair the Fintidierians had provided. "Perimeter, check. Hospital, check. All buildings have been cleared and sniffed, check. Tactical Operations Center is almost up and running, check. I think we're good here."

"You asking or telling, Mike? Hard to tell." Geni dragged a heavy metal chair across the concrete floor next to him. The chair *screeched* with a high enough pitch that Mike's skin crawled.

"Neither. Both." Mike hesitated for second. "How much longer do you need here?"

"About..." Geni tapped at several virtual icons and then depressed a couple of keys on a keyboard on the table. "...that long. TOC command systems are operational."

"Good. Have Martin, Henry, and Maksutov got the high-gain antenna in place yet?" he asked.

"Let's see." Geni turned and activated one of the new monitor screens she'd just put into place. The screen came online quickly. After a moment or so of her moving icons about, Mike could see a spectrum analyzer screen with a waterfall chart beginning. "There's the *Samaritan*'s beacon from the low-gain antenna, and... yep...feed is good. High gain is up and running."

"Great. Open a channel."

"Done."

"*Samaritan*, this is Proxima One, do you copy?" Mike could see his transmission on the spectrum waterfall jump up and down as he spoke.

"Copy you loud and clear, Commander," the XO's voice replied.

"We're good to go down here. You can start bringing down the crew at your leisure."

"Great news! We've got a bunch of space-sick eggheads up here wanting some solid ground under their feet."

"Copy that. Proxima One out." Mike leaned back in the chair and relaxed a bit. "Damn, I'm out of breath."

"All of us are. We're at about one point one Earth gravities here and we've been on the ship at a little less than a gee for years. We'll have to get back in shape, Mike," Geni agreed with him. "I wonder if the Proximans, uh, Fintidierians have barbells and such."

"We'll make do if not." Mike looked around the concrete-block building they'd chosen for the command center. "It looks like they have plenty of concrete on this planet. We can always make forms in the sand and pour some plates."

"Speaking of sand, Mike, we're only about five kilometers from the beach here. We should check out the ocean. I mean, are there alien shark monsters, or can we go swimming and fishing?" Geni laughed. "We need to figure out more about what is safe on this planet and what isn't."

"We need a guide. As soon as we get situated and through our two-week quarantine, I'm sure the Fintidierians will provide us with one."

"Right." She looked as if something had alerted her and then started swatting at icons only she could see. "Drones just connected. We've got eyes in the sky now."

"Good. What about the sats?"

"Still handshaking. Give it another minute or two; there might not be one directly overhead. The constellations give us a ten-second refresh," Geni said.

"Use the *Samaritan* as the channel. It should always have line of sight with several of the birds," Mike said.

"Are you bucking for my job, Commander?" Geni smiled at him but from the tapping away she was doing, Mike was certain she was implementing his suggestion. "There. Satellite constellation feed is online. We have a full-up operational TOC command center here."

"Well, we'll want to get more permanent perimeter cams and motion trackers out, but I'm going to take a breather right now."

"Looks like the other OSAM just dropped from the ship. We'll have people here soon." Geni pulled up a view of the air traffic system. "Look here, there are, I guess, aircraft flying about on the other main continents. They're slow."

"Remember, these people are like early 1900s to maybe 1950s. Fossil-fuel, propeller-type vehicles. How'd we ever manage that?" Mike reached out in front of him and opened up a window from the drones' lidar maps and had it overlay the complex map given to them from the Fintidierians. "Hobbs?"

"Yes, Mike?" his AI responded.

"Pull up the personnel roster for the *Samaritan* and let's start finding them living quarters based on this map."

"Right away, Mike."

CHAPTER 47

December 13, 2099 (Earth timeline)
Proxima b, aka Fintidier

Roy was a spaceship design, build, and test systems engineer. He wasn't a colonist, an explorer, a geneticist, or, for that matter, anything that this mission particularly needed. But he didn't want to spend another minute on that damned spaceship if he didn't have to. He'd pressed Captain Crosby to let him go down on one of the first OSAMs. Crosby had agreed to the third one. By the time he'd gotten to the base, Proxima One they were calling it—Roy laughed at how unimaginative that was—he was afraid all the good living spots would be taken. As it turned out, that wasn't the case at all.

The Fintidierians had built a complex designed for hundreds, not tens, of people. In fact, Roy wasn't so sure that there wasn't room for thousands there. He was given a choice of one of twenty different living spaces. They were all the same and lined up in street blocks on a perfect grid with streets between them that were wide enough for what the aliens considered automobiles. They were amusing versions of fossil-fuel vehicles. Roy was glad they'd brought their own transportation from Earth. Several electric six-seater all-terrain vehicles had already been brought down from the ship. More were on the way.

The living-quarter buildings were single-story, ten-meter-by-ten-meter concrete-block buildings with what appeared to be some type of petroleum-based roofing material. They were all painted a dull gray color and the roofing was as close to obsidian black as possible. Roy just randomly picked one of the unclaimed quarters on a street corner. He figured that way, he'd only ever have one neighbor to deal with. Each living-quarter building had a small front "yard" covered in sand about ten meters deep between the roadway and the door with a single sidewalk leading to the front door. There was an equal space behind each house with a small chest-high privacy fence made of some type of wood. There was about ten meters between each house down the street.

Inside was very nondescript. The buildings were bare block buildings with electricity and running water. In the kitchen area there was a box resembling a refrigerator and a stovetop. Roy realized that he was going to have to ask for a microwave system. The furniture looked a lot like that from old black-and-white movies from the previous century. He guessed that the Fintidierians had used the movies as references for building the complex and furnishing them. There was a bathroom and two bedrooms. The only bit of color in the entire quarters was a single painting-sized picture hung over the couch in the living area. The picture was of what must have been one of the metropolitan cities on the planet.

Roy sat the holoprojector on the alien's excuse for a coffee table and activated it. The image of his two-year-old daughter looked back at him. Roy thought that she'd have to be pushing ten by now. He was so far behind on the data from home and all that data was scrambled and he couldn't see it. He ached to know the status of his family, even a four-year-old one. But that asshole, Gaines, had seen to it that he couldn't even keep up with his wife and daughter's life. He wanted to watch her grow. And for now, he couldn't even do that.

He had taken it on as his job to build a radio telescope system so that they could receive the signals from home. He'd identified most of what he needed, but some of the parts would have to be constructed from base materials. There were some chips he might be able to "salvage" but they were all in critical systems. He had spoken to Dr. Gilster about it and the two of them had taken that project on headfirst. They had found a suitable location on the complex map. They had identified how they planned to build the components. But they were still weeks away from completion. Honestly, they'd yet to even start.

He looked at the case of issued things from the *Samaritan*.

He wasn't in the mood to unpack yet. He opened a beverage and plopped onto the couch breathing hard, and realized that he needed to get acclimated to gravity again.

"Nigel," he said. "Play the latest letter from home."

"Right away, Roy."

CHAPTER 48

December 27, 2099 (Earth timeline)
Proxima b, aka Fintidier

Ambassador Charles Jesus stood at the edge of the runway a few steps in front of the entirety of the ground team of the Proxima One basecamp that had been provided by the Proximans before their arrival. He was flanked by Captain Crosby and the rest of the flight crew of the *Samaritan* to his right—for this brief moment, only, would Crosby allow the *Samaritan* to be put on auto-AI-pilot and be crewless. At all other times, there had always been a minimum of three flight crew members aboard the ship. It had usually been Cindy and the techs who were doing much-needed maintenance and upkeep.

The SEALs and the rest of the international security force were to his left. Behind them were all of the various scientists. In all, forty-two humans from Earth stood waiting to meet in person—for the first time ever in the history of humanity—aliens from another planet. Of course, the Earthlings weren't on Earth, and the aliens looked very human, but that didn't matter. Today was the day for first contact between two alien races from different worlds and Charles intended it to go right.

"There it is." Artur pointed in the star-filled sky. "That thing is loud."

"Old fossil-fuel engines were loud," Crosby added knowingly. "It has some fairly bright lights on it. How do you imagine they know where they are going?"

"Maybe radio navigation," Victor Tarasenko replied.

"Or the stars and geography," Roca added.

"They just flew across an ocean!" someone else among the group said. Charles didn't turn to see who it was.

"Not really," Tarasenko corrected them. "There is a naval vessel off the coast about one hundred kilometers that acts as a landing platform. I have great satellite and drone imagery of them if you'd like to see."

"There're two more of them! Smaller ones." One of the physicists pointed. The name in Charles's contacts was Dr. Tasneem Faruq, a South African theoretical physicist. While Charles had met them all, he was still learning all their names and backgrounds. The virtual display through his contacts was especially useful in that regards.

"Fighter escort," the retired Space Force Chief Warrant Officer 5 Joni Walker replied. The bubble over her head when she spoke told Charles that she had expertise in spacecraft construction and repair, power and nuclear technologies, space and exo-terrestrial construction, and was a pilot.

"Commander Rogers, is there anything we should know about it?" Charles asked.

"Vic?" Commander Rogers nodded to the Russian intelligence systems expert.

"There are seven passengers in the midsection. It looks as if there are three pilots in the cockpit section. No surprises otherwise. Magnetic sensors, quantum ghost imagers, ultrasound, and penetrating radar suggest that they do have large metallic components with them."

"Probably guns of some type," Rogers said. "Ambassador, we'd expect them to be armed. We are."

"Makes sense. But let's make sure we don't need to use them, right?" Charles said.

"Yes sir," Rogers replied. "I hope the only need for them is to show that we have them."

"Right," Crosby grunted in agreement. "Rialto, make sure your firearm is visible at your side."

"Right, Captain," Mike Rialto, the chief of security for the *Samaritan*, replied.

"The other two vehicles?" Charles asked. "What about them?"

"The CW5 is right," Victor continued. "Fighter escorts. I'd say very similar to early World War Two technologies. Looks like wing-mounted combustion-powered guns. Those things under the wings aren't bombs. They're fuel tanks. I suspect they are added for the long trip across the ocean here. The carriers they have are off shore over a hundred kilometers."

"I guess they are taking the isolation overly serious," Crosby said.

"Not a bad idea," Dr. Sindi Thomaskutty, ship's second M.D. and pathologist, added. "Considering we have no idea what they are afflicted with. And we might have a cold virus that could wipe them out. Although we've checked everyone thoroughly."

"Fighter escort makes sense if that's some big dignitary," Rogers noted.

"Right," Charles agreed.

They all stood pretty much motionless and watched as the alien propeller-driven aircraft approached them. The two smaller craft peeled off into an orbit above the runway and maintained positions there in a large elliptical track around the complex. The larger passenger vehicle approached and grew louder and louder. As it got closer lights lining each side of the runway self-illuminated. On Earth they would have been bright and blue. But these lights were a dull red and didn't seem very bright at all in the visible. The contact lenses they were all wearing enhanced the visual spectrum making the lights seem much brighter. Clearly, the runway lights were designed by humans who evolved to see farther into the infrared portion of the light spectrum.

The big, noisy, metal-winged vehicle rocked and buffeted due to slight crosswinds and appeared to be turned a bit sideways like a crab walking. Then just as it neared the surface at the end of the runway it immediately straightened itself and flared its nose upward. The vehicle appeared to almost float in the air as it sank slowly to the concrete and then it bounced to ground at the end of the runway twice before all of its wheels stayed on the surface. The vehicle was traveling faster than it had appeared to be while in the air and screamed past them at over a hundred and fifty kilometers per hour. Then it slowed significantly in bursts at first accompanied by loud metal-on-metal screeching sounds. Then it slowed more steadily finally coming to a halt after braking the three sets of eight large, what appeared to be black rubber, wheels. The noisy and quite smelly behemoth then started to roll toward them, turning itself in the direction from which it had just come. Once it reached the taxiway nearest the Earthlings it stopped and the engines motivating the propellers chirped and then belched white smoke out from around their cowlings, followed by very loud explosive bangs. As the engines cut out the two smaller aircraft approached together only a few meters apart and landed much more quietly and gracefully, pulling into a stop position not far from the passenger vehicle.

"That's quite a show. I've never seen anything like that," Charles overheard a female voice behind him that he didn't have to use his contacts to identify. He'd known her long enough and recognized the voice as Rain Gilster's. He turned with a schoolboy's grin and agreed.

"I've seen them in movies, but never been to an old airshow to see one in person," Charles said.

"Can you imagine how exhilarating it must be to ride in one of those things?" Yoko Pearl exclaimed.

"Exhilarating? Hell, scary must be more like it," Dr. Renaud said. "And how *loud* must it be inside one of those things?"

"Hold it down, everyone," Rogers ordered. "Something is happening. Team on the ready."

There was another metal-on-metal screeching sound that made Charles think the first technology he wanted to bring to this planet was modern synthetic dry lubricants and seals. The large rectangular hatch on the side of the vehicle facing them popped and hissed as it opened and started slowly descending to the ground as if held up by hydraulic compression cylinders. As the hatch door lowered it became clear that there were steps on it rather than a ramp as Charles had been expecting. He wasn't sure why he'd been expecting a smooth ramp rather than steps, but he had been. His surprise to the difference was very self-amusing. What an opportunity to see things from a completely different perspective, he thought. Everything was alien and that excited him.

"Steps, hmmm." Somebody from behind him must have had the same thought. He didn't recognize the voice and didn't bother to turn to get an AI ID tag. Oh, he could have just asked his AI subvocally or with pull-down menus but he wasn't really concerned about it that much.

After a moment or so two men wearing dull gray uniforms, black boots, and hats that looked most like French-style burgundy-colored berets walked down the stairs shoulder to shoulder, taking up posts at the bottom with what appeared to rifles held at the ready position across their chests. There was something about the fashion of the uniforms that looked familiar, but Charles couldn't quite place it.

"Looks like standard guard protocols," Rogers said quietly to Charles and Captain Crosby. Then with his head on a swivel he whispered to his team subvocally, "Eyes open, team. Vic, the fighter pilots are likely soldiers. Get me some INT data on them."

"On it, Mike." The Russian intel specialist started swiping his hands about before him at virtual icons only he could see.

Two women, who looked to Charles like they might be in their late thirties or early forties, wearing burgundy-colored button-up dress jackets over noticeably short skirts came down the steps next and walked about five meters, stopped and separated, and then took station facing each other on either side of the aircraft steps like the guards did. As far as Charles could tell the two women were not carrying any weapons. He wasn't quite sure where they would hide them as their skirts were just that short. One of them held up a device about the size of handheld datapad, but thicker, and it had a small rod protruding from the top of it. The woman said something into the device.

"Radio transmission," Victor Tarasenko alerted everyone quietly. "That's a radio device. Spectrum analyzer has it around eighty megahertz."

"Can you tell what they are saying?" Charles asked.

"No. It's in their language," Victor replied. "I haven't set up my intel dashboard with a translator app yet."

"Can you pipe it to me?" Dr. Oliveira-Santos asked.

"Dah. Hold on a minute." Victor waved his hands about his head in front of him quickly and moved some virtual icons about. He tapped twice at the air and then nodded at her. Then in Russian he said, "Tanya, please transmit audio to Dr. Oliveira-Santos's AI."

Tarasenko's AI replied something to him in Russian and then Dr. Oliveira-Santos nodded that she was receiving the signal. Most modern AI systems not only could connect through contacts, but also ear implants for audible signals. There were new direct-to-mind implants being experimented with but none had been approved for use yet at the time they'd left Earth. She tapped at various virtual icons in front of her and then whispered something to herself.

"There. I'm activating the translation algorithm and sending it to each of you for visual captioning. Just tap the icon if you want to read what they are saying. If you want audible, it's in the pull-down menu," she explained.

Charles immediately tapped the icon before him and set it to quiet mode and captions only. Suddenly, each time one of the individuals spoke in the alien tongue the translation appeared in a speaking bubble graphic above their heads in his field of view.

"...the ambassador is safe to egress the vehicle..." he read over the woman on the right side of the steps.

"Alright, here we go, folks." Charles straightened up and took a deep breath. "Smile, everyone, just don't look like a lion smiling before he eats his prey."

"And for God's sake, don't look like the prey." Crosby giggled but then quickly regained his composure. "Sorry about that."

A much older woman, wearing black robes like the style seen in the first images the astronomers had received from Proxima veiled about her and over her head, began slowly making her way down the steps of the aircraft. Two men on either side of her, wearing what appeared to be black business suits with white collared button-up dress shirts and black ties, helped her down carefully. The men were even wearing tie clips with some sort of flag on them but they were too far away to make out.

Charles wasn't quite sure how to estimate the older woman's age as people on Earth now lived much longer than they did back when fossil-fuel-based propulsion was the norm. He was guessing maybe a hundred and ten Earth years old, but he also suspected he could be off as much as forty years. He was beginning to realize just how primitive in comparison this culture was and how little humanity from Earth could recall from an age similar in their history. That was only a hundred and fifty years ago or so. Charles considered how different a culture a hundred and fifty years more advanced than Earth's might appear to them. Frightening was his most likely answer.

"Their clothing is very similar to Earth fashions of the turn of the millennium." DR. RAHEEM RAMASHANDRA: HISTORIAN, POPULAR CULTURE AND FUTURISM STUDIES EXPERT, HISTORY OF TECHNOLOGY EXPERT appeared over him when Charles turned to look and see who'd said that.

"What do you mean, Doctor?" Charles asked.

"It would appear that other than the older woman, except for her shoes, they are Earthly fashion, all of them are wearing Earth-style clothing from around the year 2000 or so. I'm sending you all comparison images now," Dr. Ramashandra explained. After a couple of hand movements in the air he continued, "There, look at these comparisons."

"Amazing," Charles said. "Why that period?"

"Did women actually wear skirts that short to work?" Dr. Carrie Shavers, astrogeologist and planetary astronomer, asked.

"According to this image here they did." Ramashandra sent them a still picture of a very slender woman wearing a very short dress skirt, white button-up blouse with a large collar, and a buttoned dress coat over it. "This is from a popular television show of the time. The woman, Ally McBeal, I think it was, was supposed to be a high-priced attorney in Boston. This was what was considered highly fashionable for business professionals of the era."

"That's it!" Rain said loud enough that one of the guards leading the elder woman actually looked up. "Sorry. But that's it. The culture part of the Encyclopedia."

"Explain it quickly, Rain," Charles said while trying to maintain his disarming smile and undivided attention on the approaching dignitary. "And lower your voice, please."

"Yeah, sorry. As part of the Encyclopedia we sent them an entire volume on culture, which included popular culture from various decades. This time period must have appealed to them for some reason, so they emulated it."

"This is good to know," Charles said. "And it would explain their clothing. Maybe they are trying to make us feel more comfortable—at home, so to speak."

"The ambassador's shoes are great Nike running shoe knock-offs for that time period. Running shoes haven't changed that much since," Ramashandra added. He held up his right foot and pointed at it. "It's hard to beat a good running shoe."

"If I were them, I would have chosen the 1940s. Men in fedoras, women in knee-length dresses with padded shoulders. Classy," Rain added.

"Why am I just now hearing about this?" Charles asked to no one in particular. "This is very important diplomatic information."

"Well, Charles, I just thought of it," Rain replied with a shrug of her shoulders and turning both hands palms up.

"Mike," Victor Tarasenko interrupted them. Then they all were given an image of the Proximans with a red circle around a part of their attire. "The pilots are carrying hand combustion-based projectile weapons on their sides. They are visible here. If my analysis is correct, they each house seven rounds. They do have reload magazines on their gear."

"Got it, Vic. Keep your eyes peeled. No grenades or anything?"

"None to speak of."

"Armor?"

"No, Commander. They have no armor."

"Estimates on our armor against their weapons?"

"The projectiles all appear to be soft lead as best I can tell. Completely useless against our armor. Other than a shot to an unprotected area like the face."

"That's good to know." Commander Rogers cleared his throat, getting everyone's attention. "Alright, folks, let's hold the chatter down now and let Ambassador Jesus do his thing."

CHAPTER 49

December 27, 2099 (Earth timeline)
Proxima b, aka Fintidier

The tour of the complex was going well. The secretary general made pleasantries with all of the humans from Earth and then they all spread out and went back to the work they needed to be doing. The soldiers chatted with soldiers, shared stories, and showed each other their weapons. The scientists spoke with the women and the pilots. But, mostly, Charles had asked them all to get "back to work" and "look busy" so he could show the Secretary General around. Everywhere they went, the two younger women and the two men in black dress suits followed closely behind.

"We've had ten of your years, Ambassador." The old Finti-dierian woman smiled. Charles noted that they must not have invented dental braces yet as her teeth were very misaligned. "We all have studied your culture and language. We teach your English in our schools now in our primary education system."

"Madam Secretary, we are mostly humbled, and honored by such actions. And believe me, many of us have learned much about your culture. But mostly, we've been studying your dilemma," Charles said. "That and building a means to travel here to you to offer our help."

"Yes, we received your messages that you were coming to help with our problem. And even that you have sent a second ship to be here sometime in the not-too-distant future." Secretary General Balfine Arctinier's eyes raised a bit when Charles realized his expressions were giving him away. They had yet to be able to reestablish communications from home and weren't certain if the *Emissary* had left Earth or not. There were so many data dumps lumped in on top of each other and, as it turned out, Gaines had left them another present: about the last three or so years' worth of communications had been scrambled by some encryption algorithm that they'd yet to crack. The *Samaritan* had no up-to-date data that was much newer than their midpoint physicals.

"We had, some, uh, technical difficulties, and have yet to be able to reestablish communications from home," Charles explained. "We are working the issue and hope to have that fixed within the next week or so."

The old woman paused a moment and counted silently on her fingers. Charles guessed that she was interpreting a week into some Proximan time unit. Then she nodded knowingly.

"I am sorry to hear that. If there is anything my people can do to help, then please ask," she said.

"I'll pass that along to the scientists. I have no idea if they need anything we don't have or not. Thank you, Madam Secretary." Charles led the ambassador around the control center of their headquarters building showing her some of their amazing "magical" technologies. He found her questions very interesting and with some of them he realized that he also didn't really understand exactly how the technology actually did what it did. There was nothing like having to explain something to help you realize whether you really understand it—or not.

"About our problem, as you have perceived it?" the secretary general asked. "How do you think you can help us?"

"That is a good question. Our understanding, our science and technology, of medicine, diseases, and the human makeup is probably a century or more ahead of yours. Perhaps, with our technologies and advanced knowledge, we can find the culprit of your gender disparities," Charles offered. "Would you allow for our scientists and medical teams to conduct physical examinations of a sampling of your people?"

"Of course. We have volunteers available."

"Great. When can we go see them?"

"For the meantime, we'd prefer it if you stayed here on this isolated location while we bring them here." The secretary general turned and faced him squarely. She was much shorter than Charles, her skin was very pale as if it never had seen sunlight, and her face was far less wrinkled than he had expected it would be. "Ambassador Jesus, your people might be dangerous to ours. We do not know what ailments you may have brought with you. And trust builds slowly."

"For how long?" Charles asked.

"Until enough time has passed for our experts to be comfortable with you leaving this location. I'm afraid I cannot give you an exact date. You know how difficult politics, and politicians, can be. I don't anticipate it will be too much longer," she replied.

"I understand, ma'am," Charles agreed. "I understand completely."

"Good."

"Now, if you don't mind, Madam Secretary, I've noticed that you have a slight limp to your left side as you walk." Charles had noticed an obvious medical issue as she walked down the steps of the aircraft. He'd hoped that could be one of the inroads to take with her. "A sports injury perhaps?"

"You are quite disarming," she laughed. "I'm afraid it is geriatric. At my age, sports are quite the thing of the past."

"If you don't mind my asking, ma'am, how old are you?"

"Well, I had a suspicion you'd ask that question, so I have already converted it to your time." She smiled at him with her crooked teeth again. "I am sixty-eight of your years old."

"I see. Would you mind letting one of our medical experts take a look at you?" Charles couldn't believe how young the "old woman" was. "I believe you will be amazed at some of the treatment options we have available for all sorts of ailments."

"An excellent idea, Mr. Ambassador. Perhaps I can be the first test subject for you, although my birthing years are much a thing of the past." They both chuckled together briefly and then Charles decided to bring in the doctor.

"Excuse me just a second," Charles said. Then he reached up in front of him and moved an icon around until he found Dr. Thomaskutty. She was five buildings down in the medical center. He switched open an audio channel and connected to her. "Sindi, this is Charles, do you copy me?"

"Loud and clear, Charles. How can I help you?" The Fintidierians looked at Charles as if they were trying to find the transmitter. He turned his head forward and pulled his earlobe down and then showed them the tattoo there. "A transmitter here . . . Sindi, I'm going to bring the secretary general down there now for a physical examination."

"Wonderful, Charles. I can't wait to see her," Dr. Thomaskutty replied.

"Your technology is so amazing," the secretary general said. "You mean that mark behind your ear is actually a communication device? That small?"

"Yes." Charles nodded.

"And why do all of you wave your hands about in the air? I've noticed this."

"Ah, I should have thought about that. Those motions are commonplace for our culture now. You see, not only do we have systems like this tattoo behind my ear that is microscopic technology, but we also have lenses that we put in our eyes. They act like movie screens we can see through. In my vision right now as I look at you, there is information in front of me that I can see which you cannot. I can move the information around like books on a shelf. But they are not real books, of course, they are movies. I can show you with glasses we have if you would like to experience it?"

"Very much, please."

"Her limp is gone," Charles noted. Dr. Thomaskutty stood next to him, waving goodbye to her as she walked up the aircraft stairs without any help from her guards.

"She had a bacterial infection in her joints. It used to be quite common in the elderly on Earth even fifty years ago or so," Thomaskutty explained. "I gave her an anti-inflammatory, the right antibiotic, and a female hormone stimulant. Her endocrine system had basically shut itself down. I turned it back on."

"Wasn't that a bit premature? We haven't yet done a complete physical workup on them yet. What if she has some sort of reaction? Accidentally killing their ambassador in our first meeting would not be a good way to begin establishing relations," said Charles.

"That's what I said. After the exam, she asked me what I found, so I told her. She then asked me if there was a treatment and I wasn't going to lie, so I told her that too. It was at that point that she specifically asked if I could administer the antibiotic and the hormone stimulant. I warned her of the risks, but she insisted," she replied.

"You should have asked me," Charles said.

"Sorry about that, but when I have a patient I can help and they ask me to do so, I have a difficult time saying no. I did insist that one of her protectors witness her treatment request and I recorded it—just in case. I will send you a copy. Besides, there's always patient-to-doctor privilege. I probably shouldn't have told you anything."

"She already looks like she feels better."

"Wait until tomorrow when she starts menstruating again."

As promised, a steady and recurring stream of volunteers began visiting the basecamp for their medical screenings. As would be expected, there was roughly a fifty-fifty split in the genders, with the average age of the female Fintidierian volunteers being much older than the male. Over the next ten days, the Earth humans had poked, prodded, scanned, and taken samples from well over three hundred individuals. All of the volunteers spoke at least rudimentary English and, without exception, they were polite and completely cooperative, showing absolutely no modesty during the exams, which were sometimes quite intrusive and lengthy.

CHAPTER 50

January 7, 2100 (Earth/Proxima timeline)
Proxima b, aka Fintidier

"As far as we can tell, there's nothing wrong with them." Yoko Pearl pointed out the last graph in her slideshow to the team.

"Really?" Charles Jesus whispered under his breath and to no one in particular. He had been expecting to find some disease or something. Charles had called an all-hands meeting, including the crew of the *Samaritan* who were connected virtually. As the ambassador from Earth, he, by default, had become the leader of Proxima One Embassy—at least that's what they had been calling it. He figured that at some point they'd have to come up with an official name like the United Nations Embassy to Fintidier. But for now, Charles was fine with Proxima One Embassy.

"Doctors Nkrumah, Polkingham, I, and the medical team all agree. There is no known, or unknown and detectable, pathogen we can find, no genetic anomaly, nothing. The genetic makeup of the Fintidierians is identical to our own—which is miraculous, by the way—and suggests identical or connected origins. Even the local animals and plant life we've been able to sample show identical genetic origins, although they've evolved to slightly different species. There was a clear genetic origin for both our planets that, well, must have been from the same genetic samples. Our immune systems are slightly different due to evolution on separate planets, which is to be expected like the animals and plants evolving differently. Dr. Kopylova has something to say about that, but before he does, I have some other, very interesting news."

285

"Don't keep me in suspense."

"As you knew before we left, life here is similar to that on Earth, but an independent parallel evolution creating humans so similar to us is a near impossibility. You are familiar with the basics of evolution, and you know that human reproduction creates children who are the combined product of the genes of their parents. These combinations are unique enough that genetic testing can confirm your identity perfectly, and the threads of these genes can be traced back through generations over thousands of years. Since genetic testing began we have created massive databases of genetic data for us humans, and also virtually all the other remaining species on Earth.

"Using this technology, we can determine whether you and, say, Dr. Gilster share a common ancestor, and can also estimate how long ago they lived, up to several thousand years back," she said.

"Go on," Charles prodded.

"We now have a Proximan genetic database too, thanks to samples we have taken. We compared it to our own Earth human database, and some of those samples suggest we share a common ancestor from about 50,000 to 75,000 years ago, most likely some-where in Asia. Ancestors who strike out on their own to create a new line in a new place are called 'founders' in genetic terms."

"You said some of the samples suggest a common ancestor. But not all, then?"

"Well, some may have founders older than that, up to two hundred thousand years ago or longer. But those with Asian ancestry are more closely related. Much more closely."

"But how is that possible?"

"Honestly, we don't know. We are starting to sequence as much of the flora and fauna here as we can, to see if it also relates to those on Earth. Maybe then we will have a rough family tree of sorts."

"Thank you, Dr. Pearl." Kopylova's face appeared on the large data screen in the basketball gymnasium they used as the all-hands assembly location. Kopylova was currently on the ship at geostationary orbit above them, using the scanning electron microscope there. The team had yet to transport, unpack, and install the one meant for the lab at Proxima One—soon, very soon, there was just still a lot to be done.

Charles listened intently and made mental notes of who was on the surface and who was still on the ship and for what reasons. He understood the need to man the ship with at least a minimal crew, but if there was an issue of not getting equipment moved down in a timely manner, then he might need to suggest some prioritization. He'd give it time and see if the scientists figured it out for themselves. He listened as Kopylova continued.

"Doing a pathogen screen, and an immunity analysis, I've identified the disparate pathogens between us and have a vaccination protocol being developed for us and the Prox...uh... Finitidierians. The vaccine should be ready in a couple of days in a quantity enough for us and several hundred of the Fintidierian volunteers to come onto the complex. While none of us are currently infected with primary sickness, and the fact that we've been quarantined on the ship for almost seven or ten years relative, it is possible our immune systems are constantly defeating something within us that could be deadly to them and vice versa. We know that lower and microgravity exposure can weaken the immune response to certain Herpes viruses, like Shingles, for example. There are others that might become transferrable under certain intimate contact with the aliens...uh, Fintidierians...I don't know what to call them. So, I suggest we implement the vaccine protocols as soon as possible."

"That is good news, Mak," Crosby chimed in virtually. "Right, Commander?"

"Agreed," Rogers replied. "We've been wanting to do some exploration, even to remote areas that aren't populated, but the excuse we get from the Fintidierians is that they want to maintain the general isolation and control any exposure that may occur."

"I didn't realize. I'll push that," Charles said. "Dr. Kopylova, is it possible to spread something to the Fintidierians if we traveled to an unpopulated area?"

"I don't see how," Kopylova said. "What are you thinking?"

"Commander Rogers, could you conduct manned recon in the OSAMs without being detected by their radar systems?" Charles asked.

"Hahaha!" Victor Tarasenko laughed out loud and the screen switched to his face. "What radar systems? They have not invented them yet. Or maybe, they have the idea in a lab somewhere, but there are no radars being implemented on this planet or we would have detected them with the satellites."

"Okay, then. I'll authorize away missions for data gathering as long as we stay out of sight, to unpopulated regions, and as long as we don't get caught. I'll have to deny ever having given permission to you if the secretary general asks," Charles said. "So, be prepared for a public slap on the wrist if you get caught."

"Understood, Mr. Ambassador," Commander Rogers replied. "Been there and done that."

"Is there some place you'd like to go?" Charles asked.

"Not me," Rogers replied. "My job is to go where ordered."

"Yes, there is!" Dr. Alma Jones's face appeared on the screen as she stood in the bleachers so everyone in the gym could see where she was. That wasn't actually necessary as much as tradition. Their individual AIs would quickly handshake and point out the locations of whoever they were looking for. Old habits sometimes took a long time to filter out of culture.

The AI drone flying silently in the gym readjusted itself to get a better view of her for the video conference. Charles noted in the bubble he could see above her head through his contacts that she was an expert in archaeology, archeoastronomy, theology, and anthropology. Of course, she would want to go exploring the planet.

"Dr. Jones?" He motioned for her to continue.

"Yes, look at these satellite images here." She waved her hands about a bit and then tossed something toward the main screen set up at half court. "Here, see? Look in the southern region here of this continent."

A globe of Proxima b, Fintidier, appeared and she started zooming in on a southern continent on the planet's side farthest from their equatorial island continent. As the satellite image zoomed in, an area of heavy foliage appeared. It looked like one of the deepest, darkest jungles from anywhere in Africa or South or Central America on Earth.

"This jungle region here shows no signs of current habitation. Exhaustive infrared searches show only animal life and no human population. There are no roads, footpaths, dwellings, farms, or anything. It is currently, completely uninhabited. However, when we apply the foliage penetration filters in this region here, and overlay the lidar depth data, as well as the infrared data, we can see that there was clearly an ancient civilization here hundreds, maybe thousands of years ago," Dr. Jones explained. "At first, I thought it would be easy to find stories about this ancient civilization in the library data the Fintidierians gave us. I wanted to know—and still do, spoiler alert—*who* were these people? We've collected a significant library of Fintidierian history books. We scanned them and have had the AIs go through all of them looking for any reference to this culture. There is none that we can find. According to the history that we've been given, this continent has always been uninhabited. Nonsense."

"What are you thinking about this, Alma?" Rain Gilster asked. "A lost civilization or something?"

"Well, Rain, honestly, I just don't know. But what I do know is that from all, not some, but every single one of the history records given to us by the Fintidierians, there is absolutely no reference, zero, zilch, nada, to an ancient culture on this continent."

"Maybe they've yet to discover them?" Dr. Raheem Ramashandra suggested. "There is still debate about the age of various cultures on Earth."

"Yes, this could just be a new discovery that our technology has enabled," Dr. Jones offered. "But it might not be. All I can say is, perhaps there are clues there as to where these people came from. If we know where they've been..."

"We might figure out where they are going?" Charles asked.

"Right," Jones agreed. "But there's more to this story."

"More?" Charles asked.

"Yes, there is. Dr. Jenda actually had the idea," Dr. Jones replied. "Tanya, would you mind?"

Charles looked as the screen changed to a tall, slender, black woman with very silky-smooth skin. Her eyes were a piercing ice blue. He didn't have to look at his AI for her name because she was the kind of woman that when a man met her, he remembered. She had all the features of a runway model or a movie star. To top that off, she'd been nominated not once, but twice, for the Nobel Prize—once for economics and once for mathematics. Dr. Tanya Jenda from Tobago. Her expertise was economics and statistics and the history of macroscopic economies.

"Yes, thank you," Dr. Jenda said in a very mild voice. "After hearing Dr. Jones's discovery of this lost culture, I started thinking about our own history. Such locations always drive and fuel manifest destinies. Treasure hunters, thrill seekers, explorers, and the like always fuel the next economy. Just look how much economy we created with our insane adventure."

"Hahaha!" Charles chuckled to himself quietly. "You ain't kidding there."

"Where are the ancient artifact hunters, the gold rush seekers, the explorers looking for treasure? If they were attempting to fly there, we would see runways nearby. So, they must be using naval vessels to go there if there are exploration activities in this area, right?"

"That makes sense, doesn't it?" Alma Jones added.

"Yes, it would make sense," Dr. Jenda agreed. "So, we looked for increases in naval-based economies in the southern hemisphere going on trade routes, exploration routes, or anything in this direction. There is nothing. Next, I took all of the satellite imagery data we have taken since arrival and had the AIs mark all naval traffic, as well as all aerial traffic. Granted, their technology is slow and it will really take several months more to map with certainty, so I needed more data. Therefore, I also had a library search done on all forms of traffic lanes noted in their history, literature, and even mythologies—of which they have few. I have here a map compiled from all their traffic. The blue dotted lines are current paths and expected trajectories. The red dotted lines are from current maritime law data. The green dotted lines are from historical documents. The purple dotted lines from literature. And the yellow dotted lines are from mythology."

"That's an impressive bit of work," Victor Tarasenko said, a bit too loudly.

"What on earth?" Rain agreed.

"What are the odds of that?" Dr. Renaud asked.

"Very good question, Dr. Renaud," Dr. Jenda replied and continued. "Clearly, you have all noticed that according to this data there is no traffic to this region out to at least one thousand kilometers' radius from these ruins. This is what appears to be a quarantined zone or an off-limits zone for whatever reason."

"What the hell?" Crosby's face appeared on the screen briefly.

"Exactly." Dr. Jones stood again as Dr. Jenda sat back down. "Thanks, Tanya. I'd have never thought about that approach. Brilliant investigation. But there's more."

"More?" Charles was so intrigued. He was on the edge of his seat at this point. "Please go on."

"Once we figured this part out. The fact that there is an off-limits zone in the southern hemisphere of this planet that is

almost two thousand kilometers in diameter is absolutely fascinating and clearly deliberate. For comparison, this area is a little
larger than three million square kilometers. Texas is about six
hundred and ninety-one thousand square kilometers. This spot
is about four and a half times larger than Texas! Alaska is one
point seven million square kilometers or so. The spot is almost
twice the size of Alaska! Why? What happened here?"

"What did happen there?" Charles heard but didn't bother
taking his eyes off Dr. Jones to see who it was. This was absolutely fascinating and riveting.

"At this point I asked Victor to do a very detailed intelligence
data sweep of the region," Dr. Jones continued and then held out
a hand pointing to the intel specialist. "Vic?"

"Yes, uh, thank you, Dr. Jones." Tarasenko stood and started
talking. "Following her direction, I started at the center of this
circle and began a push-broom sweep with all sensors of the area.
We now have data of this region down to centimeter accuracy
across the spectrum. First, sensors show no signs of radioactiv-
ity or any such major catastrophe. What it does show us is this,
right here. You can see scattered in large areas—larger than soc-
cer fields, many of them—where the earth has been disturbed
and then filled back over as mounds that are now grown over
by vegetation. There are no spoils piles."

"Pyramids?" from the audience.

"Ha! That is what I thought I was finding." Tarasenko's Russian accent rolled the words together. "But nyet. They are graves.
Massive, massive, mass-grave sites. And there are many tens,
maybe hundreds of them."

"Grave sites! That many?" Dr. Faruq, theoretical physicist, asked.

"Dah, yes, and maybe there is more of them." Tarasenko nodded his head in the affirmative. "I am still looking at the data.
As of right now, the number of grave sites, and the size of them,
I can't be certain of the depth, but each of them are roughly
rectangular pyramid shapes about one hundred meters on a side
and at least fifty meters tall. Ground-penetrating radar suggests
they are equally deep with a twenty percent error, perhaps. The
volume of a rectangular pyramid this size is about three hundred
thirty-three thousand cubic meters. If it is equally deep then the
volume is six hundred sixty-six thousand cubic meters. A human
body is about zero point zero seven five cubic meters. Allowing

for dirt falling in, and sloppiness, we can say a body would take zero point one cubic meters of volume. This would mean that in each of these grave sites there are approximately six point six million bodies. Counting all the known sites suggests hundreds of millions of bodies and maybe as much as a billion or more!"

"Jesus Christ!"

"Allah be praised."

"Holy shit."

"So now you see." Dr. Jones stood up, motioning a thank-you to Victor Tarasenko. "Now you see. Something, horrible, cataclysmic, dangerous, I don't know what, happened there. We *must* go there and see what happened. It might be a clue as to why these people are dying off. Maybe it happened before."

"Maybe there was a disease like the Black Plague in the Middle Ages?"

"Well, we will not know the answer until we go there and investigate. There is nothing about this in the Fintidierans' literature, history, politics, culture. Nothing. They have either forgotten it or covered it up. Since there are actually no travel zones, it smells of cover up," Dr. Jones finished. "Ambassador, it's a clear imperative that we go and investigate this location."

"I'd like to take a team there and investigate with you."

"I'll volunteer to go!"

Charles listened as most of the team discussed going and what might be the cause of such mass death and then what reasons there could be to cover it up. He listened for a few moments and then stood.

"Alright, let's hold it down a bit," he said. "First of all, the contents of this meeting are to be kept completely confidential to Earthlings only. I cannot emphasize this enough. Until we have more information, we had better not let on that we are investigating something that could be at the very heart of this culture's deepest, darkest history. We could start an interstellar incident. Hell, they might just come kill us for our troubles."

"We have to go. You realize this, right, Charles?" Jones pleaded with him.

"Calm down." He waved a hand at her. "Of course we have to go. We have to find out what happened on this world and make sure it doesn't happen to us."

"So, we're going, then?" Jones asked again for affirmation.

"Commander Rogers." Charles turned his attention to the SEAL. "Yes, Ambassador?"

"Can you get a team, handpicked by you and Dr. Jones, geared up so that they would be protected from alien bears and snakes and the like?" Charles asked. "And ready for God-knows-what-else in the event something happened?"

"I will gear them up, as you say, sir, with a security team," Rogers replied. "We can protect them. And we can get in and out without being seen."

"Okay then. Do it. But don't tell me about it until afterward." Charles held a finger to his lips with a grin. "Understood?"

"Plausible deniability, sir. Understood."

"Okay then, on to the next front. Let's please shelve the discussion of this bizarre and fascinating discovery until we complete our business of the day here." Charles moved an icon in front of him. "Dr. Burbank and Dr. Gilster, you two are up."

"Go ahead, Rain," Roy said. The camera jumped to him briefly and then back to Rain. Charles was glad to see Dr. Burbank integrating into the team. While there was still a quietly routed suicide watch notice about Roy, there was nothing official other than everyone was worried about him.

"Right. Okay, Roy." Dr. Gilster stood so the drone could find her easily. "Roy and I have been reworking the long-range communications capability and we've succeeded. This morning, our radio astronomy assay was brought online, tested against known radio stars, and then pointed at the Sol system. We, after some fine-tuning, detected the communications beacon being transmitted from there. We decoded it. As you can imagine it was a repeating loop wanting to know if we could read them and instructions on what frequencies to find looped letters-from-home data dumps. There are also news feeds and so on in the loop. We've started full downloads and have routed them to all the appropriate public folders on our network."

Rain paused to let that sink in. There were sighs of relief, various cheers and applauding, and a few shouts of "Amen!" She nodded in agreement and could see a noticeably big expression of satisfaction and happiness from Roy. He was already updating his three-dimensional model of his daughter.

"The secretary general was right. From the top line of the news feed, it is clear that the *Emissary* left Earth about four and a half years ago, just after we went into cryo after our midflight physicals." Rain let that sink in too. "I've been looking through the data for the ship's roster along with other information. My AI has put together several days' worth of video feeds and tomes of information that we've missed. It will take some time to get through all of it and that hasn't been my main focus anyway."

"What has been?" Crosby's face appeared briefly on the screen.

"This." Rain tapped at more icons before her and the screen changed to a spectrum analyzer waterfall page. "Roy and I found this."

The waterfall chart represented an area from one to ten gigahertz. Just to the left of the middle of the chart was a peak sticking straight up far above the background noise. There were two smaller peaks on either side of the central one. Rain zoomed in on it just a bit and placed a window box over the main peak. It then zoomed in and spread the peak into what now appeared as a bell-shaped, or Gaussian-shaped, curve that modulated up and down and had ripples changing on the bell-shaped line. The curve looked like a faster rippling sinusoidal function bent upward into the bell shape. The faster smaller ripples changed in frequency and amplitude.

"This is coming from the general direction of Earth, but it is much, much closer," Rain explained. "And I'm sure any of you space jockeys online can recognize it. If I apply the blue-shift filter to it and then add a narrow waveform frequency modulation filter, we get this..."

"...*Samaritan*, this is the starship *Emissary* from Earth. This is Captain Alan Jacobs of the United States Space Force on adjunct assignment to the United Nations. We are currently inbound to Proxima. Please respond. ETA at current rate of closure is ninety-three days..."

The room cheered again.

CHAPTER 51

January 16, 2100 (Earth/Proxima timeline)
Proxima b, aka Fintidier

The scientists of the exploration team had been on-site for more than three days. Before that, Commander Rogers had made the first trip with security forces only and did a forward recon of the region. At first, they completed several flyovers and then landed at the central point of the region. In the very center area, according to ground-penetrating radar, infrared and visible lidar, and acoustic vibrometry was what appeared to be a large pyramid-shaped stone temple that was as large or larger than the great pyramids on Earth. There were several smaller adjunct pyramidal structures adjacent in particular geometric patterns. The scientists were running AI pattern recognition algorithms against other known patterns such as star maps and so on. The temple was completely covered with eons of vegetation and unless you'd already looked at the location with foliage-penetrating radar and lidar there would be no way to discern it from a geological feature.

The security recon team had spread out and covered several of the burial mounds, which were overgrown so thickly that walking over them and around them was nearly impossible. Using exfoliants, fire, and several of the ATVs with ad hoc scoops added to the front of them, pathways and gathering areas were created. No permanent structures were set up and Rogers was pretty certain that in less than a couple months the area would be completely grown over, covering nearly all traces that they had been there. The jungle was that thick, alive, and encroaching in every direction. Screams of all manners of insects, reptiles, and mammals filled the twilight daytime that practically never ended, at least not for twenty-some-odd days.

For the first two Earth daytime periods the security team set up perimeter markers, makeshift barricades, and temporary shelters. A tent was set up to act as a latrine station and a thousand-gallon plastic water tank was set in place for drinking and bathing. On day three, the scientists were brought in, and they went straight to work.

"We found an entrance to the main temple," Terrence Henry from the security force, a retired British Special Forces colonel, told Dr. Jones with excitement. "You should come see it, Doctor."

They had used the ATVs to cut a driving path around the base of the large temple and had continued to excavate upward and inward until they had hit stone. From there they had cleared away dirt and vegetation based on ground-penetrating radar data until there were clear markings and evidence of construction methods, and that led them toward an entrance. About a hundred square meters of area up the side of the pyramid that had been covered in alien oranges, yellows, and burgundies were cleared away, revealing a large monolithic stone entrance.

"Looks like the front door to me," Dr. Jones exclaimed. "Look how big!"

"I bet that thing weighs tens of thousands of tons. How on Earth did they get it in place amidst all of this?" Terrence asked her.

"I don't think it was a jungle, or at least it was more manicured when they lived here," she replied. "We need to move that rock."

"No way the ATVs will do it," Terrence said. "I don't even think the OSAM would move it."

"No, I suspect it wouldn't." Dr. Jones studied the entrance and looked about the stone steps and sidewalls for marking or writings that might reveal how to get in. There were markings, but the application that Dr. Oliveira-Santos had given them couldn't translate it. "We need Maggie down here to look at this. Maybe she can figure out a way to translate some of these glyphs. They're not similar at all to any on Earth or the AI would pick up on it."

"Want me to get the OSAM sent back for her?"

"I don't know. Let me think," Jones said.

"We could get Dr. Ash over here. She's an expert on explosives and war-machine engineering. She might have an idea," Terrence told her. "Not sure what that stone is made of, but surely we have some ordnance that would take care of it."

"Well, I was thinking about asking the CHENG about an idea," she said. "Get Maggie and Dr. Ash down here. I'm going to keep looking around. And maybe call the CHENG. Can we get some more lights here also?"

"Yes, ma'am." Terrence turned back toward the ATV, calling out to Commander Rogers on the 'net as he left her. Then he turned to one of the other security team members. "Zeke, stay with her. I'm going to talk to the boss."

"Right." The SEAL responded.

"No, Alma." Dr. Maggie Oliveira-Santos shook her head in disappointment. "I don't have a reference for these glyphs. They are a language, but not from any of the Fintidierian libraries and not of Earth. This is a different lost language. Maybe inside or somewhere else out here there might be a primer stone."

"Okay, then, take a break, or keep at it. It's up to you." Dr. Jones sighed with frustration. "I've got a meeting with Dr. Ash. We can talk in a little while."

"So, Carol? Do we have anything that will blow the stone up? Move it? Cut it? I dunno?" Dr. Jones was growing more and more frustrated with the lack of progress of getting inside the temple while the rest of the team had excavated one of the burial sites and discovered remains. They were bringing down a Carbon-14 dating machine on the next OSAM flight.

"Well, we might could move it with some high-ex compound, but it would probably collapse the tunnel or whatever else is on the other side," Dr. Carol Ash, the New Zealand weapons and power expert, explained. "We might could cut it with a plasma cutter, but that would take a very long time."

"So, 'no go' then?" Jones asked.

"No go." Ash shrugged. "How the hell did ancient people move something that big?"

"I'm working on that."

"You want me to do what with it?" Cindy Mastrano, chief engineer of the starship *Samaritan*, exclaimed.

"I want to take the spare WECAV and set it up here. We'd have to focus the projector in one direction and we'd need a means of tuning it to the right mechanical frequency. Mikey will explain." Dr. Jones spoke to a virtual projection of Cindy, who was floating inside the engine room of the ship working at something. Alma directed the viewer at the large stone at the temple door. "Here is where it needs to be. Mikey?"

"Right, uh, Alma, I can explain it from here." Dr. Michael "Mikey" James, somewhat the polymath with multiple doctorates and master's degrees in physics, mechanical engineering, electrical engineering, mathematics, and metaphysics, grabbed the virtual icon and tilted the view toward himself. "Dr. Jones has a brilliant idea here. I've done some ion and electron microscopy elemental analysis on this thing and you'd be surprised how crystalline it is. There's a lot of shock quartz—how that got there who the hell knows—and there is a significant amount of various forms of granite intermingled with, get this, bismuth. I also found significant amounts of copper, yttrium, and barium. Can you believe that? Hell, I can't."

"You think it is superconductive?" the CHENG asked.

"No. I dunno. Probably not unless it were supercooled," Mikey replied. "But it is very specifically chosen or constructed, whichever doesn't matter. I think it has specific acoustic-based metamaterial properties. I think we could use the Weak Energy Condition Acoustic Violator in conjunction with a feedhorn and hit just the right resonance with this thing and reverse its mass."

"You mean, just like the Samara Drive engine block?" The CHENG raised an eyebrow, cocked her head slightly in one direction, and then let out a large exhale. "That would be worth trying just to see what happened. I'll have to get the captain's permission to drop the spare WECAV box down to you."

"Can you do that, Cindy?" Alma asked her.

"I'll go right now. Do you need anything else from up here?"

"I don't know. Mikey?"

"Yes, we need some sheet metal, projector acoustic tiles, and a joint melder. I'll send you specs and a list." Mikey started tugging away at virtual icons in front of him. Alma pulled the camera back to her.

"You might as well add a ton of duct tape to that. I have an idea that this is going to look klugey." She laughed.

                    ✧   ✧   ✧

"So, this works how again?" Commander Rogers stood beside the other Mike, the smart one, watching the operation. It had taken the better part of three days to prepare the equipment, but the other Mike and Dr. Jones were very excited about what they were about to attempt.

"Uh, right, so, um, the big block of granite there is like a bell. It was discovered way back in the year 2020 by these scientists from Columbia University in New York, I think it was, that if you rang a bell in the right way, and if the bell were made of the right materials, that bell would reverse gravity or maybe shield it, or maybe become a different kind of matter that falls away from other matter. You see, all matter in the universe falls toward all other matter."

"What goes up, must come down," Rogers said.

"Right. Universal Law of Gravitation; Newton came up with it centuries ago. This is known to physicists as the so-called weak energy condition or WEC. Science fiction writers and scientists trying to invent star drives and antigravity machines have been trying to 'violate' this weak energy condition for centuries. In 1901, H.G. Wells wrote a story about a material that did this, allowing men to travel to the Moon. It wasn't until 2020 that it was ever actually accomplished in an extremely specific and complex laboratory setting. The Russian team that invented the Samara Drive figured out a way to build a big chunk of special material that, when rang like a bell in the right way, would really change the properties of the matter and violate the shit out of the WEC." Dr. James came up for air, it seemed, so Rogers did his best to get a word in.

"So, to make a long story short, you're gonna try and make a Samara Drive out of this rock and lift it up from the tunnel entrance," Commander Rogers said nonchalantly as if he'd understood all along.

"Uh, yes, Mike, that is exactly what we're going to do."

"Why didn't you just say that, Doc, and avoid the college lecture?" Rogers did his best to maintain a straight face. He couldn't tell if Mikey was stunned, hurt, nonplussed, or just didn't care because the scientist just kept right on directing the ship techs with what had to be done.

"Pank, get me another two-meter-square sheet of ZK60 alloy here and meld it to this one. The feedhorn projector doesn't have to be precise. Centimeter accuracy will do. We can manipulate the air flow to fine-tune the acoustic standing wave."

"Right, Mikey. Can you hold that other end? This is a three-handed job." Pankish Patel looked up from his welding mask and tossed a clamp at Dr. James. Rogers had to hand it to the other Mike on the ship. The guy didn't mind getting dirty and sweaty and working his ass off.

"Anything I can do to help, Doc?" Rogers asked.

"Just stand over there looking pretty, Mike." He laughed. "Besides, I'd rather you be watching to make sure more of those damned screeching panther things don't jump on us."

"Alright, Alma, here goes nothing," Mikey James said as he activated the feedhorns to the WECAV projector system they'd constructed in the middle of an alien jungle light-years from any decent laboratory or machine shop. Mikey looked at various virtual slidebar controllers in his virtual field of view and adjusted them upward.

"The ground is shaking; do you feel that?" Pankish slowly stepped backward from the device and behind Mikey a couple of meters more. "Are you sure this is safe, Doc?"

"Don't worry, Pank. If it kills you, it will probably be painful," Mikey joked. "Just in case, everyone get their safety goggles and hearing protection in place now. Starting up in ten, nine, eight..."

"You know, Pank," Dr. Faruq, theoretical physicist who'd come down to help, joined in the fun, "the first team to experiment with the Samara Drive concept spent the first two months in the hospital with extreme diarrhea from the affects the acoustic signals had on their intestines."

"Seriously?" Pankish stepped back another step or two. Commander Rogers was ten meters behind that. "Doc? Mikey? Seriously?"

"...three, two..."

"Odds on nothing happening?" Dr. Faruq elbowed Mikey.

"...one. Dr. Jones, maybe you should stand back behind the acoustic shielding," Mikey whispered to her. He watched the frequency spectrum of the signal coming from the monolithic stone and at first was seeing nothing but white noise, then a few spikes here and there, but once the AI saw the spikes various tracking filters zeroed in on the right frequency mix and suddenly there was a loud *gong*, like someone had struck a giant gong with a hammer. "I think we found it."

"Hey, I've heard that on engine tests before!" Pankish shouted over the now very loud rushing noise. The air around them began to whirl about with eddies and tiny dust devils. Debris blew about almost to the point where it stung the skin.

"Alright, we've found the right resonance. Now we are fine-tuning it and looking for the WEC violation to start. Hopefully, we can couple enough energy into the stone!" Mikey shouted. Then suddenly the rocks started shaking violently. Several small stones of similar makeup lifted from the ground a few centimeters and then shattered like a crystal glass. Shards of granite stone and white dust flew in all directions. The large monolithic stone made a loud *gong* once again and then the noise dropped to almost zero decibels of detectable sound. The monolithic stone began to rise from its resting spot slowly. As it rose to about three meters from the surface it stalled, fell back about a half of a meter, and then rose again.

"Shut it down, Mikey!" Dr. Jones shouted louder than she needed to. "It worked!"

"Holy shit! Did you see that!" Dr. James exclaimed. "You should've taken Faruq's bet, Pank!"

The energy dropped to zero when Mikey had all the systems shut down. He double-checked to make certain there was no energy being transmitted anywhere and then he pulled his earphones off. He turned to the rest of the team with a smile of triumph.

"We need some big-assed beams to hold that thing up or something." Mikey shrugged. "I don't think I'd trust walking in under that thing while the system is on."

"Somebody must have if this is how they did it to construct the thing," Alma said. "The rock was floating, right?"

"Yeah."

"Could we push it with a long stick and just slide it out of the way and let it fall to the side?"

"Why the hell not?" Mikey liked the idea. Simple was always better in his mind. "Pank! Go find us a four-meter-long stick!"

CHAPTER 52

January 17, 2100 (Earth/Proxima timeline)
Proxima b, aka Fintidier

"Commander Rogers, are the scientists close to wrapping up down there?" asked Captain Crosby via audio link, interrupting Mike's discussion with one of the scientists about which corridor they should explore next. The team's incursion into the now-open underground chambers was going well. They had been exploring, sampling, photographing, and otherwise cataloging everything they found once the stone had been removed—and it was a mother lode. They were not even close to being finished.

"Uh, no sir, we are not," Rogers replied.

"Well, you might want to either wrap it up and come home or start getting ready for company. There are three large aircraft headed your way. We've been monitoring their flight since they took off about two hours ago. They at first appeared to be following one of the flight routes around the 'forbidden zone' until they deviated and began moving toward your location about ten minutes ago."

"What is their ETA?" asked Rogers.

"At their current rate of speed, two hours and eight minutes. I'm sending the live radar feed to you now so you can track them in real time."

"Thanks, Captain."

"Commander, Ambassador Jesus would like to speak with you as well. I am patching him in from the basecamp. Here he is," said Crosby.

"Commander, I just want to remind you that our interaction with the Fintidierians is in its formative stages and we've gone behind their backs, going to locations other than those they requested we remain within and, I might add, to an area that may well be considered sacred to them for some reason. Your presence there might be perceived as more than just a violation of the initial agreement as to where we would remain. It might be sacrilegious or worse. It is imperative that this not escalate into violence," said Jesus.

"Ambassador, I hear you loud and clear, but I am going to do whatever is necessary to protect my team and the scientists. That's my job."

"With all due respect, your job is subordinate to mine, which is to establish peaceful relations with the Fintidierians and render medical aid to help them solve their population, dare I say, extinction crisis. It might be necessary for us, for you and our security team, to make sacrifices to preserve that larger mission."

"I understand, but I won't know what I need to do until I need to do it. I will keep that in mind, but you will have to trust me. I am here and you are not. Signing off," Rogers said as he cut the connection.

"Major Maksutov!" Rogers called out.

"Yes, sir!" said the Russian, trotting forward from the encampment where it looked like he had been grabbing some dinner and, knowing the Russians, probably a bit of vodka—even while on duty. He claimed it made him more "aware" of his surroundings.

"We have some incoming aircraft, possibly hostile. You and Lt. Kenosha need to break out the antiaircraft missiles, light them up with the radar, and get ready to take them out. The locals are sending in some aircraft and I don't want them to get anywhere near this base. The folks who like to chat are going to try to get them called off, and I hope to God they do. But if they don't, then we have to assume they are hostile and we will defend ourselves," said Rogers.

"Yes, sir!" replied the major as he began to sprint toward the pallet where the weapons had been unloaded. They had brought them because, well, "just in case" they were needed. Good soldiers plan for contingencies, even unlikely ones, because those are often the ones that might kill you.

"Major, hang on," Rogers called out.

"Sir." Maksutov stopped and turned around.

"Set one of them to fly ahead and above its target for detona-tion. If the diplomatic approach fails, then I may want to fire a warning shot before we take any of the planes out. They might just get the hint and save their own lives in the process."

"There's another one, and this one appears to be coming toward the basecamp," said Crosby, relaying the location of what appeared to be another aircraft, similar, if not identical, to the one that brought the Fintidierian ambassador the last time. "ETA at the basecamp in just a little over an hour and only about fifteen minutes before the planes headed toward the excavation team arrive at their location."

"I'll get ready," Charles replied. He was expecting something like this. Somehow their excursion to the southern continent had been detected and now it was time to pay the piper. *Stupid. Stupid. Stupid. How did they possibly think they could literally walk onto another world, move around at will, and not be found out? We have better tech than the natives and that made us arrogant.*

With well over half the complement of Earth humans some-where else, either on the *Samaritan* or the southern continent, it was going to be difficult to make their compound look fully occupied. He alerted everyone else in the compound to get ready for visitors and prepared for it being decidedly unfriendly, what-ever that might mean. He took a deep breath and tried to put himself in the shoes of the Fintidierians, or the moccasins of the ancient Mayans, as he contemplated how he might explain their blatant ignoring of the requested isolation—and explicit Fintidierian request that they remain at the basecamp. He had hoped to plead ignorance, but with so many people gone, that would not hold water. He decided it would be best to wait and see why they were paying a visit rather than worry. Worry would do no good anyway.

In the perpetual twilight that passed as daytime for the locals, Charles could hear the approaching plane before he could see it. As last time, it roared its way onto the landing strip and put-tered to a stop before the side door opened, dropping the stairs. Immediately thereafter, Secretary General Arctinier and her two protectors descended, looking not very happy.

"Madam Secretary, to what do we owe the pleasure of your

visit?" asked Charles, fingers mentally crossed. He was alone on the tarmac, having thought it would be best for no one other than himself to be visible rather than a few, which might prompt questions as to their whereabouts. He found himself wishing the SEALs were among those who remained. Both Captain Crosby and Commander Rogers were tied into the conversation, listening via his ear patch.

"Ambassador, I am here to discuss with you the blatant violation of our sovereignty, and our specific request that you and the rest of your team remain here until the requested isolation period is complete."

"Madam Secretary, I am—"

"Ambassador, please spare us the unpleasantness. We know that some of your number are in Misropos and we must ask that you have them depart from there immediately. They are in grave danger."

Misropos. That must be what the locals call the keep-out area with the ruins, thought Charles as he carefully constructed his next few words.

"Let's dispense with the formalities and get to the issue. Yes, we have a small team there investigating the ruins. We thought long and hard about whether or not to go—whether to ask permission or forgiveness. We opted for the latter. We are here to help you and unless we know what has happened here, your history as well as your biology, we might not be able to help you. And when I say 'here,' I mean everywhere on the planet."

"Ruins? In Misropos? That is news to me, but what is not news is that unless your team leaves immediately, they may die," she replied.

"Are they in immediate danger, other than from the aircraft you have headed toward them?"

"I suspected you would know about the military flights headed there. No, whether or not they are in danger from us depends upon how you and they react to our request, our order, that they depart. That area is strictly off-limits for fear of contagion, fatal contagion. It has nothing to do with our current biological problems," she said.

"Madam Secretary, please excuse me while I confer with my colleagues," Charles said. He stepped to the side and turned away from her so he could speak without being overheard. "Commander

Rogers, are you getting this? She says there is some sort of virus or something there that you might catch. I'm thinking we may need to evacuate you."

"That's a negative, Mr. Ambassador, we cannot leave now. If there is a disease here, then it is too late. Given how long we've been here, we are all exposed. If we leave now, then we might still get sick and not have all the information about this place that we want. We can have medical check us out when we get back and isolate at the basecamp until we know if we've caught something. And those military planes are almost on top of us. Are we about to be attacked?"

"I'll find out. Stand by," replied Charles, turning back to the secretary general.

"Madam Secretary, I admit that our team is there and that if they are going to catch something, then it is too late to do anything about it. I beg your forgiveness for this incursion but it is imperative they complete their reconnaissance and not leave prematurely. Once they are finished, they will return here and we will once again go into quarantine to make sure there is not contagion."

"That is unacceptable, I—" she began.

"Madam Secretary, as you are undoubtedly aware, part of our team are trained to provide security and some are in the military. Our weapons are far superior to yours and I would hate for any misunderstanding between Commander Rogers's team and your incoming aircraft to result in a loss of life—on either side. We apologize for breaking your rules and beg you to call them off before something happens that we will all regret," he said.

Secretary Arctinier's stare was among the best Charles had ever seen in any tense negotiation. For a brief moment, he thought she was going to push him over the edge and allow a confrontation.

Arctinier turned toward the open door on the airplane and called out something in Fintidier that Charles could not understand. She then turned back toward him, her gaze no less intense and her anger still simmering within it.

"I have instructed my pilot to tell our planes to divert immediately. It may take a few minutes for the message to be relayed to the aircraft, but they should veer off as soon as they get the message," she said.

"I will inform Commander Rogers. Mike, did you get that?"

Charles said to himself so that the earpiece and Secretary Arctinier could hear.

"Roger that, I'll let you know when they turn around."

"Madam Secretary, I must ask, why did you not tell us about this region and the possible risk of going there? Does it have something to do with the ruins?" Charles asked.

"I am reluctant to show my ignorance, but I suspect you have already figured out that I know nothing of there being ruins in Misropos. As for the keep-out zone, we had planned to inform you later. That region has been off-limits for as long as we have kept historical records. Entering it is strictly forbidden and punishable by death. It is one of the few capital crimes we have and your team has blatantly committed such a crime. That is, of course, if they survive the trip. Your curiosity and rule breaking have placed everyone from your ship in mortal danger."

"Thank you for calling off your military response. If you can believe me, and if we survive the breach, then I promise we will share with you everything we learn at the ruins."

"I am sure you will understand if I tell you I have a hard time believing you," she replied.

"As would I, if our roles were reversed. May I ask how you knew our team was there?"

"You may ask, but I choose to not answer. But I will tell you what those aircraft were ordered to do so you can get an idea of how serious we take this breach."

"And that was?" Charles asked, not quite sure he wanted to know the answer.

"The planes are fully loaded with incendiaries. Their objective was to firebomb your team to sterilize the area and make sure there was no chance of the contagion spreading. I will retain this option, and others, should your people get sick and bring the contagion back here. I must ask that you again quarantine yourselves and this time we plan to monitor your activities much more closely. It will take some time to regain trust."

"I hope that whatever our team finds at the site will overcome any mistrust and allow our peoples to move forward with solving your problem," said Charles.

"As do I."

CHAPTER 53

February 2, 2100 (Earth/Proxima timeline)
Proxima b, aka Fintidier

The weeks since the team returned from the ruins were filled with more than a little anxiety. Based on the warning from Secretary Arctinier, the medical team ran a complete workup on those who had been part of the excursion to the southern continent, looking for any sign of infection. The workups were performed every two days since to account for any latency period of possible infection. They were all clean and had remained that way. Whatever contagion risk that had so worried the Fintidierians either didn't affect Earth humans or it didn't exist anymore, if it ever had.

And it was clear that they were under long-distance surveillance. They had been warned that there would be multiple flyovers of the small, propeller-driven aircraft multiple times each day and that there would be spotters surrounding the camp. Rogers noted their locations, routines, and how they were able to blend in with the surrounding countryside with respect, noting that they were extremely professional and competent—and would have been difficult to keep track of if it weren't for the Earthers' more sophisticated technology.

It was clearly going to take more time to rebuild trust.

"Do they have groundhogs on Fintidier?" Charles asked.

"We saw some little rodents down in the southern hemisphere that might pass for a groundhog," Alma said. She sat her coffee mug down on the conference table they'd set out in the middle of the basketball court. The rest of the scientists were making their way to seats in the bleachers. One of the security force guys, Lyle Baker from the US FBI, was setting up the projection screen and activating the drone. They were coming together to learn the results of the analysis done on the data they collected during their foray to the ruins.

"Crosby here. Are you guys reading us?"

"We have you, Captain," Baker said and then he turned to the ambassador. "Charles, you are ready go whenever you like."

"Thanks, Lyle. We'll let them all get seated."

"The remains we found; they are all human. Since the atmosphere here is remarkably similar to Earth's, uncannily so in its composition, we measured the interactions of incoming cosmic rays with the atoms in Proxima b's upper atmosphere and found the rate at which Carbon-14 is produced, normalized it with what we are used to on Earth, and then applied the results to dating the remains we found in the burial mounds. They Carbon-14 date to over fifty-one thousand years ago. And the stories left on the walls of the inside of this temple appear to be telling us of an ancient much more advanced culture than even what we have on Earth today, perhaps having developed here tens of thousands of years ahead of us. This sounds like an Atlantis-type myth," Alma Jones briefed the rest of the Proxima One Base team.

"The myth that is recorded though, is much darker than ours. This advanced culture here just vanished. There were two different interpretations that Dr. Oliveira-Santos and I came up with after the AI cracked the glyphs. One, they left the planet. Two, they died and their spirits went to heaven. Typical kind of ancient myth debate here." Alma paused and looked to the linguist. "Maggie?"

"What we have here is *A Tale of Two Cities* all over again. No matter which interpretation we use here," Dr. Maggie Oliveira-Santos explained as her face popped up on the main screen at half court. "There appear to be haves and have nots. Whoever this... Atlantis culture, as Alma calls them, were, they were somehow different and more advanced than the others. And it appears they must have mixed their genetic line with the lesser-advanced culture for centuries, maybe millennia. For whatever reason, their advanced culture or technologies weren't shared.

Maybe they were like the Romans and the rest of the world were slaves or at least labor peasants in an extreme lower class. The story told by the glyphs isn't clear on this."

"This is where it gets interesting," Alma whispered to Charles sitting beside her at the table sitting in front of the bleachers.

"You mean it wasn't already?" he shot back at her quietly.

"Then the Atlanteans—again, what Alma calls them as we never found a name—started dying at an extremely fast pace. There must have been some disease then because the glyphs show them falling dead in rows. It was a very significant time for them and there were these glyphs here representing this." Maggie tossed an image of the wall inside the temple onto the main screen so everyone could view it and then she continued.

"You see here how there are rows of people with these ornate-looking belts and bandoliers? That is how they drew the advanced people. The normal people are always stick figures. Well look at this image here and see how the stick figures are smaller and prostrate to the others. Note how the sun behind them is illuminating them with these rays. Now, what appears to be later in the story, we see this same type of presentation but the sun is much larger and more pronounced and there are rays here coming all the way to the taller advanced people's figures. Maybe this means they were more godlike or in touch with the heavens. We're not sure about that. But it is here where we see"—Maggie changed the image—"to this one Alma found. Alma..."

"Oh, okay, yes, you see here that the larger figures with the ornate belts and such, well, some are standing and some are horizontal. Perhaps these rays from the sun are representative of their spirits going to the heavens when they died? Maybe they were sun worshipers?" Alma started to flip to the next screen but was interrupted. Dr. Gilster was standing up, waving at her.

"Hold on a minute," Rain said. Her face appeared on the screen. The little conference drone silently hovered closer to her. "No offense, Alma, Maggie, but that isn't what that glyph is telling us at all."

"No offense taken. Go on, Rain." Alma sat back down.

"Proxima Centauri is known to be a highly active flare star. We just haven't seen it flare in a while. The flares act a lot like solar flares due to energy stored in the star's extreme magnetic field. The field lines within the star get very strong and warped out of shape due to the other magnetic field lines. When there is enough of a tug on one of the lines, it breaks and reconnects to a nearby line. When this happens, there is an enormous amount of energy released. In fact, the star's brightness will increase all across the spectrum from radio up to x-rays. Solar winds are accelerated to significant portions of the speed of light. Those x-rays and accelerated ions are then slammed into the planets within the solar system. This why we weren't sure at first that Proxima b could actually house life because if the planet didn't have a strong magnetic field, which we now know it does, these flares would irradiate and kill anything over time. However, the strong magnetic field of the planet helps shield them from this."

"What are you suggesting, Rain?" Maggie asked before the screen could change.

"I'm suggesting that whoever these advanced people were, their bodies were being killed by the solar flares. The pictures don't give you a time epoch. They could have been dying of cancer from the exposure. Maybe skin cancer or something." Rain sat back down.

"Holy... Rain... you've just explained why this next part occurred!" Alma stood up. "You see, we hadn't finished the story. It was at this point, when the Atlanteans started dying off, that the peasant culture started an ethnic cleansing." Alma tossed an icon about and then threw something at the screen. "This set of glyphs here shows a family tree of sorts. Any of the lower culture that had heritage back upward through their bloodlines with any of the Atlanteans were purged. There was a major upheaval and a war here. This entire continent was divided racially, or I guess ancestrally, and hundreds of millions fought and died. The non-Atlantean line won and marched the rest into what must have been deathcamps that would have made what the Nazis did pale in comparison."

"They thought it was a contagious disease killing them?" Charles asked.

"They must have. So, out of fear and ignorance they started removing the cancer from their planet," Alma replied. "This makes perfect sense now. Before, we just assumed it was some disease. Now with this, we know that at first, well, it was a disease but it wasn't contagious. Over time, had they not overreacted, then the solar flares would have killed off those susceptible and the stronger ones would have survived. Selective adaptation would have occurred given time to do so."

"But they didn't let it. They forced it and went overboard with it," Maggie agreed. "And they cleansed their planet of whatever races were due to the intermingling of these people with their own."

"Wait, has anyone done an assessment of the number of races within the Fintidierians?" Charles asked.

"We haven't really?" Yoko Pearl stood and gave the drone time to zoom in on her. "Early on before we left Earth, we did go through as much of their video as we could to look for diversity in the genetic pool. We concluded that we didn't have a good enough sampling across their culture to know for certain. We based this on looking at our movies of that era of technology. The genetic makeup of the planet was very poorly represented at the time. At least that was our conclusion."

"I'll agree with that," Dr. Raheem Ramashandra added. "I'm aware of this effort and we concluded in parallel from a study of our own archived data that an accurate model of the genetic makeup of the era couldn't be accomplished."

"Alright then." Charles held up a hand to quiet everyone down. "Everyone, I think we are close to an answer here. And it is time I brief you all on something that the president of the United States briefed me on just before we left. Commander Rogers, are we certain we are clear of Fintidierians here?"

"Yes sir, there is no presence of them as of yet. We are expecting a food-and-supplies vessel at fifteen thirty, but we're clear," Commander Mike Rogers replied.

"And we're certain they are not eavesdropping on us somehow?"

"Vic?" Rogers turned the screen over to his intel specialist.

"Mr. Ambassador, there is no technology that these people have that we cannot detect. There were listening devices in various locations that might have been placed in malice or just as internal communications during construction that were left behind. But they have all been deactivated. We are clear to speak here," Tarasenko assured him.

"Alright then, this is never revealed to the Fintidierians and is considered to be classified to Earthlings only. I need all of you to raise your right hand and swear to this. If you can't do that, I'll have to ask you to leave the room and the channel for a bit." Charles waited and nobody left the room or cleared the channel. Then he opened up a file and had an oath displayed on the screen and sent to all of the Earthlings. "Raise your right hands, read the oath out loud, please. The AIs will record it for the record." Charles waited until his AI showed that all of them had read the oath and digitally signed it.

"Very well, before we left, I was briefed by a Dr. Jason Faheem, an expert in pandemic and population studies. What he told me was that there are actually three locations on planet Earth to date that have for generations shown a tremendous gender discrepancy in their population census data." Charles paused and then ticked them off on his fingers. "Those are: one, Saudi Arabia; two, Oman; and three, a small area in Asia known as Bhutan. Dr. Faheem went on to show us that at times the female percentage of the population has dipped as low as thirty-four percent in each of these places. He even showed that the birth data portrays a significant difference in the number of female babies born versus male babies born each and every year for the past century. Whatever is causing this, nobody has an answer for it. Fortunately, for us anyway, Earth is extremely racially diverse and has many people moving into these areas to make up for the problem. However, we don't know if it could spread or not as we don't know yet what is causing this."

"Jesus..." Charles heard Alma whisper next to him.

"So, as you can imagine, the governments of Earth are extremely interested in what the cause of the problem here on Proxima b is. Not only are we here to save them, but potentially ourselves as well."

CHAPTER 54

March 5, 2100 (Earth/Proxima timeline)
Proxima b, aka Fintidier

It wasn't the Lunar Farside Radio Observatory, but Rain thought it was beautiful, nonetheless. She and Roy had taken the crude radio receiver that they had cobbled together to reestablish communications with home, added some additional spare electronics, printed equipment, and then some repurposed radio antennas made by the Fintidierians and made a pretty decent radio telescope. The first radio telescope facility on Fintidier. She immediately dismissed the internal comparison to Karl Jansky, the man who discovered that you could use radio as an astronomical tool, and smiled at the thought of comparing herself to Jocelyn Bell Burnell, the woman who discovered radio pulsars, which later led to the navigation system they were supposed to use on their journey here.

The system had been online for roughly three days and most of that time was spent calibrating the results with observations taken from Earth of known deep-space radio sources. Being closer to Proxima Centauri than Earth was to Sol had to be considered—there was much more noise coming from Fintidier's ionosphere than her Earth-based counterparts had to deal with and orders of magnitude more than she had to contend with on the radio-quiet lunar farside. Pointing was also a bit of an issue given the quite different day/night cycles and orbital period of her new home planet. The software would take care of most of that, but someone, thankfully not her, had to do all the programming.

The good news was that it worked and the calibration cycles were now complete.

"How does it look?" asked Mak, momentarily pausing the neck-and-shoulder rub he was giving Rain as she looked over the data. Rain had requested the rub. She had been sitting in the chair, poring over the data for hours, and could feel the tension in her neck and upper back. Besides, over the last few weeks she had learned that Kopylova gave fantastic back rubs and seemed to enjoy providing them.

"The system is working and the calibration runs are complete. When the constellation gets about twenty-two degrees above the horizon, we'll see if there is anything there," she said, easing her body back into Mak's firm hands. "That's the spot, right there, hmmm." If she weren't careful, he would put her to sleep.

"And it is on automatic? You don't have to be here to start the scan?"

"That's right. I've got it set to alert me if anything unexpected comes in. The odds are extremely low that we will detect anything on the first pass, even if something is there. SETI researchers had scanned hundreds of thousands of possible targets and heard mostly nothing until we accidentally picked up the signals from here—and we had to be on the lunar farside to that, with much more sensitive equipment, I might point out," Rain said.

"Did the SETI searchers look at the constellation you found in the Atlantean temple?" Kopylova was referring to the lone odd piece of astronomical data the team had photographed during their incursion into the burial mounds on the southern continent. Other than the image of the flaring Proxima b, the constellation was the only visible reference to anything astronomical found in their excavations there, so, of course, it piqued Rain's interest.

"I don't know and we won't have any information about that for several years. I made the request by radio in the last batch of updates sent home and you know how long it will take for the signal to get from here to there and then for the data to be sent back. Who knows? I suspect not, or there would have been some sort of news about it a long time before now."

"How much time do we have?" Mak asked, pausing the back rub to scratch his chin, which did not look all that easy to do through his beard.

"Two hours, give or take," she said.

"Then we have time for lunch," Mak said. "I will prepare my famous soup, some pasta, and allow you to try my latest attempt at making *kompot*. I promise it will be better than the last, and not so bitter. I'm finally getting used to what fruits to use."

Rain smiled. She had been spending a great deal of time with Mak these last few weeks and enjoying each time more than the last. As she rose to leave, their eyes locked and she knew he felt the same way. She so much wanted to lean in and kiss him through his scratchy beard, but she restrained herself. Rain was all too aware of Mak's deep love for his long-dead wife and she did not want to rush him. The moments stretched to a few awkward seconds.

"Ah, yes. Lunch," Mak said, adding a smile to his face. "Perhaps when we return and you examine the data, we will have reason to celebrate with dinner tonight as well."

"That would be wonderful," she said as they walked out the door.

They had just finished the *kompot*, which was, to Rain's delight, much better than the last attempt, when the automated alert from the radio telescope came to her ear patch and sounded. They quickly exited Mak's spartan apartment and hurried across the compound to the observatory.

Rain sat at the console and then looked straight ahead, poring over the processed data being sent to her contacts. Mak quietly stood behind her.

"Oh my God," said Rain after a few minutes.

"What?" asked Mak.

"There is something there, near the twenty-one-centimeter band, just like the early SETI researchers claimed there might be. Clear as day," Rain said.

"Is it like what you detected on the Moon? Some sort of radio leakage?"

"No. This is definitely not an analog transmission. The computer ran it through all the algorithms and says it is digital, and highly sophisticated. In fact, so sophisticated that it was almost classified as noise, but not quite."

"I don't understand."

"The more sophisticated, in other words, the more information that is packed into a packet of data, the more random it seems.

The encryption algorithms generated by our quantum computers make the signals we send appear to be nearly random. That is why they are not so easily decoded unless you have the key and is the reason we couldn't figure out how to read the signals coming from Earth in the last half of our trip thanks to whatever Gaines did to the *Samaritan*'s communications system. This signal is clearly artificial—the computer pegs it with a ninety-seven percent probability."

"But we can't read it," Mak said.

"That's correct. But, by God, there's someone else out there and they're signaling us."

"Signaling us?"

"Well, maybe not us, but someone here, on Fintidier or nearby. The message has to be directional. It's too strong to be otherwise—strong enough that if it were omnidirectional, then it would have been seen at Earth a long time ago. The constellation of stars we are looking at is visible from Earth and the signal strength is high enough that the lunar radio telescope would have heard it like someone yelling in a quiet room if it were directed toward Earth or emitted at this strength in all directions. No, whoever this is wants their signal to be heard by the Fintidierians or someone else in this general direction."

"Do you know from which star the signal comes?"

"Not yet, this hardware isn't directional enough to pinpoint a specific star, just a general group of them. If there were another telescope on the other side of the planet, then I might be able to triangulate and narrow it down. Of course, the best way will be to send one of the ships to the outer solar system and let them listen from there. That would give enough of a baseline to narrow it down considerably."

"We need to notify everyone," said Mak.

Rain rose from her chair and right into Mak's embrace, which was quickly followed by a very scratchy kiss.

"We must celebrate," Mak added as he caught his breath.

"I am looking forward to it, but after we tell everyone. Tonight, we will celebrate!" she said, leaning forward to initiate her own kiss.

And celebrate they did, for more reasons than one.

CHAPTER 55

Roy was an aerospace systems engineer. He was trained to design and build things that worked good enough and apply that thing pragmatically as a solution. He thought the hubbub about the three small spots on Earth that had gender-birth issues had a solution. The very large diverse population of humanity was Mother Nature's very own feedback control loop that was keeping Earth's numbers growing rather than declining. The solution was most likely, to him, already in place on Earth. And his take on the entire problem was that the Proximans—he was still having trouble saying Fintidierians—had brought this on themselves. He agreed with the ambassador and that economist lady that trade and commerce with Proxima bringing in new genes into the gene pool would be the cure for them. The *Emissary* was already on the edge of the system and would soon be bringing even more people down. Soon, the Proximans were going to have to start mixing and mingling on a larger scale.

Roy was walking through the greenhouse, observing a row of corn they'd brought from Earth. It was growing well and right next to a row of something the Fintidierians had given them that was orange-brownish and looked like an alien vegetable to him. The three-dimensional hologram of his two-year-old daughter walked beside him. He'd been doing his best to catch up in order with his daughter's growth since they had managed to get the new data dumps from home. He wouldn't let himself move

319

ahead, because he didn't want to miss a moment if he could avoid doing so.

"Good morning, Roy," Dr. Joey Zimmerman, the botanist and plant expert managing the greenhouse, said. "Want to try one? I did. They are kind of like a cross between a turnip and a beet, if you ask me."

"Sure, Joe. Why not?" Roy replied.

"She's getting big now." Joey looked at the hologram as he pulled one of the ugly stalk-grown, tuber-looking vegetables and handed it to him. "How old is she here?"

"She's about two and a half at this point." Roy took the vegetable and rolled it over in his hands, inspecting it. "Of course, she's got to be nearly ten by now or will be in June."

"Yeah, that's tough." Joey didn't say much else about it. Then he turned to a row across from them. "Hey, you should try one of these things. They are actually good."

Roy took a bite of the first vegetable that he'd been given and had to agree that it was nothing to write home about. He followed Joey to the next row of plants that were directly underneath some white lights. The plants looked like thick vines with broad leaves spread across them so plentifully that they reminded him of grapes from Earth. In fact, there were bright red fruits or berries dangling in bunches all along the vine.

"Here, these are great. I'm thinking of seeing if I can ferment them."

"They are a bit bigger than grapes." Roy popped a couple of them in his mouth and was surprised by how sweet they were. "Very good."

"Roy, auld boy, you have an incoming call," his AI Nigel told him.

"Excuse me a moment, Joe." Roy stepped a couple of meters away. "Okay, Nigel, let's have it."

"Roy, how are you doing today?" Captain Crosby's face appeared in his virtual view.

"I'm fine, Captain Crosby, how are you?"

"I've got something I want you to see up here. I need your expertise for the nav systems. We might have cracked what was done to it. Or, well, we have a new solution," Crosby said.

"Cindy can't handle it?"

"Nope, this is a task that I'd like your expert eyes on," Crosby told him. "There's an OSAM on the pad ready for launch. It's waiting for you."

"Alright," Roy sighed and swallowed the last bit of sweetness from the red grape things. Maybe they should be called "reds," he thought. "I'm on my way."

"Duty calls?" Joey asked.

"Sorry, Joe. I've got to go do something on the ship. I'd ask for more berries but microgravity makes me queasy for the first thirty minutes or so."

"Isn't that the *Samaritan* over there?" Roy pointed out the viewport of the Orbit and Surface Access Module at the starship he'd spent so much time on, against his will. "Why the circuitous route?"

"Look out the other side, Roy." Bob Roca tossed his head toward the porthole across from them.

"What am I looking fo—holy shit!" Roy's jaw dropped. "That the *Emissary*? They're here already?"

"Yep. Just came to a stop over the complex a few hundred kilometers from the *Samaritan*. Cap'n wants you to get some spares from there and bring them with you."

"Jesus, that thing is twice as big as the *Samaritan*."

"Yeah, and it was a hell of a lot faster. They say it took them only six years to make the trip. It was like only three years relative to the crew. Can you imagine how much easier that was?" Roca told him.

"Wow," Roy agreed. He thought about how he was supposed to have been the test engineer for that ship too. He was supposed to have tested the nav system, the engine operation system, and all of the overall ship functions under simulated flight conditions. And then he was going to retire with his wife and maybe start a family.

Roy started to drift back into that depressed-funk state of mind where he pitied himself. He reached down to one of the pockets on his jumpsuit and felt the little holoprojector and thought about his daughter, whom he'd never meet. He thought, briefly, just briefly, that maybe he could convince one of the starships to take him back. If the *Emissary* took him, he could be home before Samari was twenty, maybe sooner. He'd miss her childhood, but maybe, just maybe, he could get to know her as a young adult.

After several minutes of quietly fantasizing about a way home, or another life in another time, he pulled himself back into the real, more pragmatic world. The ships had come to Proxima for a mission and they were always expected to be a one-way trip. Roy was jarred out of the fantasy by the OSAM locking into the docking ring with a metallic *cathunk* sound.

"*Emissary*, this is *Samaritan Three*. Docking complete. All indicators are in the green and pressure is regulated. Are we clear to ingress?" Roca spoke to the docking control of the larger ship. "Be advised we have Dr. Burbank here to receive the package as planned."

"Copy that, *Samaritan Three*. You're clear to come aboard, Bob."

"That's our cue, Roy." Roca floated past him and tapped a few buttons by the docking hatch. It swished open and the light on the panel above and to the right of the hatch turned red, showing it was open.

"Alright." Roy unbuckled and floated upward. He gave a kick against his chair, propelling him through the hatch. He and Roca floated into the main corridor of the loading bay and then Roca activated his magnetic shoes, pulling him to a stop on one of the bulkheads where there were two soldiers standing post. Roy followed suit.

"Mr. Roca. Dr. Burbank," one of the soldiers said. "Come with me, please."

"Roy, I think you're gonna like this," Roca said as the door behind the soldiers opened.

Standing on the other side of the door was Chloe. And beside Chloe was a little girl with long, curly red hair with her head just about at Chloe's waist. The little girl looked to be about six years old. The two of them were wearing light blue jumpsuits and Chloe had a medical insignia on her shoulder patch.

"Hello, Roy." Chloe smiled. Roy could see her eyes filling with an expanding tear. He looked down at the little girl beside her. "I'd like you to meet your daughter. Samari, say hi to your father."

"Hi, Daddy!" The little girl bounced off the floor into Roy's arms followed by Chloe. The momentum from the two of them nearly knocked him over. Roy pulled them to his chest and squeezed them. Tears grew in his eyes and stuck there, fowling his vision in the microgravity. He didn't want to let go to wipe at them.

"I have missed you so much!" Roy cried. "But, Chloe...how?"

"They needed doctors. And, well, we needed you."

CHAPTER 56

May 3, 2100 (Earth/Proxima timeline)
Proxima b, aka Fintidier

"Just thought you'd like to know, Dr. Burbank." Captain Alan Jacobs shut the videos down and turned to Roy and Chloe. Samari was in the backyard playing with one of the Fintidierian boys about her age. Roy had requested some children come to visit the complex and Charles had agreed it would be a good start to public outreach. Roy's motive was much more selfish: Samari needed a playdate.

"Thank you for showing us this, Captain," Chloe replied to him and turned to her husband. "They finally caught O'Hearn, the bastard. He slipped up when boarding one of the ships making a run to Mars—his fingerprint tripped an alert and they had him in custody within minutes."

"Well, they were well funded. O'Hearn, or Gaines, or whoever the hell he really is, he will be in prison the rest of his life for the murder of Thomas Pinkersly and for what he did to your family. Dr. Luce...well, he's been arrested and who knows what the outcome of that will be. And certainly, somebody was pulling his strings. It took a lot of money to pull off what they did," Jacobs told them.

"We may never know. And you know what?" Roy stood and held out his hand to shake the Space Force captain's hand. "No hard feelings. You didn't know me and never met me. Gaines is in prison. Luce, hopefully, will be. We are light-years away and my family is here with me now."

"That's a very gracious attitude, Dr. Burbank," Jacobs said, shaking the offered hand.

"After the long duration of darkness I've been wallowing in, this is heaven, Captain Jacobs," Roy said. Chloe squeezed his arm and slid a little closer to him. "Absolute heaven on, uh, well, Proxima b."

CHAPTER 57

June 13, 2100 (Earth/Proxima timeline)
Proxima b, aka Fintidier

"There have been three pregnancies, including mine." Chloe rubbed her stomach, which was just now starting to bulge. "None of them cross-breeding with the Fintidierians, although I suspect that is coming before long. Several of the crew have been getting very cozy with the locals that have started extended stays here."

"What does Samari think about it?" Dr. Thomaskutty sipped at a glass of the newly minted wine that Dr. Zimmerman was so proud of.

"Well, Sindi, it *is* what she wanted for her birthday." Chloe smiled at Roy across the room as he lit the candles on Samari's cake. There were seven even though Samari had insisted that she was ten. "But the fact that, so far, all the pregnancies are boys...well...not a big sample space but the odds are starting to be suspicious."

"Yes. Dr. Kopylova and I have each seen two miscarriages. I don't recall the last time I even heard of a miscarriage on Earth. What if they were female?" Dr. Thomaskutty said with an ominous tone. "What if?"

"'What if' is right."

ACKNOWLEDGEMENTS

We would like to thank Cathe Smith and Dr. Cliff Gooch for their insights into genetics and genetic drift.

We must also give a big shout-out to all the exoplanet scientists out there who are giving us a myriad of new worlds to work and play in. When we were young(er), back before about 1992, there were no confirmed planets outside of our solar system—can you imagine that? When Captains Kirk, Picard, and Janeway were gallivanting around the universe, visiting one habitable planet after the other, the only people who knew such planets existed were the science fiction writers! Well, in all honesty, the astronomers were also pretty sure they existed, but they did not yet have the proof. Now they do. It is a big universe out there, so we better get busy and start exploring it.

—Travis S. Taylor and Les Johnson